COMPLETELY COMPLICATED

THE BOXED SET

BY JULIA KENT

TABLE OF CONTENTS

AUTHOR'S NOTE

This collection is not a standalone book, but rather is a continuation of the series I started with the *Her Billionaires: Boxed Set* book, and continued in *Random Acts of Crazy* and *It's Complicated*. While new readers are absolutely welcomed into the world of Laura, Mike and Dylan and Laura's best friend Josie and her boyfriend, Alex, this collection will make more sense if you've already read the *Her Billionaires* boxed set and, especially, *It's Complicated*.

This boxed set contains the originally-published novellas:

Complete Abandon
Complete Harmony
Complete Bliss
Complete We

Sign up for my mailing list to get information on new releases, sales, and special exclusive excerpts at http://www.jkentauthor.com

Praise for Julia Kent

the finale overwhelming. Very well worth my heart palpitations."

"I just can't imagine how you come up with this stuff, but am so glad you do!"

"I finally had to write to you and tell you that you are simply one of the most amazing authors. Your humor is perfect. I really do bust out laughing out loud. My family thinks that I am crazy when I do it but I can count on a good read from you especially when it has been a rough day. There hasn't been a single thing that you have written that I haven't fallen in love with the characters. They become real and some of your lines have become a part of our family language. Thank you for sharing your amazing gift."

"Having another fantastic evening as I just finished your latest book and now the fam can go to sleep since the laughing/screaming out loud has stopped...Stomach muscles are sore. Better than sit-ups! :-)"

COMPLETE ABANDON

LAURA

SHOULD HAVE NAMED HER RENESMEE.

All those baby books lied, or they committed dramatic sins of omission. Either way, nothing prepared you for motherhood. Especially not for nursing. Little Jillian performed baby acrobatics during most feedings, attached to Laura's nipple with tiny little glass-like protrusions masquerading as teeth ripping into her six, seven times a day. No one had warned her about this. None of the baby books *really* emphasized the fact that at some point, you would be nursing a baby with teeth like the edge of a razor. If nipples were meant to look like shredded, bloody, Chinese lanterns, then Laura had perfected the art of breastfeeding a six month old. Her daughter might as well have been named Renesmee, and Laura might as well be nibbled to death by a great white shark.

It was just like when Jillian was a tiny newborn and Laura had come to the startling realization that she was a fart hostage, trapped with this little rear end that emanated deathly biological weapons-grade methane, inches from Laura's face. And she had nowhere to go. She was this little being's source of food, and the food was what fueled those noxious gases wafting up into Laura's face, making her a fart hostage.

Thank God for her eReader. And thank a slightly lesser god for the *Fifty Shades* phenomenon. While Laura was no fan of that particular book, or that particular series, she had found a wide array of books that allowed her to escape into a completely different reality while she was trapped on the couch.

Sylvia Day made the bondage of motherhood tolerable. So did Melody Anne, and Lexi Blake, and Shayla Black. Sara Fawkes and Georgia Cates, and so many other authors who wove these amazing tales of women who needed to lose control in order to gain it. It was fascinating even though, in so many cases, the plot line seemed the same. She could take a book, a series like Sylvia Day's Crossfire series, or Julie Kenner's Claim Me series, or Maya Banks' Breathless Trilogy, and go off into another world. Laura found herself devouring these books, and then imagining herself in the role of the heroine.

Not like she didn't have two heroes right here, right now, at her disposal whenever she wanted them.

Somehow that made it all *worse*.

Loving Dylan and Mike was more than she'd ever expected. Living with them day to day was like being divinely inspired on an emotional, and psychological, and spiritual level. But the reality of a messy house, an infant with high needs, of a postpartum body that reminded her of two hundred pounds of jelly stuffed inside a giant balloon—that? That made her just reach for the eReader.

While she'd always felt insecure about her body, and had always been overweight with curves on top of curves, now, six months *postpartum* she still felt six months *pregnant*. It was as if her curves had rebelled and multiplied in her sleep, as if some sort of mitosis had taken place against her will. She felt ugly, and fat, and stretched out, and so thoroughly undeserving of the two very sculpted, lean, and exceptionally hot men who claimed to love her.

They did love her, and she knew this. It wasn't as if they were lying—it's more that they were being *nice*, right? They were saying all the right things that you're supposed to say after someone's given birth to your baby. But she knew. She knew they didn't find her body attractive. It must have been a chore to sleep with her. It must have involved a lot of imagination, thinking back to how she'd been when she'd met them just fifteen months ago. That body was the one that they really loved.

This body? No one could love this body. *No one*.

Letting her mind float off to other men and women, people far more together than she was, and finding something predictable, comfortable, and yet racy and mind expanding, was safe. The few times she'd made love with Mike and Dylan since the birth of Jillian should have been wonderful, but it was as if there were only two people there. Laura had to check herself out because she couldn't believe what she had become. She couldn't fathom that they *really* wanted her.

As she sat on the couch, there was one person who did want her, one-hundred-percent. Laura's love for Jillian was so deep and so intense that it guided her through those first few months. The love that the three of them shared for her was unbounded, untamed, and every day felt new.

What receded, though, what had firm boundaries around it, ever tightening, was Laura's sense of sensuality, of being something other than Jillian's mom. She figured that was normal. She figured that's what everyone went through. As the idea that she could be seductive, and attractive, and draw Mike and Dylan to her the way that she had when they met, as that faded...she hoped that they could still love her unconditionally the way that all three of them so thoroughly loved Jillian.

Her books didn't let her down. They were like her ice cream, always there, welcoming her with a smile, and never demanding anything of her. If she had to be in control, if she had to manage one more detail in her life, she was going to explode. It was easier to withdraw. It was easier to pour everything she had into Jillian, and to micromanage her baby, so that as a part of her died off, another part could blossom.

Guilt could be overwhelming, especially when Dylan placed a loving hand on her ass, or Mike came at her with a kiss that had more heat behind it than affection. From the outside, she was so all-consumed with Jillian that she just didn't have room for more than affection. It was a facade she carefully constructed, and to some extent the guys were going along with it. Every time she imagined making love she felt twin emotions that battled for domination within —and not the heady, come-fuck-me domination in her books.

Oh, no.

It was the kind of overwhelming oppression that guilt possesses. She didn't feel worthy of sensuality, so she evaded their passes. They slowly pulled back, confused but unsure of how to talk about it, and when they tried she brushed them off. Stayed up late until they fell asleep. Took extra long with Jillian in the rocking chair in her bedroom.

Waited them out.

Tears threatened to fill her tired eyes as Jillian reached up and grabbed a fistful of Laura's blonde hair. The baby giggled, mouth full of breast, and spurted milk everywhere, which made Laura laugh and cry at the same time.

Another set of emotions battling within.

Books let her feel something about anything *but her life*.

And that's where the love remained unconditional.

JOSIE

"I know you didn't invite me here for the mint cannoli or the fried pickles with guacamole-horseradish sauce," Josie announced, eyebrows so high she thought they'd be permanently wedged in her hairline. What was this all about? A summons to Jeddy's was always welcome, but usually it was Laura doing the summoning. The call from Mike had been interesting, the request to meet just him and Dylan—sans Laura—a tad odd.

The looks on their faces now confirmed it. Oddities abounded. And not like on the television show. Unless Dylan had a three-headed pig in a jar in his car and had recently learned to eat flames. Nothing would surprise her these days...

She glanced at her smart phone. "Waiting for a call?" Dylan asked as he scanned the menu. Madge had just thumbed Josie over to the guys when she came in; the new menus featured a smorgasbord of new culinary delights.

"No," she said, tearing her eyes off the menu. Coconut sweet potato soup with fried wontons sprinkled on top and a dollop of paprika sour cream? Yum. "Alex is joining us."

"Why?" they asked in unison, manly brows instantly frowning. *Hoo boy*. Whatever they wanted to talk about must have a testosterone edge to it. Even Mike's neck tightened.

"Because he wants to invite you to join us and act out some scenes from the book *Their Virgin Princess*," she cracked, returning to the menu. "Except I'm not the one who'll be wearing the butt plug in the desert." She tried to stare down Dylan, but he wouldn't make eye contact. Didn't even react to the bad joke.

Hmmm.

"What's that?" Mike asked, bewildered.

"Never mind." She looked at the dessert specials. Candy cane ice cream with chopped chocolate truffles and a local dairy's sweet cream whipped with Madagascar vanilla, drizzled with a reduced blackberry sauce? Double yum.

"You can't just drop virgin princesses and butt plugs into a conversation and not explain," Mike protested.

"Sure I can!" Josie ventured. "Especially with a menu like this to distract us." She buried her face in the specials page. Holy smokes, Madge had outdone herself.

"Want one of everything?" Dylan asked, barely holding back drool. "The homemade mac 'n cheese made with lobster and asiago," he moaned.

"Who doesn't?" a wonderfully familiar voice asked, coming up from behind her. A warm hand pressed against her shoulder and Alex's stubbly jawline caressed hers as he planted a kiss on her cheek. Alex's brown hair was in need of a haircut, curling up slightly at the nape of his neck, and he looked like he hadn't slept in a day and a half. Which was true—he hadn't. Warm, brown eyes locked with hers, affection and love pouring out of them. *A woman could get used to this,* Josie thought, delightedly—though actually she hadn't. Her mind and heart still marveled, unaccustomed to the fact that *every single day* she got her internal love cup filled to overflowing from him.

"You look like shit," Dylan said to Alex in a voice that could have just as easily been saying, "How's it going?"

"Same back at you," Josie jumped in. "Fatherhood has not aged you well." Alex shoved his ass against her hip, buying real estate in the booth. She squeezed a butt cheek through his scrubs. "You smell like blood," she commented absently.

"I'll smell like you soon enough," he said cheerfully.

Mike groaned. "Braggart."

"Just stating the facts, man."

Dylan snorted. "I remember when I had *facts* that often. Lately, though, *facts* elude us. *Facts*, in fact, are hard to remember."

"You mean *sex*," Alex said. It wasn't a question.

Laura's guys sighed. So that was what this meeting was about. Josie's protective senses went into overdrive. Laura was her bestie. This could get...*complicated*.

"Do I really need to know this much about your sex lives? Seriously?" Josie whined.

"Do you guys *ever* keep it in your pants?" a gravelly voice added. Madge, the eighty-something waitress and, it so happened, Alex's grandfather's girlfriend, skittered by. Her nurse's shoes squeaked on the faded—but clean—linoleum at the stalwart diner.

"Only when you're around, Madge," Dylan shot back. She pointed her stylus at him and winked. He slumped back in the booth and grimaced, making Josie snicker.

"That's because you couldn't handle all of me, Pretty Boy."

11

Alex looked green suddenly. "Uh, Madge, do you mind?" His grandfather, Ed, had Alzheimer's, though a recent med change had given Ed a much better prognosis and a better memory overall. His filter about his sex life had faded, though, and Alex couldn't handle the truth.

Especially when it turned out Madge and Ed used Dan Savage's column as a bucket list.

That they were rapidly making their way through.

Madge opened her puckered smoker's mouth to say something else to Dylan, shot Alex a sidelong glance, and then snapped her lips shut. "You want one of everything?" she asked the group. "All the new specials?"

Everyone groaned.

"What's with the menu?" Mike asked. "This is amazing."

"My grandson, Caleb," Madge answered, puffing up her chest like a silver-back gorilla after eviscerating another alpha. The effect drained a little of Josie's appetite. "He's come to Boston to help out more, and look at the difference."

"You really think we should get one of *everything*?" The specials page looked like it held at least fifteen different dishes. Josie would need to be hauled out in a wheelbarrow if she ate as much as she wanted.

"How about you pick for us, Madge?" Alex asked affably, his face friendly with a smile. "You know better than anyone how to please the crowd."

Her tight prune face lit up and she patted Alex on the cheek. "You're just like your grandfather. You always know how to butter up an old lady." She zipped off, clicking on her electronic order pad.

"I'd hate to know how those two use butter these days," Josie muttered.

"I'm going to be sick," Alex mumbled, picking at a napkin.

Everyone laughed. Mike and Dylan sounded sick, too.

"While we all make jokes and pretend you didn't invite us here to talk about your non-existent sex life, let's just get it out in the open. Why do you have a non-existent sex life?" Josie asked.

"Ask your best friend," Dylan muttered.

Mike shook his head, giving Dylan a look of disappointment. "It's not that simple. Something's wrong with Laura. And it goes deeper than sex."

"Like what?" Josie had just seen her a few days ago. Laura was exhausted and harried and smelled like baby shampoo and milk. Wasn't that how all new mothers were for the first year? Josie had held Jillian for twenty minutes or so here and there, letting Laura shower and go to the bathroom alone. Then again... from Laura's effusive praise and thanks—more than Josie had heard out of her own mother's mouth in twenty years—she should probably have assumed Laura was especially overwhelmed.

"All she does is sit on the couch, nurse Jillian, and read."

"What else can a breastfeeding mom do? She's attached at the nipple," Alex interjected. Madge appeared with two plates of fried pickles, a pitcher of water, and glasses for everyone.

"Coffee?"

"Yes!" they all hissed. Dylan shoved a pickle in his mouth and promptly spat it out, raking his palm across the table to grab the water pitcher. Frantic hands poured ice water and he shoved the glass to his mouth.

"Do I really have to tell a grown man who has been coming to this diner for nearly a decade that a plate of fried food straight from the kitchen is hot?" Madge said in a disgusted tone.

"Ad dow by tug id bunt," Dylan whined.

"Whatever. Your tongue will recover. Here's the dipping sauce." Madge set down two cruets. "The.Sauce.Is.Cold," she said slowly to Dylan, then rolled her eyes, marching off.

"Her compathun ith udduhwhemming," Dylan sputtered.

"Dat waskly wabbit went dataway!" Josie answered, pointing at Madge's rapidly moving form, now filling another table's coffee mugs.

Alex elbowed her. "Milk," he said to Dylan. "Some milk will help." Pushing the cream pitcher to the poor suffering guy, Alex looked at Josie and said, "Speaking of compassion..."

"It's his own fault!" She pulled the platter of fried pickles closer. "Besides, more for me."

"Ad least I don't need a fully-functioning tug these days," Dylan said after cooling it off with water and milk. "Nod in bed."

Josie pushed the platter back to the center of the table. "C'mon. That was just mean," she said, deflated.

"I know." Dylan's evil grin made her grab the plate back. No way he was winning this one.

"If you're having problems in bed," Alex said, carefully dipping one pickle chip in the sauce, holding it in his hand to cool off, "maybe Laura needs to see her gynecologist in case she's having pain or dryness issues."

Josie stuck her fingers in her ears. "*Lalalalala* can't hear you talking about my friend's vagina like it's a motor on a car."

14

"If it were, the engine would be seized," Mike said quietly.

"LALALALALALALA!"

Dylan took the mature route, surprising Josie. "Laura already went. Everything is fine. Lube isn't an issue; we bought a 55-gallon drum of it a few months ago."

"There's a visual," Alex said, dropping his chip.

"See? You've grossed out an OB-GYN, guys. Congratulations. That takes some effort." Josie dipped a now-cooler fried pickle into the creamy green sauce in front of her. The taste was exactly as she imagined, only a thousandfold better. Who knew you could combine avocado and horseradish and produce *this*?

"I never said I was grossed out," Alex protested. Josie was too involved in the savory delight assaulting her tongue to argue.

"Is this just something we have to suffer through?" Mike asked Alex. Sad puppy-dog eyes made her heart go out to him.

Her hand, on the other hand, reached greedily for another piece of pickle.

"Six months postpartum? For some women, yeah —they're still not that interested. Especially if she's exclusively breastfeeding."

"She is," sighed Mike.

"What are we talking about in terms of lack of interest here?" Alex asked.

Josie gagged audibly.

"Once a week?" Alex continued.

Dylan snorted.

"A...month?"

Mike cleared his throat. "We've had sex twice since Jillian was born."

"HOLY SWEET JESUS!" Josie shouted. Thank goodness she'd finished swallowing, because the shock of that little detail would have required Alex to perform the Heimlich if she'd still been chewing. "What on earth is wrong?"

"That's not quite true," Dylan said, turning to Mike. "There were a few blow jobs—"

"STOP!" Josie ordered, just as Madge delivered plates filled with cannoli, a crock pot of what must be the mac 'n cheese, and an array of delights.

"Blow jobs, huh?" the waitress cracked. Alex turned beet red. So cute he could blush under circumstances like this. Josie wasn't sure if he could get any sweeter.

But right now she wanted to kill him as he so dryly talked about Mike and Dylan's penises as if they were commodities. And Laura's vagina were a department store shelf.

An empty one.

"TWICE?" Josie couldn't get over that one. Sure, she'd had dry spells herself. But not while living with Thor and a guy who looked like a romance novel cover model.

"Nothing wrong with two blow jobs," Madge muttered as she walked away.

"See why we called you?" Dylan said plaintively. He reached for the ice cream sundae and stuffed a spoonful of creamy cold sweetness in his mouth, closing his eyes. Josie imagined it was the closest to sex he'd come in, well...a lot longer than she'd imagined.

"Poor Laura."

Alex looked at her like she had two heads. "Poor *Laura*?" He gestured to Mike and Dylan. "How about poor *them*?"

"Poor *everyone*," she conceded.

"Not poor me," Alex whispered, his hand snaking around her waist, sliding up her ribcage to—

"Hey!" Dylan snapped. "No PDAs."

"What is this? Catholic school?" Josie snuggled up against Alex's warm form. Scrubs were thin enough to show that he was pretty warm for her form, too. She patted Alex's hand. He took hers and put it on his thigh. Nice and high. Then squeezed. Twice in six months? Try six times in one week. Even that wasn't enough these days, with Alex's crazy work schedule. Mike and Dylan had every right to look so sad, but now Josie was on high alert about her best friend. Time for an intervention of some sort.

"Might as well be," Mike grunted. "We're celibate."

"And not by choice," Dylan added, now halfway through the sundae.

"What are you doing about it?" Josie demanded. "Do you give her breaks? Compliment her? Take her out for nice dinners? Give her massages?"

"Buy her a nice new sex toy?" Alex added.

Josie's turn to blush. "That doesn't work for everyone."

"Works for you!" he said. "Snaps you right out of a bad mood. That fourteen inch—"

Mike put both palms out flat in a gesture of *halt*! "We get it. And yes—we tried that. No go. We've sent flowers. Chocolates. Gotten extra cleaning and errand help. You name it. All she wants to do is play with the baby, nurse, and read."

The group went silent as they ate their way through two continents' worth of plates filled with amazing culinary feats.

As they picked at the remainders of the desserts, Josie had an idea. "You said she just reads all day, right?"

"Yep." *Unison*. The frequency with which those two answered the same word or phrase was eerie.

"What's she reading?"

Mike's face folded into an expression of consternation. "No idea."

Dylan shrugged, eyebrows coming together as he frowned, near-perfect muscles attuned and thinking, all focused on her question. He might be an arrogant ass but he was a damn attractive one. Shaking his head he looked at Mike. "Me too. I can't say."

Josie chuckled. "I think," she said, scooping the last dregs of truffle shavings out of a tall sundae glass, "you might find some answers on her eReader."

Alex crossed his arms over his chest, then groaned, removing his arms and placing a flat palm on his full stomach. "What do you mean?"

"Don't you think that knowing what she's doing for most of her waking hours could help Mike and Dylan to understand what she's feeling?"

All three men bent in, leaning toward her, as if she were divulging the secrets of the Dead Sea Scrolls.

"Seriously, guys? The woman spends eight or ten hours a day reading and living in a fantasy land in her head and you didn't even think to *ask* her what she's reading?"

Mike blinked rapidly, his strong, Nordic jaw set in concentration. Piercing blue eyes met hers, buried under a brow furrowed in understanding. "She is living in that little machine. And in her head. I never thought to ask what she's reading, frankly. I just ask about her and the baby."

18

Dylan sighed, his face so different from Mike's, dark and swarthy, yet no less concerned. He was also the scruffier of the two, with a torn t-shirt from some '80s band covering his toned body, and a face that hadn't been shaved in a good three weeks. "Beard" wasn't quite the word for the train wreck of whiskers that covered his face and neck.

"No, I didn't ask either." He ran a frustrated hand over his face. "Jesus. How could we miss *that*?"

"Because you're men," Josie declared.

Six eyes stared at her, gone to stone.

"It's true!"

"You're saying women are smarter than men about relationships?" Alex asked, his voice fighting to stay neutral. Her heart soared. She loved a challenge.

"Do you have a penis?"

"You know damn well I do."

"Then yes."

"You realize that you're the one who was so terrified of my monster of a mother that you—"

"HEY!" Mike growled. "This is our relationship mess we're deconstructing. Not yours. Go book a slot on Dr. Phil if you want to untangle your mess."

"We're the ones who should be on that show," Dylan grumbled.

"You're better suited for Maury," Josie said.

"Who?"

"Nevermind."

"Nice diversion," Alex cracked, elbowing her in the rib, "but let's get back to the point. Go read her eReader. See what she's been reading. Maybe it will give you some ideas and you can go from there."

"I can already guess," Dylan groaned. "Breastfeeding books and baby signs and how to make homemade baby food. Sew your own cloth diapers.

How to make a Maya wrap from leftover moss and shredded placenta. Shit like that."

"It's not shit!" Mike retorted. "It's a perfectly valuable way to bond with your kid."

Dylan rolled his eyes. "Co-sleeping and breastfeeding is fine. But she's going on about sherpa fleece and buying a sewing machine to make more absorbent cloth diapers and my mind goes zzzzzzzzzzzzzzzz. And now she's asking about 'elimination communication.'"

"What's that?" Josie was almost afraid to ask. "Like, announcing when you have to pee?"

"OK, she's going overboard," Mike relented. He turned to Josie. "No—it's not using diapers on the baby and reading her signals when she needs to go, then holding her over the toilet."

"Laura is doing *that*?" Josie's jaw dropped.

"No, thank god," Dylan exclaimed. "But she's thinking about it."

"She really has thrown herself into the whole Attachment Parenting thing," Josie agreed.

"Nothing wrong with that," Alex said. "Every parent has to pick the approach that works best."

Silence. That anyone anywhere was holding a baby over a toilet every hour so it could pee was an eye opener. If Alex wanted that for their kids... Wait. *What* kids? She didn't want kids! Josie scrubbed her mind. She needed to focus on Laura.

"But you might want to broaden your expectations," Josie mused. "I think you're in for a surprise when you see what she's been reading."

"You know something we don't?" Dylan asked.

"No. It's just...I'm a woman."

Three balled up napkins hit her head at the same time.

DYLAN

"**A**re they asleep?" Mike closed the bedroom door slowly and looked at him, a finger pressed to his lips. Turning the knob slowly, he managed to close it entirely with just the faintest *click*. "Yes."

Finally! Josie's suggestion had been a good one, he had to grudgingly admit, but getting Laura 1) away from her eReader 2) away from both of them and 3) Jillian away from both of them all at the same time had proven to be a logistics nightmare worthy of air traffic control at LaGuardia Airport. What a mess. Ten days after their meeting with Josie and Alex at Jeddy's they finally had their chance. With Laura sound asleep, and Jillian snuggled up with her, they could take a long look at what was going on inside Laura's head.

Literally.

The eReader powered up quickly and Dylan zipped his way through the screen to find her library.

Well, now.

Josie was right, much as Dylan was loathe to admit it.

"It's like a giant online porn shop!" Mike hissed. His eyes bugged out of his head as he leaned over Dylan and held the corner of the machine.

"This one has 'fem dom' in it. What's that?"

"Beats me."

For the next ten minutes they scrolled through page after page of book covers in full HD color. *Blush* by Lauren Jameson. *Anything He Wants* by Sara

Fawkes. A bunch of books by someone named Maya Banks. He suspected the book *Burn* had nothing to do with firefighting.

Surrender by Melody Anne. *Bared to You* by Sylvia Day. *Release Me* by Julie Kenner. They all had tasteful little objects on the covers, with pearls and cufflinks and shadowed faces, but as Mike opened one and randomly flipped through to what looked like a sex scene—

My, oh, my.

Laura had quite a little kink going on here.

In her *mind*.

Dylan's pants tightened as his eyes skimmed over the words. Women in bondage. Long, drawn out scenes that went on page after page. Master/sub contracts. And then...

"*Their Virgin Princess*! That's the book Josie was joking about at Jeddy's," Dylan pointed out. Mike had remained remarkably silent as they stood there, transfixed.

A few taps and they scanned the first few chapters. Three bodyguards for a princess in a land where three men and one woman was the norm.

"THREE?" Dylan grunted. "Do we need to make room for another razor in the house?" He snorted. "Then again, it'd be just another guy who *won't* be getting any."

"Shhhh," Mike whispered, entranced. Dylan could see his eyes racing across the page, eating up the words. And those were some words. You name a descriptor for male and female genitalia, it was there. And the dom in the story was—whoa.

He made Dylan feel like a wuss.

Butt plugs. Three ex-military bodyguards. A plane crash in the desert—Josie wasn't kidding! That meant *she* was reading these books, too. Were all women reading this stuff now that *Fifty Shades of Grey* and eReaders had unleashed something? This wasn't his grandmother's romance novel. Noni had always read bodice rippers, with covers that showed a gleaming man's bare chest next to a damsel whose dress was pulled down around her shoulders, his mouth pressed to the woman's neckline for a kiss.

"My stories," she called them. Noni invested a lot of money in her stories. When she had died, they'd found more than four hundred paperbacks, mostly Harlequin books, stacked neatly in grocery bags in her guest room closet.

The local nursing home residents had been thrilled to get them.

Now Dylan wondered what the hell was between those covers. This was like crack for romance lovers.

And Mike was quickly becoming addicted as he gently pulled the eReader from Dylan's hand and walked over to the couch, settling in for a good, long read.

Good and *long* being the operative adjectives.

Those three bodyguards knew how to please a woman.

Holy BDSM!

For the next twenty minutes Dylan was transported somewhere else.

And so was his cock, which twitched and grew, straining against his jeans. While his hand, a bottle of Laura's coconut-scented lotion, and YouPorn had held his needs at bay for a bit, he was desperate for the old sex life he, Laura and Mike had shared. Thoughts of Laura filled him, pumping through his mind as he imagined she was the princess in the book, being readied for her three (no, two...) men.

What—two wasn't *enough*?

By the looks of it, Laura needed hundreds of men. Pages of long, drawn out temptation and longing, then fevered denial and brutal—yet passionate, and loving—bondage and domination greeted his eyes as he drank it in. Mike sat next to him, their bodies touching, breathing even and steady as they comfortably read through the next few chapters of the book, shifting occasionally in what Dylan imagined was arousal.

Or shock.

Or, more likely—envy.

The men in these imaginary worlds got everything they wanted. Sex. Love. The woman. A forever ending that he, Mike and Laura already had.

Minus the sex.

It wasn't about the orgasm. Really—it wasn't. What he missed most was the sound of her breath hitching in that oh-so-sexy way she had, the little give that told him she was getting ready for him. How her face flushed with need when she was aroused. The wetness of her walls as he slid one finger in her, his mouth eager to taste her juices.

Everything sensual and alive and skin was missing right now. Collapsing into the goodness and animal need of a world where the bedroom made everything else fade, where the three of them could just be raw nerves and want and naked lust was...gone.

Dried up.

As if it had never happened.

There was no lack of affection in their lives. Hugs and kisses and cuddles abounded. But when he or Mike tried to turn a peck on the lips with Laura into something deeper, she went shallow. Neither wanted to push because, well...they were respectful. Nice. Honorable.

Learning that it turned out she'd been filling her head with *this* every day, for hours and hours, made him re-evaluate the last few months. Not in the sense that he should ever violate her boundary—if Laura didn't want sex, Laura shouldn't have to have sex. Period. End of discussion. No meant no, *always*.

But what did all this BDSM reading *mean*?

"Where did we go wrong?" he asked Mike.

Mike shook his head slowly, not taking his eyes off the screen. Running one hand through his shaggy, blonde hair, he mumbled, "I don't know, but damn, this writer can write." A long, slow sigh poured out of him, his lips pursed, face deep in a frown. He looked like a Norse god troubled by thoughts of war.

"No shit. You as worked up as I am?"

Mike looked longingly down the hallway, toward their bedroom door where Laura now slept. "Yeah."

Unable to stand it any more, Dylan stood and marched over to the kitchen, willing his erection to go down. *Heel, boy*, he ordered it. Reluctantly, it began to fade. Reading all that had triggered more in him than any porn ever could. The words elicited reactions and emotions far stronger than any image or video ever could.

Maybe that's why romance novels were so popular. If that was why Noni read so many...

He shook his head like a dog trying to brush off a burr. *Don't think about Noni aroused. Gross.*

The new espresso machine gave his hands something to do, scooping the coffee in, tamping the grounds, and then—yes! The familiar hiss of manna being brewed. Two little cups later, he brought Mike one and reclaimed his seat. Browsing through a new book, Mike took the cup in one big hand, his other cradling the eReader.

"I can't believe this is what Laura's reading!" Mike whispered.

"We need to do something about this," Dylan insisted. "It's obviously her fantasy."

"We can't engineer a plane crash on a desert island and have a suitcase full of sex toys wash ashore magically," Mike said dryly, taking a sip.

"No, but we could get Josie and Alex to babysit for a night while we get some velvet handcuffs and drip some hot wax on a blindfolded Laura!"

The air rang with Dylan's words, and...yup. Hard again. A quick glance at Mike told him he was in the same state.

"If this is what she really wants," Mike mused, "why doesn't she just ask for it? She knows we're about as open as anyone can be in the bedroom."

Dylan shook his head, then took a good, long look at Mike. "You look like hell." Hair overgrown, a scruffy beard, and a button down with a missing top button greeted his eyes.

"You're just a shorter, darker version of me." A not-so-gentle set of fingers brushed against Dylan's overgrown cheek.

"We've let ourselves go," Dylan said. Aside from quarterly meetings with the Board of Directors for his new charity, an organization designed to help families of cancer victims with services and grant money, Dylan didn't have anywhere he had to be that required cleaning himself up. When Jillian was born he'd stopped volunteering at the fire station, so now he was basically a professional dad.

And trust fund dude, a fate he and Mike had settled in to, finally. Even Mike had handed over most of the day-to-day operations of the ski resort to his management. No one really needed to look presentable for society. Other than basic hygiene, they just hadn't cared.

"We can fix that right now. A quick haircut, shave, and some decent clothes would go far. You clean up nicely when you bother," Mike said, smiling.

Dylan frowned. "Not enough. It's not like we've looked like this forever. I think we need to go further."

Mike finished his espresso and set the cup on the end table with a grace that belied his size.

"How far?"

Dylan tapped on the eReader and pulled up a page full of sex toys. "Let's start here."

"Alex was kidding when he suggested we get her a new sex toy!"

"I don't think it's a bad idea, though. Except the toys are for us to use on her. Not for her to use on her, you know? How about we read more of these stories and buy some of the...*implements* they use, and give Laura a taste of what her imagination is creating?" Dylan presented the idea to Mike with, he hoped, a sense of urgency and excitement that would convert him.

"Hi, honey!" Mike hissed. "Now that you spent sixteen hours breastfeeding all day and are coming to bed covered in vomit and smelling like sour milk, here we are with the Baby Jesus butt plug and a Sybian!"

"Not like that," Dylan insisted. "And what's a Sybian?"

Mike took the eReader, flipped back to a different book, and pointed. "Start reading here. I'll be back in a minute." Dylan looked up and watched Mike leave the room, his frumpled t-shirt and the shaggy blonde curls over his ears symptoms of benign neglect, and sighed.

They really had let themselves go.

But that shouldn't matter. And what the hell was a Sybian?

Ninety seconds later Dylan knew exactly what a Sybian was, and he was ready to go order one if there was any hope he could watch Laura use it. And there was that scene with the sex swing....

Where was she hiding this crazy, uninhibited side of her? Under those soft curves, that dimpled smile, those lips she bit at the moment of orgasm? The mere idea that she'd ride a machine with a dildo attached to it and like it made him nearly come in his pants right now. Flipping frantically through the eReader, he opened another book with a woman's hands bound on the front. Then one where she wore a mask and was draped in red silk. Yet another with a cuff link and pearls on it. And another...

Ropes and handcuffs and melted candle wax and dildos and dilators and butt plugs.

His very own Laura had an active, healthy, amazingly wonderful inner sex life.

Unleash the woman, for fuck's sake!

Or, he mused, perhaps what she wanted was to be *leashed*.

"Are you a Sybian expert now?" Mike asked as he returned from the kitchen, chomping on an energy bar.

Dylan shifted himself in a way that made Mike laugh. "Oh, you laugh, but you know exactly how I feel right now."

"Yup."

"That Sybian..."

"Yup."

"I'm thinking about ordering one."

A cocked eyebrow was Mike's calm response. "You are?"

"You in?"

"I say order one of everything from those books and see what happens." The devilish gleam in Mike's eyes was so different from his droll manner that even after ten years together, Dylan was amazed the man could surprise him.

"You realize you're talking to a guy with nearly unlimited money and zero impulse control?"

"You realize you are talking to a guy who has had sex twice and exactly one blow job in six months?" Mike's face was serious, eyes gone dark and smoky. Mischief was gone. This was a man determined.

Dylan's jaw dropped. Thank God they were in agreement. Whatever it took to unlock the passionate woman they'd met fifteen months ago and to regain the intimacy they all seemed to crave—but couldn't quite find their way to—was what they needed to do now. Something had to give.

"What are we wasting time talking for, then? Let's start clicking."

Crreak. The telltale sign of their bedroom door opening made them both freeze.

"Shit!" Dylan hissed. Mike put a finger to his lips and stopped chewing on the energy bar. Both stood there, ears cocked. The sound of footsteps, and then the baby began to babble.

Mike looked at the eReader. "It's been nearly two hours!"

"No way!"

Mike tapped and slid his fingers wildly, getting the machine back to the Home screen. "You order whatever we need later on from your phone. You have carte blanche. Get whatever you want."

An evil laugh bubbled up inside Dylan as he rubbed his hands together.

This was going to be fun.

ALEX

"**A**re you crazy? Let Josie watch the baby overnight? That woman can't keep a houseplant alive with a growlight, fertilizer, Google, and a team of highly-trained pot farmers at her disposal." Laura's high, reedy voice could be heard from across the room, as Josie had the phone on speaker mode. Josie had insisted that Alex spend the night at her place—fortunately, Darla was at a gig for Trevor's band. Joe was still in law school, though all Darla had talked about for weeks was how he'd be home soon for winter break. For Alex, it meant a nice night together away from his roommate, John, who had returned from his medical fellowship full of talk of medical genetics and one-upmanship politics as he tried to get a coveted research spot for next year.

Alex, meanwhile was on the decidedly less ambitious family physician/obstetrician track. The more surgery he performed, the less he liked it.

"I heard that!" Josie shouted at the phone. Alex winced. Even in a bad mood, Josie would still be interested in sex, but a bad mood could ruin his chances for something a bit more *risqué*. Like a romp outside.

"But she loves Jillian." Dylan's desperation made Alex cringe. His deep voice was a stark contrast to Laura's nervous, high voice.

"And I'll be here the entire time in case she drops the baby!" Alex added, followed by Josie's marching across the room to elbow him in the gut. "Ow!" he shouted.

"Jillian will be fine, Laura," Josie crooned. "This will give me a chance to see how I do at this whole pretending I have a maternal bone in my body thing."

"Not the best thing to say to convince a brand-new, first time mother, Josie," Alex hissed, taking the phone away from her unceremoniously.

"Overnight?" Alex asked. "That's quite an honor, Laura." He took the phone off speaker and decided to talk one-to-one. Dylan and Mike needed this night. Hell, he and Josie needed it, too. After six months of dating he was working on convincing her to consider the next step in their relationship, though he wasn't quite sure what that was. Moving in together would displace Darla, and his own lease had another six months on it, anyway. Josie had grudgingly let him keep one set of work clothes at her place these days, while he'd cleared out half his closet for her.

If she really, truly never wanted kids, then he'd have some hard reckoning ahead of him, because he most assuredly did want children. Maybe not right now, but in a few years...and so this could reveal a lot about her. An entire day and night with a six month old.

Plus, Dylan and Mike needed this. He could practically see their eyeballs floating, they were so backed up.

"Laura, I have a medical degree. I've helped birth more than two hundred fifty babies, and I'm CPR certified for infants. I even have perfect pitch for singing happy songs that soothe babies. Plus, Jillian loves my hair."

"You have perfect pitch?" Josie interjected. She looked at him with one eyebrow raised, her eyes sparkling with a look he couldn't name, but that instantly made him fall more deeply in love with her. "Is that why your voice is so melodic when you cry out my name?"

Damn it. His body hardened in all the wrong places right this moment. His brain returned to Laura, scrambling to find the thread of discussion again. Ah, yes. Baby. Watching the baby. Overnight. Helping to see how Josie would be. Giving Dylan and Mike a chance for something after six months.

And then Josie's hand snaked over his ass and gave him a squeeze as she began a slow hip curl down to the ground then back up, unbuttoning her shirt from the top down, one *sllllloooowww* button at a time.

While licking her lips.

Brain shattered.

"Alex?" Laura's confused voice brought what little bit of cohesive thought he had back to center. "Are you and Josie really willing to do this?" Sensing a need, a desire to give this a try, and something deeper, he put his entire being into convincing her that this was going to be alright.

"Laura, we'd love to. And," he said conspiratorially, cupping his hand over the phone, "it would be a real favor to me."

"To *you*?"

"You know how skittish Josie is about the idea of settling down and having kids—"

Hysterical, barking laughter filled his ear. Josie moved on to her second button and he waved her away frantically even as he hardened. If more blood went south he was going to need a transfusion.

"Josie," Laura gasped, "have kids?"

"See?" he said darkly as Josie walked out of the room, tossing her shirt in his face. "That's why this would help me. Give us a day with a baby, warm her up to the idea."

Laughter halted. "You two are that serious?"

"Not yet, but..."

"But you'd like to be."

"Yes," he said, his breath escaping and elongating the *sssssss* as Josie returned, now nude, carrying the biggest vibrator he'd ever seen.

It was the size of his forearm. She stuck her tongue out *à la* Miley Cyrus and he half expected her to reach for a foam finger and—

"So Laura? Just trust us, OK? Um, I'm getting buzzed right now," he said, nearly yelping as Josie turned the vibrator on and pressed it against his hip. That wasn't a lie.

"Oh, a patient?"

"A future mother who is out of her mind right now," he gasped into the phone, grabbing Josie's wrist. With very little effort he managed to push her against the wall and pin both wrists above her head, his hip holding her pelvis in place as he struggled not to wipe that wicked grin off her face with his—

Waaaaaaaa! A baby's cry pierced the air and Laura said, "Gotta go—talk later!" A merciful *click* set him free.

"You are so going to pay for that," he growled in Josie's ear as he hit "End" on the phone with a practiced thumb, then tossed the device behind him. It landed with a soft *thud* on the couch. His wriggling, naked girlfriend, all flesh and sinew and tight body, moaned as he tightened his grip on her wrists with one hand and used the other to slide down between her legs, finding her wet for him already.

"You want to play a game, young woman, you need to be ready to play to win."

34

"I'm," Josie gasped as he slid his thumb along her clit, fingers sliding down, then up, lubing her warm folds, "not younger than you."

"Then you cradle-robbing cougar, you," he said as his cock pressed against her hip, clothes suddenly a hindrance, her eyes half-lidded and face pinkened with a hazy, unfocused look that told Alex more than any words could. This was not how he'd thought the next hour of their day would go; Laura's phone call had interrupted their walk out the door to grab a lovely meal at a local Greek restaurant. A striptease and a little hand bondage, however, could replace dinner.

He could dine at the Y and have a lovely meal.

Wiggling her shoulder, Josie tried to get out of his grasp. He rather liked this, the muscled difference between his body and hers making this unanticipated encounter more masculine, more animalistic, than any they'd had before. He knew she enjoyed his dominance in the bedroom, but it had been a more genteel, modern-era dominance.

Right now he wanted to go all-out Don Draper.

After all, she had transgressed, right? Cockteasing him, interrupting his call, misbehaving and all that.

"You've been so bad," he whispered, running his tongue up the side of her neck, sucking her earlobe with his wet, warm bottom lip, then biting as she groaned. His fingers were slick with her heat and response, and he used his thumb to stroke her swollen nub in soft, unyielding circles. Her grinding against his hand was all he needed to know.

If she pushed her soft, naked body against him much longer, he'd come in his pants.

Time for no pants.

As he removed his hand from her vulva, she cried out with frustration, then leaned forward to kiss him as

35

he deftly unbuttoned and unzipped himself. There wasn't much time—for a change their dinner plans were at a place with atmosphere, and a dinner bill that would probably equal a day's pay—a place where tables were by reservation only. No time like the present, then—especially when your girlfriend offered herself up like something out of a Penthouse fantasy letter. If she wanted to shift the power balance by sending him off kilter with her nudity as he struggled to maintain composure on the phone with Laura, two could play at the unequal game.

Before she could react to his releasing her hands, he lifted her easily into his arms, walked to the couch to grab an afghan, then carried her to the door.

"What are you—ALEX, WHAT ARE YOU DOING?" she shrieked as he juggled a flailing, nude girlfriend, a front door knob, and his own sliding trousers. The blanket began to fall off his arm, and one move and the house of cards would come tumbling down.

That was fine.

As long as someone came.

"We're having sex on the porch!" he said in the same tone one might use to say, "We're getting a popsicle from the ice cream truck!"

"Are you crazy? I'm naked!" she squealed.

"Should have thought about that," he answered—squeezing her ass with more force than was needed for a turn on, knowing the added pain would help bring her to the edge—"before you started that dicktease." Six months of sleeping together had given him considerable experience in getting Josie to express her boundaries. It turned out they were as flexible as she was—in bed.

"Stop it!" she hissed.

He froze.

"If you're going to do this, you have to be naked, too!"

A deep chuckle rose out of him as he laid her gently on the porch swing he'd helped to install a few months ago. The November chill made her nipples turn to pink peaks in seconds, a fine gooseflesh beginning on her arms and thighs. God, he could stare at her body forever.

Oh, how his erection said otherwise. *Now now now now.*

Grabbing the afghan, Josie threw it over her naked form and a laugh burbled up. "Seriously? Now we're air fucking on my fucking porch? You got a thing for having the mailman look at your naked ass?"

What amazed him—what made him love her—was that she wasn't horrified, or angry, or offended that he'd just assumed she'd be fine with being poured onto a very public piece of furniture and be fucked outside, in broad daylight, where someone might find them.

She'd questioned whether *he* should be naked, too.

But hadn't questioned the premise of danger sex one.tiny.bit.

Could he love this woman any *more*?

"Not *my* naked ass," he murmured as he pulled his pants down so that his eager cock was laid bare for her. Sitting carefully, he pulled her into his lap, holding one of his hands to her mouth. She sucked on two fingers, taking her time as her tongue ran down the sides of his index and middle finger, the sensation making his abs tighten. Something had to go rigid—if his erection were any more taut it would slingshot off his body, hit the moon, and land somewhere in the Indian Ocean, tracked by NASA.

A shift of his hips, a nudge of her perfect, round ass and then he felt himself at the edge of her deep warmth, her body leaning into his as she straddled him, the afghan a warm, thick, knitted cover he draped over their bodies. She was on the pill and for the first time in six months of being together he felt a tug as that detail floated through the periphery of his mind, a hint of a life not yet lived. Cars lolled by and dog owners played across the street in the dewy, foggy late afternoon as the touch of sun wisped away into gray.

Sliding in her, he felt the cool air against his neck, her hot breath setting his ear on fire, his hands under the blanket caressing her breasts, each fitting perfectly in one of his palms with room to spare. With one foot braced against the porch floor be began to gently rock the hanging swing, his motion met with a throaty laugh from Josie, who lifted her hips up, then slid down, impaled by him and yet he was the one pinned in place by sheer lust and overwhelm.

And then she tightened.

If kegel muscle control were an Olympic event, Josie would be the US team captain, on the cover of Wheaties boxes every four years. For life. The feeling was brutal and glorious at once, as if he were being milked by a hot, wet cave of Josie's love.

"I love you," he murmured in her ear, her pants of concentration and shifting hips his only answer. When she was this close—and they both were, really—she stopped speaking, fingers digging into whatever part of him she touched. Bare breasts pressed against his clothed chest, and his pants pooled around his knees as she writhed, nude, on top of him, the curve of her shoulder under the wool blanket blending with his heated gasp, white clouds of condensation lifting away from them as if moans could take actual, tangible form.

She licked his neck, then suckled, the pull attached to a sinew and muscle trail straight to the base of his cock, like a line she discovered and played with impunity. "Oh, God," he shuddered, her own orgasm so close he could taste it.

How he wished he could.

Something to save for later.

A shattering clamp was her response, twinning with the suck of her mouth against his jugular, and all the blood flowed to his arms and legs in a great whoosh, receding back and pounding into his core with a rhythm and crescendo that became so insistent it lost definition, growing outside him, blending with the air, the trees, the sky, and with Josie's trembling form. Only she could bring him to this, in this way—sitting under a blanket, rocking lazily as passersby strolled on, unaware that their world imploded and transformed through a joining borne of connection and shared risk.

And *kegels*.

Verbal, linear thought eluded him as he became an expanse of skin and nerves, centered at his heart and the base of his shaft, connected by her body. So sweet. Being in her was the ultimate welcome, an invitation to join with a woman so special he couldn't imagine living without her, a love that would transcend her lifetime, lingering on in children and grandchildren imagined, in an extraordinary choice to embrace something more than either of them could be without each other.

Thrusting up, ever so incrementally, as she plummeted down on him, the micromovements managed for social respectability, controlled by structure and discovery, each push into her felt like a pilgrimage to some holy place, a chapel of love and trust where acceptance and blind need all mixed together with passion and lust to form *this* thrust.

And *this* groan.

And *this* gasp.

And then, just when the feel of her fingertips on his neck was like fire, as her lowered head and parted lips blended with her thighs pushing against him, at that moment when she levered him deeper in with her bearing down—it was then that his climax took over, all red and white and black and grey behind his eyes, the white-hot star of explosion and disbursement a sweaty, fevered affair that hit him not like waves but, instead, on one giant *crack* of decision.

All of her on him, his whole being in her, the rasp of his cheek against her neck, the scent of pussy and her soap filling the air between them—and the soft slushy sound of car tires wheeling by, mingled with horns and trains and carefree calls of owners to dogs said one, singular thing whispered through the lips of this gorgeous woman stretched over him, jellied limbs around his neck, spent nerves twitching in little residual movements:

"I love you, too, you pervert."

He chuckled and squeezed. "We both are."

Peeling herself off his chest, the afghan slipping and threatening to bare her back to the guy getting out of a cab across the street, he reached for the cloth and pulled it back up, cocooning her. "We're a perfect match."

"I could get used to you."

"After six months, you haven't broken me in yet?"

Squeeze. He was spent and fading fast, but the thrill of her enveloping him made blood rush down again. "I can just peel this off you right now and—"

The press of her lips against his caught him off guard, the heady feel of his hands and body and mouth overflowing with Josie like a second climax. Her tongue parted his lips and he drank her in, her hands buried in his hair, lips nipping at his. She planted a cute little kiss on his nose.

"How about that Greek place?"

"We probably lost the reservation."

"How about take-out Thai and we spend the night with The Determinator?"

"The what?"

She flexed her arm and made the wrist flick quickly back and forth. "The Determinator. My new toy."

"What does it determine?"

A sly grin from her. "That's what we need to explore."

The steady clomp of footsteps startled him, Josie's arms snaking about him and pulling tight against his chest to hide her naked front. Instinct kicked in and he pulled the cloth around them both, covering any hint of her nudity. While their position was a bit less dainty than might be appropriate, it was nothing close to what a full reveal under covers would expose.

"Good day," said the mailman cheerfully.

"Hi," they replied together, Alex's voice stronger, Josie's hampered by a giggle fit. Burying her face against his neck, Josie bit his collarbone, the vibration of barely repressed laughter jolting through him.

With a weak wave of his hand he tried to create a modicum of decorum, and when the guy turned the corner Alex exhaled slowly, with relief. Standing carefully, he let Josie wrap her shaking legs around his hips as he rolled them both in the afghan and guided them inside.

"You're crazy," she chided.

"I'm adventurous."

"You're awesome."

"Awesome enough to move in with?" the words came out so fast he surprised himself.

She said nothing.

Shit. And then:

"Awesome enough to babysit Jillian for a night and see how we do together in domestic harmony."

"Really?" Surprise infused his voice as a warmth spread through him. Even agreeing to such a thing was a huge leap for Josie. This tango they danced recently —he pushed, she pulled back—had become wearisome enough that he was beginning to wonder if this would define their relationship. Always surprising him, he found this sudden shift a sign that perhaps he had been hasty in judging her intransigence.

"And you can bring a toothbrush you can leave here."

Double surprise.

"Why don't you just get my name tattooed on your breast? A toothbrush? Wow." His words were sarcastic, but there was a ring of truth in it.

Josie looked down at her chest. "Not enough room," she mugged.

"Enough for me." One palm stretched out to fill it with her soft flesh. She inhaled sharply. Too soon? His cock grew—not too soon for him...

"Take it or leave it, porch sex boy."

He dumped her on the bed with a satisfying *plop*, her arms and legs splaying out like a daddy long legs.

"I'll take it." He stripped down quickly.

"What about dinner?" she asked, turning on her side, her hip jutting up, breasts calling out for his mouth.

His palms ran up the length of her calves, over her knees, opening her to him. "I'm coming for seconds right now..."

MIKE

No amount of meditation would make his erection subside. Visualizing the Dalai Lama, Pema Chodron and Thich Nhat Hanh—nope. Imagining suffering—nope. Conjuring images of dancing teddy bears and foam fingers—OK, that helped...

The doorbell rang. Josie and Alex. All five adults had jointly decided that the best approach to the overnight would be for Jillian to stay at the home she was most accustomed to; uprooting her to Cambridge for the night might add to the potential for disaster. All of the baby items that Laura, Mike and Dylan used to manage one twenty-pound infant filled the cabin to the brim, from a bouncy seat to the high chair to the crib that the baby never actually slept in. It was currently filled with clean, folded laundry and a six-foot bunny rabbit Dylan had bought on a whim. Yesterday.

Orchestrating this night away had involved a logistical operation worthy of a five star general. Convincing Laura had been the hardest part.

"You what? You want to what? I can't leave her overnight!" she'd protested, though a flicker of interest, barely noticeable, flashed in her eyes. He had struggled for the past few days not to say anything about her reading habits. A quiet calm descended over him, his way of processing the new information. On the other hand, his libido screamed with the knowledge of what she had been reading, making his mind chaotic with questions, so many they threatened to burst from his veins.

Twenty mile runs didn't really help.

Nothing, he suspected, would help until he and Dylan had her naked and alone for nearly an entire day.

They would all have to fight the urge to sleep. Sleep had replaced sex as their preferred bedroom activity. He stopped that line of thought cold—if he kept being so pessimistic, what he thought would become what he lived. *No. Absolutely not.* Of course, it already had become what he lived, but he was not going to let his thoughts rule him.

Mind over matter needed to become hands over thoughts. Hands over Laura's sweet, creamy skin. Her fingers wrapping around his shaft, their lips mingled in a kiss as his palms explored her body, loving the woman who had brought him so much joy.

Not thoughts of sleep. Fuck *no*.

His will was stronger than his worry.

When had life become so odd? Even Dylan seemed...diminished somehow these days. Less cocky. Tired. Beaten down. They all were, and as much as he wanted to blame it on the transition to parenthood, something else accounted for it. Even the discovery of Laura's BDSM reading couldn't quite make everything add up.

Something deeper was troubling Laura, and the preparations for Josie's and Alex's arrival had helped him to understand more.

She was altered. Different. Completely consumed with Jillian and yet it was more than that, as if she were consumed precisely because she was running away from something. It was familiar to Mike, of course—he literally ran away from problems. Pounding feet on pavement took his worries and troubles away. At least for the time he was running.

Laura's form of running was the baby.

And when you were away from the distraction you used to escape your problems, they all came back in one full, enormous rush.

Were he and Dylan doing more harm than good with their crazy scheme? He hated overthinking plans, but right now his mind raced as he watched Laura talking with Josie and Alex, Jillian resting in her baby wrap on Laura's hip, reaching out to play with Alex's sleeve. Serious and frowning, Laura was explaining something about how to warm up breast milk without using a microwave while Josie's deer-in-the-headlights look visibly increased. Alex was charmed by the baby, whose hair was the exact blonde shade of her mother, Jillian's little bow lips pouting as she concentrated on accurately grabbing a button on Alex's cuff.

Mike could watch Laura forever. How could someone so beautiful and loving have found her way to them? Being given a second chance and, now, an opportunity to parent seemed more surreal than becoming a billionaire. The horrors of Jill's cancer and death seemed somehow cleansed by the baby, as if her little soul were here to wash away grief and sadness. Rich beyond his dreams, deliriously in love, and content with a family of his own making, he found himself pausing and pulling back, watching the scene not from an emotional point but, instead, with his wise mind.

Laura's nose turned up a little when she smiled. Her cheeks looked like apples when she laughed. The skin at the edges of her eyes folded in a way that conveyed compassion and empathy when she listened. Her body moved with grace and purpose, whether she was changing a diaper or talking to the woman who baked fresh bread for the farmer's market. From the blonde beauty they'd met online, to the woman timid and fearful they were making fun of her, to the broken-hearted person who'd been too upset to reveal her pregnancy, Laura had shown them so many sides of herself.

And he loved every damn one of them.

So why hide *this*? Bondage and domination and cravings and control while naked and steamy and full of temptation—how could she think he and Dylan wouldn't be on board? Give him a collar and some rope and every sex toy you could imagine and he'd be ready, willing, able and hot.

What made her read so much, allow her mind to feed off this, but kept her from telling the two men who were her life partners, who wanted to please her and share every intimate experience you could imagine?

Had they done something wrong?

The questions killed him, ricocheting around like errant fireworks, careening aimlessly but ready to explode on impact, far off course. And then he realized people were speaking to him.

"Helloooo!" Josie waved one arm, the other struggling to put on the baby carrier Laura was offering. "Earth to Mike!"

He ran a hand through his freshly-clipped hair. It felt good to have shorter hair, no beard, and a clean, pressed shirt. What joy the little things in life held. "Sorry. Thinking."

"Too much of that is bad for you," Laura joked, eyes panicked. Dylan was loading their overnight bags into the jeep, and he could tell from the tension in Laura's voice that she was about to—

"C'mere," Mike said, pulling her into his arms. The sobs poured out. Alex now held Jillian and deftly turned away so she wouldn't see her mother crying. Finding a blanket, he put it on the floor, and then gently set her down. As Mike soothed Laura and smoothed her hair, he realized he hadn't been this close to her, bodies touching the full line from shoulder to knee, in far, far too long. Recent hugs had been more perfunctory. Kisses had been simple pecks.

That was far too little.

No more of too little.

They deserved caresses and pats, longing looks and playful smacks, deep kisses in the kitchen, pushed up against the counter, tongues and hands exactly where they should be, holding flesh and promises of rendezvous later in the night between the sheets. He wanted frenzied quickies during naptime and slow baths in the huge Jacuzzi on the deck, the first whispers of snow in the mountains hinting at a winter wonderland, making love beneath an audience of stars in the inky sky.

Watching Alex play with the baby, who was decked out in a red and white striped outfit with hearts sprinkled randomly in the cloth, he closed his eyes as Laura reached up and wiped her eyes, laughing sheepishly. "What's wrong with me?" she asked. "I want to go away. I need to be with you and Dylan."

Josie grunted next to them, wide chocolate eyes beseeching as the tangled multi-colored cloth and brass rings of the baby sling twisted her arm behind her. "Is this really some sort of strange sex toy? Because I'm totally tied up now."

That got Laura chuckling, a genuine sound of amusement that made Mike feel better about having her pull away from him, the loss of the heat of her skin

47

against his making him all the more determined that tonight needed to be theirs—nothing but the three of them.

"Let me unravel you," she said as she helped her friend align the contraption. Alex turned back and waggled his eyebrows at Josie in a comically overdone lascivious look that made Mike burst out laughing, his body suddenly content. More than content—right. He felt right. Everything would be just fine, he knew, if he and Dylan could get Laura out of her head space and into a more sensorial, explorative frame of mind.

With the set up she was about to discover, there was no way she could stay in her own mind.

He and Dylan had put a lot of effort into *that*.

Laura unraveled Josie and was poring over a four-page, single-spaced, handwritten set of notes, complete with diagrams and charts, for how to take care of Jillian for the next eighteen hours.

Josie shot Mike a look that said, *Kill me now.*

He shrugged. She mouthed, *You owe me.*

No kidding, he mouthed back.

"You guys taking mime lessons?" Dylan asked, hands full of Laura's purse and her coat.

"Done packing?" Mike asked, avoiding the silly question.

"We're ready to go!" Dylan replied.

Laura looked up, eyes wide, hands reaching for Jillian. Alex gently transferred the babbling baby to her mother. Laura's half smile vanished, her cheeks going pale, as the moment had come.

She had to trust Josie and Alex to watch the baby.

But most of all, she had to trust Mike and Dylan to go back to that time when it had just been them. To give herself a portion of a day to be Laura. *Just Laura.*

They wouldn't be Mommy and Daddy and Daddy and roommate and errand runner and burper and diaper changer and breastfeeder and soother.

For eighteen hours they would be Mike, Dylan and Laura.

Mike hardened at the thought.

LAURA

"**I**f you huff the baby's head any harder you'll make her go bald, Laura," Josie said as Laura sniffed Jillian's head. Inhaling deeply, Laura used the gesture to center herself. This really was ridiculous. Everyone would be fine.

Josie wrapped her arm around Laura's shoulder and squeezed. "We really will be fine. Just hand her over and go have fun with your guys. Get your groove on."

Groove? Was this the '70s? The comment made Laura laugh again, and Josie took the opportunity to slide her hands around Jillian's little striped ribcage, expertly guiding her little feet through the baby wrap and—*voila!* The baby rested on Josie's hip as she tightened the cloth to secure her on.

"That was perfect!" Laura gasped, genuinely impressed.

"Gah!" Jillian gurgled in agreement, bright eyes turning to Laura, then focusing on the ends of Josie's hair.

Warm fingers slipped through hers. "Let's go," Mike urged, pulling gently. With feet feeling like concrete, she lurched along next to him, feeling both heavier and lighter with each step away from her little girl. As they crossed the threshold, she willed herself not to look back, knowing the baby might cry.

Instead, it was Laura who cried as they walked to the Jeep. Dylan was standing next to it, arms outstretched toward her. As his arms enveloped her, the scent of aftershave and his musk mingled in her senses as she inhaled, throat shaky.

He smelled so good. So *man*.

And all *hers*.

A dull ache emerged deep inside, a desire for something she hadn't even thought to want in a very, very long time, emerged with such force she closed her eyes and tried to hold it back. It was too much, too fast, and too hard.

And...so was Dylan.

Her hand, as if driven by a will of its own, slid over his hip and down the front, fingers finding the outline of his straining erection against his pants. His sharp inhale pleased her. Ah, yes—this power. She'd forgotten about the thrill of arousing a man, how a simple caress could drive him to a frenzy, the promise of more and the tease of not now so intoxicating.

Knowing they could complete whatever she suggested pleased her, too.

A sharp stab of doubt hit her as he leaned in for a kiss.

Her hands found the same man she'd first touched fifteen months ago. What did his hands find when he reached for her? A very different Laura, with a body that had changed too much.

She was too much.

And just like that, the light turned off inside and she pulled back, leaving a very confused Dylan. Mike, thankfully, saved her.

"Let's go! The minutes are ticking, and we have a surprise for you, Laura," Mike said, voice a little too tight to be cheerful as he slid behind the steering wheel. His eye cut to the rear-view mirror and met Dylan's, in the back seat. They both seemed to alternate between compassion for her and ruthless efficiency. She couldn't blame them; they were probably worried she'd back out. She dutifully buckled herself into the front passenger seat, and as the Jeep peeled out of the driveway, gravel kicking up and pinging against the sides of the vehicle, all three shared a huge, deep, loud sigh of relief.

"My God, we did it!" Laura laughed. Each foot away from the cabin made her feel conflicted, yet she breathed easier. Maybe the conflicted feeling was what she thought she was supposed to feel, and not actually what she really felt. An entire day with no baby attached to her seemed unreal.

Leaving the cabin behind felt like a kind of escape, too. It wasn't that she didn't go out; she and Jillian went to stores, shopped, played at playgrounds, and took a weekly baby swimming class. But this was different. And as Mike's hand snaked across the gear shift to hold hers, she remembered that her guys were waiting with bated breath to get into bed and unleash some pent up desires, too.

When had she become "that woman," the one who wasn't interested? Every sex toy you could imagine had once lived in her bedside table, and her rich inner fantasy world had created sex positions that just plain old defied the laws of physics. She, Mike and Dylan had collectively explored about half of those—and now...nothing. She was happy to please them, but not really interested in *being* pleased.

Why? What had changed?

Within five minutes, Mike was pulling in to a small driveway at the edge of the ski resort. "What's this?" she asked, curious. "I thought we were going in to the city for the night."

"It's a surprise," he said in a low, suggestive voice. As the road narrowed, the brown leaves clinging to trees that should have released their burden by now, large pines appeared, tall and foreboding.

And then—a tiny cabin, the size of a turret, with a winding staircase around the outside. Made of unfinished timber, it looked like a fairy cottage, delicate and sturdy all at once, like a handcrafted home out of a fantasy movie.

"What is this?" she marveled. The cabin was two stories, but small. A wall of glass faced south, and she could see a small deck near what appeared to be the front door. On the deck sat a wooden hot tub, like something you'd see in Finland.

"A new property for the resort. We're testing out little eco-cabins, to see if we can encourage ski tourism."

The Jeep came to a halt and they piled out.

"And this is where we're staying? Boy, this sure is remote," she said, intrigued. The driveway was a good eighth of a mile, and as she scanned the full circle of the site, there wasn't any sign of civilization as far as she could see. The cabin itself almost seemed to have sprung up out of nature, Laura's view took in the timber steps, made from solid logs cut to fit, and the solar panels on the roof.

"Solar?"

"I said it was an eco-cabin," Mike reminded her. "We have electricity, running water, and a grey water recycling system."

"Is there a bathroom?"

"Yep. No worries. It has all the luxuries!" he assured her. A deck light glowed and she realized how close to winter they were. It was just barely 4pm and already dusk was settling in. They had to be back at

10am tomorrow. An image of Jillian hit her, how soft her skin was, how her chubby fists felt in Laura's hair.

"We have everything we could possibly need," Dylan added, a bit cryptically, hefting some luggage in each hand. Mike grabbed a bag as well, his other hand reaching into his front pocket. Watching him fumble and dig for the keys, Laura saw ample evidence of just how excited Mike was for this night. The two men emptied the Jeep in two trips. Laura hung back as they finished unloading, joining Mike on the front deck when they were done; Dylan remained inside. Mike's arm slid about her waist, confirming what his jeans had already hinted: this night was planned as a sexfest.

Mike gave her a look of warmth, love and teasing that made her toes tingle and—for one lovely, fleeting second—she felt transformed. All her worries and insecurities disappeared as if desiccated and blown away on the wind, carried off like dust she needn't ever worry about. The thought of making love with him made her body rev up reflexively...

But her mind quickly ground to a screeching halt. Sex was the last thing she wanted to want. As if dragging her limbs through concrete, she moved toward him, a sense of dread and angst filling her. She wasn't supposed to feel like this! Making love was what she was supposed to want, right? Stalling for time, she pretended she was still admiring the cabin. She noted there were no curtains on any windows, and why would they need them?

They were completely isolated. Only a deer or a fox would see them if they walked around nude.

Poor deer. Wouldn't want to see me naked, either, she thought, and then clamped down on the negative words. *Stop it!* This intrusive voice wouldn't stop cutting her down, and she wished desperately she could spend the night curled up with her eReader, even here. The only time the voice went away was when she kept her mind occupied with books. Crawling into someone else's sensual world, where the hero and heroine possessed so many faults, and love overcame all...

"Hey," Mike said gently, unlocking his knees to level himself with her, hands cradling her face. "What's going on inside that gorgeous head?"

Panic kicked in to high gear. How could she admit what she was feeling? Impossible. She didn't want him to doubt that she loved them. Or wanted them. Or needed them. But how could she say what she was really experiencing? The fissures in their relationship that this kind of revelation would bring were just too dangerous.

Better to keep it to herself.

A shaky, deep breath and she caught his eyes, making herself fake a brightness and freedom she definitely did not feel. "Just...thinking about Jillian." Not a lie. Well, not...technically.

"You can think about her tomorrow," he said in a dark, steamy voice, his lips taking hers. His hands were on her, fingers sinking in to her waist, lips owning her and then his tongue seeking to find her, all the motion so fast she felt a fire flare within, making every cell warm instantly.

As his tongue traced her teeth and his arms tightened around her, whatever train of thought she had until that moment died quickly. Melting into his arms, she was dimly aware of a light vanilla and sandalwood aroma mixing with the taste of Mike, making her wonder... Their sex life as a triad had morphed over the past year. Sometimes she slept with Mike. Sometimes Dylan. Sometimes both. No one seemed to get jealous or bitter or angry: they made it all up as they went along. Often if she was with one of them like this, the other would join in, a second set of warm hands were on her, always very welcome if not expected. A flash of memory, of Dylan's palm on the small of her back, then riding down to grasp her ass, made her smile through Mike's kiss, which seemed to ignite him. Her mind began to nag more and more insistently, urging her to note the absence of Dylan's hands on her, and finally made her break away from Mike and ask, "Dylan? What is he—?"

Smiling, Mike pushed the door to the cabin open. As she turned, she saw the answer.

Candles.

Hundreds of them. Dylan had been lighting them, encircling the interior of the round little house, a glow that warmed her further. How precious. How startling and wonderful. As dusk settled in out here on the deck, the warmth the candles cast over the interior made the cabin seem like a sanctuary.

She and Mike stepped through the door just as Dylan crossed by it, pecking a quick kiss on her as he walked past, his target the fireplace. The care they'd taken to set up this moment made her appreciate both men.

Mike stared down at her, eyes ablaze. "Some wine?"

"I'd love some," she replied, giving his arm a caress of thanks, of affection, of appreciation. She took in the rest of the interior. Sexfest, indeed. The bed was enormous—bigger than a California King—and dead center in the middle of the circular room. A cream-colored net, suspended from the ceiling, draped down over the huge, down-comforter-covered mattress, more pillows sprinkled about than an entire Bed, Bath and

Beyond could even contain. Underneath the scented candles' perfume, the room smelled like the fresh cedar the cabin was made of, a scent of comfort.

Mike brought her a shining wine glass half full of a lovely rosé. She gulped half down without thinking and he chuckled. Eschewing alcohol because she was nursing, she hadn't had more than a sip here and there since Jillian had been born. Drinking so much so fast would hit her hard. Loosening up couldn't hurt, right? "Same old Laura," Mike laughed. Her lack of appreciation for good wine had been a joke when they'd met, and now it was a running tease between them.

The answering laugh came out of her unbidden, her muscles relaxing, the room like something out of a fantasy, all a pale, creamy glow, with the darkened forest peeking in through the wide windows like a protective mother, tree branches embracing the tall, circular building. It really felt as if this cabin had grown out of the ground like a tree, the knots in the wood visible in the walls, the scent of cedar filling the room.

Laura sipped the rest of her glass and said nothing when Mike, after pouring a glass for Dylan, refilled hers without asking. The three stood and faced the large picture window, eyes unfocused and lost in the splendor of the view as the dusky, pink-streaked sky faded with a sepia tone.

It was the most time she'd spent just *being* with them since the baby had been born.

The baby. Jillian. Motherhood. For a short half hour she'd somehow pushed all thoughts of the baby aside and taken halting steps toward just being Laura again.

And it had felt good.

Reproach and guilt poured in. She batted it away. Jillian was fine. Fine. Alex and Josie could manage just fine.

Fine.

And she *still* felt good. She felt damn good.

Speaking of things that felt good...Dylan's arm found its way around her waist and he kissed her neck, the scent of wine and citrus mixed with his earthy, spicy aftershave. A deep inhale and another kiss, this one below her ear, and she felt her heart pick up, her body responding with a finely-tuned keening that made her feel empty, wanting him in her. The sudden rush of warmth and eagerness surprised her, making her smile, for it also pleased her.

Maybe more of the old Laura remained than just her wine cluelessness.

Maybe she really could find her way back, for one night, to the way they were.

Dylan turned her toward him, finished his glass of wine in one big swig, and with a tight power in his face that she would have thought was anger if she didn't know otherwise, reached for her hand. He pulled her toward the bed. He didn't ask.

This wasn't up for discussion.

Mike—to Laura's deep amusement—finished the rest of his wine with an audible gulp and joined them. The air in the room was suddenly cold and hot at once, the candles making the bed seem to float in the middle of the room. Acutely aware of every muscle in Dylan's hand, the way the hair at the top of his chest peeked out from the V of his shirt, how Mike's tall, lean body cast a shadow in the ever-darkening room, Laura felt transported. Loved. Wanted.

Desired.

Four hands made ready work of removing her clothes as Laura closed her eyes, so vulnerable and accustomed to the two men, yet hesitant and a bit shy. Dylan eased her heathered-lilac shirt up over her head, hands sending the shirt to the ground, then cupping her full breasts with a sense of want she could feel in her core, her body tightening and opening at the same time, ready for what he so desperately seemed to want to give. Mike's fingers pulled at the zipper at her waist, letting her skirt drop to the ground. She slid her shoes off, now in her panties and bra, hating how awkward and self-conscious she felt.

It had been so long. Her fault, entirely—Mike and Dylan had asked plenty of times for more sex, though over the last month they'd backed off, probably tired of her endless rejections.

Mind looping with all these thoughts, she couldn't just relax.

Even worse, she struggled to hide that fact. Because who gets uptight and awkward around the men you've pledged to love forever? Their bond was sacred, the three connected and forged into one soul, it seemed. If Laura had been told two years ago that she would soon meet two protectors who would love her forever and unconditionally, and would give her the greatest gift ever in baby Jillian, she would have scoffed at the sheer impossibility of such a life.

Yet here she was, now, living it. With Mike's intense eyes raking over her nearly-nude form, Dylan's hands effortlessly unclasped her bra, sending shivers down her spine as he moved the lingerie across her shoulders and let it slide, useless and unwanted, to the ground.

She froze, and it wasn't from cold. Looking at Dylan, Mike frowned and reached down, one arm going under her knees, the other under her neck and then—she was in his arms.

"Put me down!" she gasped, impressed by the feel of hard muscle against the back of her knees. You would think she weighed nothing, the way he held her, as if she were a hundred pounds lighter.

"I'm about to," he murmured in her ear, eyes closed off, making her feel unsettled. What was this? Depositing her on the bed, Mike nodded to Dylan, who appeared at the headboard with a small box, the size of a laptop computer.

"What are you doing?" she asked.

And then silk scarves appeared, the same color as the netting that surrounded her now that she was on top of the down comforter. The feel of the feather bed beneath her nude skin was like being reborn, the comfort and sensuality a balm that cut through her trepidation.

"What's this?"

"You tell us," Mike said, sitting on the bed next to her. A chill poured over her exposed skin, knees bent and thighs pulled up against her waist. One nipple stretched, lazy and languid, toward the bed spread, her body on display for her fully-clothed and—she now saw—very determined men.

"Tell you...what?" she asked, sitting up, pulling her knees to her chest. This felt wrong. Different. Not what she'd expected.

Dylan fingered a silver silk scarf, pulling it between his fingers, the action so powerful and suggestive she found herself licking her lips for no conscious reason. "Shall I be Gideon?" he asked, looking at Mike.

"Sure. And I can be Cooper."

Fuck.

They knew.

61

"Been reading my eReader?" she squeaked, taking a stab in the dark.

Dylan snapped the silk like a cord, making not so much a sound, but a gesture that left her confused. He didn't answer her question, but instead asked one of his own, dark hair mussed, mahogany eyes bold and in control. "Do you want a contract?"

"Contract?" Laura repeated, brain on fire.

"And a safeword?" Mike crooned.

"A what—?"

"Because Laura," Mike said, interrupting, his own hands now filled with a different silk scarf, this one bright, China red, "we're the ones who should be your book boyfriends."

"And *only* us," Dylan growled.

Book boyfriend? How did they know that term? How did they know what she'd been reading? Did they read her eReader and find all those erotic romances on it? Gideon? That meant they'd read Sylvia Day's BDSM books. Cooper? The extraordinary Dom? Oh, God—they'd found *Their Virgin Princess*—and oh, holy mother of—*what* was Mike pulling out of that box?

Was that a vibrating butt plug and a bottle of lube?

Uhhhh. Her mind went blank. Completely, hopelessly empty.

Both men now sat on opposite sides of her, twenty throw pillows in various hues of cream piled around them, the netting thrown back so that they lived in a little bubble. A tense, sexually-charged bubble of her own making.

"So, I can draw up a contract if you'd like," Dylan said.

"Why would I want—"

"Because, Laura." Mike cut in, his face serious. "You're getting *every* fantasy tonight. Right now. Here.

62

You get to have ultimate control by handing over every shred of it to us."

Every cell in her body turned from hot to cold, her skin like a live wire.

"I don't—they're just books," she laughed, her voice tinny and utterly unconvincing. The promise of what they were offering was readable on their faces, both men hard and ready to play out what she'd only read. What they, *too*, had read. It made her wet to think about it, and she squirmed, trying not to be obvious. "Just something to read while I'm bored," she choked out.

"We won't make *this* boring," Dylan whispered in her ear, making her jolt. They were serious. This was real. What they offered her was...

Impossible.

Neither of them had shown the slightest inkling of interest in BDSM in the bedroom before. Why now? What was this?

"I, I'm sure you won't," she stumbled, face bright red with a flush of embarrassment and incredulity, breasts smashed against her knees, her panties her only clothing, "but we don't need this to be intimate," she said, her voice trailing into a hush as she gestured toward the box by Mike's hand.

"We don't need it," Mike agreed. "But you want it."

"I never said that!"

"You didn't have to."

An excited rush of embarrassment filled her. Telling her deepest desires to Mike and Dylan should be part of their relationship, right? If you can't share that central part of yourself with the person(s) you choose to spend the rest of your life with, then who can you share it with? Inhibition was normal; being

63

mildly shy and a bit hesitant made sense, because sexual fantasy was a funny thing. Dreams and wishes didn't have to make sense. They were hers. And if they asked too much of her guys, or seemed silly or self-indulgent or—her greatest fear—were something they found unappealing, then the risk of asking and being rejected was too much.

Letting the mind wander to places where you lost all control, where a man wanted to dominate your body and completely pull your sexual strings muscle by muscle, gasp by gasp, was a kind of world that she should be able to access with a single request to her men.

So why was it so hard to look Mike in the eye right now? Or to even glance at Dylan? They offered her a willingness to give her some wonderful sex play that she'd been too...something...to request.

And now...they'd read her mind.

Or, at least, her eReader.

"Laura," Dylan said gently. "We love you. We want you. We desire you. Tonight isn't just about the sex. It's about being intimate and feeling whole with you." He took her chin in his hand and tipped her eyes up to meet his, pupils dilated and so full of heat she felt her skin tingle. "When I touch you, the connection makes me feel like a better Dylan. Stronger, more real. And when the three of us are together, we go places none of us can go as individuals."

"Let us make love to you the way you want to be loved," Mike added, stroking her back.

Bzzzz. The sound of a phone interrupted before Laura could answer. Her phone. The phone! Jillian! Something was wrong with the baby. Laura's sexual self died in half a second as Mommy Brain kicked in.

"Where's my phone?" she shrieked, the moment ruined as Mike and Dylan deflated, Dylan's disappointment registering in her mind briefly, while Mike appeared to be angry. She couldn't think about them; something might be wrong at home. Heart racing, her chest suddenly chilled with a flush of sweat, she fumbled for her discarded skirt, dropped the phone, picked it back up and answered, running for the sanctuary of the bathroom.

"What's wrong? What's wrong?" she shouted into the phone.

"Shhhhhh!" Josie hushed quietly. "You'll wake Jillian. She's right here and sound asleep."

"THEN WHY ARE YOU CALLING? WHAT HAPPENED?" Laura bellowed.

"Did I interrupt you guys?" Josie said, the sly tone in her voice making Laura want to rip her ears off and wear them on a chain around her neck.

"Why are you calling?" Laura snapped. "And no, you didn't interrupt anything," she lied. "We've only been here for what? Half an hour?"

"Shit," Josie said, "it sounds like things aren't going well there."

And with that, Laura burst into tears, sat on the toilet lid, and realized she was wearing nothing but panties.

"Aren't going well is...oh, hell, I don't know," Laura whispered through a sob.

"Oh, honey," Josie said, her voice so comforting it made Laura cry harder. "Are you guys having a hard time?"

"You told them to read my eReader?" Laura asked quietly, wiping her tears with a piece of lavender-scented tissue from the box built into the log-cabin wall.

"I...shit." Josie blew out a long sigh that gave Laura a chance to blow her own nose. "Yes, I'll own that. I did."

"Why?"

"Because Mike and Dylan told me and Alex you have only had sex twice in six months."

The hand holding the piece of tissue curled into a tight fist. "They WHAT?" she hissed. The distinct sound of a champagne cork popped in the distance, and Laura heard Dylan's muffled voice say something with urgency.

"And they said the only thing you seemed interested in were your books, so..." Josie's voice faded. A sharp inhale came through the phone. "I never realized how good a baby's head can smell," Josie said, as if naming an embarrassed confession.

Snorting, laughing, and fuming all at once, Laura felt like a vortex of too many emotions crammed into one body. What a mess. Her two amazing men were out in the living room of this gorgeous cabin, getting champagne ready, with hundreds of candles lit and an assortment of pleasure-driven sex toys purchased based on her deepest desires, and here she sat sniffling into the phone and berating her best friend, who was watching her precious baby.

Could she be any more screwed up?

"She's really OK? No problems?" *Please say yes*.

"Laura," Josie ventured, "don't ever tell Alex I said this, but I think I like this whole baby thing. Jillian is adorable and even when she cries—"

"She cried? Why?"

"Because she's a baby." Josie snorted. "But don't worry Alex just stripped his shirt off and latched her on."

"Ha ha." Even that cut through Laura's malaise.

"I swear the man would lactate if he could," Josie joked.

"You like the whole domestic thing?" Laura wasn't surprised. She knew Josie had it in her.

"I like the baby thing more than I want Alex to know. Yet."

"OK. Shhhh. I won't spill *your* secrets."

"*Touché*. I'm sorry."

"So why did you call?" Now Laura was flushed and mussed, confused and overwhelmed.

"We couldn't remember whether you said to use the butt cream on her rash or to just let it air out."

"You called me for that?" Laura said through gritted teeth.

"The way you gave us instructions made it seem like we'd have nuclear bombs shoved up our asses and your foot would trigger the explosion if we didn't do exactly what you said," Josie replied in a sing-songy voice.

"Is Jillian awake?"

"No. But your angry voice made her stir."

"Air first. Butt cream second."

"M'kay."

Silence. But Josie didn't hang up.

"Anything else?"

"Yes." Pause. A quiet, softer side of Josie came out in her words. "Laura, what are you doing to those guys? But most of all, to yourself, honey?" Josie didn't use words like "honey." That was the second time in one conversation. Either her niece, Darla, was rubbing off on her or Laura was in worse shape than she ever possibly realized.

More tears. "You're the one who called," she sniffed.

"And you're—what? Sitting in the bathroom talking to me?"

"How could you tell?"

"The echo."

Laura looked around the bathroom and laughed. "I don't know what I'm doing, Josie. It's not that I don't want Mike and Dylan. It's just that—" she choked on her next words, but forced them out anyhow—"what if they don't want me?"

"Why wouldn't they?" Josie whispered. "According to both of them, they're slobbering all over themselves to get you in bed, but you're not interested."

Gah. Even more tears. "Because..." Her mind rushed with excuses and reasons why she wasn't interested, and then—like a wrist flicking away a gnat —she shooed her own flimsy rationalizations away. "Because I don't know. Because I don't feel desirable."

"Maybe you should just fake it."

"*Fake* it?" Fake what? An orgasm? No need to do that—they were plentiful when the mood struck and she was really into sex.

"Make it 'til you fake it. Wait. No—got that backwards," Josie chuckled. "Basically, be willing to start having sex and see whether your interest catches up."

"You mean pretend I want something I don't?" Laura could hear her own voice go flat.

"I mean be willing. Show up for your own sex life. The guys are there with a fucking 20-foot billboard that says "Make Love to Us" and hard-ons the size of tree trunks, all pointed at you! Be willing to touch them and let them touch you, Laura. Just start with that. Don't overthink it."

Don't overthink it. "Easy for you to say."

"No, it's not."

68

"You have the libido of a seventeen year old boy."

Josie didn't argue. "I had to get over myself, though, to let Alex love me and to love him back," Josie reminded her.

"You think I'm the same way with sex? Because I a m *so* not as fucked up in my sex life as you are in your emotional life."

"Nothing has to be 'fair and balanced,' here," Josie huffed. "This isn't Fox News."

They both laughed. "Now get off the phone and go get into a mess of six arms and legs and tongues—"

"Six tongues?"

"You know what I meant. Go get dirty, Laura. Have raunchy, awesome, mind-blowing sex with the fathers of your baby. Enjoy yourself. Alex and I have Jillian and we sure as hell won't be having any sex tonight, so go be the ones getting some for once." *Click.* Josie ended the call, leaving Laura no choice. Only a best friend could do that.

Leave you to your own devices at the exact moment when you just want to be an ostrich and pretend you don't need to deal with real life.

Laura loved her and hated her for it.

"Laura?" Mike called out from the living room.

Josie was right. It was time to show up. Catching a glimpse of herself in the full-length mirror on the back of the door, she gasped—and then stopped. The mental torture dissipated. This was silly.

And the whole mascara-raccoon look really didn't do it for her. Giggling (and enjoying the sound from her), she wiped her eyes, splashed some cold water on her face, and used the magic of the lavender-infused tissues to clean herself up. A deep, shaky breath or two and she opened the door, walking toward the bed, and looked up to find:

Dylan and Mike, completely naked, stretched out on the bed. Mike dangled a pair of handcuffs from one finger, while Dylan held a large champagne flute in his hand, stretched out for her to take.

"Subtle," she said, taking the drink. She downed it in one huge gulp.

"That's Taittinger—" Mike protested as Dylan interrupted him with a dark look.

Laura couldn't stop herself from laughing at the scene. Mike's long, tan, taut legs didn't even come to the end of the enormous bed, his erection standing proud, making Laura feel a prickly heat flow through her as her eyes took him in greedily. As if that weren't enough, Dylan lounged on the bed like a model in the middle of a shoot, one knee up, the other stretched out, his own massive cock at attention, as if it were the focal piece for a photograph.

In her mind, it was.

And between them, a space just right for her. Instead of climbing into the bed and over one of the guys, she started from the base and crawled up, her eyes shifting from one man to the other, their bodies and coloring so starkly different yet blazingly rich. Tall, blonde Mike and thick, muscled Dylan, with his swarthy complexion and riveting eyes. Both made her smolder, and both made her see that all her fears were baseless, her insecurities an old relic left over from a time when she hadn't felt loved enough.

No need for those thoughts any more.

Dylan's warm palm slipped under her panties, cupping her ass, and then Mike's nimble fingers made quick work of the wisp of cotton and silken cloth, leaving the three of them completely nude on the huge bed, the room hushed and warm, the candles lending an eerie, contemplative glow as Laura relaxed—*really* relaxed—for the first time in ages.

"What do you have planned for me?" she asked Mike, eyes flitting from him to the handcuffs he held over her as Dylan teased one nipple, the shock making her shiver.

A crooked half-smile teased his lips, making her wet and, suddenly, very wanting. "We had more than enough planned for you, but we thought we would have to pry whatever's wrong out of you." He gently set the handcuffs down on the end table, twisting his torso in that maddening way that made muscles pop out from his waistline, the effect artistic and graceful and *hot*.

"Pry?" Now Dylan peppered her shoulders with tiny kisses that made it hard to think. Ah, that wet, warm mouth. What he could do elsewhere...

"We know you've been so quiet, honey," Mike said, cupping her chin, as Dylan's kisses continued. "We just want you to be happy. We both feel so complete when we're with you. You light us on fire. We want to do the same for you."

She swallowed, hard, as Dylan stopped the butterfly touch and curled around her, legs pulled up, glorious cock ready for its own set of kisses—from her.

"This is when I feel most connected to the entire world, Laura. Right here. Right now. With you," Dylan added, brushing the hair off her face with little touches of love.

What should have happened next didn't. Laura expected to cry, to make a bunch of excuses, to apologize, to cringe—to *deflect*. But it didn't happen.

"I could sit here," she said, fingers lightly stroking Mike's shaft as he gasped, jaw tightening, struggling to listen to her, "and tell you all about why I've been so

71

miserable." In fairness, she took her other hand as she stretched out on her back, and gave Dylan a set of finger strokes that made him inhale sharply. "Right now, though, I don't want to do that. I don't want to tie myself in knots trying to unravel the past six months and ruin what we have right here, right now."

"So," she said, letting go of Mike and turning to Dylan, the press of her lips against the tight, warm skin of his pecs so luxurious and so sensual she wished she could do it—and nothing *but*—forever, "let's read and talk later. We have six months of catching up to do."

Strong hands pinned her to the bed with such speed she couldn't think, her wrists pressed deeply into the mattress. "Six months, huh?" Mike asked, now looming over her, body folded on his knees, the thick thigh muscles bulging along with another very bulging muscle that glistened with need. "Which fantasy is your favorite, Laura? Because Dylan went shopping and we can do anything you want right now."

Whatever control she thought she had over both of them with her taunting touches dissipated in seconds. Holy shit. They were *serious*. A deep, shaking sense of profound joy filled her.

"If you're the one who is dominating, you're the one who calls all the shots," she rasped.

"No. Wrong," Dylan said, his voice hoarse with desire. "You decide everything. We have only one thing we control."

"What's that?"

"Your orgasm."

She groaned involuntarily, already squirming with a white-hot need that she'd assumed could be quelled with a mouth or a cock within a few minutes. They were going to draw this out amidst the splendor of the room, the greatest gift before them handed to the three by their friends: *time*. Oh, the grand joyful prospect of an entire night stretched out in infinite glory for nothing but this—pleasure and sensual pain and whatever these men did to her as the three of them explored uncharted territory in bed.

Her clit swelled with a craving to be touched and nibbled and licked and loved, the emotion so buried and unfamiliar it claimed her in full. *This* is what it felt like, to be in a state of wanting all the time. She'd hardly recognized it, having repressed it for so long, and yet here it was, laid bare just as she was, her eyes being covered by that red, silk scarf Mike had just played with minutes ago in his hands.

"You need to pick a safeword," Dylan whispered.

"Safeword?"

"It's something you say to stop us if—"

The giggle bubbled up inside her as someone—Mike?—adjusted the scarf. Unable to see them, her senses sharpened as she worked to know where they were in space. Dylan's voice sounded like brandy.

"I know what a safeword is. Do we really need one? You guys aren't going to—"

Bzzzzz. Except that wasn't her phone. What was that? It sounded loud.

And *big*. She felt the covers shift slightly, and then the bed began to vibrate a bit. Good hell.

"OK, OK, a safeword," she gasped. How big was that vibrator? Racing through the set of books she had on her eReader, she wondered which sex scenes the guys had read. The possibilities were endless. Stifling a moan of ecstasy at the thought of reliving some of what she'd read, she tried to gather herself.

"Um, *Madge* is my safeword."

"*Madge*?" She almost laughed at the incredulity in Dylan's voice.

73

"Yes, *Madge*."

"That will halt everything permanently," he mumbled. "And—yep. There went my erection. Good choice."

Mike's laugh erupted to her right as someone—she guessed him—turned the buzzing off.

"I can take care of that for you," she murmured, fumbling with her hand for him. He was just there a moment ago, and now that he wasn't talking, she could only go by touch and sound. The shuffle of skin on cloth as someone moved beside her tickled her ears; the muffled sound of lit candle wicks flickering as air moved, and the rasp of muscle against the sheets again all filled her with anticipation. Without vision she was acutely and frustratingly tensed for whatever came next.

Hopefully, it would be *her*.

Strong hands slid up her calves, to her thighs, and then a gentle push apart as her breath flowed in with an increased rush at the end, clit ready for the expected sensation of a finger, a mouth, of attention lovingly delivered the way she most wanted and needed it.

The warmth of a body—Mike's, she could tell, from the way his leg brushed against her knee, the pattern of skin and hair somehow ingrained in her, her mind marveling that she could know that, blindfolded —was between her now and a heated ache spread from her belly on down, body awakening. To her surprise, Dylan's lips were at her ear, teeth nipping her lobe, and he whispered, "I want your mouth."

Biting her lower lip, her core swollen with need, this was almost too much. "Of course," she said, and as her eyes rolled and she felt her body relax, layer by layer, at the same time the feel of Dylan as he moved to put his erection close to her face made a keen wave of pulses pour through her, nearly pushing her to climax by the mere thought, the hint, of what was next.

Wet, eager, and wanting, she was hardly the same woman from thirty minutes ago. And she loved it that way as the tip of Dylan's taut cock touched her mouth. Fumbling, unable to see, she pulled one hand to his shaft, but a strong palm wrapped around her wrist and stopped her.

"*Tsk, tsk, tsk.* Dylan, we forgot to tie her wrists," Mike said, his body catlike and stretched out, half on her and off, the massive heat from his body now covering two thirds of her as he'd stretched up from between her legs to grab her.

"Guys, you don't have to do this," she said in a sheepish tone. "It's not like I need thi—"

"You have a safeword," Mike hissed, her wrist encased in a soft coating around something metal. Click. Her shoulder adjusted, then Mike did the second arm. She was spread out on the bed and felt somewhat silly and yet more turned on than she'd ever been in her life. "Feel free to use it whenever you need. But until then, Laura, your pleasure is completely in our hands."

A wall of pure lust pounded through her veins as Mike's words sank in. Dylan's hot, pulsing cock came to her mouth at the same split second Mike's warm lips descended on her clit, the twinned tactile treasures shoving her out of her own head and back into her body, where all that mattered was her lips wrapped around Dylan's erection, the push of Mike's fingers on her wet folds, the heat of all three bodies working in concert with no interruptions, no plans, and nothing to do but *this*.

Hips bucking up, she found her orgasm standing ripe and ready, the tease of Mike's little laps bringing her there as she tightened, his finger sliding inside to find a wall of muscle searching for some welcome visitor to embrace.

And then...he stopped.

Dylan's gentle gliding in and out of her mouth, balanced above her chest, slowed down as she moaned from frustration, wanting more of what Mike had to offer. He wasn't kidding—he was going to draw this out and bring her to the edge, then pull back, over and over until she begged.

Maybe if she pleaded now he'd relent? It had been so, so long. *Too* long.

"Please," she mumbled, hips straining up.

Bzzzz.

Oh, dear.

Warm liquid poured from a single drop that fell with exquisite perfection on the tip of her engorged clit, and then a river of lube poured down her folds, the feeling so lush she rolled her pelvis up to capture more. Everything felt more right now, without her hands or eyes, and she wondered what the buzzing and the lube meant.

The push of something hard sliding in the lube around her ass made her core tighten, kegels excited and pulsing. The three of them had never been shy in using Laura's extensive sex toy collection in bed, but whatever Mike had at her spread-out ass was big.

She pushed against it, body eager on a level that her mind hadn't quite caught up to.

"Good," Mike said, his voice thick with emotion. "You want it."

Who was this? Mike could certainly take charge in the bedroom but he seemed to...*revel* in exerting so much sensual control over her. Dylan wasn't exactly a wallflower, either, his hands buried in her hair, fingers lovingly massaging her scalp as he gently rode her mouth. His legs tightened and she knew that it was *her* body, *her* lips, *her* tongue, and the essence of her that brought him to this kind of free hedonism, the easy, open sensuality that they shared right now. It made what Mike was doing to her all the more intense as he edged whatever vibrating device he used toward her puckered hole, sending her pussy walls into spasms that weren't quite orgasms.

Unfortunately.

And then the live wire of her entire body coalesced into one pinpointed strand of pure presence and enjoyment as he breached her tight ring of muscle and
—

Aahhhhhh. The feeling of fullness was so powerful that she faded to a white cloud in her mind, existing as nothing more than pure touch. A ball of nerves, a set of lungs that panted, and an ass and pussy that throbbed with short bursts of pounding blood and roaring cravings. Dylan's slow, shallow thrusts gave her tongue an opportunity to find the ring of his mushroom cap and to give it the languid, centered attention it deserved until suddenly he was gone, her hands itching to touch him, body one long bundle of need to give.

Receiving so much pleasure was hard. Harder than she'd ever imagined, and as Mike slowly inserted the vibrating device past her point of comfort she found a thick wall of soft pain heightened everything, making the pleasure achingly better. Ears perked, she could hear birds outside, the rustle of vibrant late-fall leaves floating to the forest ground, the wind whistling against tall pines.

Just as she began to undulate in waves, her hips moving in a perfect sine curve, Mike slid the device out of her, leaving an emptiness she couldn't bear.

"No! Please!" she cried out, her words silenced by the voracious press of Mike's mouth on hers. Thickly muscled arms slid under her as deft hands released her wrists from the handcuffs. Aloft in the air, she felt her self-consciousness kick in as Mike's mouth broke away and she felt herself moving through space.

"What are you doing?"

Dylan's voice whispered in her ear. "You up for some swinging?"

A cold terror shot through her. *Swinging?* "Swinging?" she gulped.

Mike laughed to her left. "Not that kind."

Her belly rolled in on itself and her breasts pressed against Mike's perfect chest while Dylan held her and Mike moved her feet into some sort of odd, suspended strap in what seemed like midair. It was as if all the extra flesh on both her men had been conferred unto her and she felt it again, that familiar, slightly-sickening diminution of what should have been a near-holy moment.

Dylan tensed and stopped. "What's wrong?"

"Nothing," she said airily, trying to recapture the mood.

"Time to pry." Mike's words came out as if he'd expected to say them all along.

Blinking under the silken cloth of her blindfold, Laura was at a crossroads. She could tamp down her feelings and pretend they weren't there, which was her default mode these days. Or, she could do what she'd always wanted to do in her heart—in her soul—and extend the benevolent, sensual wholeness that Mike and Dylan had brought into her life and trust that it would be there when she opened her mouth.

Slipping her right arm into some sort of leather belt thing, and then her left, she felt Dylan release her and she faltered, her core muscles struggling to find balance where, it seemed, there really was none.

Hands reached behind her neck and untied the scarf, revealing her lovers, still naked, now face-to-face with her as she found herself suspended in front of them, her full body on open display, legs split apart by the laws of physics and the designer who made what she now realized was a sex swing, attached to a special anchor in the ceiling near the fireplace.

"Eco-cabin?" she said, arching one eyebrow.

Mike had the decency to look a bit sheepish. "A perk of being a billionaire. I can build my own sex den." As the words "sex den" poured out of his mouth he went from sheepish to wolfish, the transformation so erotic and entrancing.

One of the guys had lit a romantic fire, and the glow of the flames mingled with the hundreds of candles as Laura gawked in disbelief at how this night had unfolded. Her little red nub thrummed like a lighthouse beacon, screaming for attention but it was the only part of her that seemed to maintain any sense of what she really wanted.

"A swing? Seriously, guys? I'm going to rip the roof off if you don't get me out of this," she joked. Her hands reached for her belly, eyes focused on staring anywhere but down.

"And there it is, Dylan," Mike whispered. Reaching for her, he splayed his palm over the curves of her breasts, her belly, her ass, making Laura inhale a slow, deep breath that came out shakier than she'd intended.

"Look at her, Dylan." Both men raked their eyes over her now as she was completely naked, vulnerable and left with nowhere to hide. *Oh, God*. It was like that high school nightmare where you go to school wearing only your socks, except right now? She wasn't even wearing *those*.

What the hell was wrong with her? These were her guys.

"I'm looking. She's even hotter than the day we met for the first time." Like Mike, he reached for her and began caressing her, hand tracing the swell of her hip, the curves of her waist and ribcage, the smooth flow of palm across her torso like warm honey. Melting into it was not what she thought she would do. The involuntary reaction allowed a new layer of tension to disappear, her body sinking into a little more peace, a deeper connection with these two amazing men who were looking at her like she was eye candy.

Gloriously nude Mike stood before her like a god at Asgard, his height perfectly matched to her position in the sex swing. He grasped her shoulders and looked down over her nude body, eyes lingering over each inch, the rock-hard need in his cock—and moreso in his expression—making her tighten and release with a rhythm within her own core that connected with a deeper tone in the universe, as if she were becoming less defined, more integrated, and more a part of something so much larger and more primal than herself.

"You," he said in a hoarse tone, "have always been perfect." His torso pressed against her open legs, the shaft of his cock aligning perfectly with her wet lips, swollen slit so sensitive she jolted. "You will always be perfect, and your lush body is exactly what I want."

80

"*We*," Dylan interrupted, suddenly behind her, his own rigid manhood pushing against the cleft of her ass.

"*We*," Mike whispered. His eyes were magnetic in the candlelight, golden skin made luminous as he consumed her completely, her skin alight with the feel of Dylan behind her, warm and eager, with Mike at the helm. Being enveloped by their bare skin on both sides was an all-too-familiar reminder of the importance of *we* in this moment, of the blending of three souls, hearts—

And bodies.

"This," Dylan whispered, moving his hand from the side of her breast down to her belly, "is the most amazing body in all creation. You were sensual and sexy as fuck long before you had the baby, but knowing you built an entire baby, and that you nurture that baby from here"—he touched her breasts—"is the sexiest damn thing I can imagine, and all you do, honey, is make me want you more and more with each day that we spend together."

He was a thick wall of hot muscle behind her, her shoulder blades pushing against his pecs as his arms wrapped around her and roamed over her breasts and belly, joy and wanting obvious in the way he relished each line, every bend and turn of her skin. "Not being able to have you ride me every single day is torture," he added in a murmur that made her shiver. "We want you, Laura. The whole you. Every damn day. And we need to show you that and love you enough that you believe it."

"I do!" she cried out as Mike nuzzled her neck. "Of course I believe it!" God, it had been so long since she'd had this much flesh on her, surrounding her, wrapping her in complete abandon. The swing made her feel naughty, like a wilder Laura she wanted to explore. Whatever else Mike and Dylan had in that magic box of devices, she'd love to find out—but later.

Right now she wanted to make love to Mike and Dylan and let loose. It was high time, and the old Laura, the woman she had been before the baby, came roaring back, fast and hard.

And really in need of a good fuck.

Arching her back, she let go of all her inhibitions and lifted her pelvis as high as she could, leaning back against Dylan for leverage. His chin brushed against her neck and she swore she could feel his smile. His cock—*that* she most definitely felt, nudging against her ass. Would they be up for a quickie after all that build-up? Was it fair to ask them to—

"Ready?" Mike asked, hands cupping her face, his lips coming in for a kiss.

"For what?" she asked, starting to tremble.

"Me." Centering his thick pole in front of her wetness, he slowly entered her as Dylan held her in the swing, then began to rock her forward and back, inch by inch.

"Aren't you," she gasped, "supposed to hang this swing in front of a,"—*gasp*—"door?"

"I *am* the door," Dylan hissed, now placing his rigid cap right at the base of her tight ring. Mike filled her, the slow thrusts and the gentle rocking motion of the swing making her clit feel like it would burst if she didn't come right this very instant.

Bzzzz.

Cold metal and lube licked against her hot mons in random starburst of explosions as Mike stroked her red nub with a small, bullet-shaped silver vibrator. Gripping his shoulders, she screamed in extraordinary pleasure, imbued with the relief of knowing she could be as loud as she liked, and tightened, releasing just as

Dylan slowly, steadily entered her ass, the fullness slow and sensual, the feeling unlike anything they'd shared before.

Breasts molded against Mike's bare chest, his face intense and jaw tight, the languid strokes of the vibrator brought her to a gasping mess in seconds, the push of a massive orgasm making her pussy and ass push out, then pull in, long and tight, luring Dylan's cock deeper in her, adding to the sense of an enormity within her that was now connected to everything else.

Simple touches, like the push of Dylan's flexing thighs against the bottom of her glutes, how his lightly-stubbled cheek grazed through her hair, the mingling of her breath and the feel of his gasps against her closed eyelids—all made time stand still, made love seem stronger than she'd ever imagined, blended with her sense of self and purpose as rays of pure pleasure radiated down her body, making her mind leap into the unknown and trust that what they shared would transcend all.

And then Dylan's groan and Mike's own grunt as both tightened, the thin line of skin separating them becoming something otherworldly within, like a second clit as Mike thrust a little faster into her, Dylan touching some spot in her so deep she had no words, and then Mike took the vibrator and pressed it against the thin sliver of skin and she bucked against him, kinetic force turning her into a pendulum that swung between their throbbing shafts, each plunging into her as the buzz of the metal bullet made her climax roar up and claim her.

"Harder!" she called out, Mike bowing his head down and gritting his teeth, neck muscles standing out as he stayed with her movement, Dylan behind her and rock hard, the only sound he made now a grunting keening of animalistic desire.

The wave hit all three at the same time, Laura babbling in some language she didn't know she knew, the words nonsense as the vortex of pain and pleasure and entirety slammed into her, making a burst of color appear behind her opened eyes, as if she were transported to a different dimension, secured to reality by their joined bodies.

"Ah, God!" Dylan shouted from behind, driving deep and fast into her in a way that should hurt but that instead felt like a homecoming, her muscles expanding to accommodate him, her body shocked by the ferocious need and wanton drilling—yet perfectly happy and eager for more. Mike arced his back, hips pointed in between her spread legs, the sum total of their combined movements mere inches and yet the thrusts of two cocks inside her felt like miles of friction.

"Oh, Laura," Mike rasped, his voice coming out through parted lips, eyes unfocused now as he came, the luscious slide of his rod in and out of her made slick by his orgasm. At that same moment, her abs tightened into a ball, then a long, twisting knot inside her, as if every muscle from pussy to upper back coordinated in a fluid motion, rolled in and up, body then letting go in a microburst.

Waves of pleasure poured out like huge ripples, carrying whatever remained of consciousness out in emanating circles, love driving her to come again and again, over and over, too many orgasms to count all blending into complete acceptance, complete love, complete ecstasy.

Complete abandon.

Dylan's body loosened behind her, his arms now stretched around her shoulders in embrace, and Mike leaned against her body, still in her. Without their tight control the threesome swayed, listing forward and back as Laura felt her own core muscles adjusting to the rhythmic motion.

"Sex den, huh?" she whispered in Mike's ear. He looked up, hair tousled, eyes so deeply pleased she felt like a better version of herself simply from being looked at that way.

"You like it?"

Her calf began to cramp, and a stretchy piece of leather cut into her ass. Shifting, she tried to get comfortable, but to no avail. "I do, but—"

"Let me help you," Dylan said, moving quickly. Between the two men she was soon down from her perch, under the soft covers, and the three nestled in bed, bodies aglow from the fireplace and candles.

A quick glance at the clock told Laura they'd only been here for a mere two hours. "Two hours!" she whispered to herself.

"Two hours what?" Dylan murmured into her right breast.

"We've only been here for two hours!" she marveled. Desire rushed back into her. Bring it on. Sexapalooza.

"Then we have plenty of time for more," Mike mumbled.

"More what?" Laura's body shook with the muscle memory of what they'd just done. And yet, she found herself warming to the idea of more. Already?

"More sex. But first," he yawned, Dylan copying him within seconds, "let's nap."

"Nap?" she asked, incredulous. "We get an entire night together, alone, and have mind-blowing sex and you want to nap? Why are you so tired? Jillian's been sleeping through the night."

"We were up late the past few nights," Dylan said. *Yawn*. "Reading your eReader."

"Jus' a lil' nap," Mike muttered and then...out.

Gaping, she turned to Dylan to find his eyes closed, too.

You have got to be kidding me. She was on fire now, one big walking bundle of turned-on nerve endings, and they wanted to sleep?

Peeling Dylan off her, she climbed out of bed and wandered to the kitchen. A cup of water and a shot of espresso later, she surveyed the scene.

Two hot, naked men? *Check.*

Romantic cabin? *Check.*

Alcohol, good food, and coffee? *Check.*

Baby well cared for? *Check.*

More time for more sex? *Check.*

Light snores from the bed made her chuckle, and then, out of the corner of her eye, she saw it.

The sex box. Stepping carefully across the room, quiet so as not to make a sound, she lifted it and took it to the couch.

If they could snoop on her eReader, she could snoop through their box of sex toys.

Opening the lid carefully, she couldn't believe what she saw before her. The breadth. The depth. The—why did that...thing...have six attachments? And who knew you could get a dildo carved out of that?

The footstool she'd placed the box on shifted, as if it were on gliders. How odd. She moved the sex toy box off the ottoman and placed it on the couch. This was no ordinary ottoman. Tracing the edge of the top of the fake leather, she realized there was a lid. When she lifted it off, she found—

A Sybian?

A sly look at the bed, then the "ottoman," then the bed.

Oh, guys.

You have no idea what you've unleashed.

COMPLETE HARMONY

Laura

MAMA.

The word was so perfect. So delicious. So utterly sweet and endearing it was like helium pumped directly into Laura's heart, helping her float and fly, sweet little Jillian looking at her with those wide green eyes, her brown hair now darker and curled at the ends, and that button nose flared as her bow-tie red lips moved in concert with her little vocal cords.

Mama.

No word anyone ever spoke could be as precious.

"Shit!"

Especially not that one. The sound of Dylan cursing from the living room, hands balled up over his crotch, bouncing from one bare foot to the other in a dance of pain, made her bite her lips and laugh. Not out of meanspiritedness, but out of the comical nature of what was going on. Now that Jillian was crawling and grabbing small objects, she'd become quite accomplished at tucking tiny items into seemingly impossible spaces.

Like Dylan's car keys into the heating vent.

"Is that some sort of ritual dance, like calling for rain? The key dance?" Mike strode into the living room and began to imitate Dylan, bent over his crotch, head tipped back in a mock-painful howl, as Dylan sucked a sore thumb and glared.

Jillian's giggles made Mike dance harder.

That made Dylan glare more.

"*Your* daughter put my keys down the grate!"

"Why is she always *my* daughter when she shits up her back or bites you or puts your keys in things? Quit leaving your crap all over the house. We have a key rack." Mike's answer came in an even-toned voice, a deep chuckle behind the words.

"Because *my* daughter would never do such things."

Their daughter let out a juicy fart. Both men scattered, suddenly busy in other rooms.

"Why is she always *my* daughter when she does that?" Laura called out, sighing as Jillian gave her a drooly grin, sitting up on her well-padded bottom like a stinky Buddha.

Mike reversed course before Laura's eyes, his pivot far more graceful than any man six feet and a half had a right to be. He scooped up the baby and made her fly in the air like an airplane. Jillian rewarded him with laughter that could have doubled as fairy dust.

"I'll change her if you take out the garbage," he called back.

"Deal!" she replied. "I got the better end of the deal," she added under her breath. They'd hired a lovely housekeeper, but they all wanted to keep it real, too. No live-in help. Besides, they didn't want the added scrutiny. Trying to explain the situation would be awkward at best, fodder for tabloids at worst. Creating a threesome dating service had been iffy enough, giving the three more potential exposure than any of them wanted.

Dragging the overloaded, diaper-laden bag of stink out to the huge cans in the garage felt like a mini-vacation compared to changing a teething baby's poopy diaper. Keeping it real, all right.

A quick wash of her hands and a check in the mirror showed a more refreshed version of herself than she'd seen in months. Good. About time the old Laura came back.

Mike and Dylan, with a little help from Josie and Alex, had seen to that. A month ago they'd taken her off for a night of sex. What they'd actually gotten out of that crazy, staged, over-the-top night had been, well...

An awakening.

And a lot of really awesome, inspiring, devilishly delicious kinky sex.

As if their *menage a trois* weren't kinky enough? Guess what. It turned out there were levels of kink Laura didn't know existed. Maybe others did and she was just naïve, but the realms they'd entered recently had—

Damn. There it was. Her libido, tapping its foot, demanding to be acknowledged. Its return had shocked her—a night with a sex swing, a week with a Sybian, another week with a Liberator and Determinator, and then a week of all of them should have tempered her desire, right?

Nope. Not one bit. In fact, the guys had actually offered up a schedule where they took turns. One day with Dylan, one day with Mike, one day together.

"What do you mean, 'day'?"

"Now that you want sex two, sometimes three times a day, we figure this is the best way to, um..."

"Pace ourselves," Dylan had finished for him.

"You want to *ration* my access to sex?" she'd asked, incredulous.

"We're tired," they'd said in unison.

Dylan had tried to be helpful. "And you can always use your toys if you—"

She had cut him a death glare. "Are you fucking kidding me? You two went to my best friend and her boyfriend and did the 'poor me' act to find out how to get more sex in our lives, and now you're acting like I'm the freak?"

"No one's calling anyone a freak," Mike had soothed.

"Actually, that thing you did with the pearls last night was pretty freakish," Dylan had countered, one eyebrow cocked at Mike.

"No one is calling *anyone* a freak," Mike had repeated archly.

"Boo-hoo. Too bad, so sad," Laura said.

"You sound like Josie!" Dylan had protested.

"On this topic, I'll take that as a compliment," she'd challenged.

The two men had whispered something to each other, infuriating her.

"This is so unfair!" she'd declared. "It's two against one."

Both had shrugged at the same time, as if they'd planned it. She'd stormed out of the room. Sex resumed that night.

But the guys prevailed. They had a schedule now.

Other women didn't have to deal with this. She'd been a one-man woman for her entire life until a year and a half ago. The sense of wonder and unreality in her relationship with Mike and Dylan could be overpowering at times, counterbalanced only by the exceptional feeling of being loved more than enough.

If she complained to Josie, she'd hear her own words echoed back.

"Too bad. So sad."

Completely absorbed in her thoughts, she was caught unaware as warm, rough hands wrapped around her waist and yanked her into the playroom as she wandered absentmindedly down the hall to check in on Mike and Jillian. Dylan's scent filled her as he nuzzled her neck, then he pulled her to the ground.

Squeak! A little rubber giraffe protested as they fell on it. "A different kind of threesome," Dylan said in a low voice that never failed to make heat pool in her belly. And lower. Of course, it didn't take much these days to arouse her. She was like an eighteen-year-old boy assigned to check bathing-suit seams at a beauty pageant.

Perpetually excited and very, very motivated to make sure every detail was perfect.

"You want me to put that giraffe *where?*"

Booming laughter filled her ear, then hot hands slid up under her shirt, his palms venturing forth and pulling back, clenching her curves with a primal ownership. Faster than she realized, his mouth was on her nipple, biting lightly, sending white-hot signals straight to her clit, her body so ready for touch she seemed custom-designed for nothing but sex. Hot monkey sex, the kind you do seven times in twelve hours and then go eat ice cream in bed while watching '80s movies on cable.

That sounded even better than the sex cabin right now.

Hot monkey sex wasn't on the table, but Dylan's mouth was on her clit now, his hands unrolling her yoga pants and undies with ease, the soft carpet a lovely cushion for her bare ass as his intense face dove between her legs, tongue on a mission as Laura arched her hips and groaned.

As she rolled one hip, eager for his tongue on that spot, she yelped in pain.

Hot giraffe sex after all.

The damn toy cut into her thigh, the pressure making her leg muscle spasm. Dylan slid it out from under her and flung it across the room, where it struck a musical toy, the sound of bells and whooping alerts alternating with green, red, blue, and yellow flashing lights.

Giggling, she pushed him back in place, warmth flooding everything as his little groans of pride from giving her pleasure made her want to climax even more. Nothing turned her on as much as the sounds they made during sex—so real, intimate, and primal. Dirty talk was great, but the sighs, the moans, the licks and smacking sounds of really juicy sex was a layer of her own enjoyment she hadn't known existed until recently. Being even more real with Mike and Dylan meant being a sexual being who was open, willing, and realistic about what sex really was.

And right now, sex really was about grabbing fistfuls of his hair as his tongue danced on her and elicited an afternoon delight she hadn't seen coming just minutes ago.

But she could see herself coming, right—*now*.

The sound of a baby show on the television in the muted distance barely registered as Dylan's hand traveled up over the curve of her belly, the rounded slope of one breast, his finger and thumb teasing her nipple in time to the rhythmic strokes of his pointed tongue, the rapid flicker bringing her to her own hum, and she tipped over the edge into a writhing orgasm, riding his face, the man so caught up in the pointed focus on making her lose it that his intensity became her and drove her climax further and deeper.

"Dylan," she gasped as her ab muscles clenched into a wall that took over her ass, her clit, her internal passages, and every core muscle from pussy to navel, turning them into a steel vise of pure, unadulterated pleasure.

The push of her hips against his face and his determination to make her multiply satisfied made her relax completely into his mouth, knowing that he was at the ready for more, her hand reaching down to stroke his thick cock through his pants.

The gasp of hot air against her folds, the baring of his teeth that rested against her as he reacted, made her smile as she pushed his head away, her orgasms peaked and leaving her panting, something animal inside her wanting to wrap her lips around the base of him and give back at least—if not more—what he'd just given her.

Squeak.

Halfway down to his cock, her head tipped toward Dylan's now-bare, tantalizing navel, the sound made her halt. Dylan's legs tensed and his sharp inhale this time had nothing to do with her. Following his gaze, which looked…guilty?…she turned toward the doorway, where she found Mike towering over them, two steps in the cheerful room, his face anything but.

Before she or Dylan could open their mouths to explain, he held out a palm. Mike said exactly three words before he turned on his heel and left the room.

"It's my day."

***

Laura had to find a way to fix this. Day two of polite interaction with Mike, no affection, and a tight smile that reminded her of her old Republican congressman being forced to share a lunch table with Dan Savage. And his husband.

Dylan wasn't having much luck either.

97

"I've tried," he'd hissed over coffee that morning, both attempting to talk about what Mike wouldn't.

So they'd been playful and spontaneous and had sex on a plastic giraffe. That whole "assigned days" thing had been a general guideline—not the equivalent of tax policy, right? It wasn't like they could be audited and emotionally fined for sexing outside the box.

Right?

Mike, though, was acting as if she and Dylan had committed sex fraud. Tongue violations galore. Blatant disregard for orgasm limits. If their sex life had an alternative minimum tax, this would be Mike applying the formula and forcing her to give up a share of her last handful of climaxes.

She was taking this way too seriously.

Or personally. Likely both.

Then again, so was Mike.

Marching into the kitchen, determined to get more than three consecutive syllables out of him, she found him blending some ungodly green glop and pouring it into an ice cube tray.

"What is that?" It looked like something she'd vomited up after having her wisdom teeth removed after college.

"Kale/pear sauce. I figured Jillian could give it a try next." The slow march toward solids was not going as well as planned, as Miss Jillian The Milk Vacuum had decided that warm and directly from the tap was how she liked her nutrition.

Like an Irishman and his Guinness.

"Sounds delightful," she lied. "Now, can we talk about something other than the latest vegan baby trend and get to you let me in? I am so sorry, and I've said it a thousand times, but I can't apologize if you won't hear me."

"I hear you."

"No, hear me. Really hear me. Let me understand what's going on and tell me how you're feeling and then let me reflect and all that gooey interpersonal interplay that the Mike I thought I knew was into."

"I'm sorry I'm not being the person you thought I was." His voice was pleasant enough, but the words felt like little poison darts aimed right at her soul. That kind of detachment chilled her and made a deep part of her suddenly very, very vulnerable and afraid.

"What does that mean?"

"It means exactly what I said."

Oh, *this* game. She knew what he was doing. Saying words she was supposed to turn around on herself and take on, as if she were the one acting like a different person, as if she were in the wrong here, when all she'd done was had a lovely romp with one of her men. Mike's head games weren't going to work.

Maybe he's right, her guilty conscience chimed in. *You haven't been as eager in bed with him as you have with Dylan lately.*

Fuck off.

The voice skittered away.

She must have been glaring at Mike, because his eyes narrowed and matched hers. Great concentration was the only way she could relax, and as her face muscles shifted down to neutral he mimicked her subconsciously. Whatever was going on inside him wasn't intentional—that was helpful to realize.

Didn't make this any easier, though.

Glop delivered and smooshed into the trays, he put the entire mess in the freezer and washed his hands. Was he pretending the conversation was over? Acting like she wasn't there? Uncertain and confused—and also quite upset—she stood in the doorway. Dylan had

Jillian right now, so they could avail themselves of all the time in the world. Talk. Sex. Coffee. Even—God forbid—a few runs down the slopes. Laura hated skiing. Hated it almost as much as childbirth. But she'd do it for Mike.

She'd do damn near anything for him and Dylan, and he knew it.

Which made this all the more perplexing. Had she been unfair? Yes. But they'd never treated their relationship as something to be equally doled out, as if each needed exactly 33.3333333333333 percent of some kind of relationship pie. This wasn't about making percentages add up. Emotions and time and sex and attention weren't like that. If they'd tried that kind of math they'd have failed long ago.

Instead—she thought—they'd all loosely fallen into a less-distinct process, a more cooperative way of living that involved everyone giving their best and hoping it would work out. Take when you needed to take and give when you needed to give. For nearly a year and a half that had worked, but this breakdown now showed her that clearly, something wasn't working.

As his strong back faced her, arms scrubbing furiously as he washed his hands, the scent of orange mint floated over his shoulder, the new dish soap inviting and fresh. Too bad life couldn't really be as clean and open as that soap seemed to promise, as if a scent could make the atmosphere happier than it really was.

Hesitant, then plunging in, she raised her hands and touched his shoulders, gradually laying her palms flat against the broad crossbar of the T that made up his shoulders and backbone. She expected him to stiffen, knowing that breaking through with Mike could be a slow-to-warm process.

Having him slump forward and rest his hands on either side of the sink as a slow, deep breath changed the landscape of his entire body was definitely a surprise. This was the act of a man deeply conflicted, of someone grappling with a core issue.

"Laura," he said with the rush of an out-breath, his tone of voice so hard to read. Was that passion? Exhaustion? Discord? That he said anything at all, though, was good.

Had she miscalculated? Invalidated his feelings? Misjudged so badly that she'd compromised the very center of what she held dear with him? Tears filled her eyes before either said a word, and as he turned to her there were so many layers of emotion in his face that she could spend an entire year alone with him before she could unpack all those messages.

"I'm not jealous," he said, the words coming out around a second sigh. His head tipped down and alarm shot through her at the way he said it. The hair on the nape of his neck was a golden brown, the same color as Jillian's, and much like her own blond locks. His shoulders slowly released as he added, "I am hurt."

Oh.

Ouch. Her hands would have started to shake if they weren't firmly flattened against his shoulders. She closed her eyes and took a deep breath.

Lean in. Her heart told her what to do. One step forward, so awkward and hard, and she rested her cheek against his spine, her belly pressing into his thigh.

"I'm sorry," she whispered, the teardrops mottling the back of his shirt. She reached the middle of his back like this and it made her feel childlike, small and wrong.

One out of three was true.

He turned around and somehow, the unbreachable was broken, the wall of thorns stripped away, the wall vanquished, as his arms wrapped around her shoulders and she twined hers about his waist. The heady aroma of orange and mint on his hands now had the scent of hope and renewal, of wholehearted love and faith.

Mike was so tall, so stalwart and steady, that she had taken for granted that his sheer size meant he was unbreakable, never shaken, always strong. Selfish of her to think it, she now realized.

He was fallible. And soft and vulnerable like her, too.

On the inside.

"When you acted like it was no big deal and Dylan said I should get over it and just take two nights in a row you both really made me feel as if my feelings didn't matter. How I felt in that moment has nothing to do with divvying up everything. It was a feeling, and they can't be spreadsheeted."

Her smile made her lip catch on of the buttons on the front of his shirt, which made her sniffle, which made her snort, which made him laugh.

"Sorry." She coughed. "I always get a stuffy nose when I cry."

"I know."

She loved that he knew. He pulled her back and gently wiped each tear from her face, the pad of his fingers tracing the path, working to give the rolling drop eternal companionship, a traveling partner in pain.

"Thank you."

"For what?"

"For telling me why you've been so closed up. And for having the courage to open up after I didn't treat you well."

Dylan's voice surprised her from behind. "*We* didn't treat you well." With a half-turn she could see him, a sleeping Jillian on his shoulder. "I'm sorry, dude. I had no idea you were that bothered."

Mike arched an eyebrow and Laura got it. Got it. What Dylan said wasn't an apology. She thought it was, and Dylan probably did as well, but seeing someone else deliver it like this gave her a new perspective.

"Dylan," she said quietly. "The fact that he was bothered at all is something we all need to deal with. It's not just Mike's issue."

Mike nodded quietly, his chin bobbing against the top of her head. "You get it," he whispered, squeezing her gently.

Blinking hard, Dylan shifted the baby to the other shoulder, resettling her head on his shoulder as she snored lightly. Absentmindedly, he stroked her hair, cupping the back of her head in a soothing manner that made Laura so ridiculously happy she couldn't put words to it.

"I think I understand. I basically just fake apologized, huh?"

Mike nodded.

"Like 'I'm sorry you were offended'? Where I'm apologizing for your emotional reaction and not for my action?" Dylan's lips pursed with the intensity of his realization.

"Someone's been watching Dr. Phil," Mike replied, as if impressed. Laura bit her lip, trying not to laugh.

Dylan pointed to the sleeping baby. "Blame her. Three o'clock nap." His brown eyes went soft as they jumped between Laura and Mike, friendly and apologetic. "I'm sorry, Mike."

"Much better," Mike said, a sad smile on his face.

"But...?" Dylan and Laura said in unison, drawing out the word like a question.

"Something's off. I don't know how to put it in words." Mike pulled back, leaving Laura frantically scrambling inside, like a gerbil on a wheel. Not knowing how to get off, but getting nowhere by being so panicked.

Dylan looked as worried as she was, which was a comfort. *It's not just me.*

"And maybe it is me, but it's not *just* me," Mike said. "We've been through so much in what feels like a short time span." The look he gave Dylan made Laura focus on Mike's eyes, so dark and conflicted, yet childlike in their openness and blessedly hopeful nature. The churning inside him was coming to the surface and she could taste his fear. What could be the source of this?

"Jill died, then we struggled, we met Laura, we screwed up—"

Her sudden laugh was like a guilty bark, making the baby jolt on Dylan's shoulder, waking with a start and grousing. No amount of head stroking made a difference, and Dylan gave Mike a sympathetic look.

Mike seemed determined to continue now that he'd given himself permission to really share. "—Laura shut us out, we missed so much of the pregnancy, then the fire...and that's not even the half of it."

The fire. *That's right*, Laura thought. The fire. Sometimes she blocked it out—needed to forget it—because the implications of what could have happened were too strong. Raising a baby without her mom was hard enough, but remembering how her grandparents died, her own confusion in the flames and smoke in her little apartment, how Dylan preternaturally knew what to do, instinct kicking in for him in a way that it should have for her...ruminating on it was too much.

She felt like a failure. The thought made the smallness return, a tiny ribbon of shame slipping into the cracks of her consciousness, where insecure dragons lurked behind every corner, waiting to attack.

"I can see you pulling away," Mike said quietly, and she flinched. "It's not just me." A storm of emotions bubbled inside her, each feeling flying past as she tried to identify it, too slow and too late. By the time she could even feel anything, the feelings turned into a blur, like a tornado of chaos inside that was so enormous she needed to numb it. Kill it. Cover it.

Feed it.

Pretending it didn't exist never worked, because the steady spiral of ever-moving tumult inside had a sound of its own, a high-pitched whine that made her vibrate from within. And not in a good way. Leaving her shaky and filled with trepidation, she knew this state only as discomfort.

Mike studied her; she felt his eyes lingering on hers, knew he sought to understand what she was thinking and feeling, and in that moment what she had always felt as extraordinary discomfort turned into a completely different sense.

Authenticity. Vulnerability. A peaceful, if painful, settling in that she could only do with Mike and Dylan. Only.

Ever.

"Hey," Mike whispered, and then Dylan interrupted as Jillian let out a loud, juicy sound from her diaper region that broke the contemplative moment, shattering the deep resonance she had just begun to feel. Leave it to a baby to strip you bare of any sense of decorum or deep anything. They lived on the very surface of life, all sensation and experience, without any of the baggage adults drag around like anchors weighted with pain.

"Whatever I was thinking has been replaced by a fleeting thought of baby wipes. Do we have enough?" she asked Dylan, who just shook his head with a healthy dose of good humor, waving his hand in front of the stinky baby's bum.

"We hit Costco last week, so we'd better." A quick look rippled among the three, an acknowledgement that pragmatics trumped all. And, she hoped, a promise to revisit what had just been a turning point inside her. What it meant, she didn't know.

Its evolution was more important than its purpose.

"I'm going to go take care of Stinkbug here," Dylan said quietly, his voice modulated in an attempt to keep the baby calm, though she began to wiggle and fuss, rendering his attempts fairly useless. "I'll change her and feed her and we'll go for a nice, *long* walk," he declared.

If he'd wiggled his eyebrows and thrown glow-in-the-dark condoms with lit sparklers attached, he couldn't have been more obvious.

Mike managed to nod, frown, smile and sigh—all at once. "Thanks," he said. Laura watched Dylan's back and Jillian's face as they faded down the hallway, his cooing adorable and Jillian so settled in (one of) her daddy's arms that she could complain and still be taken care of and love.

That shaky vibration within settled a bit, too, especially when Mike took his hand, large and warm and so assured in its grasp as he reached for her hip and guided her toward the bedroom.

Oh.

Oh.

This was, most definitely, not where she thought their conversation would lead them, and yet it made her breath hitch in a radically different way, her jumbled emotions all convening for a brief meeting to talk amongst themselves, only to emerge twenty seconds later with extraordinary consensus:

Yes.

He wasn't commanding, but he was clear in his intent, and as Laura felt the familiar need rise up she decided to flip this scenario and focus entirely on him. Maybe she'd taken him a little too for granted when it came to sex and bedroom intimacy, too. Focusing too much on her own newly resurgent sexual needs might have left her a little blind when it came to Mike. Dylan tended to ask openly for what he wanted, more assertive and dominant, while Mike could certainly go alpha when he needed to, but today was an example of how complex he was.

Deep layers and a quiet surface meant that she needed to be more incisive, infer more, when it came to truly being there for him. Right now, what she needed was to give selflessly. Fully. And not take one iota.

Not one bit.

Not even a drop.

Climbing on the bed, she pulled up onto her knees and yanked with more force than she expected, pulling him on to the bed, then straddling him. Without a single word, she untucked his shirt and began to undo his pants.

"Hello there," he said with a sly purr, hands lacing behind his head, his triceps popping from under his sleeves. The look on his face said, *Please, continue.*

With a twinkle she hadn't seen in a while.

"This all right?"

"When is this ever *not* all right?" he asked, an incredulous tone in his voice, but something unspoken was in the tone. A thank you. A touch of gratitude for knowing what he needed without being asked. Her fingers slid the waistband of his jeans over those carved hips, pulling down, setting him free and unencumbered of the burden of any layers between them. Just what he wanted.

Exactly what she wanted.

"What about you?" he murmured, hands firmly in place beneath his neck, arms stretched up, chest and torso long and elegant, cock at the ready. Winter had dimmed his skin from a burnished gold to a more sedate hue, though his face remained tan from being on the slopes more than one would expect an owner to be.

"It's your day," she said without snark or bitterness, a smile tickling her lips. His wary look made her glad, too, the neutral way she spoke coming from a place in her that wanted the world to work in harmony. "Let this be about just you."

"But—"

"And it will make tonight that much better."

"Tonight?" His voice went mellow and rich, into a register that made her neck tilt and her belly ache with desire, but no—this was about giving.

Tonight, though, she would take, take, *take*. The heat between her legs confirmed it.

Mike enjoyed long, dry strokes at first; she'd learned over their time together that everything she thought she knew about blowjobs—and everything that *did* apply to Dylan—didn't mean anything when it came to what turned Mike on. Relearning how to give a man this kind of pleasure felt like an advanced seminar in sexuality, the kind of upper-division course you think will be a complete blow-off (no pun intended) but that shakes the core of your knowledge paradigm, making you question the entire framework upon with your expertise hinges.

And that was perfectly fine.

A few strokes and then she clasped the root of him, her fingers closing and squeezing far harder than she would imagine any man would enjoy—but Mike groaned, a sound of ecstasy. Her other hand went under his balls and her thumb pushed against the thick wall of muscle between his scrotum and anus, her mouth covering just the tip of him, his hips thrusting up a few inches, though settling right back down.

Her mouth—her control.

The hand around the base of him let go and she took in his muscled buttock, the thick lines of his powerful ass turning her on more than she wanted, making it so much harder to focus solely on him. Squirming a bit, she wanted his hand—his mouth... hell, *her* hand—on her own clit for a quick release, but that would have to wait. The steady throb of her own soaking wet self was a reminder that there was no isolation of pleasure. She couldn't just give, any more than she and Dylan could make love with Mike in the room and not have him react. All sensuality was connected.

The idea of disconnection was the mistake.

There should be no "my day" at all. That was where the three of them had erred.

Time later for philosophical discussions, though— right now she had him in her mouth, her tongue performing a lazy walk around the cock's cap, one hand on his sac, the other up over his washboard abs and now teasing his nipple, which peaked at her touch. She looked up at him to find closed eyes and a frown of deep concentration and focus. Whatever she could give him now, she hoped, would make him trust her to give a complete release, open and bare to her.

A naked body was fairly easy to share with someone else. A naked self? Damn near impossible.

His inner thighs went tight as a shift in his hips made his glutes rock hard, chest a lovely, hard-cut expanse of man she never tired of watching. The tightness was a sure sign that his release was coming any second now.

Not yet, she thought, wanting to draw this out. A long, slow, wet stroke down, her throat relaxing to take him in, and then a slick suck going back up made him buck and moan "Laura!" through gritted teeth.

"Not yet," she whispered, blowing air gently on his wet tip, making his body shiver. Hands buried in her hair and he made a sound of gratitude and frustration, twinned forever together in her mind.

Now she pulled both hands back to his base, one stroking him up to the rim, her mouth deep throating him, her other hand rolling his balls. A dip down to suck one into her mouth felt like a guilty pleasure of her own, the harsh hush of his breath sucking in through his teeth followed by a full-body clench, and then—

"Oh!" he gasped, the hot flow of his pleasure into her mouth surprising her, his climax coming sooner than she'd read, her ability to catch and interpret his signals clearly off. Following his movements, she caught it all, and as he twitched and panted, movements slowing, skin rasping against the sheets as he relaxed, she pulled her mouth off his hot, wet cock in a slow, studied movement, keeping her lips together at the end, and then swallowed.

He groaned again, this time with a touch of humor and playfulness. "You look very pleased with yourself." He chuckled as she sat up and just looked at him, eyes taking in his perfection.

"I am." The salty fluid tasted a bit like mango and crackers. How odd.

"You should be." With open arms, he beckoned to her, and as she settled against his bare chest she reveled in the incongruity of her entirely clothed body against his utterly naked one. The balance of power was off.

Kind of fun like this.

Mike took deep belly breaths, Laura fixated on his navel and watching its rise and fall, the tranquility of the moment making her slip into a hypnotic state. If they'd had more time she could have fallen asleep, so peaceful were his breaths.

"Thank you," he murmured.

"You're welcome." She crawled up him, sleek and catlike, and planted a kiss on his lips.

"About tonight," he added.

"Oh, don't you worry," she said in a low, determined voice. "I haven't forgotten about tonight."

And then her ass buzzed.

Fucking phone. She looked—voicemail message. Josie. Holding up one finger, she walked out of the room, dialing as she went to the bathroom and shut the door.

"'lo?"

"Josie?" Thank God. She needed a friend. A voice. An ear. Someone sympathetic and empathetic who could just listen. Let her talk and unwind all the tangled thoughts and feelings that made every part of herself feel so confused.

111

"Who else would it be? You got Joe programmed in your phone next to my name, too? Because if you're calling for law school advice—"

"Joe?"

Josie snorted. "Darla's been sexting me."

"That's an interesting relationship you have there," Laura said, coughing.

"Ha ha. 'Joe' and 'Josie' are next to each other in the contacts list on her phone. I'm ready to change my name to Zandramander at this rate if it gets her to stop." Josie's voice went low. "You wouldn't believe the pictures they take of each other."

Laura shuddered, the taste of Mike still sharp in her mouth. She needed to get off the phone, fast. "What's up? You never call this time of day unless you have a business question."

Half the time Laura forgot that the dating service even existed. Then she felt tremendous guilt, because the venture was backed by money Mike and Dylan readily gave her, expecting nothing in return and not really caring whether it generated a profit. The unspoken secret between the three was that the two billion plus change that the men had in trust, and the millions they earned every year in income payout, was more than enough money for Laura to spend as she pleased on whatever she wanted, for Dylan to fund his foundation, and to support Mike's work at the ski resort.

In other words—and this was where she cringed, but gritted her teeth and faced the truth—Good Things Come in Threes was just a pet project. It never had to turn a profit. In truth, it could bleed money forever and all would be well.

"Just calling to say 'hi'," Josie said in a voice so friendly Laura almost started crying. She missed her friend.

"I need to meet for coffee." Laura said the words before she realized it was exactly what she wanted and needed.

"Fake meeting?"

"Yep. But make sure it doesn't seem like a fake meeting."

"Gotcha. I can't today, though. How about tomorrow?"

Laura did a mental scan. Shit. Tomorrow she had a doctor's appointment for Jillian and a playgroup. "Can't tomorrow."

"Day after? I'm free," Josie said.

Mental scan again. "Yes! I'm free."

"See you at Jeddy's. One o'clock." Click. That was easy. A little too easy.

Laura needed *easy* right now.

The fact that the company existed at all was its own reward in such a scenario. When you took away the standard economic trappings that the bottom 99.9999999999999 percent of the world assumed to be a permanent, fixed, and universal part of the structure of society, what Laura and Josie were doing with the dating service made zero sense.

Who starts a new business in a down economy, with an extremely limited niche clientele, with no simple way to advertise, and with people like the Westboro Baptists as likely to generate negative publicity as the local start-up incubator in Cambridge?

There wasn't a huge support network for threesomes, after all. That wasn't conjecture. They'd learned the very hard way since news about the company had spread as it had become the butt of bad jokes on Reddit and BuzzFeed, at one point going viral —but never getting the attention dinosaur porn or *Duck Dynasty* had captured, thank goodness. What she, Dylan, and Mike viewed as a simple attempt to help people earnestly searching for something hard to attain had become corrupted by the views of a small minority that viewed the very existence of a desire for love out of step with society as an abomination.

Dylan weathered it best, somehow able to compartmentalize and view the negative press as "their fucking problem, not mine. Assholes." Mike had gone quiet, angry, and disappointed, though Laura shouldn't have been surprised. His own family rejected him for the same reason; why should he expect strangers to hold him in any higher esteem?

But Laura had needed to put herself on a strict media diet. A news fast. Josie read everything because she seemed to be made of Teflon ("Plus, it's my job now, Laura," she'd explained in a kind, though troubled, voice).

Why all of that mess invaded her thoughts now, as Mike surprised her in the bathroom wearing jeans and nothing else, sliding his hands over her shoulders and sinking one into her hair, bringing his mouth to hers, was a mystery. All she knew was that he needed and wanted her to help heal a rift between them (among them?) and she was here.

"I love you," he sighed against her mouth. He winced and pulled back.

"I love you, too." She saw the funny look on his face. "You okay?"

"That's quite a…taste." He reached for a glass of water and turned on the tap, filling it. After chugging a glass, he refilled it and handed it to Laura, who just chuckled.

"What about you?" he asked in a slow, lazy voice. She knew he didn't mean love. Lust, on the other hand...

"You can take care of me later," she said, laughing in a manner she'd only recently been able to reach, a tone of playful understanding that everything in this household would balance out in time. No niggling need to get what she wanted while she could. It would come to her eventually. As if the universe were somehow conspiring to make her happy.

In a way, it was. Good karma was flying her way, and if she slowed down enough to grab on to a piece, the ride was amazing. So was the view.

"*We* can take care of you later," he said, making her eyebrows arch. *Men.* First he spent two days pouting...sulking...stewing...eh—pick a word—because she was sexual with Dylan on Mike's "day," and now he acted as if that was all over and of course she'd sleep with both of them.

Of course.

And then there was Dylan, who had confessed he knew it was Mike's day, and further knew that Mike would be upset, but had jumped her bones—in his words—"because your tits looked so fucking scrumptious when you walked past me wearing no bra." So evolved. She'd strained an optic nerve rolling her eyes.

What was she? A piece of meat?

The anger that would have rushed to the top in a wave of pure, primal fury wasn't there. In its place uncoiled a slow, deep breath, one of experience and a carefully developed pause button on her temper. Reactions would get her nowhere.

"What if I don't want *we*?"

Blinking hard, Mike seemed taken aback. "You don't?" The lush moment in the bedroom just now faded. Fast.

"Maybe I just want *you*." On firmer ground now, she was balancing on the razor's edge of being an adult and focusing on forging alliances and connections with mindfucking him. She didn't always choose the mature path, no matter how hard she tried.

Right now, maturity was barely winning out.

Barely.

With intent, she held back from touching him or sitting within physical proximity. Sometimes she wanted to nurture her anger. Defensive? Yes. Unfair? To everyone. But when she was outnumbered two to one and there was no blueprint for how to navigate living with two men in a balanced (supposedly), permanent, loving threesome, she had so few options that gave her any sense of equilibrium, no matter how misguided at times.

If being angry and embracing it was a stepping stone to a better understanding of who she was within this crazy relationship, then so be it.

Besides, if Mike could be pissed for two days and take it out on her, she should be able to have a couple of hours where the guys were in the wrong, right?

Balance and all that.

Balance was increasingly overrated.

MIKE

Run. Run and just...run some more. His body started the low, deep rumble, the vibration that made his soul scream out for release. Whatever was going on inside him didn't have words, and that made interacting with Laura and Dylan so damn hard.

Words were hard.

Running was easy.

The pounding of his feet on the pavement, the blur of trees and sunshine and clouds. Or, hell, rain pelting him while he ran in the heat, stripping off his shirt and being as close to nature as he could. Within public nudity laws and basic physics, because naked running would, um, hurt. Rebound effect and all that.

As Laura's speckled green eyes glared at him, he stood shirtless and commando, his jeans an afterthought, his body pulsing now with the desire not to escape, but to push his body into a zone where emotions could be handled one by one, instead of on top of each other in a giant pile.

Right now, his inner world looked like a fucking garbage dump.

And no one wanted to smell that.

"What's wrong, Laura? What did I say?"

"It's what you don't say," she said with a sigh. Mike knew that sigh. He'd thrown it around these past few days. No name for it, unfortunately. It just was, like a stray cat that shows up on your door and proceeds to piss all over the perimeter of your home, claiming its territory and making life miserable for you.

Until it decides to leave.

He had no control over these feelings. None. It made his jaw tighten, because holy shit—if he couldn't control his own feelings, how could he reach out and help Laura with hers?

It made him feel like a giant failure. As he towered over her, standing behind her at the sink, he saw their height difference and realized that compared to her, he really was a giant.

Failure, too.

These damn feelings...and talking. Laura had been content, when they'd first met, to have him be silent and to just be with him. In fact, she had seemed to like his stillness. Years of meditation, practice, and thousands of miles eaten up by his legs had gotten him to that point. The reality of being centered on the inside was that it took a lot more work than it seemed from the outside.

And now, Laura had worked to pierce his shield and succeeded, not just with sex but with the expression of caring, of wanting to ride out his confused mood with him. Not just to help, but to walk alongside him on his psychological journey as he plumbed whatever these emotions were.

That was love.

That was *rare*.

She tilted her head to the side and the expanse of her creamy skin, where the neck and shoulder met, called out for a kiss. Not knowing what else he could do without screwing this up more, he planted a tiny kiss there, his tongue slipping out to taste her. Salty, with a touch of something more. Laura seemed to have an essence about her, and not just in her sensual juices when they made love.

She tasted like *Laura*. He couldn't describe it any more than he could detail what an orgasm felt like, or how he'd experienced the moment Jillian's head had crowned, watching his daughter emerge into the word. Like trying to define love, it couldn't be contained within something so rudimentary as language.

It was a flavor he savored.

Her anger—he guessed it was anger, at least— melted as his lips caressed her neck, dipping over her to the collarbone. The jeans tightened, his shaft down his leg and pressed against his thigh, now thickening.

Already? Not bad for a guy in his thirties. When he was seventeen he could be rock hard ten minutes after a rousing batch of sex. Lately it took longer.

Apparently, this was different. He took a deep breath half filled with pride and amusement, his lips turning up in a smile he couldn't stop.

"What's funny?" Laura asked. Could she feel his smile on her skin?

And then he looked up. The mirror. Of course. Yet it wouldn't surprise him if she could read his emotions purely by touch. Their connection was that strong.

All three of them.

"I'm thinking about how hard I'm getting."

"Again?" Her voice turned up with a questioning surprise and a sultry tone that made him remove one hand from her shoulders and dig into his jeans, adjusting himself as the seam irritated the head of his cock.

Oh, yeah. Again, all right. He was hard as granite.

"You said you didn't want *we* right now. How about *me*?" he asked, his tongue now seeking the sensitive spot beneath her earlobe, the part he knew she could barely tolerate having touched. That spot made her wet, though.

And Mike definitely wanted her nice and wet for what he was about to do with her.

Something that required very few words, half of them variations of "Oh, God."

Those words he could handle right now.

Laura spun around and reached up on tiptoes. He slid his hands over that hot ass and, cupping it, lifted her up. Just as he hoped, her legs wrapped around his waist as her hands plunged into his hair, mouth slanting across his and tongue burying itself. His tongue sought her heat, craved her touch, needed more connection than they'd just had.

And he'd thought *that* had been just fine.

Tired of accepting *just fine*, Mike shifted into some predatory mode that fueled him, his body taking everything she gave and insisting on more, his hands hungry on her ass, her back, prowling over her breasts and stroking each nipple to a peak, the way he claimed her absolutely and utterly complete.

He owned her.

He wanted her to know that. While he and Dylan shared Laura, and she shared them, there was no reason she shouldn't also know that she was his one hundred percent. Relationship math did not have to balance out.

Ever.

There was room for New Math in plenty of places.

Barreling out of the bathroom, he threw her onto the bed where she'd just sucked him off, where his body had shimmered and convulsed under her steady and knowing hands.

His turn.

This really was his day. In full. He raked her clothes off, hands moving so fast they felt like a blur. Making love with Laura, with or without Dylan, was always passionate and sweet and loving, but sometimes...sometimes he wanted more of an edge.

The thought passed through his mind that he needed to slow down, to contemplate, as her bare body wiggled under his, her gasps and wide eyes telling him she was aroused and excited, and then when her hand unbuttoned his jeans and he kicked them off, the full length of his muscled heat pressed against her hot, lush curves, he kicked that thought away like a ninety-yard punt.

Through the fucking goalposts, man.

Balance was so overrated.

Laura was on the pill, one of the first things she'd done after having Jillian, so he knew he was safe, and he reached down between her legs to find her slick and ready. Her moans as he moved his thumb in lazy, wet circles over her swollen clit told him she was ready, but he wanted to be sure.

"Fuck me, Mike. I want you in me," she whispered.

Okay...sometimes words worked.

With his arms on either side of her, he steadied himself above her, dipping down for a heated kiss as she lifted her hips up, wrapping her legs around him. She was so soft and tantalizing, a gift that kept on giving, and as she shifted just enough and used her hand to guide him in, he said the only words he could think.

"I love you."

The moment of pushing into her was like looking up to see a shooting star, as if the heavens made it just for you and you alone. That was how Mike felt as her

121

wet warmth encased him, his head bent down next to her neck as her little gasps and moans fueled him. All he wanted to do was to take, to be free and uninhibited, and something primal pounded through him as a low heat singed his skin, sweat forming on their chests as he thrust into Laura, her body moving up to meet his, her hips tipping in concert.

He pinned her to the bed with each deep thrust, imagining he was burrowing into her soul to combine his and hers, to create a new love that would pulse through them both. Watching her was like seeing the world for the first time, her face glowing and eyes unfocused, brow furrowed with concentration and the epic sense that his body, his will, his touch was driving her to a place no one ever took her before.

And then she clenched deep inside, encasing him, the power of her sex muscles so strong he cried out her name, the deep grooves milking him like a determined hand, the wetness and the warmth and her power making his release so close.

"Oh, Mike, oh," she shouted, her voice low and smoky, like a woman who knew herself and how to make him hers. He took one rosy nipple in his mouth and nipped, the bite stronger than intended, and she came with a force that made him smile through her orgasm, matching her rhythm, never letting go of her pebbled flesh.

One of the final spasms inside her tipped him over, too, and he finished with deep, almost-frantic thrusts that burst through with a growl, like an animal making his mark on his mate, the feel of his hot seed pouring into her so ungentlemanly that he wondered at the power he possessed, ever at his access, her arms around him and scratching at his back as she tightened around him and came again, this time with God's name pouring out of those luscious, beautiful lips.

He collapsed on top of her, breathing hard, her breasts sliding against his chest, the feel of her goodness pinned under him like a prize.

He balanced himself on his elbows and looked tenderly at her, the animal instinct all gone, replaced by a slyness.

"What was that?" she whispered, breathless.

"That," he said, kissing the tip of her nose, "was *me*."

* * *

Maybe it was time to hand off the reins to someone else, Mike thought, as Shelly calmly explained that their liability insurance would increase twenty-three percent when they renewed the policy, and that the lodge restaurant really needed to add a gluten-free menu, because their competitor across the mountain had just added one, and customers were asking.

Laura's scent filled his brain, taking over.

"Earth to Mike? We need some decisions," Shelly chided. Young and bold, his assistant had this way of being that demanded obedience, even when she was the subordinate.

It was unsettling, but she kept the place going, so he tolerated it. On days like this, he reveled in it.

"You know what, Shelly? It's time to give you a promotion."

Her neck pulled back in shock. "A what?"

"A promotion. How about…operations manager? A move up from administrative assistant." He paused for a second, realizing he had no idea what he would pay her. A promotion had to come with a raise, though, right?

"But the operations manager job...you're still taking resumes and the interviews start next week. And I don't have a bachelor's degree. The job requires one." The arguments surprised him. She almost didn't seem to want it. Weird.

Too bad.

"You're more qualified than any of the applicants, and it's easier to get a good administrative assistant than it is to find an operations manager who can run this place smoothly."

She snorted. "You think finding a good admin is 'easy'?" She brushed a piece of her overgrown red hair out of her eyes. He wondered if she was growing it out. There was a scraggly look to it. Appraising her, he realized she was looking thin and stressed. She was twenty now. No one should be stressed at twenty.

"You want the job or not?" Truth be told, he didn't want to make liability insurance decisions, or deal with finding cooks who could be retrained to deal with food allergies. All of those issues were important to the ski resort, of course.

But did *he* have to be the one in charge of making those decisions?

No. Hell no. Time to delegate.

"Uh, yes!" She reached for a file on Mike's desk and pulled it out. "The job description," she said, waving a piece of paper in his face. "You realize the salary is...I'd get a sixty percent raise."

He smiled wide. "You deserve it."

"You are fucking kidding me." Her eyebrow cocked up. "What kind of CEO are you, throwing jobs around like candy and hiring someone who doesn't meet the qualifications on paper?"

124

He looked out at the fresh powder on the double black diamond trail, the tip of the mountain calling his name.

"The kind of CEO who needs to do quality control on his own mountain."

"Mike!"

He shrugged into his coat, ignoring the messages and paperwork that would keep him here for ten hours. "You can take over a lot of this," he said, gesturing at the pile. "Leave the things I need to do. And start your raise and promotion immediately."

"But—"

"I think that you're struggling to find the right words, Shelly."

"The right words?" She looked at him like he was crazy.

"Thank you. Just say 'thank you.'"

He heard the words in a faint shout as he made his way to the outer doors, texting Laura and Dylan.

* * *

"I am going to die," Laura said in a low, shaking voice.

"It's skiing. Not BASE jumping. You aren't cage fighting. You're riding down a tiny slope on skis." Mike sighed. People let their fear get in the way of the exhilarating push down a mountain. The control, the easy glide, the heart-pumping challenge of the slopes— nothing was better.

Well, sex was better. And fatherhood. And love. But aside from those…

"Death on sticks," she grumbled.

Try as he might, he couldn't get her off the bunny slope. This was a source of endless teasing from his staff. When Mike had been "just" a ski instructor here for all those years, he'd had a reputation for being the only instructor who could teach *anyone*, and have them up on the lower trails within hours.

Fear? Fear had no place in skiing. Yet Laura was the hardest student he'd ever faced in well over a decade of teaching on the slopes.

"Laura," he whispered in her ear, "there's no reason to be afraid. Worst case, you fall. And we've practiced falling."

"*You've* practiced falling. I've just *actually* fallen. Over and over." She eyed the bunny slope with trepidation. Someone had put small barrels out to help new skiers to handle turns.

He couldn't help but laugh. That just made her scowl. She looked adorable with her ski goggles, white jacket, and tight white pants. Her golden hair peeked out from under a knit hat, and a white helmet with purple stripes topped her head.

A pink nose poked out from under her goggles. It wasn't cold enough for a balaclava, and the new powder made this a perfect day to spend hours out here instead of chained to a desk. Dylan was in the lodge, playing with Jillian in the new Kid's Korner they'd installed shortly after she was born. The added playroom pulled in a lot of parents of small children, and by letting one couple share a single ski lift pass, he'd gained a huge following among parents of little kids.

And why not? He, Dylan, and Laura knew how hard it was. Firsthand. When Mike watched the parents of two little ones come in, he always smiled. A bit wistfully. Jillian was pulling up now, and that meant she would walk soon, babyhood fading.

Maybe she needed a sibling.

He hadn't said those words to anyone. Those were words that were very, very dangerous. Yet he knew they needed to be said one day.

Just not yet.

"I am going to snap a knee and it will be your fault," Laura said in a tight voice as she looked down the puny hill. Before she could say anything else, Mike took the little bunny slope in ten seconds and cut at the bottom, sending an intentional spray of snow out like a giant fan.

"Showoff!" she called from above.

He couldn't argue. "That's right! And you'll get to my level soon enough." A lie. A complete lie, but he said it anyway because he knew that half the battle with becoming a competent skier was in the mind.

"LIAR!" she screamed down the hill. A four year old whizzed past her and gave her a thumbs up, doing a credible imitation of Mike's maneuver and filling Mike's mouth with snow.

Deep, loud laughter came out of him, the feeling coming from the bottom of his lungs, a release his body needed. "Awesome! High five!" The little kid shimmied over to him and jumped up on the skis to land a high five, then skittered off, bent over in that crouched way kids with lower centers of gravity had. No poles, either; Mike taught the young ones that way. Made them less dependent on the poles and—more pragmatically—less likely to poke themselves or anyone else.

"You're both showoffs!" Laura called down.

"Quit stalling!"

She planted her hands on her hips and shook her head, then put the poles down. Her legs went into snowplow position—like an inverted V—and he groaned. She was still stuck at that level.

127

And then she pushed off, and to his surprise she pulled out a bit from the V, keeping the skis parallel as she slowly descended, her calves turning enough, tight muscles working to get around the first barrel. Good! Then she managed the second and third like a pro, gaining speed.

"Good speed!" he called out. The shout unnerved her, he could see, and he regretted it instantly. No longer in control of her legs, her core muscles and arms didn't give her enough balance, and he could predict, with pinpoint precision, what would happen next.

Once you let fear take over, the muscles freak out and aim for what they know. When you're in a situation so unfamiliar, and gliding on snow on wooden sticks in a body that's only done it a handful of times, there is no easy "normal," so the muscles go crazy and the brain can only see one option.

Get on safe ground.

Except you can't, because falling on skis has its own set of dangers.

And so panic hits, control abates, and you just— crash.

Laura made it to the bottom of the hill and Mike skied quickly to her, to try to break her fall, but she crashed smack into the orange construction netting his staff had placed there to stop kids (and adults) from sliding off into the abyss and snowballing down into a culvert.

Suppressing a smile, he stood over her and said quietly, "You did a great job until the end."

"Oh," she groaned. The same word she used sometimes during sex sounded nothing like its aroused form. "I think I broke something."

Alarm shot through him and he looked up for a medical responder. "Leg? Wrist?"

"Ego."

Adrenaline burst through him as her self-deprecating laughter clued him in that she was safe and unhurt. "Don't joke like that!" He bent down and began untangling her ski from the orange mesh. "How did you manage to get the ski through three separate holes?"

"I'm talented that way," she grumbled, settling on her back, right leg twisted in a suspicious manner as Mike worked on the left leg. Seeing her in repose, eyes hidden by amber goggles but lips spreading in a sheepish grin, made him love her even more.

Trying. She was trying to join him in his world, his love of skiing, and he loved her for it. His gloves were in the way of unraveling the mesh, so he pulled them off and she reached out to hold them.

"I think we need to pop off your skis and figure out the rest."

"Good." She laughed. "You do that and I'll hobble over to the lodge for a latte."

"No way," he said firmly. "You need to own this hill before I let you take a break."

"I will dominate the bunny slope! I have the power!" she shouted, tipping her head back as he stood and reached down to pull her up.

"You can't handle the bunny slope?" a kid with a snowboard said, pushing past. Twelve or thirteen, Mike guessed, a light sprinkling of pimples on the part of the face not covered by goggles or helmet. His voice dripped with condescension.

"What?" Laura joked back, not letting him get to her. Mike admired that. "I *own* the bunny slope. Watch out! Bunny slope today, Chuck E. Cheese climbing

129

structure tomorrow. I will dominate!" The kid shook his head and glided off, one foot hooked into the snowboard bindings, the other pushing himself to the ski lift.

"Double black diamond for me!" he shouted back.

"You can have it!" Laura responded, then looked at Mike. Without thinking, he reached down to kiss her, their goggles clanking against each other, pain shooting through his brow and ears.

"Ow!" she said, giggling. Both pulled their respective goggles up over their helmets and the kiss was awkward. Heartfelt, but awkward.

"What was that for?" she asked.

"For joining my world."

"Well, then, thank you," she replied.

"For what?"

"For rocking mine."

JOSIE

The text simply read: *You ever been on a plane before?*

Darla.

Yes. You haven't? she texted back.

Josie could easily imagine that Darla hadn't, because it wasn't like Aunt Kathy was a platinum club member of any frequent-flyer club. Living in a trailer in a tiny town in Ohio on the Pennsylvania border hadn't given her niece Darla a life of luxury.

When the hell would I? Between my champagne and lobster buffets when I worked midnights at the gas station and my caviar dreams when I slept in the trailer with the pipes all frozen? Darla texted back.

That was about what Josie expected.

What's up with planes? The guys ask you to go somewhere special? Josie responded, ignoring the sarcasm. Darla was in a permanent, loving threesome relationship with Joe Ross and Trevor Connor, members of the band Random Acts of Crazy. She worked now as the operations assistant for Good Things Come in Threes, where Josie was the...hell, they didn't have a name for what Josie did.

She ran the place.

A dating service for women who want two men and want the triad to work out forever was one hell of an anomaly in today's world, but then again, Josie was, too. Assembling a family of her own out of good friends who were all living a little (or a lot) off the beaten path was about all she could manage, aside from the incredibly normal boyfriend she'd stumbled into finding eight months ago, at her best friend's birth.

How did she snag *normal*? Thinking about Alex came as easily as breathing or masturbating. You just did.

Aren't you working right now? Josie asked. She needed to get her mind off Alex and masturbating, because she was going to get that hot, tingly flush that would dog her for hours, making her clit scream for attention and driving her to rub one off in a bathroom if she didn't divert now.

Yep. New lead! A chick named Callie. That makes six new signups from women and three from men this week, Darla replied.

You coming home for dinner? Josie asked. Mundane details. Ask about mundane details and make the rising swell inside her go away. Was this what it was like for guys who thought about baseball statistics to keep from prematurely ejaculating during sex?

She would have to ask Alex later.

And...there she was, back at thinking about Alex. That tight, inviting body. The smattering of dark hairs over a chest with muscles that swelled, his cobra back hot and chiseled. How his muscles curved in at the hips, making her drool just to imagine him. His fevered breath hissing her name as he thrust into her...

Damn it.

She was at an office supply store, picking out a printer stand, the most mundane task on the planet short of choosing curtain rods. Who gets horny in an office supply store? Maybe Steve Carell. Who knows. But for Josie, just the fact that thinking about Alex could get her into this kind of throbbing state was a huge warning bell and source of tremendous joy.

Both. Warning and joy. Because Josie was that fucked up on the inside.

Nope. Back to planes. Help? Darla texted.

Didn't Trevor and Joe give you advice? Josie responded.

No, the guys didn't. Just asking. What do I need to know? Darla replied. Something about that sentence did not make sense, but Josie didn't feel like prying when she had a big old red clit like a button that, if pressed, would scream out something other than, "Yeah, we got that."

Don't joke about bombs, Josie texted back.

Haha, Darla replied. A chill shot through Josie, helping to quell her need for Alex, for an electronic vibrator, for her own hand. If Darla made a joke in front of a TSA agent, she'd get the cavity search of her life. Though, Josie assumed, Trevor and Joe had probably done quite well in that area...

THAT killed off her arousal lickety-split. Whew.

No—seriously, Darla, don't you make a single fucking joke about a bomb, she typed back, slamming her fingertips against the phone as if Darla would realize her emphasis. This was serious stuff.

Like I look like a bomber, Josie. What am I going to do? Eat a can of beans and sit on the pilot's head? That's about the only bomb I can manage, Darla said with a smiley face.

No one looks like a bomber, you idiot, Josie replied. *That's the point.*

Especially me, was Darla's response. You could take her out of small-town Ohio and put her in classes at Harvard, and have her in a long-term relationship with two guys in Ivy League law schools, but

133

sometimes Josie wondered about Darla's provincialism. Being blond and curvy didn't mean anything when a TSA agent was concerned about abnormal behavior.

And while Darla was no terrorist, she cornered the market on abnormal.

So help me motherfucking God, if I have to come bail you out of federal prison and explain that shit to Aunt Kathy because you couldn't shut down the short circuit between your funny bone and your mouth, I will make you sponge bath my mother when she is too old to care for herself, Josie answered in two texts.

Silence.

More silence.

And then: *Point received.*

Whew.

Any more advice that doesn't mean I need to go poke my eyes out with a hot car cigarette lighter after reading it? Darla added.

Josie thought for a moment, imagining Darla at a TSA checkpoint.

And then: *Yes. Don't wear an underwire bra.*

WHAT? Darla texted. *WHAT does my bra have to do with flying? I'm not going to stab someone to death with my underwire.*

The thought made Josie giggle, and she looked down at her own modest chest. *I read it somewhere*, Josie answered. *Research it for yourself.*

K. Tnx. was the only response.

She tipped her head up and her neck muscles groaned with the stretch. How long had she been bent over her phone, a texting zombie like half the population of Cambridge and Somerville? Slapping one hand on the printer stand she was sure would work, she realized it would be easier to order it on her phone and have it delivered to the office than to buy it here and haul it there on her own. The order took all of five clicks.

Done.

Ah, technology. She heard they even had vibrator apps on smartphones these days. Alex had come home from work one day telling her all about them, a weird smirk on his face.

Alex. Back to thinking about Alex and sex.

She needed to go do something about that.

Right now.

* * *

Outdoor sex was their thing, but this was going way too far. "I am not fucking on a public ice-skating rink, Alex!" Josie said as his hands pawed at her jeans, trying to work the button with fingers so cold she feared having one slip inside her, like a vagina popsicle.

"Why not?" Hot breath tickled her ear. What tiny sliver of ear skin she allowed to touch the air. Boston was experiencing one of the coldest weeks on record and it was twilight, the air temperature dropping more with each breath.

She had to hand it to him—the setting was amazing. An open-air pond that had frozen just right, leaving skaters to play on the ice for free, bare trees surrounding the little alcove he'd pulled her into. Streetlights dotted the landscape on the road above them, but otherwise the only light came from the full moon.

Full moon. It always brought Alex outside, his cock hard as a rock, his mind in single pursuit of her body and her heart, unencumbered and outside, air a strong aphrodisiac, the pull of which she found hard to fight.

Like gravity.

Like sexual tension and need, all rising up inside her but abruptly cut off by his icicle fingers.

Bet his tongue is nice and warm, though, her little devil inside said. "Devil" was a euphemism for clit. Her clit said it, and she was unabashedly out for some action right now. Unable to get home after her earlier shopping trip, Josie had walked around town with fire between her legs.

And Alex had just the right hose to put it out.

He took her glove off and shoved her hand down the front of his jeans. Ah. Commando. How could guys go around without underwear when it was six degrees outside? Seriously? Didn't their mushroom caps turn into little push-up bars? How could you leave so much to the cold elements?

Her hand warmed up instantly as she brushed against his soft, thick goodness. "Who needs hand warmers?" she murmured, and then slipped on the ice, her hand caught in his pants and dragging him down with a lurch and a strangle cry.

He sounded mutilated. Her fingers were tangled in the thatch of his hair and one testicle was clenched in her fist that she'd involuntarily made as she struggled to remain upright.

"Did I break something?" she said, worried now— unable to stop giggling at the absurdity of what they were doing, though.

"If you did," he said with a choking sound, "I know a way you can fix it. And," he muttered, looking at his package, unbuttoning his jeans, "after what you just plucked out, I won't need to be waxed for months."

Her giggles increased and she couldn't stop, overcome with wet eyes and whooping gasps as Alex tried in vain to get her to re-engage in some semblance of sex.

"How about on the shore?" he finally asked, struggling to stand. In the moonlight he was quite a sight, knit cap pulled over his unruly brown hair, crystal-clear brown eyes full of lust.

And his pants were hanging open under his ski jacket, like some kind of flasher.

"Snow is way better than ice. I think I wrenched my shoulder when I fell," Josie admitted.

Alex reached up under her coat and shirt to cup a breast.

"That's not my shoulder."

"Really? I'm so sorry. I'm really bad at anatomy." He teased her nipple until she gasped and began to tremble with need.

"You're a doctor and you don't know the difference between a shoulder and a breast?"

He pulled her hand over his now enormous erection. "Can you give me a neck rub? My neck really needs you."

"If that's your neck, then what have I been kissing all this time?"

A rush of power and he was on her, Josie's back crunching against fresh snow, the cold somehow shifting to warmth as his body was over hers, bare abs rubbing against her own as her shirt pulled up, his hands fevered against her skin, unclasping her jeans and pulling them down.

Cold. Frozen buttocks. "ALEX!" Josie squealed. "The snow's all over my ass."

"Let it go," he whispered.

"I'm not some Disney princess," she hissed, but his hands warmed her. Then he sat up, pulled off his coat, and draped it on the snow like a blanket.

"Get your frigid ass on there. Now," he commanded.

"Frigid! You want to see frigid? I'll show you—"

He leapt on her, pinning her arms to the ground, her ass stripped bare of panties, jeans around her ankles as he took a deep breath and inhaled against the groove between her breasts. Josie's shirt was inelegantly shoved up, along with her now-unzippered coat. She didn't wear a bra today simply because, and now she was glad as his mouth found one nipple and he plucked it with his tongue, making her wet and hungry to have him in her.

The moon agreed, watching over them as always, a celestial voyeur. And they were giving it an eyeful.

Alex pulled up, balancing himself on one arm, his hand deep in the snow, wrestling with his back pocket, which now rested somewhere around his knees. The clumsy way they were made her smile, a deep sense of goodness and comfort infusing her, making the night chill an afterthought. Their breath mingled visually, puffs of white essence twining together like a visual manifestation of their relationship, and even as they fumbled like teenagers, she found herself.

She found herself.

"I love you so much, you dork," she said as he fell on his side, his ribs hitting the cold snow, his yelp of surprise sending her into a fit of giggles. At this rate she'd be laughing so hard he wouldn't be able to enter her. She'd shoot him back out like a blow dart.

"I love you, too." But he was distracted, the reply robotic.

"You're such a romantic. I'll bet you say that to all the girls whose asses you dip in snow."

"I'm trying to find a condom," he huffed, tossing a handful of snow at her bare belly. Josie's turn to yelp.

138

She clapped a hand over her own mouth, then a single finger.

"Someone's going to find us!" she said.

The all-too-familiar sound of a foil wrapper tearing in the night made her stop laughing and her insides went liquid with white-hot desire. He handled the basics and then hovered over her, trembling.

"Are you cold?"

"Let's make our own heat," he said as he slowly entered Josie, her legs going wide by pragmatics in the way, jeans holding her to one spot. The rub of his thighs against her own as he slowly thrust in and out gave her shivers, like a fingernail tracing up her spine.

Or maybe that was the beginnings of frostbite.

Masterful and patient, Alex had this way of being during sex that gave the impression he could do this all his days, until they were ancient and timeless. At the same moment, he was dominant and feverish, wanting and needing with a near-violence that spoke more of deep trust than sheer control.

They didn't have much time, so the latter man emerged above Josie, her clit gaining a rapid slick from their movements, the push of his abs against hers, the tilt of his hips driving her to sensual insanity. Josie's own orgasm crashed first, careening as her hands found his bare ass and dug in, cupping the sculpted flesh and feeling his power as he used it to push into her, to drive them closer to each other.

As she held in her screams through gritted teeth, the stars sparkling above, a squirrel skittering across branches a few trees away, Alex tensed and heat poured through Josie as he came, a glorious rush of emotion and animal tension released because of her.

Her.

"Hey!" a voice shouted as Alex panted over her, eyes intense. That wasn't Alex's voice, and his eyes shifted to alarm. With lightning speed, they pulled apart as a flashlight flailed its beam in their direction.

Josie's panties tore as she pulled them up, her fingers too cold to button her jeans, so she simply zipped her coat over them. Alex shoved his condom-covered cock into his jeans and pulled them up, deftly snapping them and pulling his coat shut just as a man's form rounded a thick tree and Josie was blinded by light.

Her hand went up, palm facing him. "Do you mind? I rather like my vision!"

"Oh," he said, dropping the beam. Heavy breath filled the air, a panting that definitely wasn't her boyfriend. Josie looked down, and in the non-flashlight-holding hand a husky on a leash panted heavily, looking at them. That dog looked really familiar. A little too familiar.

If dogs could smile, it did.

"Sorry, folks." The guy looked to be the age Josie's dad would be if he were still alive. A bit gray, and slim like hers was. Tall, and with a lean runner's look. His face was guarded, but you could tell he was naturally friendly. He reminded Josie of someone, but she couldn't see his face.

"John?" Alex choked out.

The flashlight hit Alex's face and he turned away, like something out of an alien abduction movie.

"Alex! What are you—oh! And Josie!"

She peered deeper into the dark and realized...

They'd nearly been caught air fucking by Alex's stepfather.

If you could actually see a man blush in moonlit darkness, Alex would have glowed right about then.

His hands smelled like Josie. He was still wearing the condom on his rapidly deflating erection. What a day to choose to go commando.

Don't laugh don't laugh don't laugh, Josie chanted inside, using every muscle at her disposal to keep her face even and neutral. One comment, one joke, one anything and she would crack.

Like Darla at the TSA counter, she imagined.

"What are you two doing out here this time of night?" John asked, coming closer, an easy grin on his face. Noi, the dog, came up to Alex and began licking his hand eagerly. Alex snatched it back with a confused, horrified, completely helpless look on his face, and rapidly shoved his hands in his gloves.

Only then did he pet the family dog.

"We're ice skating."

Alex had lured Josie here with that promise, and they'd actually had two sets of skates sitting by the ice, which Alex pointed to, like an errant child lining up his evidence to get out of being in trouble.

"Oh, nice! Meribeth doesn't trust her knees anymore, so I can't get her to come out on the ice with me these days. Next time you guys decide to do this, please let me know. I'd love to join in!"

Don't laugh don't laugh don't laugh.

Alex's eyes were so wide they might compete with the moon for the largest orb in the sky. "Will do, John." Josie bit her lips and gave one of those smiles where you just pray you won't turn into a raving lunatic, and John's eyebrows twitched just the tiniest bit when he looked at her.

"What are you doing out here?" Josie managed to ask, trying to look polite. She shifted her hip slightly and felt her panties slide down from her hip to her knee, a large bunch of cloth that had not just torn,

141

apparently, but been shredded into a pile of uselessness now.

A pile that threatened to get caught at her jeans cuff and come peeking out. Kind of hard to hide bright red, satin panties, even in just moonlight. Leaning against Alex on that side gave her some safety, so she looped her arm around his waist and hugged.

Really hard.

"We're only a few blocks from home." He pointed, and then her eyes took in the road. Now Josie realized where we were—about a quarter-mile from Meribeth and John's place.

Damn. Did that mean Alex knew this alcove would be quiet? Had he planned this?

"I thought you walk Noi down at the dog park," Alex said casually, though Josie knew the real message was for her. *I didn't mean for this to happen*, he seemed to say.

But if his mom lived nearby, and he knew about this little place, had he...been here before with other women?

Suddenly the moon seemed more a conspirator than a voyeur, and a smoldering began inside her.

Not the good kind, either.

"You two want to come over for coffee, or something stronger?" John looked at our discarded ice skates. "After you're done, I mean."

Oh, we're done.

"Thanks! Um, maybe?" Alex turned to Josie, his voice going up like a question. She hated when he did this, because it put all the pressure on her. If she said "no," she looked like an asshole, and she felt like every time she said what she actually wanted, if it wasn't the "right" thinking in terms of being with Alex's family, that it gave them ammunition against her.

Reality and what she felt were two radically different states, though. Her rational brain knew that Meribeth and John would understand if she turned them down. And right now, she didn't want to be around anyone.

Not even Alex.

"I…"

Her hesitation seemed to make Alex kick into gear. "I shouldn't put that on you," he said, apologizing as if reading her mind. "John, can we just show up if we decide to? We might be too tired after skating."

Gratitude and fury fought inside her.

She didn't know which one would win.

"Suit yourself. You know your mom has a standing invitation for you two. If you don't come over then it's just an extra night of wild sex for us."

Jim had an odd sense of humor.

Alex blushed again, though he seemed to recover, this role more familiar. "Just don't do it on the kitchen floor by the back door. Don't want a repeat of what happened when I brought the soccer team home after practice that one time." Low chuckles, then a wave from John as he disappeared, dragging Noi off by the leash.

A long, audible exhale from Alex, and then he turned to her with amused eyes. "Can you believe that?"

Josie snorted.

"Oh, that snort sounds dangerous," he said, turning away. He reopened his pants, but if he thought they going in for round two after that, he was crazy.

Nope. He tied off the condom and found a trashcan nearby. This was a well-known area along a trail, but it fueled her anger that he knew exactly where the trashcans were, right here in the woods.

143

How about that?

"So, come here often?" she asked him.

He took that as a joke, an invitation to sidle up and snuggle. Her body went stiff with anger.

"Oh," he said archly, taking a step back and holding his hands above her, as if dealing with something he had to handle gingerly. Which, he did. "You're upset about something."

"Perceptive." She had been reduced to single words now, the churning cauldron of fucked-up emotions inside her spewing nonsense. Josie knew if she tried to explain why she was upset, she couldn't be coherent. Hoping that Alex understood that, and would somehow just ride out this mood with her and be gentle and understanding, she went quiet.

ALEX

Josie didn't *do* quiet. He knew he'd screwed up somehow, but damn if he could figure it out. Coming here had been some sort of mistake, and having John discover them left him reeling. While John had always treated him more like a friend than a father, it was still damn intimidating to have your stepfather nearly find you balls deep in your girlfriend in the woods in public.

"You're upset that I stuck you with answering about his offer to visit after we…" His voice disappeared. After they what? They'd just completed what he'd come here to do. Mission accomplished. His guilty eyes cut over to the ice skates and hope resurged in him.

Maybe he knew exactly what to do next.

"After we…" she repeated in a mocking tone. Uh oh.

"You knew why I brought you here," he replied, voice as neutral as possible. They had an implicit agreement that outdoor sex and all the thrills and risks that came with it was a joy they both were privy to indulging in. The shock of finding that the other enjoyed the slightly voyeuristic sexual kink had been a revelation. Alex fell for Josie that first time they'd been together, kissing at the hospital while her best friend Laura was giving birth. The impromptu sex by the river a few days later had clinched it.

The rest, as they say, was history, and seven and a half months later, here they were.

Fighting.

He and Josie didn't, generally speaking, fight. They bickered and argued about small details, but the big concepts weren't an issue. Both fell into a pattern of just living life together, and as the relationship deepened they found, layer by layer, that they were even more compatible than either realized from the start.

It felt like they were somehow getting away with something. And outdoor sex most definitely fell into that category for Alex. As his breath made clouds that floated up to kiss the observing moon, he took deep, piercing breaths to steady himself. He wanted more. Not just more sex, but more.

However, he didn't like more *fighting*.

"What about the others?" she asked in a soft, heartbreaking voice. Others?

"Others what?"

Josie's arm swept out from her, extended like an announcer at the circus making a grand gesture. "You knew exactly where to go so we couldn't be seen. You grew up around here. And the trashcan. Ether you have a strange inborn echolocation system for finding the nearest garbage can every time we have outdoor sex, or you know because you've been here before with someone."

He cleared his throat and drew upon the only response he could think of. "You're right," he said in a low voice.

She looked stricken. It made his chest hurt. "I am?"

"Yes. You've discovered my secret. I'm..." He paused for dramatic effect. "Garbage Can Locater

146

After Public Sex Man." He unzipped his coat and pulled up his shirt. "I forgot to wear my uniform today."

"Oh, Christ..."

"Professor X rejected me for the X-Men school. Didn't think my powers were sufficiently designed to help mankind. I argued that, in fact, they are uniquely designed to aid mankind! I mean, what better skill would a person want as a superpower?"

"Alex," Josie said, lips twitching. He was getting to her, and then she punched him in the chest, right at diaphragm level. She practically had to jump to do it, their height difference that vast.

It felt like having a plush animal thrown hard at him.

"Ouch," he said weakly, which made her laugh.

"I know that didn't hurt."

"Then why did you do it?"

"Because you're an idiot."

"An idiot with unique trashcan-finding abilities."

"Alex."

"What?"

"I love you." Without even looking at him as she said the words, Josie walked over to the ice skates and sat on her ass. She began to shake one leg like a dog, and he frowned, wondering what on earth she was—

And then she pulled a piece of red silk cloth out of her ankle.

"What is that?"

"I just gave birth. Congratulations! You're a daddy." She threw the item at him, hitting his cheek. He bent down and picked it up. Her panties. Shredded.

That would have made him laugh, but her words made his heart stop and speed up all at once.

147

You're a daddy.

Someday, he wanted to hear those exact words from her as they huddled around a pregnancy test, eager for a positive result. In the not-too-distant future, when his residency was over and he worked reasonably normal hours (though there was no "normal" for an obstetrician, ever on call for babies who didn't follow schedules), they would talk about marriage and children and...

A family.

Josie slipped her feet into the set of ice skates he'd brought. Thankfully, they were the right size. Frankly, he'd brought them for show, never imagining she would actually want to skate. As she laced them up, she looked out over the pond. God, she was beautiful. Tiny nose, sharp bones in her face, the kind of woman who would age gracefully and even at sixty look like she was forty. Not that he cared. She could look like an ogre's pet boar for all it mattered.

She was Josie.

And they would have babies.

He walked to her, and plunked down on the ground, and put on his skates, the toes pinching a bit, making his feet feel swollen, but for an hour on the ice he could suffer. His ankles would take a beating, and his old failed ice hockey seasons—all of two, in middle school—gave him enough muscle memory to manage this.

Standing carefully, Josie balanced well and impressed him as she glided on the ice, taking care. Her ankles wobbled and she caught the toe of one ice skate on a bump in the very uneven ice, but soon was skating with decent control. Not circles or triple axles, but she could move with a level of grace that surprised him.

She could always surprise him.

His turn. Being well over six feet, close to seven, meant his center of gravity was far different than hers. *BAM!* His ass cracked hard against the ice, the moon laughing at him as he looked up.

The *snick snick snick* of Josie's skates on the ice told him she was coming to his rescue. Or something like that. Her petite form couldn't possibly pull him up without the two of them wrecking each other in a painful pileup.

"You need to talk to Professor X again," she said, her face over his now, grinning. The moon spilled light over the back of her body, framing it like an aura.

"Why?"

"That superpower of yours needs to include better ankles."

He slipped and slid, finally giving up and turning over onto all fours, ass in the air as Josie dissolved into giggles. Aching move by aching move, he toed his skates and pulled up to standing. He felt like a toddler wrapped in bubble wrap, trying to run.

Those two failed seasons of ice hockey came back to him. They had been a failure precisely because of this.

He couldn't skate worth a damn.

At indoor ice rinks he could cling to the wall for help, but out on the open ice his only option was Josie, and he'd snap her like a twig if he used her to balance on.

CRACK! He was down again, helpless, like a turtle on its back. Alex wasn't accustomed to this sense of impossibility. The ice was defeating him, and a simple matter of physics ought to have allowed him to figure this out. Millions of people, from tiny toddlers to elderly folks, could ice skate. Why on earth was this eluding him?

"You're too big."

"That's what she said," he joked.

Josie rolled her eyes as she looked down at him, then glided away. "Dr. Perfect isn't so perfect at something," she teased, her voice floating through the still night.

He blinked for what felt like one long minute, and then began to crawl to shore, her laughter twinkling like the stars.

When he reached the snow, he sat and watched her as he took off his skates, her face luminous, her body in rare form. Controlled. Hesitant and cautious until she got it right. But skating with abandon, navigating the new and uncomfortable, the ice as nature intended.

Pausing, he took her in, legs taut as she made a turn, her mind and body in complete harmony.

In that moment, he realized, he had no choice. The universe had made it for him. She carried his heart with her, encased inside, and whatever remained of his natural life was hers, and only hers.

The moon seemed to glow a little brighter, as if agreeing.

DYLAN

If men could have PMS, then lately, Mike was the poster child for whatever drug the pharmaceutical companies would debut for it. Fucking hell. His moods had always been erratic, even as he used medication to chill.

That, and running until he destroyed a pair of shoes in six weeks. Too many miles.

Not that Dylan couldn't keep up. If he wanted to. But why destroy muscle when you could lift and bulk up?

He thought about the gym. Hadn't been there in forever. Same with the old firehouse. The grapevine told him Murphy's wife was on the mend, and those volunteer shifts he'd grabbed for a while ended once Jillian was born. You stay up all night with a baby a few nights a week and you're a complete wastoid when it comes to handling a twenty-four at the station.

Hell, he couldn't manage a twelve-hour shift any more. Sleep when you can sleep. Jillian's latest bout of teething meant the handful of weeks where she'd started to sleep through the night felt like a dream.

Mike and Laura came out of the bedroom a hell of a lot happier than they'd been going in, he noticed. Jillian had dropped off to sleep, and he looked on the counter near the coffee maker. Sitting at the tiny kitchen table, sipping a cup of much-needed Joe, gave him a rare moment to just think.

Sometimes thinking was overrated. But not when you felt like you never had the time to do it.

His cell phone and car keys were in their newly designated spot, the phone plugged in to charge. Training himself to put them there would take a few weeks, but it was better than the hack he and Mike had finally devised to get his cell phone out of the heating system.

He was telling that story to Jillian's prom date some day.

Yesterday had to go down in the history of their entire relationship—his and Mike's—as one of the weirdest. And that was saying a lot, because after Jill died, Mike turned strange. Then, again, after they thought they had lost Laura. He had this hidden ball of something badass deep down in the dark reaches of himself, and while most guys deal with it by being assholes, competing for who's the bigger man, or just blowing it out through weightlifting or pickup basketball, Mike used running and meditation.

Dylan thought punching something was so much better.

He'd spent the afternoon in a haze in the Kid's Korner of the lodge as Jillian found new ways to pull his hair and tug at his heart. Toddlers wobbled on new walking feet around her, and she tilted her head, wide green eyes following the movements of the kids, a drooly grin ever at the ready for whoever looked her way. He'd become accustomed to the other parents cooing at her and then looking at him quizzically.

"She takes after her mother?" they'd say, and something in his throat would tighten. Jillian had dark blond hair and green eyes, and looked like a blend, as if genetics really had somehow taken three sets of

152

DNA, put them in a Vitamix, and poured them out into a live newborn.

But she didn't look at all like him right now. You could see it in her shoulders and the way she tilted her head. Her expressions, too, especially when she frowned and tipped her eyes up, lips pursed. The looks was so quintessentially a Stanwyck trademark that he'd taken pictures whenever he could and sent them to his mom and dad.

They'd responded with scanned pictures of him at that age with the same exact look. Laura and Mike had gawked, and something about the look they gave him, Jillian, and then each other had made his throat tighten, too.

Home was a sanctuary. He didn't have to worry about what people thought (not that he did…much). Mike and Laura and he had a pact to raise the baby together as one unit, and they hadn't given him even a hint that Jillian's paternity meant one tiny damn. Whether he was her biological father or not, she was his heart child. Embedded forever and holding a piece of him, it was like she was his soul, raw and naked, crawling through the world.

And right now she was sitting up in her toy room, her hand clutching something she munched happily on.

Wait.

He hadn't fed her a snack.

On well-practiced feet, he moved like a lion across the room, sleek and graceful, not wanting to scare her.

A crumb-filled grin was his reward, five teeth poking out in odd syncopation. Those five teeth had cost him, Mike, and Laura plenty of sleep.

"Whatcha got there, Jelly Belly?" he asked, cooing.

"Aga da!" she pronounced, holding the fist high like a victor's.

A well-gummed teething biscuit and a long insect's wing poked out between chubby, dimpled knuckles. Oh, gross.

Eh. Wouldn't be the worst thing she'd eaten, he surmised. But after peeling her fingers back, he took the day-old (at least) biscuit out of her hand, murmuring condolences as she wailed.

"I know, I know. The teething biscuit is better after a couple of days. It's aged to a fine tone, isn't it? Like wine." He ran to the kitchen and zipped back in seconds with the box of new biscuits, handing her one.

She threw it into the ball pit.

"Wah!" she shouted, like a ninja throwing a star.

"Jillian for the Olympic softball team in 2032!" Laura said, clapping. "That was quite a throw."

The baby heard Laura and stopped, mouth open, eyes wide and rimmed with the beginnings of tears. She scowled.

"It's Dylan's twin!" Mike said, holding two cups of coffee, extending one to Dylan.

Yesterday they'd been in the bedroom or skiing, Dylan on kidwatch, and this morning had been no different. It was not that he didn't enjoy it, but looking at Laura's v-neck sweater, so like the one she'd worn for their first date, he began to feel decidedly less Daddy and more *Hey, hot mama, come to daddy...*

The doorbell rang. Mike startled, spilling some coffee on his hand and yelping in reaction.

The sound made the baby giggle uncontrollably.

"All you have to do is burn yourself to drag her out of a bad mood!" Dylan declared as Laura answered the door. He did a mental check. They'd all showered. Mike had given more control to Shelly (and about time...). Jillian could manage without breast milk for six hours or so.

Time to put himself at the center of this relationship again. To put all three in the same circle, really.

One side of his mouth crooked up in a smile. But he'd happily take all the credit.

He was an Evil Fucking Genius.

"Josie!" Laura cried out from the other room, the door shutting and the thump of rapid footsteps filling the hall. Mike batted at the coffee stains on his jeans and sucked the webbing of his thumb where the coffee had burned.

"Hey!" Mike said, giving Josie a ginger hug as she approached the playroom. "To what do we owe the privilege?"

"Zombies."

"Huh?"

"It would take a zombie apocalypse for me to do what I'm about to do for you."

"For...me?"

"All of you." Josie winked at Dylan and he groaned. She lifted one eyebrow and stared at him.

Mike and Laura turned and imitated her. Six eyes asked a lot of questions.

Dylan fished in his pocket and pulled out a set of keys, dangling them.

Jillian started to bounce on her ass and shouted, "Aga hbbbbb mama da!"

"These are not for you," he chided, wagging a finger toward her.

She gave him a raspberry.

"Oh, for God's sake. He's taking you to your sex cabin. I'm here to make sure your baby doesn't get taken away by wolves or eat a spider or throw the Hope Diamond in your garbage disposal."

"She is capable of any and all of those things," Mike deadpanned.

"Sex cabin?" Laura whipped her head to stare at Dylan. "You planned this?"

Josie bent down and rubbed Jillian's head. The baby looked up and reached out with a grubby finger to snag the hem of her sweater.

"Six hours! I have to get home to..."

"To what?"

"To help Alex move in."

They all froze. *Great*, thought Dylan. Trumped by the damn best friend. Wanting the spotlight for a moment was asking too much, it seemed. Laura's eager look a second ago faded fast as Josie dropped her bomb.

"Alex is moving in?" Laura squealed.

"Practically! He's leaving a toothbrush and a spare set of clothes at my place." Josie took a deep breath, one that seemed never to end, and let it out slowly. Dylan looked at her like she was crazy, which was accurate.

She really was.

"That's not 'moving in,' Josie," Mike said. Captain Obvious always knew exactly what to say.

"It's close!"

"Have a child with him and tell me about—"

"Shut your whore mouth, Mike!"

His booming laugh filled the room. "That is the first time I've ever been called a whore."

"You continue to joke about my uterus being used for anything other than blood storage and I'll call you worse."

Mike just lifted his eyebrows as he walked away. "Thanks for watching Jelly Belly!"

Laura closed the space between her and Dylan and took his face in her hands. "You arranged this? You went behind my back and called my best friend to come over here to watch the baby for six hours so we could go somewhere and fuck?"

When she put it that way, his plan started to feel tawdry. Cheap. Unseemly.

"Hell yes!" he said with gusto, because hey—he was a guy, after all.

"Thank you!" she whispered, kissing him hard, her tongue parting his lips, the aggression making him submit for a few moments, until he found himself and took over, leading the way and leaving her invaded. Touched. Enraptured.

When they pulled back from each other, breathless, they found a startled Josie with her hand covering the baby's eyes.

"Ix-nay on the ex-say in unt-fray of the aby-bay."

"Aba bah!" Jillian said.

"Great. Her first sentence will be Pig Latin. Why don't you teach her something more useful, like Klingon?" Dylan snapped.

Laura began tugging his hand. "Let's go. Mike! Load up the Jeep. We're about to have an adventure!"

But as Dylan passed the big picture window in their living room, he saw Mike already at the Jeep, loading a small gym bag, waving furiously at them to get in the car.

A man after Dylan's own heart.

The drive to the cabin was exceedingly short, as Mike sped there. Dylan raced inside and turned on the tap to fill the tub. Earlier that day, he had come over with the baby in tow to turn on the heat and stock the fridge. The "eco-cabin" Mike's resort had developed was really a sex sanctuary for them, and—at times—

just a sleep sanctuary when one of the three reached a point of half-psychosis from sleep deprivation.

It was so much more fun to use it for sex, though.

He'd attached the swing to its harness, fingers stroking the leather, remembering the last time they'd used it, his cock growing hard at the image of Laura's wet lips open with orgasmic pleasure as they'd found new heights of sensation and exploration.

Six hours was just enough time to fuck each other silly and shower. All this deeper meaning of life crap that plagued Mike could wait.

When Dylan found himself at odds with his own sense of self, he found pounding it out—and not through his feet—was a form of salvation.

Laura uncorked a bottle of a nice white Chardonnay and poured three glasses, looking around the bright cabin.

"Why is it so warm in here?"

Dylan's smile went sly again. "Jillian and I came here earlier to prepare."

She threw herself at him in a huge embrace, drinking wine over his shoulder. "This is the best surprise I've had in ages."

"This is the first surprise you've had since the last time we were here," Mike added, his voice warm, body relaxed. *Good*, Dylan thought. *So much better than the way he's been acting lately.*

Laura pulled back, her mouth stretched into the kind of vibrant smile he loved to see, and she moved in for a kiss just as her juicy ass began to buzz.

She jumped and laughed. "Shit. My phone." The look on her face as she read the screen made Dylan's stomach fall, and his erection soften just a bit. Uh-oh.

"Josie?" This was a call, not a text. "What's wrong?" Laura's voice was guarded but resigned, and as he heard the tinny sound of Laura's friend saying words like "puked," all their shoulders began to slump.

Mike drank the rest of his wine in one long gulp. Parenthood had changed him that much.

"She puked up a what? An insect?" Laura's voice went up half an octave and she spun around to give Dylan a death glare. "A giant wing from a what?" Josie continued as Laura pulled the phone away from her ear and hissed at him. "Did you see the baby around any insects?"

Just as he was about to craft the smoothest, best PR-spun answer ever, he heard a baby wail in the background of Laura's phone. Laura listened for a second. "And she's warm, too? Insects don't give babies fevers, do they? Could she have picked up some God-awful disease from eating"—GLARE—"something as disgusting as a bug? How big was the bug? Oh my God, what if she ate a cockroach!"

Laura descended into hysterics as Mike calmly pried her fingers off the phone and said to Josie, "She'll be there in five minutes." He ended the call and slowly, deliberately pressed the Jeep's keys into Laura's hand.

"Go," he ordered. Dylan had to admire his chillness. Not cold. Just in control and considerate.

"But..." Laura's eyes were wild and a bit crazy. She looked at the wine, the swing, which now looked like a limp dick in Dylan's eyes (joining his own), and the bed, made neatly and begging for action.

"But nothing. You won't enjoy a single moment if you aren't with our sick baby. Dylan and I just need to unload the fridge so the food won't spoil. We have backpacks. It'll do us good to hike home. It's not even two miles."

Internally, Dylan groaned, but he said nothing. He was already in the doghouse for letting the baby eat an insect (or...maybe she only ate that wing...).

"I—" he blurted, guilty conscience kicking in. Apparently, he had one. "She found an old teething biscuit this morning and there was this insect wing..."

Mike rolled his eyes and crossed his arms, now joining Laura's glare. "And you didn't say anything?" You would think that years of living with Mike would give him some indication of what the guy thought, but no. He was either royally pissed and ready to rip him apart, or barely keeping it together to not laugh.

Dylan could have flipped a coin.

"I don't even know what to say!" Laura screeched as she zipped out the door and slammed it behind her. He'd never seen her run as fast as she did to the Jeep, spewing snow-covered gravel as the tires spun over ice patches until they caught and she drove off.

Mike winced at the grinding sound his poor engine made.

"Smooth. Really smooth," he said, pouring another glass of wine. Dylan watched with growing amusement as Mike downed another half a glass.

"You working on your frat-boy skills? Is beer pong next?" he asked.

Mike smiled wistfully over the top of his wine glass, then downed the rest, carefully swirling the stem between his thumb and index finger.

"No. Just...relaxing."

"Let our baby eat a bug and you're sucking down wine like it's coffee. What the fuck has happened to us?" Dylan plopped down on the bed and stared at the ceiling, the swing in his peripheral vision, taunting him.

"We're parents."

"We're boring."

"You tried. Thank you. This was a great idea."
Mike handed Dylan his glass of wine, and Dylan
figured when in Rome, do what Thor does.

And drink the fucking wine.

"Cockblocked by an insect." Dylan sighed.

"That's a first," Mike said, nodding. "And your
lobster tails are in the fridge now."

Fuck! He'd forgotten about that. "You seriously
want to stuff them in a backpack and hike home?"

"No. Let's just boil them up and eat them. We can
get more some other time. Laura's not coming back."
Mike's words stung.

His plan was a failure.

Chugging the rest of his glass, he eyed the final
third of the bottle. "We could steam the lobsters in
water and wine and have the meat with some butter.
Bring the steaks home."

"Deal."

And while the rest of the afternoon did not involve
sex whatsoever, it turned out to meet one of Dylan's
needs.

Time to just *be*.

LAURA

The day after the Great Insect Ingestion Disaster of 2014, as it would forever be known, Jillian's fever was long gone, and Laura had let go of her annoyance with Dylan. You couldn't catch that baby before she did anything—she was so fast! And cunning.

Just like her parents.

Washing dishes with Mike while the baby played with a set of plastic rings, Laura heard something. In the distance. Her ringtone. Josie's ringtone, actually.

Mike shook his head. "'Superfreak'? Got that right." But his tone was playful. A quick shrug and she was running down the hall on tiptoes, trying to anticipate whether Jillian would have a fearful reaction to the ring (a new development in the baby), where the phone was, and how to locate it quickly and quietly.

The mother's phone dance.

By the time she found it, it was too late. Josie left no voicemail, but the texts told the story.

Problem at the office.

We have a PR issue.

Meet me at Jeddy's.

Not a fake meeting, either.

"What does she mean, 'fake meeting'?"

Laura hadn't noticed Dylan behind her as she read through the quick messages. There were just too many men in this house! The affect in his voice was accusatory, yet joking. But not really.

"Nothing." Laura pocketed the phone and frowned. Could Josie be a bit more obvious? WTF? "What could be so important? A PR issue? As if I need more shit with the company. This is getting out of hand," she complained. Had to be convincing.

"You guys create pretend meetings so you can just hang out?"

"Of course not!"

"That's what it seems like." *Damn it, Josie.*

"And I suppose that folder on your computer marked 'Tax Documents 2001' is really tax forms," she shot back.

"Fuck," he muttered under his breath, stretching out the word. She'd accidentally stumbled across his porn collection a long time ago. Didn't care, but she knew the knowledge would come in handy some time. Like now.

"We don't really do a lot of fake meetings," she said. "And most of the time I bring the baby. It's just... sometimes I need to sit and have a cup of coffee with a friend without making a big deal out of it."

"Of course—"

She cut him off as two more texts came in. "But this sounds really bad. Can we talk later?"

"We're talking?" He smiled, dimples and all, and cupped her chin.

"Ha ha."

"Mike okay?"

That made her pause, even in her rush. "I don't know. He's really grappling with some deep issues. Questions about how we operate, what our relationship means, how I relate to him alone and to both of you...that kind of stuff."

"I just block that shit out when the worry bubbles up," Dylan muttered.

164

"What a great strategy. I'm sure that's working so well," she deadpanned. "You're just deferring all your emotions and in ten years Mike and I will pick up the pieces."

"That's the plan. Thanks in advance." The smile in his eyes made her grateful she'd paused, the joke sinking in on many levels. That they would be together in tens years was a given.

And what a wonderful, loving given it was.

These moments were what made life the chaotic, messy, loveable, astounding shambles she'd always wanted it to be. The days of being lonely and licking her wounds from guys like Ryan (Ryan who?), working in a windowless office, living life as if it were meant to be a series of transactions to get through rather than a buffet of experiences to taste and devour, were long gone.

And then—Dylan's ringtone.

Echoing down the hall.

"What's that?" The sound of something country made a tinny reverberation, as if Blake Shelton were stuck inside a tailpipe. The two followed it, and Mike appeared in the hall, watching them as they perked their ears and followed the sound. His still-shirtless chest made her mouth start to water.

"What is that?" he asked.

"Shh!" they said in unison as they got closer, the sound increasingly louder in the living room.

"Weird," Mike said. "It's like your phone is trapped somewhere."

The ringtone ended. Then—*Bzzzz*.

"Call it for me, would you?" he asked Laura, who pulled her phone out. Three more messages from Josie. *Hold on*, she thought, and then called Dylan.

More country music stuck in a tin can.

Mike found it. Pulling a pop-up toy off one of the heating vents, he pointed down through the slotted metal. "Look."

As she and Dylan clustered around the beige-painted metal vent, they both groaned when the reflection of the glass screen glittered up at them.

"Jillian!" all three exclaimed.

"How did she get my phone down that tiny little slot?" Dylan huffed, his face twisted with incredulity.

"Pure evil," Laura answered.

"Your daughter!" Mike and Dylan said to each other.

Laura took this as her moment to exit, leaving the two grousing and making plans involving duct tape and rope to retrieve it.

What a waste of perfectly good duct tape and rope.

* * *

"Do you have the key lime pie today?" Laura asked the cute guy who seemed to have taken over the place. Madge wasn't always at Jeddy's these days, and if Mr. Hottie Hot Chef Dude was her replacement, then he was a fine upgrade on the eyes over the crotchety old institution.

"We do, and I have a new blackberry glaze to go with it, on the side if you don't like the drizzle," he added, grabbing a coffee pot and two mugs. "Your friend joining you? The brunette?"

A flush of something prickly and unfamiliar crawled over Laura's cheeks and chest. Oh, yeah. She remembered this. It was called attraction. Had he noticed her and Josie? Was he interested? How was she supposed to act? She was taken. Twice over!

"Um, you mean Josie?" she stammered.

166

"Is that her name? The one my grandma told me liked to defile the warlock waitress?" When he smiled there was a dimple on one side.

Ah. Not attraction. Notoriety. *Stupid stupid stupid*, she chided herself, mumbling, "Uh, yeah, she's coming, too."

"Two mugs, then," he said cheerfully, slamming them down with the coffee and a creamer pitcher, then moving with a muscled grace that made her eyes linger a little too long over his denim-covered ass. If Josie was going to be late, at least she had a fine view while she wasted a few minutes. Wow. She'd been out of the market just long enough to forget what it felt like to find someone other than Mike or Dylan attractive.

What did that mean?

Ruminating on it wasn't in the cards, for Josie careened into the booth, a blur of sinew, her single-digit-sized body making Laura feel big and bumbling. Not that Josie was responsible for that—it was simple comparison and all on Laura. This was her own insecurity she was slowly shaking.

One coconut shrimp at a time.

"Key lime pie?" Josie huffed, reading her mind. As if on cue, her friend poured a cup of coffee, fixed it just so, took a sip, made a frantic burned-tongue gesture, and sat with wide, expectant eyes, fanning her open mouth. She looked like an Affenpinscher with a caffeine habit.

The waiter dude happened to walk by at that moment and stopped on a dime. His sneakers actually squeaked. "Two pieces?" he asked, nodding toward the door. "We're about to have a huge crowd come in, so if you want to order now, you can get ahead of the crush."

167

"Two coconut shrimps, two pieces of the pie, and..." Laura looked at Josie, who shrugged.

"And?" the waiter asked.

"And that's enough," Laura added definitively, touching the rim of her mug. "The coffee's fine."

"Sounds good." He ran off, and Josie gave her a look of appraisal.

"That's it?"

Laura patted her stomach. "Not eating for two any longer." She actually wasn't nearly as ravenous now that Jillian had started solid foods, and her appetite was diminishing back to normal. "What about you?"

"Alex and I had lunch an hour ago."

"You don't have to eat with me."

"Give up coconut shrimp and key lime? You crazy?" They shared a good-natured laugh and settled into a very weird, awkward silence that stretched on. And on. And interminably on, until finally Laura broke.

"Why are we being quiet?"

"You're being quiet. I'm waiting."

"What are you waiting for?"

"For you to tell tell me why you *needed* to be rescued from Mike and Dylan."

"By the way, Dylan read my texts. Thanks for the fake meeting comment, you dork."

Josie snickered. "Sorry. Is the fact that he's reading your texts one of the reasons you needed a meeting? Too controlling? Men like that are total assholes. If you have to control your woman to that point, or send her hundreds of texts a day, you've got a screw loose."

Laura waved her hand dismissively and took another sip of coffee. Her shoulders began to relax. "No. He just happened to look over my shoulder at the wrong time."

"So you're here because..."

"Because I need help with my relationships."

"*Pffft*. Wrong person to ask!" Josie crowed, taking a long, nervous gulp from her mug. "Wrong, wrong, wrong."

"Says the woman who runs a dating service. So inspiring."

"You hired me!" Josie shot back. "No accounting for your taste."

"Speaking of which, how is business? I assume you made up the PR comment in those texts."

Josie went from joking to uncomfortable. Uh-oh. "I did, but there was an element of truth. Some online forum like Fark or someone's Tumblr made fun of us. We analyzed the inbound traffic to the website and followed it backwards. Just nasty stuff."

"Let me guess. A bunch of guys moaning about how the only good threesome involves two women and one man."

"Something like that."

"Whatever. That we can handle. It's when the gossip sites get hold of the whole 'billionaire freak' meme that we need to worry." Laura could talk a good game, and was significantly calmer about the occasional bubbles of scandal, but it still hurt. When the gossip sites ripped into the life they chose, it was still *her* life. Her men. Her child. The jokes she could chuckle at. The barbs, though, drew blood.

And always would.

Jillian wasn't an "abomination." Her threesome life with Dylan and Mike wasn't "unnatural." The folks who spewed intolerance came from such a wide cross section of people that she found herself studying it from a distance, because sociologically it was fascinating. Christian, Muslim, Jewish, atheistic, southern, New Englander, male, female—there were equal-opportunity haters out there, and all had an opinion.

Good Things Come in Threes soldiered on, though, gaining a steady clientele as Mike, Dylan, and Laura did everything they could to stay out of the limelight, going as far as hiring a PR specialist who had a sub-niche speciality: keeping clients *out* of the press. What irony.

So far, so good for the two months since they'd hired her.

And Darla was a treasure. An absolute treasure, and a bargain, from what Laura understood. They'd worked together occasionally, but their schedules never gelled well. Laura lived on Jillian time while Darla seemed to need her nights to play with her guys and their band. Josie said life was working well for her niece, and that the move had been good, which was fantastic. Laura knew how hard and radical giving up your known life for uncharted territory could be.

"I can't prevent people from finding out that you three are, in fact, freaks. Did you ever get that hip injury checked out?" Josie's eyes were filled with merry mischief.

Laura blushed. "I'm fine."

"Alex had to go into a lot of detail that involves physiology and anatomy terms I haven't heard since college when he was on the phone with Dylan that day. You guys really need to stop abusing that sex swing." The last words came out of Josie's mouth just as the hot waiter dude appeared with their shrimp and pie.

His jaw was on the floor and he stood, blinking furiously. Dark hair, gorgeous eyes, and the muscled upper body of someone who did hard work for a living. His shirt fit nice and tight against his pecs and his hair was cropped short. Forearms bulged under the strain of the serving tray, but he didn't seem to struggle with the weight.

And he stared.

"Hello?" Josie said, half standing to help. "You're keeping us from a mouthful of your luscious stuff."

"Excuse me?" He choked, nearly sending the tray onto Josie's lap. A quick movement from Laura held it in place, the pie balanced precariously on the edge.

"Caleb, what the hell?" Good old Madge appeared, eyes clear and blazing as she jumped in, delivered the food, and tucked the empty tray under her arm. "You planning to throw the food at people now in an effort to streamline efficiency?"

"No, it's just—"

"And you!" Madge snapped at Josie. "Are you talking about balls and threesomes and did I hear a sex swing comment?"

"Yes, ma'am." Josie's face was a careful mask of restraint. If Madge weren't her boyfriend's grandfather's girlfriend (say that five times fast...) then Laura knew Josie would rip her a new one. Instead, she demonstrated remarkable tact, and it made Laura realize how much they'd changed.

Both of them.

Stunned silence from Caleb, who—in Laura's humble opinion—could sit there and look shocked and pretty all day long. Stealing a chance to study his rugged cheekbones and noting the alarm in those perplexed eyes, she noticed the similarity between him and...Madge? Wasn't a grandson helping to run the place and develop new menus? Bingo. She put it together all by herself, all while eyeing a guy whom she had no right to admire.

171

But hey—a girl could look as long as she didn't touch, right?

"Good." Madge cracked a wide grin and patted Josie gently on the cheek. "I'm glad to see Alex is being well taken care of."

Josie's turn to choke. Literally. The bite of pie she'd started to munch on went down the wrong pipe and she whacked herself in the chest several times as both Caleb and Madge beat a hasty retreat.

"Heimlich?"

"How about bleach?"

"Bleach? For what?"

"My brain. I don't need sex tips from Madge. Not about Alex." She whooped her way back to a normal respiration pattern, then cringed as if she'd tasted something that had gone bad.

"Seems like she and his grandfather have a healthy sex life."

"Lalalalalalala, I can't hear you!"

"It bodes well for you, actually."

"What the hell does Madge's sex life have to do with me?"

"If his grandpa's going at it in his eighties, then when you and Alex are in your eighties, you have a sense of what to expect."

Josie froze, her eyes going huge, her breathing stopping. Leaping to her feet, Laura came to Josie's side of the booth and leaned into her face. "Josie!" she shouted with alarm. "Are you choking again? Can you breathe?"

"Why are you screaming in my face?" she gasped. "Have you lost your mind?"

"Your eyes...and you stopped breathing!"

"Because of what you said. Your fault! Not the pie!" As if to prove a point, Josie stabbed another piece and shoved it in her mouth, chewing pointedly this time and not gagging, thank God.

"What on earth did I say?" Tears threatened her nose and eyes, her face suddenly swollen and puffy, feeling too big for her bones. Knowing this feeling, she realized she was overly sensitive and on edge, in need of a friend and a pow-wow. What she hadn't expected was an edgy Josie. If the rule said only one of them could fall apart at any given time, then it was Laura's damn turn right now.

"You implied that Alex and I would still be together in fifty or sixty years!"

"Why would that make you freak out?"

"Because I only recently let him take up an enormous amount of my apartment! Nearly half!"

"Josie, a toothbrush in a drawer and some underwear is not 'nearly half.'"

"Says the woman who defines half a piece of key lime pie using the same metrics."

"*Touché*." At least they had their own pieces this time. "So you're still *that* commitment shy with Dr. Perfect? Why? He's...perfect." He really was, and Laura never thought she'd say that about any guy Josie dated. The handful of men over the years that Laura had been allowed to meet were suspiciously familiar at the time, and months later she'd catch a rerun of some reality show about cheaters and realize, oh—that's why.

Not Alex. Every time she thought about the two of them together, she smiled. Just like her and Mike and Dylan. The fit was so...perfect that there was no need to search any longer. Done. Signed, sealed, delivered.

And Josie knew it. Knew it deep in her dried-up little terrified peach pit that masqueraded as her heart. She just needed to give herself permission to let go and be with it, giving Alex a lifetime to get her to let go of the shield that was looser each day.

"We're not talking about my relationship," Josie said archly. "You're the one with problems."

Hearing it stated that bluntly didn't sit well with Laura. "Not problems. Complications."

Josie pointed her fork at Laura's head. "Don't you say it!"

"What? That it's always complicated?"

Josie groaned and threw a sugar packet at her.

"It is, though. It really is. The complication comes part and parcel with the love." Both took deep sighs and filled their mouths with blackberry drizzle and key lime perfection. Food was truly perfect with greater consistency than men. And it didn't hog the bed or leave beard shavings sprinkled all over the sink. Food didn't leave the toilet seat up or shove balled-up dirty socks between the couch cushions.

Food also couldn't fuck you silly and whisper dirty love sayings in your ear while it asked you—begged you—to share a fantasy you'd never told any other person in the world. And then give you that little naughty dream right then and there with strokes and licks and squeezes and pinches and moans that lingered in your mind for weeks.

But man, if food ever could do that, then men would be done in a second, replaced by kitchens with insemination stations.

So men better be on their toes.

"Alex is really pretty simple. As a body, I mean. But that brain of his gets in the way," Josie said in a tone that made Laura wonder if she was just a microchip implanted in a human body.

"What about his heart?"

"Even worse! He expects me to be all touchy-feely new-agey and all that shit." Eye roll.

"And you are too cool for that," Laura said in her best neutral voice.

"I thought we were past it. Hello? We watched your daughter overnight. I gave him a few inches for his toothbrush and he took a mile."

"He keeps one spare pair of underwear in your nightstand."

"Squatter."

"Now you're just being argumentative."

Josie gave her a blank look. "What does that even mean?"

"You're arguing for the sake of arguing."

"You've been my friend for nearly a decade and you're only now realizing that? Gatorade. It's what plants crave."

"What the hell does that mean?"

"Let's just rename you Princess Obvious. Of course I argue for the sake of arguing. It's in my DNA."

Laura's turn to fling a sugar packet at Josie's head. "You are the worst person to talk to when I'm having a man crisis."

"Men. Plural. You don't have a man crisis. You have men crises."

"Yeah." Laura sighed, pushing the last shrimp away. Her appetite really had diminished. "Plural."

Josie looked a bit sheepish, leaning forward and giving Laura that tilted-head kind of look that made Laura feel as if her exterior matched her interior when it came to the level of confusion she felt. Was she exuding it? Did her eyes shine with some kind of needy bat signal?

"You need to talk to someone," Josie declared.

"Like a psychologist?"

Josie frowned, considering that one. "No. More like a friend. A buddy who's been there. Done that. Has the sore body from two at once."

"Hey!"

"What? It's true."

"Like you'd know."

"Only that one time."

"Just...don't."

"Don't what?"

"Make fun of me." Burying her face in her hands, Laura almost cried. Almost. Raw and one big twinging nerve, she wanted to have the freedom to talk about her problems like a normal person. Just because she had unconventional relationships didn't mean she wasn't normal.

"I'm not making fun of you. Really." Josie's brow furrowed and she almost looked like she really cared.

"Yes, you are."

"But not in here," Josie said, pointing to her heart. "I'm just teasing. I'll stop."

"Thank you. And good attempt at actually looking sincere. Your fake sincerity has improved by leaps and bounds."

Josie stuck her tongue out at Laura in response. "You need to find another woman who's in your position." Josie poured a cup of coffee and shook the pot, listening for the telltale slosh. Nope. She set it on the edge of the table, and Laura knew Madge or Caleb would come by soon for a refill.

"No pun intended."

"No pun...? Oh. Ha."

"It's not like the city is swimming with women in my spot."

"If the dating service takes off, though, it will be..."

"I can't turn Good Things Come in Threes into my own personal pity party."

Josie seemed to mull that over as she fixed her coffee and took a sip. The light was fading outside and Laura wasn't hungry. Too much coffee earlier in the day made these extra cups just fuel a jitteriness she didn't welcome. She needed to get home soon and beat rush hour. Plus, who knew what life was like at home? Hopefully, Mike was satisfied with the extra attention she'd bestowed on him earlier, but that just meant Dylan would want more.

And then Jillian would need a nursing fest.

So many people. So many demands. So little time for Laura to just sit and think and breathe and figure out who Laura was. How did she ever hold down a full-time job before, and date guys, and have a life?

Oh. That's right.

She didn't. Have a life, that is. Or date many guys...

"What about Darla?" Josie whispered, making a skeptical face, as if weighing the quality of her own words and finding them wanting.

"Darla? *Darla* Darla?"

"You know another Darla currently in a threesome relationship like yours?"

That made Laura nearly spit out her mouthful of coffee. "Like mine? You can't compare some kids barely out of college who met on the side of the road with me and Dylan and Mike."

"Yes, I can. I was there, Laura. You typed some words on the internet and rubbed a genie's lamp. Poof! Insta-billionaires fawning all over you."

"It didn't exactly go like that."

"Yes, it did. It went exactly like that. So don't judge Darla's own threesome weirdness. You have more in common than you might imagine." Laura realized Josie was defending Darla, as if Laura had said something condescending. Had she? If so, she didn't mean it. It was just that comparing her relationship, where the three were committed and raising a child together, seemed so...wrong.

"I have nothing against Darla!" Laura protested, raising her palms. "Don't bite my head off. The comparison caught me by surprise."

"You two really should talk," Josie said. "Alone. Of all the people in the world right now who could empathize and help you, I think Darla's pretty much it."

"Really?"

Josie nodded. "And I'll bet she could use someone to bounce ideas off, too."

"I just...we're in such different places." Laura nearly gagged on her next words. "Darla, Trevor, and Joe are more like I imagine Jill, Mike, and Dylan were. You know. Early twenties, figuring it all out one day at a time. I met Mike and Dylan a decade later, after they'd figured out all the basic rules and..." What would life be like if the three of them had met ten years ago? What if she'd been their third instead of Jill? Would it have been difficult to be with them as they figured out their relationship with each other, and then their joint connection to a woman? Jill did her a favor, in some ways.

For the first time in her relationship with the guys, Laura felt a sense of kinship—and not competition—with the late Jill. She'd paved the way for the most important experience of Laura's life. To be fair, Laura's daughter was named after Mike and Dylan's dead partner, so it was not as if Laura didn't honor her. And yet she never felt a closeness to her memory.

178

All those questions about sexuality that Laura faced were just Laura's issues. The actual threesome relationship was completely different from Laura's own individual sexuality, just as Mike and Dylan were separate individuals with their own internal definitions of how to function in society and within the private sphere of home (and bed).

Big and small compromises and joys came out every day in their life together. How new, how different it must be for Darla, Trevor, and Joe.

Thank you, Jill, she thought as Josie stared at her.

"You are a million miles away," Josie declared, shoving her plate away and taking a long sip of her coffee.

"Thinking about Jill." Laura took a long drink of her coffee. Tepid now. She pushed it back, looking over the dirty dishes. Her appetite stayed away.

Josie's face softened. "She pulling up yet? Started driving? Producing grandchildren? They grow up so fast, so treasure every moment!"

Laura laughed. "Not Jillian. Jill. Mike and Dylan's old..." Old what? Lover? Girlfriend? Not wife. A woman couldn't marry two men. Whatever label Jill had was the same one Laura had.

Which was...nothing. No word could contain the expansive sense of what she was to them. "Girlfriend" and "baby mama" were the closest, and they made her want to throw up.

"Jill's closer to Darla in some ways," Josie said, nodding slowly. "You're right." The comment caught Laura completely by surprise. It was as if Josie had read her mind.

"And they're making it all up as they go along," Laura pointed out. "So it's not like me and Dylan and Mike."

"I don't think you have much choice, Laura."

"Huh?"

"If you want to talk to someone about the specifics of life with two men, Darla is it." Josie pulled out her phone and started tapping, while Madge zipped by and slid the check case onto the booth table like she was an Olympic curler. It landed smack between the two of them, curving around the coffee pot.

"And the U.S.A wins the gold!" Josie muttered without looking up.

Laura paid as usual (because, seriously, why not?), and she got up to check her buzzing phone.

Josie had texted, *Call Darla*, and her number.

"I know Darla's number," Laura muttered.

"Then call her! Invite her to lunch here. Do the whole girl-chat thing where you talk about how to handle two hoses and one fire hydrant."

"Josie!"

Her friend waved her hands dismissively. "Or whatever you talk about." She paused and frowned. "Do the guys cross swords? I know they're not gay, but doesn't that sometimes—"

"JOSIE!"

"Just call her." A quick hug from her friend did not melt her one bit, her body rigid with overwhelm. "Dial the number now. I want to watch you."

"Voyeur."

A strange look passed over Josie's features. Laura couldn't name it.

"Call!"

Against her better judgment, and yet needing to do something, Laura dialed the number slowly, then hesitated before pressing "Send."

This would be awkward at best.

A disaster at worst.

"Hello?" said Darla.
Laura opened her mouth to begin.

COMPLETE BLISS

Darla

The phone rang. Darla let it go for two rings as she cleared her throat, let the flush of surprise die down a bit, and picked up the receiver. "Good Things Come in Threes," she said, smiling, hoping to inject that perfect balance between friendliness and discretion into her not-quite-smooth voice. "How may I help you?"

A nervous, twitchy silence almost always greeted her. Of course it would. Who picks up the phone, calls a number they read on the internet, and says, "I'm looking for a threesome and I heard you do that for people"?

Okay, so *one* person already had, and now Darla had to engage her. But that was a rarity. Generally the potential clients were nervous as all get out and stumbled over their words, and about half the time the call dropped off midway, whatever ovarian fortitude the caller had assembled splintering into thousands of tiny pieces.

And yes, they were *always* women. The men seemed more comfortable, by far, with reaching out and asking for what they wanted.

Wasn't that how it all too often worked?

But Darla, Josie, and Laura had agreed that this service needed to be different.

And if Darla could do anything right, it was *different*. Different was her middle name. (Not really. *Josephine* was, but you get the drift.)

"Um, I, uh...is this the dating service?" A young woman with a high, scared voice was on the line. "The one I heard about on Mike Mayhearn's podcast?"

God bless Mike Mayhearn, whoever he was. This was the third call in so many days that referred to him by name. Darla jotted the name on her *To Do* list. The ways word had spread online had been so intriguing. Podcasts seemed to be the crazy new thing that brought people to Good Things Come in Threes.

"Yes, ma'am," Darla said as brightly as possible.

The woman laughed. "I'm not a ma'am! I'm only twenty-five years old."

"Well, I'm twenty-three, so sorry about that." Darla chuckled, trying to make a connection. "It's just a formality."

"I don't think we need formalities for, um, something like this," the caller answered.

Darla's smile widened and she gripped her pen. So far, so good. "I assume you're calling to get more information about our dating service?" she replied, keeping her voice neutral.

"Yes."

"What do you know about us?" Asking that question was dicey. Over the past few weeks a slew of hate calls had come in, which prompted Darla to record them all. Turned out to be from one guy who had been rejected as a client by Josie after he said he wanted sex only, and not a long-term emotional relationship. A hate campaign followed on social media and via phone. A public relations firm had been brought in. Damage control hadn't been easy.

Hell, it was *ongoing*. No one wanted to see this place tank before it ever got off the ground, least of all Darla. She knew how fucking awesome being with two men could be. Parts of her soul had been out there, and

186

instead of killing one with her car on that turnpike road one night in Ohio, she'd picked it up by the side of the road, naked and high as a kite. Trevor's sudden appearance in her life had preceded Joe's, but having them both was like learning she'd been missing something she didn't ache for until she had it.

Other women must feel the same way. Men, too. Helping them made sense to her.

Plus, this was the best damn paycheck she'd ever had in her life. Long live threesome dating services, even if Good Things Come in Threes was the only one...

"I've heard you were founded by that woman who is with the firefighter billionaire. And the other one. The ones in the news."

Darla's eyebrows shot up. Very few people knew anything about Laura, Mike, and Dylan's ties to the agency. She needed to tread super-carefully now, because Josie was ultra-protective of her best friend, and by extension, so was Darla. You didn't fuck with her peeps. Loyalty was her middle name.

Okay, so *Josephine* was. Apparently, she had a lot of middle names.

"Can I ask how you learned that?"

"Is there a problem?" The caller's voice shook.

Oh, shit. This was the part where people drifted off. Or hung up.

"No, it's just that I'm in a permanent threesome and I'm surprised to hear what you said." Deflect. If Darla could get her off topic, she could keep her on the line.

"You *are*?" the woman squeaked. "Are you a client?"

"Not quite," Darla replied. "But I was hired because of my background."

"What's it like?" the caller asked, breathless. This time her voice shook from excitement.

Hold on there, sister. Before I tell you about getting licked and dicked at the same time, I'd like to know your name.

"Before I tell you all about my love life, we might want to be on a first-name basis," Darla said cheerfully. See? She was learning tact. "I'm Darla. What's your name, hon?"

"Callie," the woman said quietly.

"Callie, it's nice to meet you." Tact. Darla was practically Miss Menage Manners.

"I didn't mean to offend you!" Callie said, clearly horrified. *Way to scare off the potential clients with her smart mouth*, Darla thought. Such job security. At this rate Darla'd be back home living with her mama and clicking on pictures of donkeys at a hotel website trying to win a free $5 Subway card.

And that would be on date night.

"No offense taken. I understand your curiosity. It's not like you can just go on the internet and find articles about women who are in loving relationships with two men," Darla replied in the most soothing voice she could muster. No one taught you these kinds of customer service skills in…um…*anywhere*.

A long sigh poured out of the phone. "Don't I wish! It's all about swingers and one-time hookups and…you know." The conspirator's tone Callie used set Darla's teeth a bit on edge. Actually, Darla *didn't* know. It was not as if she went out searching for a permanent threesome. It fell into her lap. And that was the major difference between her and their female clients: Darla never sought out what she had.

It occurred to her, suddenly, that the same was true for her boss, Laura. Hmmm.

Her cell phone buzzed. A text. Ignoring it, Darla kept Callie on the line. While Laura and Josie had told her the business could lose money in the first year—it wasn't like Dylan and Mike didn't have enough cash to buy her hometown ten times over—it was a matter of principle for Darla. She wanted to succeed. Clients meant success.

And Callie wanted what Good Things Come in Threes sought to succeed in: nonjudgmental love that happened to use a relationship math that society didn't necessarily understand. Like being metric in an imperial world. Or being Darla at a Pilates instructor convention.

You didn't really fit in.

But that didn't mean you couldn't exist. And thrive.

"I understand," was the best Darla could say and remain honest. In some tangential way she did understand. If she had been searching for what Darla had with Trevor and Joe, she'd have thought it impossible to find. And would never even try. Because why torture yourself with dreams of something that was so inconceivable that all you did was abuse your heart with so much wishing?

A smile played on Darla's lips as she explained how the company worked to Callie.

Making dreams work was her job.

It sure beat working at the gas station back home in Ohio.

After a few minutes of explaining how the registration process worked to Callie, Darla got off the phone and sighed, taking a handful of moments to process what she had just done.

Talk to a woman about her desire to find two men as life partners for a permanent threesome? *Check.*

Gently persuade the woman to sign up for a trial of their service? *Check.*

Explain that the company was so new they didn't have many matches and it could take months (ahem…a year at the current trajectory) to begin to make matches? *Um…*

Yep. Unfortunately. And so Darla felt like a big old fraud.

Then again, lately she felt that way all the time.

The phone rang again. Pushing her own emotions aside, she geared up for another call. Josie and Laura never saddled her with quotas, but she knew they weren't twiddling their thumbs running this bizarre business either. She had to earn her keep, and it was a good enough keep that it helped pay for a lot of her mama's issues back home.

Picking up the phone, she realized caller ID labeled this call from:

"Laura! How are you?" An instant sheen of sweat broke out all over Darla's body like liquid heat, except this wasn't that nice, blazing feeling you get when you catch an unexpected picture of Joe Manganiello appearing on Facebook.

This was pure nerves. When the owner of your company calls out of the blue, you freak out, right? Because they only call like this for one reason.

Because you did something wrong.

"Hi, Darla. How's business?" Laura had a breathy voice that was pleasant to listen to but had an undercurrent of iron to it. Darla admired the flat accent, which was like a linear line without a single deviation. Darla's own voice sounded like Silly String coming out of a can.

"I signed up a new client!" Darla crowed, thrilled that fate threw Callie her way today. That was the first client in four days, and of all the days and moments to report back a success, well...

"You did! Male or female?" They needed more men. Lots more men. Well, double more men than women, at least. And a few extras, because sometimes women asked for three men, which made Darla feel exhausted. Two were enough for her.

"A woman. Very nice. Nervous," Darla said with a giggle.

"Aren't they all?"

She could feel Laura's kind, calm smile through the phone. But there was something more in her voice. A hesitation. The kind of sound you definitely don't want to hear in your boss's voice.

The sound of trouble. Darla's mind raced through the past three weeks, since her last sit-down with Laura. She hadn't done anything wrong, had she? A mental inventory of all of Darla's responsibility left her with nothing. Nada. Zippo. Running the register at the convenience store and gas station back home had been a job that she'd mastered and could do in her sleep, but being the operations assistant with Good Things Come in Threes required skills. Attention to detail.

A major bullshit detector.

And, ideally, someone in a permanent threesome.

Which meant Darla was perfect for the job. *Calm down*, she told herself. *You're not getting fired. You're not.*

"Darla, I'm wondering if we could get together for lunch some time."

Darla's heart leapt into her throat and began drowning in the puddle of tears that filled her larynx.

"Talk?" she choked out. Talk? Laura wanted to talk? Talking meant concerned looks and deep discussions about failed metrics and unfilled goals and a bunch of corporate-speak that was so full of fail it made Darla cringe. Joe talked that way when he discussed business law, and it always made her laugh.

Then again, most of what came out of her mouth made Joe laugh, too, so they were even.

"Yes. Talk." Laura sounded so restrained. Embarrassed, even. This was getting weirder and weirder, and Darla knew weird. Lived weird.

Invented weird.

"Josie suggested—"

Ah. The source of the weirdness.

"—that I reach out and invite you to lunch because you and I have so much in common."

In common? Laura was a well-educated former financial analyst for a massive corporation that wouldn't employ Darla to change the urinal cakes in their executive bathrooms. Laura was blond and curvy and sweet and feminine. Darla was a wild, untamed mare with a mane about as tangled and unkempt as a '70s porn star bush.

In common?

The only thing they had in common was—

"Ohhhhhhhh." The sound came out of her mouth before she could think and use impulse control (*hah! What was that?*) to stop it.

Laura let out a long sigh, like a balloon being slowly emptied of air. "Yeah. *That.*"

Darla blinked about a thousand times, then said, "Huh. Josie's right. I don't know nobody else who has two boyfriends." Wait—that sounded so stupid, because Mike and Dylan weren't just Laura's boyfriends!

"Er, two *baby daddies*, I mean. Not that I don't know plenty of people back home with two baby daddies. Hell, one of my friends from high school is my age and has four of 'em, each baby with a different man, and..." Her mouth just detached itself from her head, running off like it was at the start line of the Boston Marathon, *blah blah blah blah blah*, spewing toxic waste along the way.

"Darla! Darla!" Laura's insistent voice cut through the floating sense of horror Darla had about her mouth.

"Yes?" She shut herself up by slamming a fist in between her teeth.

"You okay?"

"It's just—"

Darla paused, trying to figure out how to behave here. As usual, she had no idea, so she blundered through it. Truth was an absolute defense against stupidity, right? Wasn't that part of law school Joe and Trevor talked about?

"Are you going to fire me? Because you never call and ask to—"

"No! No!" Laura exclaimed, laughing. "God, no. You're fabulous. Josie and I don't know what we'd do without you!"

"Then does that mean I get a raise?" Darla blurted out. *Jesus, woman*, she chided herself. *You do not know when to stop.*

Laura laughed again, only this time she sounded more secure. "We'll talk about that a different time. This time, though, I'd like a chance to talk about—"

"Threesomes. And bein' in one. And how fucked up it can be." Darla felt more comfortable now. *Not getting fired. Not getting fired.*

"Um, I might put it a bit more diplomatically..."

"Laura." Darla snorted. "You've met me. 'Diplomatically' isn't in my vocabulary."

193

"Is *Jeddy's* in your vocabulary? Josie says I should take you there for lunch."

Darla paused, mouth drooling without provocation. "Are you serious? Lunch with the boss at Jeddy's to talk about being in a threesome relationship with two men? When did I bang my head and go into this dream about work?"

"Not a dream," Laura said, laughing gently. Darla could feel the relief in her—in both of them. Her brow tightened; this felt like the tip of some iceberg Darla didn't know was underneath deep ocean waters. "How about next week? Thursday? I have limited babysitting for Jillian, but that day is open. We can do it on one of your work days. It's on the clock."

On the clock? Jeddy's? Talkin' about threesome life?

Best. Job. Ever.

"Sure. Lunchtime?" Darla asked, assuming.

"How about two o'clock? We can come after the rush crowd and get a quieter place."

Laura's words made her pause. This was intriguing. People didn't invite her out under such mysterious circumstances. Hmmm...

Less full of people to hear, Darla thought, but wisely shoved that fist back in her mouth.

"Two o'clock works for me," she said evenly.

"Yes. Perfect. I'm putting it in my calendar. Want me to come get you at work, or meet at Jeddy's?"

"Whatever works for you, Laura."

"Let's just meet there, then."

"Okay." Darla's body relaxed in increments. She wasn't being fired. She wasn't having her hours reduced. Everything was right in the world. Laura just wanted to get to know her better.

"And Darla?"

"Yep?"

"Thank you."

Click.

Darla stared at the phone.

Now she had two phone conversations to nominate for weirdest fucking call at work, *ever*.

LAURA

Dylan raced from the Jeep into the little sex cabin Mike had built for the three of them last year. "I think we still have a few beers in the fridge!" he exclaimed from the deck, stripping down to just jeans in seconds.

And then nothing at all. Out here in the woods, in the remote mountain area of the ski resort Mike owned, there was no one but the deer and the occasional bear to see all of Dylan's delicious parts.

And oh, how delicious they were. While parenthood had made her a bit squishier in all her curvy parts, Dylan and Mike had stayed the same. Even better in some ways, carved and curved in hard, steely ways that complemented her abundant figure.

Over the past six months she'd worked so hard to let go of her self-conscious inhibitions, and was largely there. For the most part.

Almost.

The sex cabin Mike had built really helped. And so did adding a part-time nanny two months ago. Cyndi was a doll. A dream. Mary Poppins without the uptight attitude. She didn't have to be practically perfect, because she was loving and warm and safe and beyond good enough. The guys wouldn't settle for anything less than the loving grandmother Cyndi was for Jillian, and as their little baby turned into a walking, jabbering toddler, they'd all done better with a little space.

Twenty hours a week, Laura could just be. *Just be* all by herself, while Dylan handled his foundation's charity work, or while Mike managed the ski resort. *Just be* while she worked with Josie on the threesome dating service she'd created.

Just be with her e-reader and her imagination.

And now—just be with Dylan and Mike in the sex cabin.

The lost libido that seemed hopeless to try to find six months ago had come roaring back with a deafening rush of need when Jillian had turned one year old last month. Certain she was meant to enjoy affection and sex but not desperately want it with that gnawing, alarming need that makes the shared release of sexual touch and connection, Laura had found herself blossoming in new ways.

And "blossom" sounded so demure. Prim, even.

She was turning into a fucking animal—and the operative word was "fucking." This went beyond the mild exhaustion Dylan and Mike had exhibited as her sexual desire reawakened. This new feeling was like being a nineteen-year-old boy. She hummed with urges and cravings and—oh, my...

Dylan was naked, on the cabin's deck, chugging a nice cold one down like something out of a really fancy clothing-optional resort commercial.

Not that she'd ever seen one of those commercials, but if they ever made them, they needed to hire Dylan.

Just like this.

"Why are you naked?" Mike shouted as he grabbed a cooler of food to put in the cabin's fridge. Cyndi was back at the house for five hours today, and they intended to take advantage of every single second. Mike's idea of "taking advantage" was decidedly different from hers and Dylan's. After the first round of sex Mike would make tenderloin steaks and grilled vegetables on the giant smoker he treated like a second child, while Dylan and Laura would make fun of him and, maybe, have a little round of lovemaking to themselves.

That was what her mind filled in. But as Mike trundled through the doorway carrying a fifty-pound cooler on his shoulder like it was a pillow, she wondered how he'd look grilling naked.

I need to get a life, she thought.

I have the best fucking life, she corrected herself. *Don't need another one.*

"What are you waiting for? Didn't you get the memo? It's naked country life day," Dylan joked. The sun covered his slightly-less-tan body in a way that was so appealing. Her own skin was so white these days you could use it as a reflector to guide search parties.

Mike was the only one who managed to stay tan year round, and Laura was beginning to suspect he'd given the devil his pinkie toe in exchange for looking *that* good, even in the dim month of February when the sun didn't come near New England.

"You want me naked?" she teased.

Both men shouted, "Yes!" It was like having boyfriends in stereo.

Two baby daddies, she thought, Darla's words echoing through her mind. The phone call earlier had been odd. Halting. A bit much, but a relief to have it done. Josie might be right. Maybe talking to another woman who had two men in her life—permanently— was a good idea.

Right now, though, she didn't want to think about the future. Or worry about implications. Her present mind was right here, right now, and she wanted to lick and touch and stroke some flesh. To get back what she gave. And to have an orgasm...or twenty...so powerful she would scare small woodland creatures.

She might very well accomplish that feat right now by stripping naked, but by God, as she removed her underwear and hung them on a deck railing, she was going to obey Dylan's request.

"Two out of three of us are—oh!" Dylan said as he corrected himself, Mike strolling out of the cabin completely buck naked, holding two glasses of wine by the stems. "I guess all three of us are in uniform."

"Uniform?" Laura asked, laughing as she peeled off her socks. "The sex cabin has a uniform?"

The cold air stung at her ankles, the not-quite-summer sky a pale, hazy blue through the treetops. If they stayed outside for much longer she'd begin to shiver, but the warm rays of the sun homed in on her shoulder, her forehead, her belly, her calves, and she enjoyed the good with the cold.

The cold had no effect on Dylan and Mike, who had very distinct parts of them standing at attention. If they had the ability to point with them, she'd be the target.

"Sex cabin?" Dylan sputtered, laughter making his ab muscles roll in mesmerizing patterns. "You call this a *sex cabin*?"

"Isn't that what it is?" she asked with faux innocence, biting her lip suggestively.

"You coming inside? Because the sex cabin is most certainly ready to be used as its name suggests," Mike said with a suggestive leer. His eyes ate her up, and she let him, feeling the genuine love and lust in him.

"Inside, outside, on the deck, bent over the kitchen counter, on the couch," Dylan mused, finishing his beer. "She's coming, all right."

Talk like this used to make her blush.

Now she upped the ante.

"That a wager? How many times can you make Laura come in five hours?"

Mike choked a bit on his red wine. "You want to place bets on *sex*?"

Dylan's shoulders straightened, arms curling out a bit, forearms curved like they were carved by a woodworker with a lathe and fine artisanal tools. "Why not? Sounds friendly and fun."

"What about you two? How many times do I have to make *you* come?" she teased.

Mike looked skyward, his face twisted into a very thoughtful expression. "I think my refractory period is..."

"Math?" Dylan gawked. "You're doing sex math?" He marched into the cabin and returned with another beer, his ass so fine Laura felt hypnotized by it.

"What's wrong with sex math?" Laura asked. Mike acted like they weren't even there, now touching the tips of his fingers and shaking his head, muttering to himself.

"It's...math! Who brings math into the bedroom?"

"Math can be sexy," she protested. "One breast," she said, holding hers toward him. "Two breasts," she added, cupping both and pushing them together to make cleavage worthy of the best Regency dame.

Dylan stared at her nipples. "Okay. You convinced me."

"Five!" Mike uttered.

"Five orgasms? You want me to give you *how many* in five hours?" Laura gasped.

"At your age?" Dylan added, laughing his (fine) ass off.

"What do you mean *my* age? We're the same age!" Mike protested.

Dylan paused. His turn to do math. Laura opened her mouth to make a comment about it when Dylan said, "You're older than me by a few months. And *I* can't come five times in five hours."

Mike and Laura asked in unison: "How would you know that?"

He turned bright red and muttered, "Just trust me."

"YouPorn," Mike and Laura said, in unison again.

"Quit ganging up on me!" Dylan grabbed Laura's phone, which she'd set on the deck railing, and held up the display. "We've wasted seventeen minutes talking about refractory periods and making bets. When are we going to have *sex*?"

"After we enjoy a nice glass of wine," Laura said. She was enjoying the view, too. And not just the trees swaying in the wind. Her nice view was decidedly of the human male animal variety.

"The clock is ticking, there's a bet I might lose if we don't get busy, and you want to drink *wine*?" Dylan said in a tone of outrage. Indignation, even.

"You want me to drop everything—"

"No. Just to your knees," he said in a charged voice with such a commanding tone that she sashayed over to him, pulled a cushion from one of the redwood chaise lounges on the deck, and threw it on the ground in front of him. Handing her wine glass to him, she put her hands on his shoulders and bent down to lick one tight nipple, his body tensing with her touch. His erection bobbed up with a tight, craning motion that made her feel like it was tracing a line on her leg.

"Your wish is my command," she whispered as she bent down before him. She could feel his surprise as she grasped him at the base and stroked lightly upward with a feather touch. She reached up and squeezed his shoulders, her fingertips trailing down his large, muscled chest that was sprinkled with a touch of dark hair in all the right places.

Her palms cupped the long line of ribs that were so cut, muscles built out in layers from his back, the sheer animal power inherent in those muscles making her wet. Looking at Dylan from a sexual place was fun and purely sensual, but it wasn't just the eye candy that she appreciated. The protectiveness, the power, the promise of being cared for and rescued—of being *safe*—made his body a symbol for so many emotional states.

Her fingers reached down past his waist, unencumbered by clothing. His eyes were on her, burning a hole in her head, and if she tipped her chin up to greet them she knew she'd find his dark eyes burning for her.

She didn't need to look up, though. What she needed was to listen to his request and fulfill it. Having so much time together—all three of them—was a new luxury. *Some day this would be old hat*, she thought, as her lips grazed his belly button, making Dylan inhale sharply and clench his abs, which rolled like steel balls under silk.

Knowing she provoked that in him—her, and her alone—made Laura grateful for this time, this cabin, for the fact that all three of them were willing to carve out space for their relationship.

They needed this.

Her mouth slid up from his sac with a warm, wet kiss on his shaft that made him grasp the deck railing and tighten, legs bending slightly at the knees as, she knew, he braced himself for the pleasure she was about to give.

"Five hours," she murmured. "Plenty of time to recover." Laura knew *he* knew exactly what she meant, because the groan that vibrated through him, reaching her mouth as she engulfed him in full, was the sound of a man who could unleash and relax, unfold and de-stress. Most of their sex life involved quickies and halfway blow jobs, everyone eager to preserve the climax for intercourse, which meant this simple act of giving from Laura was simply that. A gift.

And now, in the middle of the thickly filled woods, the sound of birds and leaves shaking in the breeze filling her ears, she could give him complete release. Complete bliss.

Out of the corner of her eye, Laura saw Mike watching with a half-smile on his face, wordless and clothing-less, gorgeous and stately. He sipped from his wine and watched patiently, knowing his turn would come, just as Laura knew hers would, too. Being in a long-term relationship like this—the longest ever for her—meant compromising. Calibrating. Knowing that even if things were out of balance sometimes, in the long run everything would even out.

She took her time, tongue enjoying the exploration of skin she normally skimmed over, his shaft hot and silky at the same time, rigid as a steel rod yet delightfully flexible. Inside her, she knew, it could pump life into her, love infusing her body, release coursing through her like the rush of whitewater rapids provoked by a melting spring thaw. Her own blood began to pulse through her, ripe need gathering at her clit, the soft folds of her labia swelling with heat and want, getting ready for Dylan.

And Mike.

Cupping his balls, Laura found that sweet spot where her finger could apply pressure and—

"Oh, God, that feels incredible," he rasped.

Victory.

Lubing the shaft with her mouth's slickness, she pumped slowly, tonguing the cap, the tight tip of her tongue slicking the underside of his cock right where the shaft ended and the ridge began. She'd discovered this technique a few weeks ago and learned to use it when he or Mike were *almost* ready to come, the rapid flick of tongue combining with her encasing hand and finger pressure an instant path to—

Dylan's body tightened with such primal force she nearly fell backwards, the coiled strength in his thighs, back, and shoulders like a nuclear reactor of sexual thrust. His hips began to move in bursts toward her, and within seconds he was fucking her mouth, all inhibitions gone.

He'd become a man seeking ultimate ecstasy, and she was along for the ride, mouth and fingers keeping up the rhythm, his hot seed spurting into her mouth as she eased up on the tongue pressure, slowing her wrist movements on his shaft, bringing him down as gently as possible from his climax.

Dylan rested against the deck railing and buried his fingers in her hair as she finally tipped her face up, then swallowed.

He laughed. Mike began a polite clap. "That was quite a performance," Dylan said as he scooped her up, pressing her into a full-body, vertical hug that—oddly enough—felt more foreign than giving him a blow job outside in the woods. The feel of so much skin against so much skin, outside in the fresh air, and in the daylight—it was a series of incongruities that added up to a shift in her consciousness.

She felt more alive than ever. The taste of Dylan still filled her tongue. She loved it. Loved him. Loved *this*.

Eyes on Mike even as she hugged Dylan, who slumped against her and whispered a string of dirty thank-yous, she mouthed, *Your turn next.*

Mike winked. *I know. I can wait*, he mouthed back.

"I can hear you two," Dylan announced. "Quit talking behind my back."

"How can you hear us? We're mouthing the words!" Laura exclaimed.

"I just can. Call it my superpower."

Laura gave him a jaunty grin as she pulled back and drank in his beautiful face. "That is *not* your super power."

"Oh yeah? Then what is?"

She reached for Mike's hand, then Dylan's, pulling them into the cabin. "You're about to show it to me," she said.

Mike swept her up into his arms and carried her across the sliding door threshold like a newlywed, making her giggle and squeal.

"Superpowers abound," he said, setting her gently on the bed.

"Not there," Dylan said from the kitchen, where he was drinking a glass of water now. *Fortifying himself*, Laura thought with a grin.

"Where?" Mike asked.

"There," Laura and Dylan said in unison.

Both were pointing at the Sybian.

"Great minds think alike," Mike said drolly.

"But first, you!" Laura insisted, at Mike's side with three steps, hands wrapping around his waist. He eyed the Sybian, then Laura, then shared a look with Dylan she couldn't quite pinpoint, but which generally meant some mischief was about to unfold.

Good mischief. Sensual mischief.

Orgasmic mischief.

"How about we both get our first orgasm out of the way?" Mike suggested.

"'Out of the way'? You say that like it's a root canal," Laura teased.

"How about we try being direct," Dylan interrupted. "Laura sits on the Sybian while giving Mike head."

Stunned silence was Laura's only answer. Mind-blowingly stunned silence. "You want me to do that?"

Her answer was Dylan's hungry hands on her, sliding around from behind, cupping her breasts and tweaking her nipples to full attention with one little brushstroke. "We do."

Mike's only response was a raised eyebrow, a gesture that echoed inside her and made her bloom with heat.

The tidy little ottoman in the middle of the living room was so unassuming that the average person would never—*ever*—guess the kink hidden within. And that was precisely the point.

Hide the fun in plain sight.

Hide the source of judgment from those who did not—or willfully *chose* not to—understand.

Mike pulled the lid off and exposed the wonder underneath, making Laura's breath slow down just as her heart sped up. Time always changed here in the cabin, unlike anywhere else—even their bedroom at home. Sex was different here. Completely planned and yet utterly spontaneous. Dylan's hands continued their slow tease from behind, his cock rubbing up against the cleft of her ass, the hair on his chest tickling her back. Mike embraced her from the front, and the heat of his skin, all six-plus feet of him, made her feel complete.

She had them both.

Well—more technically, *they* had *her*.

Hands began their well-worn path down the curves of her body, those dry and supple and those wet and wanting.

The Sybian was a simple device, with a dildo attached to a rocking seat. She was more than wet enough as she eased her way down, muscles clamping tight at the slick entrance of something much smaller than either of her men, and yet tantalizing as she felt Mike's hot flesh in her hand, Dylan's own hands on her back and breasts now, connecting and adding to the loop the three shared. Like electricity, something flowed between them when they were in touch together, though Mike and Dylan drew a strong boundary at touching one another. Laura had wondered about it but never asked. Sometimes privacy within relationships had a place, and this was one of those times.

No complaints came from anyone, though, for what they *did* have—so she stopped thinking about what wasn't there.

A shudder of shock and heat ran through her as she lowered herself and clasped her thighs and knees along the device, Dylan straddling her from behind, on his knees and encircling her. His hand traveled down to find her hot, throbbing nub.

Oh, this would be over fast.

Mike's cock was thick and ready, and as her mouth enveloped it his thighs tensed. Primed to know his signals as well as she knew Dylan's or even her own body's triggers, she figured she had a minute, Maybe less.

Better make it good.

Dylan gently rocked her forward, the Sybian slipping and moving with such grace that she felt a moment of feral self-consciousness, as if the device were too prim and proper for what her ragingly wild arousal was about to make her flesh release. An orgasm swept over her and only sheer force of will kept it back, her brain firing wildly to make sure she remembered Mike's pleasure, the fullness of him in her warm, wet mouth now too much. The combination of so many sensations on her body and the need to meet his sexual release made her circuits overheat.

Desperate to give him pleasure, she slid her fisted hand along the fine, soft skin of his shaft, Dylan's fingers on her, her tongue traveling well-worn paths until Mike uttered her name and released into her just as her own tidal wave of climax made her groan deep in her throat, the sound making Mike jolt with more ecstasy.

And just like that, they had knocked out Climax #1 for all three of them.

Strangely energized, Laura swallowed and smiled up at Mike. He looked down from quite a distance, given his height, and smiled broadly.

"Four hours and six minutes to go. You up for more?"

She most certainly was.

Both of them were on her as if she'd sent them some telekinetic signal, as if she'd summoned their bodies by pure desire to come to her, the length of so much flesh pressing into her curves with such impulsive need that they shocked her.

"You're ready...*already*?" she asked Mike as Dylan stole her words away with a breathtaking kiss, tongue sweeping across her mouth like wind and fire. She couldn't breathe, couldn't speak, and Mike's answer was two hands that took her breasts like he was staking a claim on them.

Ah. Well. So.

She guessed he was.

A burst of wet heat turned her legs to jelly, and the thrumming sense of pounding as her blood rushed to and fro, building to something so much greater, took her rational thought and shattered it to shards. Reaching for Dylan, she found his thick, strong shaft, and he groaned against her teeth as she stroked him, a simple reuniting that made the fire inside them all flame higher and higher.

Sex wasn't just sex anymore. Not after two years together. It wasn't just intimacy or connection or some necessary act that they indulged in for pleasure. It was, instead, a constant, consistent re-commitment to be each other's heat, to make each other tremble in awe, to use fingertips and tongues and smiles and groans in order to be the most important soul for each other.

Acceptance is the greater part of intimacy.

How much more accepting could three people be when exploring the bounty of flesh, tendon, bone, muscle—and the pure frenzy of driving someone to a release that catapulted them out of their mind?

Trusting both, she sighed deeply, Mike's touch between her legs making her gasps turn to his name, cried out in sighs and moans, a language of arousal and more.

Trust.

Mike was in her first, hard as rock, his lips on her face and neck like a hungry man who was touching a woman for the first time in decades. His hands were rough against her back, her ass, the globes of her breasts, the sensation just on the edge of her comfort zone but so raw and real she couldn't stop wanting more.

Heightened senses and the sound of their breath in the room, background noise coming from the woods in the form of the rush of leaves pushed by wind, the calls of birds she could not name, and it all turned into a tunnel-vision pinpoint of nothing as Dylan entered her with aching slowness, patient gentleness, from behind, stretching her to the point of oblivion, a kind of disintegration of the self that came only after so, so much pleasure.

When the moment of climax came for all three, the combined explosion sent them all whirling into space, so separate from the very slick skin that twisted and flexed, adjusted and morphed, their spirits in another realm that could only be accessed by the very primal acts of flesh and want that their bodies committed.

It felt like a sacrament and a sin.

Like blasphemy and atonement.

Most of all, though, it felt so fucking *good*.

* * *

If she and the guys smoked, Laura could imagine this scene quite differently. Sandwiched beautifully between both men, their bodies twisted together in a pile of limbs and torsos that resembled a human pile of stretched taffy (*and was just about as sticky...*), she reclined in pure harmony with long, lean, blond Mike and compact, musclebound, swarthy Dylan.

All were completely sated. Sexually, that is.

"Who's getting up for the ice cream?" she teased. Sort of. It had been a longstanding joke among the three of them to share a pint of something gooey and sweet right after sex, but they hadn't done that in

211

months. Too many quickies, too many hot, frantic sex sessions done under the watchful timeline of a baby who might wake up at the slightest noise.

"How about steaks and shrimp?" Mike asked, peeling the covers off him and moving like a human gazelle toward the kitchen, his strides more than double the length of hers. That dimpled ass always made her sigh. His body was a series of gears and pulley lines, all muscle under skin, and watching him was better than anything on Netflix.

"Sounds incredible," Dylan murmured, turning over on his stomach, stealing the pillows Mike had just abandoned. His leg slid up against Laura's, and she found a warm, tingling sensation beginning at her "V". Again? Again! How could she still want more?

Mike wandered out to the deck and opened the top of the grill that was, conservatively speaking, the size of a small compact car. Built-in refrigerator, four gas burners, an espresso machine with a blender, and separate shelves for bar items. You could live in the damn thing in a pinch. The next version of the grill probably would come with a bomb shelter attached.

"Fired up!" he announced.

"Sure am," Laura muttered.

Dylan snorted, then turned on his side, propping his head up on his elbow. One eyebrow arched slowly, with suggestion. "You ready for a little something else to top you off?"

Her breath caught in her throat. She felt so vulnerable suddenly, so exposed. Not in the same way she'd felt postpartum, but more that the inner self in Dylan saw *her* inner self. Like they weren't just naked together.

They were *naked* together.

Caught off guard, she uttered a little white lie. "No. Just joking."

The eyebrow lowered and Dylan's eyes narrowed. "I can tell when you're hiding something, you know."

"Okay! Okay! I spent $300 on a new Coach bag last week! It was a splurge!" she confessed abruptly, knowing that was absolutely, positively not what he was talking about.

The diversion did not work. "I don't care about purses. I care about pussies," he crooned, reaching down her belly, hand sliding to the spot she needed him to touch—again. Again! Her body warmed—revved, really—under his steady command, fingers finding the spot where she needed them, and the surge of pleasure that pounded through her made her grin.

"Happy?" Dylan asked as he glanced up at her, hands parting her thighs, face flush with want.

"More than happy."

"Is that possible?"

"You make it possible," she whispered, her voice catching on the last syllable as his hands caressed her belly, his mouth paying attention to the soft folds of tender skin a bit lower. When he went down on her it was like being transported to a slightly different universe, one where feeling and sensation replaced thinking and talking. If only you could live in this world forever.

Too bad it took sex to teleport oneself into it.

Note to self, she thought. *Need more sex.*

And those were the last coherent thoughts Laura had until she called out Dylan's name, cried for mercy as the climax grew to be a force so big she couldn't release it. Muscled hands pinned the soft flesh of her hips, holding her in place, not letting her buck away from her own clenching climax. Emotion and pure kinetic energy tried to find its way out of her with a controlled sort of letting go, and that was the hitch: you couldn't control a supernova. You couldn't control a superstorm.

You could try, but you'd only be left frustrated.

And very, *very* wet.

Dylan's tongue strummed her like a stringed instrument, the butterfly movements making her arch up and shift into higher, deeper, finer levels of arousal and build-up, the layers interwoven and seeming not to be related until suddenly the climax was there, at the ready, a big wave of orgasms that made her move without will, grind against his mouth without humility, seek pleasure where pleasure was offered and trust that Dylan would give and give and *give* until she was sated.

That was intimacy, right? The ability to be completely bare with another person, raw and real.

And if you were lucky, like Laura was, you got love *and* intimacy, too.

Times two.

Her pussy walls moved of their own accord, like they had a hive mind that made them twitch with delicious glee, paroxysms of ecstasy slowly, lazily finding their way out of her, drawing out the joy of what Dylan had just done. She rested on her back and closed her eyes, reveling in pure sensation.

Mike sauntered back in, whistling some tune that Laura knew was a pop song from one of the smaller college radio stations in the area. That was the only way he could possibly know that short melody. "You two done?" he asked, not at all seeming to be bothered by the fact that she had just gotten one of her orgasms in quite nicely, *thankyouverymuch*. And was now in the lead in The Great Orgasm Race.

"She is. I'm not," Dylan said, pulling the sheet up and peering down at his own upright cock. "Looks like my refractory period is a bit faster than yours."

"I wasn't hanging out in bed with a luscious piece of ass for the past ten minutes. I was busy putting marinated steaks on the grill and making garlic bread." Mike reached down to give Laura a quick kiss, and she tasted garlic, oregano, basil, and something else.

As if reading her mind, he whispered "Marjoram" in her ear, and she giggled.

"It's true, Dylan. Mike was playing Anthony Bourdain while we were just having more orgasms."

"'Anthony Bourdain' and 'orgasm' don't go in the same sentence," Dylan declared, checking under the sheet again. "And...gone. Bye bye, refractory period," he whispered to his own penis with a little wave.

"You wave at your body parts?" Mike teased.

"Only the ones I name."

Mike had been walking to the doorway, but came to a dead halt. Laura loved how the muscles down his back, ass, and thighs all stopped with pinpoint precision, a long assembly line of kinetic perfection.

"You named your—your *penis*?"

"Yep. Every guys does."

"Uh, no," Mike announced. "No, we don't. Quit claiming to speak for all men. How did I not know this about you? We've known each other forever."

"You know damn well I named it. You've heard me call it by its name a million times."

Laura's turn to get confused. "We've been together now for long enough that I'd know you named it. What's its name?"

"'My appetite.'"

Laura and Mike shared a WTF? look. "My appetite?" they asked in unison.

Dylan nodded. "That's right."

"Why?" they asked.

"Because it's my appetite!" Dylan said the words as if they were self-explanatory, hands outstretched in a gesture of emphasis.

"What do you mean?" Laura asked slowly.

Dylan sighed, looking at the ceiling. "A long time ago some friends and I were joking around about what to call our cocks."

Mike placed a hand on Laura's arm and squeezed. The look on his face was priceless. Wide ocean eyes looking at her with incredulity. "Men don't really do that. Don't believe a word he says. I think he binge watched too many bromance movies and this is the result."

"Not! Not!" Dylan barked. "I knew loads of guys in college who named their dicks."

"And they tended to be assholes," Mike drawled.

"Sure, that's true, but—hey, wait a minute!" Dylan muttered, still not getting up from his position in bed with Laura, furry legs rubbing against hers, her fingertips massaging the soft skin at the nape of his neck. She could stay like this all day, but a quick glance at the clock told her they had exactly one hour and six minutes before they needed to be in the Jeep and driving back to the main house to take over with Jillian.

"Assholes. All of them. Frat boy weirdos," Mike continued, clearly enjoying working Dylan into a tizzy.

"You're just goading me," Dylan said with an eye roll.

"Like shooting fish in a barrel."

"Who does that? I hate that saying. It's so strange, because would you seriously dump a bunch of fish in a barrel of water and start shooting at them? Wouldn't that be the epitome of stupid?" Dylan groused. Mike waved a dismissive hand his way as he left. Laura saw him in front of the grill on the deck, turning steaks over.

"You two sound like a couple of teen boys having an argument," Laura said with a grin.

"You couldn't pay me enough to go back to being a teen boy," Dylan said. "Even with a better refractory period." He looked under the sheet again with a concerned expression. "Up, boy, up!"

"Your appetite isn't very big right now, is it?"

He groaned. "Foiled by my own joke."

"You make it so easy, honey. Like shooting fish in a —"

"Don't say it!" He grabbed a pillow from under her head, making her thump onto the mattress, and began beating her chest with it, the pounding fun at first, until he started tickling her.

"Stop!" she screamed, the sound coiling out of the bedroom and up over the mountains. At least, that was how loud it seemed. To her.

"Quit tickling her," Mike called out. "You know she hates it."

Dylan pelted her with the pillow a few times, making Laura roll over onto her stomach and bury her head under an unused white puff. Mike came to her rescue by laughing and throwing pillows from the couch at Dylan, until the distinct scent of charred steak wafted into the room.

Laura sat up and said, "Something's burning!"

Mike bolted outside, and she and Dylan froze, waiting with bated breath to see whether their meal had been ruined by playful fun. Wouldn't be the first time, but marinated steaks lost to overcooking were a tragedy.

"They're fine! Just in time!" Mike called out, and Laura took the distraction to jump up and throw on her clothes.

"Why are you getting dressed?" Dylan asked with a pout.

"Because the last time I wandered around the deck naked, I had about two hundred mosquito bites the next day. One of them managed to get on my labia! You ever try to scratch *that*?"

He leered. "I have a very scratchy tongue. Next time you get one there—"

She threw a pillow at him and left him to laugh. The scent of spices and charbroil made her mouth water. Mike's naked body was covered in a red chef's apron, his hand filled with a plate of half-bloody steaks.

"Salad's over there," he said, pointing with the grill tongs, "and the steaks are coming up."

"Dylan should be coming soon."

"Again? He is so damn competitive sometimes. Three in four hours should—"

"I meant coming *here*. Not, you know...."

Mike's ire faded quickly. He looked quite adorable standing tall, the apron covering his happy bits, the strange mixture of culinary convention and nudist subversion making her nose twitch with laughter. She couldn't stop eating him up with her eyes.

"What?" he finally asked. "Why are you staring?"

"The Nudist Chef. You could star in your own reality cooking show."

"No way. Can you imagine if someone found a hair in the food? Try explaining that when you cook naked."

She looked at the steak with a stink eye. "Do we need to get you a little hairnet for down there? I'd be happy to design one and help tweak it."

"Tweak it? Lots of fittings?" He reached over with his empty arm, steaks now in her hands on the plate, and kissed the top of her head. "Sounds interesting, but I'll pass. The idea of fitting a hairnet over my balls is one of many reasons not to have a nude cooking show."

Dylan sauntered out in his jeans, barefoot and inhaling deeply from the fresh air. "Nude cooking show? Where? What channel? I'm in. Let's binge watch!"

"*I'm* the nude cooking show," Mike explained as he made sure the food was set and began pouring red wine for everyone. Laura held her hand over her glass.

"No thanks. I'll be nursing soon."

Mike nodded. "Got it." He poured glasses for him and Dylan, then winked at her. "I'm a wee bit underdressed for this gathering, so if you'll excuse me..."

She spanked his tight ass as he turned around. "You're wearing an apron. That's enough. And it shows off your finest assets."

Dylan snorted, apparently inhaling a noseful of red wine. "Ow ow ow ow ow," he hollered as Mike howled with laughter. By the time Mike returned, wearing jeans and some old Coldplay t-shirt Laura hated, Dylan had cleared his nose and was eyeing the wine with suspicion.

They dug into their steaks, and within minutes had wolfed down the lovely dinner, which was fine with Laura. The sooner she told them, the better, and it was so much nicer to face a full, sated set of guys when she had a minor bomb to drop.

"So..." she began.

Both came to an abrupt halt in their movements.

"Yes?" Mike asked slowly. She saw his eyes flick toward Dylan and then return, the micro-movement so rehearsed she might never have noticed it if she weren't so intimately familiar with the two of them.

"What the *hell* do you think I'm about to say?" she demanded, the air charged suddenly, leaving her imbalanced and agitated. Like a switch had been flipped, she went from lightness to dark. Why would they look at each other that way?

Neither of them answered her, instead looking at her with such intensity her heart turned into a cyclone.

"Guys?" she pleaded. This felt so far out of the range of normal.

"Are you..." Mike began. He stopped and looked at Dylan.

"What?" Laura practically screamed. What the hell did he think she was about to say?

"Are you pregnant?" Dylan asked.

A huge stream of air poured out of her lungs, the relief evident in the way her shoulders relaxed, her body poured the worry out through her sigh. "God, no. No!"

Dylan's face relaxed with relief.

Mike's collapsed with disappointment.

"Oh!" she said, looking at Mike. "That's not the reaction I expected." When had this turned into a conversation about having another baby? She thought she was going to spend the next half-hour convincing them to come to Jeddy's and talk with Darla's boyfriends.

He shrugged but said nothing. Dylan turned and gave him an arched eyebrow.

"You want another one? Already? Thirteen months of interrupted sleep, colic, teething, and no time alone with Laura isn't enough for you? You masochist."

Laura felt the hair on her arms and neck begin to prickle. The nasty undertone in Dylan's voice made Mike's hackles go right up, and she hated when both of them argued. It was rare—most of their sarcastic comments were tossed back and forth in jest—but this one had so many layers to it that Laura felt a dangerous sense of calm pour over her, one of those moments when everything you know can turn on a dime.

"And what about the pure joy of watching our daughter come into the world, of cutting the umbilical cord and watching her settle on Laura's chest, of smelling her little baby head and being the only one who knows how to rock her the exact right way to get her to sleep? And the sleepy milk burps that always came with a happy smile afterward? Watching her grin at you, her eyes lighting up when you held her? What about snuggling with her on the couch and knowing that you'd helped to make an entire human being, a new life that will go out into the world and make it a better place if you raise her right?" Mike's words flowed over Laura like a waterfall. He'd never—ever—spoken for so long or with such emotion.

Dylan's jaw hung quite low.

Mike went on. "When she crawled, we all cheered. When she took her first bites of solid food, we were there. When she started saying 'Mama,' we were jealous."

"You were?" Laura interrupted.

Both men looked a bit embarrassed. "We'd read in the baby books that 'Dada' was more commonly the first word, so..." Mike explained.

221

"I half expected her first word to be 'Jeddy's' or 'Madge,' because we took her there so much," Dylan added.

Laura squashed a laugh because Mike's eyes were blazing. He wasn't done yet.

"And now Jillian is babbling and happy and wandering around on those fat little legs, arms in the air, so curious about the world and open and eager. She's the best teacher and the most wonderful embodiment of pure love I have ever seen in my entire life." Mike's voice was choked with emotion, eyes glistening, and Laura stood, went to him, and gave him a hug.

"So yeah," he ended with a ragged sound, "I would love another one." Mike pulled away from the hug and, with soulful eyes, regarded Laura tenderly. "Not until you're ready, of course. But if you did tell me you're pregnant, I would be thrilled."

"Shit!" Dylan shouted. "We're late!" All three of them turned to look at the clock, and Laura made a squealing sound of alarm. He was right. There was no need to clean the cabin—Mike's resort crew would handle that—but they did need to tidy and bring their own belongings out of there. The cabin was used, occasionally, by resort guests (*sex items were carefully removed*), so they had to do a quick check of everything and get out.

Five minutes later, Laura marveled at how quickly they had all acted, and as the Jeep rumbled down the rutted dirt road back to their home, she let Mike's words rattle around in her head. It wasn't that she didn't want another baby—she was an only child and had always wanted siblings, and was determined to give Jillian at least one. Right now, though, she didn't feel ready. Maybe in a year? There really wasn't a timeline.

Mike didn't demand an answer, and Dylan was in the back seat alone right now, staring out the window, his jaw locked so hard it might as well have been a safe at Gringot's.

He clearly wasn't ready for more. She knew he adored Jillian—loved her to pieces, in fact—but she also understood what he had said. Being bone-weary and at the constant ready to attend to a child's needs in its first year was an experience she would rather not relive right away. And pregnancy! The joy of swelling with new life, the feel of a growing baby inside her—that was all amazing.

The ballooned legs, the polyhydramnios she'd experienced, and all the aches and pains, along with morning sickness, made her want to be pregnant again about as much as she wanted to listen to Josie talk about data plans for the office.

"There's no rush, is there?" she said softly, not quite realizing the words were out of her mouth until they were. The sound of the Jeep's tires on the rocky road may have covered her voice, because maybe Mike didn't hear her.

But he did.

A slow smile split his lips, cheeks shining with a warmth she loved so much. He patted her knee. "No. Never a rush. I'm not really ready, either. But if you were pregnant right now, my reaction wouldn't be negative."

"I just don't think—"

He squeezed her knee gently. "Just tell me you want Jillian to have a sibling."

"Of course I do! You know I've always wanted at least two. I don't want her to be an only child."

He nodded. "I know. We've talked about it. I just... needed to hear it again." His eyes flicked over to her and then returned to the unstable road, but in that split second of eye contact she saw all she needed.

Love. So much love a pair of eyes couldn't hold it all.

And maybe one child couldn't hold it all, either, though that thought seemed so silly to Laura. Of course one child could be enough. It had been enough for her mother. For plenty of people.

But not Mike, it seemed.

A cold thought of such alarming clarity hit her between the eyes. It felt like a tiny little pinprick of pain so startling it traveled down to her heart.

Another baby.

Was Mike afraid Jillian wasn't his, and that was why he wanted more? Was this about jealousy or competition, or...something unnamed?

The glow of their happy afternoon began to fade a bit as reality intruded on her thoughts. The heat of their skin against hers had been so immediate just moments ago. And now...

She had to think. Not just feel. Not just touch.

As they pulled into the driveway, Cyndi played with Jillian on the giant swing set Mike and Dylan had installed last month. Their baby was perched at the top of the slide, Cyndi's protective arms on her waist, and as Jillian's fat little hands waved in the air, Cyndi guided her down. Jillian's face tipped up to look at Cyndi, and those baby hands clapped with joy, cheering herself on for her great slide victory.

Suddenly, all was right in Laura's world.

JOSIE

"What in the hell were you thinking sending my boss to me to talk about my sex life!" Darla screamed in Josie's ear. Pulling her smartphone back from her head, she stared at it, fully expecting Darla's holographic image to appear in spectacular, angry form.

"It was a perfectly reasonable suggestion," Josie retorted. "Perfectly reasonable because you two are in these crazy threesome relationships, and you're both struggling."

"Struggling?" Darla roared. "I'm not struggling with Joe and Trevor!"

"You meet Joe's parents yet?"

Fuming silence was all Josie got from her niece.

"I didn't think so," Josie added. "And Laura's got her own set of problems with Mike and Dylan—"

"Problems? Problems? You mean you can find yourself not one, but two billionaires, have their baby, live in luxury with them, and spend your time opening a crazy business for weirdos like me, and have problems? Nice life. What kind of problems does Laura have? Whether to buy lavender-scented car fresheners or verbena-scented car fresheners at Whole Foods?"

"Meow." Josie's arched tone said more than the single word.

Darla backpedaled, fast. "You won't tell her I said that, will you?" she said in a panicked voice. "Because I like Laura. A lot. And I don't think she's spoiled. That not what I mean. I know she worked hard and had a degree and a job before she met the guys and oh my God, Josie, say something, because if Laura's on the line with you and just heard me say that I am going to die from—"

"No, dumbass, she's not here. But you have some learning to do. Just because someone has a ton of money doesn't mean their problems go away. In fact, sometimes you end up with more problems."

"I'll trade."

"Hah! Anyhow, you guys should meet. Lunch at Jeddy's sounds like fun."

"How do you know what we're doing?" Darla asked with suspicion.

"Because Laura asked me to be there," Josie answered matter-of-factly. Being asked wasn't a surprise, but what Josie had in store for Trevor, Joe, Mike, and Dylan sure would be. First, she'd asked Laura if she thought the plan was worth it. Laura agreed. Now, on to Darla...

"You'll be there?" Relief flooded Darla's voice. "Thank God."

"And I need some help from you," Josie added.

"Help?"

"Laura's going to get Mike and Dylan to come, too. Just to hang out and have a meal nearby. I think you should bring Trevor and Joe."

"Why?"

"Because it's like meeting an albino moose."

"You just lost me. You on something? Because the last time I heard someone talking about albino moose it was Joe, who licked some piece of handmade pressed fair-trade paper from Mexico that had some LSD or something on it, and soon the whole world went albino and he was—"

Josie cut her off. It was a well-developed skill. "No. What I mean is, if you heard about an albino moose in a zoo, would you go see it?"

"Maybe."

"If you owned an albino moose and heard about a second one, wouldn't you go see it?"

"Well, sure, because that would be so rare that— *ooohhhhhh*. I get it."

"Good. Because I was about to pull out the hand puppets and leotards and do an interpretive dance to explain."

"You don't have to get pedantic."

"Can't help it."

They both laughed.

"You have any idea how hard it's going to be to convince Joe to go to Jeddy's and sit at a table with two other guys who do what we...do? He can't even tell his mom we're dating."

"What about Trevor?"

"I've met his parents. Nice people. We all met up at some town concert and walked around eating ice cream. They think me and Trevor met at an online dating site."

"There's a lie." Josie's words were true, but she knew they stung Darla.

"If you count being a fangirl as 'online dating,' it kinda works. They don't know anything more than that." To Josie's surprise, Darla wasn't defensive. A little sad, though. It made Josie even more determined to make sure Laura and Darla talked.

"He won't tell them the truth?"

"Would you?"

Josie tried to imagine calling her mother, Marlene, back in Ohio and explaining she had two boyfriends. At the same time. No, really—at the *exact* same time.

"Uh, no. But then again, with my mom, I'd probably get some story about how she'd had five men at once, and exactly which holes you can use for—"

"*Lalalalala* I can't hear you talking about Aunt Marlene that way!" Darla shouted.

"You asked."

"Question retracted."

Josie let out a long, slow sigh, the kind you can only release openly with someone who knows you inside out.

"I know that sound," Darla cracked. "That's the sound of Mama going to get the belt."

"Aunt Cathy never whipped you!" Josie protested, knowing this was all a joke.

"No, but she'd pull out Daddy's belt and tell me that if he was alive my ass would be tanned."

"And then what did she do when you didn't listen?"

"Huh," Darla uttered, the phone popping with the force of her sound. "I don't know. I always obeyed. I think I figured if she was calling on the belt of a dead man to get me to do what she wanted, I'd better do it."

They shared a chuckle, and then Josie returned to the matter at hand. "You need to get Joe and Trevor there. They can eat pie with Mike and Dylan."

Darla made a choking sound. "Excuse me?"

"Get your mind out of the gutter, Darla Josephine Jennings. Not that kind of pie. Jeddy's may have some weird things on the menu, but they haven't come up with a flavor *that* savory."

"Pussy Pie has a ring to it," Darla said through laughter.

"People would think they were baking strays from the alley behind the restaurant."

"I've eaten in some dive joints here in Boston that probably are," Darla muttered.

"Quit stalling!" Josie insisted. "Get Joe and Trevor to meet you there. Laura's doing the same with Mike and Dylan, and then we'll—"

Two strong, muscled arms wrapped around Josie's waist as Alex appeared from behind, her ass nuzzling up to an alarmingly large sign of how happy he was to see her.

"Hey there," she said in a low voice. "I've missed you. And I can feel how much you've missed me."

"You coming on to me, Josie? 'Cause that's a new low." Darla's voice had gone flat.

"Hi, Darla!" Alex called out, then kissed a trail of little pecks from Josie's ear to her shoulder. "How's it going?"

"Josie's crazy!" Darla shouted.

"Oh. Good. Everything's normal," he said, hands sliding up Josie's front, finding her breasts like they were made of iron and he had magnets in his palms.

"No, I mean *crazy*!" Darla insisted. "She wants me to get Trevor and Joe together with Mike and Dylan!"

"Quit screaming," Josie said, distracted by what Alex was doing and by Darla's shouts through the tinny phone speaker. "I'll put you on speakerphone."

Darla came through loud and clear as Alex spun Josie around for a deep, warm kiss. "Together! The four of them!"

"You're setting the four guys up?" he murmured in Josie's ear. "That's...inventive. Good things come in fours?"

Josie hit his pec through the stained scrubs he wore. After a typical twenty-four-hour shift he showered and changed at work, but had come straight home this time. She looked at the clock. More like a thirty-three-hour shift.

"Why are you covered in—ah, God, is that blood? And you smell like rancid amniotic fluid."

"How do you know what that smells like?"

"You two have the weirdest conversations," Darla added.

Alex and Josie both stared at the smartphone. "Like you don't?" Josie snapped. "You are the queen of weird discussions."

Darla backed off, voice sheepish. "Fair enough. But c'mon—you know how hard it will be to get Joe and Trevor there? And what the hell will they talk about?"

"Double penetration positions?" Alex suggested. "Best sex practices for threesomes? How to make a schedule on Google Calendar to balance it all out? What to do when—"

"Stop!" Darla and Josie shouted at the same time.

"You just managed to offend both of us," Josie said, laughing and trying to look stern as he lifted her shirt and kissed her belly. A flood of heat pooled between her legs and her fingers wove through his hair, then down his muscled back.

Except he smelled funny.

"Off to the showers with you!" she ordered, regretfully pushing him toward the bathroom. Her bathroom.

Um, *their* bathroom. Alex had moved in two days ago.

His lease had been up and his roommate was long gone on some fancy residency fellowship, again, leaving Alex with a tough choice of either finding a new roommate or getting a smaller, cheaper place.

She'd expected him to suggest moving in with her, but to her surprise, he hadn't. As days had turned into weeks of watching him scour Craigslist and roommate sites, she'd finally caved in and asked.

This was an experiment. A testing period. It was not permanent.

At least, not for now.

He gave her a big, sloppy, sexy kiss and stripped his shirt off over his head, leaning forward as he peeled the v-neck scrubs over his neck and head, the ripple of muscled layers like soccer fans doing the wave. Only this was better.

"Earth to Josie? You there? Alex still there making pervy comments about my sex life?" Darla's voice startled her.

"No," she sighed, watching him untie his scrub pants and shake out of them, leaving him in boxer briefs that outlined every vein, every curve. Thumbs hooked into the waistband, he gave her a big, sultry wink like a stripper, and then he pulled them off, giving her a mouth-watering view.

"Is he doing sex things to you right now? On the phone? Because that's just plain rude."

"No, Darla, he's not doing—'sex things'? You have the vocabulary of a twelve-year-old boy."

"It's about all I need to have a conversation with you."

The sparring normally would have made Josie laugh, but watching her boyfriend's ass stride toward the bathroom to take a soapy, steamy shower rendered her quite speechless.

And intolerant of being on the phone.

"Do whatever you need to do to get Joe and Trevor to Jeddy's."

"You make it sound life or death."

"No—but I think it's worth a try."

"Why is it so important to you?"

"Come here!" Alex shouted as the distinct sound of the water being turned on filled the walls. Josie scrambled to get out of her clothes while talking with Darla.

"It's important because I see my niece and my best friend in really unique relationships and sometimes it's nice not to be the only freak. If it turns out there's another freak just like you, you're not a freak anymore. You're a tribe."

"A tribe of two?"

"Oh, oops! I dropped the soap!" Alex called out from down the hall. "Josie, can you come pick up the soap for me in the shower?"

Darla giggled. "You two play games, too? Me and Joe and Trevor have this one game we call the 'Tortured Romance' game, where Joe is the Russian hit man who is 'sposed to kidnap me, and does, and then Trevor is the Special Ops dude who has to rescue me. But then the hit man and the Special Ops dude find—"

"I do not want to hear about your sex games!" Josie screeched. Her excited clit made a face of horror worthy of an Edvard Munch painting. Or worse, Macaulay Culkin in *Home Alone*.

"Like I wanna hear yours!" Darla huffed.

"Just—goodbye!" Josie stabbed her phone screen repeatedly with an angry finger and fell over as her foot caught in the hem of her pants. *Might as well strip on the ground,* she thought, and she made quick work of it, completely naked in seconds, ass cold on the hard tile of her kitchen floor.

She stood, just long enough to get a good, long look at the UPS guy delivering the latest item she'd ordered online.

A good look because her—their, *their*—curtains were wide open in the front picture window.

UPS Man got an eyeful, too.

She ran down the hallway, body flushed with embarrassment, excitement, and a lingering sense of disgust from her conversation with Darla.

"What was that all about?" Alex asked as she slipped into the tiny shower with him, her face coated with the shower spray. He was so tall she had no choice. It was like showering under a very misty waterfall, and she kept her eyes closed most of the time.

Which was sad, because right before her was one of the seven-inch wonders of the modern world.

She opened one eye.

Make that eight.

"Darla started telling me all about some sex game she plays with Trevor and Joe—"

Alex's entire body shuddered.

"Yeah, about right," she confirmed, her hands running in opposite direction to the water's flow on his arms, stretching over his shoulders, sliding down his back, ribcage, to his hard ass. Filling her hands with his flesh, she pulled him hard against her, and found him *hard*.

Against her.

The kiss he slammed her with was insistent and unyielding, the kind of claiming that only two people who have been together for a while can exercise. She opened her lips and he was inside her, tongue reacquainting itself with her warmth, telling her about his day, reuniting after so much time apart.

His long shifts were part of the deal in loving him: being with a doctor, she knew, carried the constant separation, and never knowing exactly when he would

233

come home from a shift in the labor and delivery ward, or the ER, meant getting accustomed to ambiguity.

But he was here. Now. Hot and strong and wet and in her arms, and that—by God—was what she was going to think about right now. Not her silly niece's sex life, or about the client shortage that Good Things Come in Threes was experiencing, or her flashing the UPS delivery dude, or the fact that she had just taken a ginormous leap forward in trusting Alex with a bigger piece of her life.

And her heart.

Right now, there were decidedly more delicious body parts that Alex could have pieces of, and my, oh my, was he finding them quite nicely without needing to use a map.

Josie was learning, stroke by stroke, caress by caress, lick by lick, that sex with the same person could be infinitely interesting given enough time and enough desire. While that should have been obvious, and she wondered how she'd managed to reach mature adulthood without really registering that little piece of wisdom, it was quite different when you lived it. Day by day, encounter by encounter, orgasm by orgasm.

The water's mist was like an audience, watching and omnipresent, demanding access to their skin, their breath, their very essence, as Alex dropped to his knees and buried his face between her parted thighs, her hands reaching for the balance bar screwed—she hoped—tightly into the shower's wall. *Thank heaven for safety features*, she loosely thought as his tongue found a way to make quite a show for the air that surrounded them. Her head tilted back as her neck muscles tightened and loosened, imitating the pattern of her sex as it clenched and released, and as she shifted slightly her movements were greeted with a face full of hot water.

Sputtering, she tugged lightly at his hair, and he moved up, hands on either side of her, caressing her calves, then knees, thumbs digging in possessively as he traversed her thighs, then hips, ribcage greeted by palms that enveloped her breasts with a nearly feral touch. By the time his hands cradled her face for a kiss that tasted like her, like rain, like everything, she was ready to have him inside her.

More than ready.

Always thinking ahead, she thought as Alex turned away and gave her a spectacular view of an ass that was either forged in a Bessemer furnace or hand-carved by a sculptor. The condom he put on made her smile. No babies.

Not yet.

His touch was more insistent this time, her last view of him fleeting but unfurling a rosebud of need inside, his wet hair and determined, dark look making him dangerous. A force of nature. Her dangerous force of nature, of course, but as he centered her and lifted one leg into place for her, his shaft sliding in from behind and making her core grab hold of him like a velvet glove, she *wanted* danger.

Wanted *him*.

Her fingers curled in on the tile, eyes unfocused and body one cloud of wet, hot skin, pumping blood and tingling with the kinetic frenzy of having Alex behind her, all muscle and flow. He did all the work, and that was just fine, a tacit agreement that was forged through time. You do the work this time; I'll ride you tonight…

Their climax hit within three breaths, smashing them against the tile wall, their ability to calibrate it swept away by the mind-blowing, involuntary nature of impulse, biology, and release. She screamed, the sound guttural and base, low in her throat but raw, as Alex murmured her name over and over in her ear, the rasp muted by the shower spray and steam that applauded and shouted "Bravo!" at their performance.

Gasping, she slumped against the shower wall, Alex behind her, the wet hair on his thighs prickling her ass, the feel alien and intriguing.

"Too bad we can't have porch sex again," he said as she turned off the shower and slid back the curtain, reaching for two towels. Handing one to him, she paused for a moment to marvel at the casual domesticity of it all. Shower sex. A towel offered as if it were so natural. Part of the flow of time and building a life with another human being, to share for decades and beyond, all the way until the fire of mortality was gone, and the soul moved on.

Deep in her pensive moment, she missed Alex's comment. Then he cleared his throat and said, "Penny for your thoughts?"

"They're worth way more than that," she said with a funny laugh, a sound choked with emotion. He had a radar when it came to her, which only made the moment more infused with emotion. Two days. He'd lived here for two days and already she was thinking about forever.

Abstract forever and real-life forever were two very different concepts.

So far she thoroughly enjoyed both.

"You have that look in your eyes," he said in that warm, whiskey-laden voice that was so smooth it made her wet. The man could recite the *Physician's Desk Reference* manual and she'd be writhing in sexual ecstasy in minutes.

"What look? The crazy cat-lady look?" As if on command, her skittish cat, Crackhead, darted out from underneath the couch and fled into the sanctuary of her—um, *their*—bedroom, ensconced under the bed, two shining orbs staring at them.

"Crackhead will never get used to me," Alex sighed.

"Don't make me choose between the two of you," she joked. Alex gave her a sour face and disappeared into the kitchen, and from the sounds of it, he was brewing coffee.

A woman could love this man deeply. And she did.

Josie finished toweling off and walked naked into the bedroom, rummaging through her dresser for clothes. A second dresser, one that didn't match (*and yet belonged there*), rested under the window across from hers. Alex's meager furniture had fit in so well with her eclectic possessions that it was creepy. Creeptastic, in an overly perfect kind of way. As if he were made for her. Even his coffee mug set with the little wooden stand matched the one she had found at a yard sale a few months ago.

Creepy.

"You look like you want to bolt out into the street and run away from me. Like I have tentacles and crawl into your body at night to turn you into a pod person."

"You have one tentacle that crawls into me at night," she said suggestively.

"And if I had more, they would join it." As if his cock were listening, it rose slowly, cockeyed (*no pun intended*) at first, then slowly straightened out, long and strong, the sedate politeness of his foreskin turtlenecking down.

"Seriously?" She made a dismissive, but joking, sound as she stared at his rod. "You're ready again?"

"Always ready."

"I know that's not true, because there was that one time—"

Alex grabbed some underwear and quickly put them on, as if his penis were offended by the conversation and needed to have its ears covered. "That one time I'd just come off an unexpected thirty-eight-hour labor, drank five beers, and you rolled over and started humping me! Give a guy a break." He stretched a simple, moss-green t-shirt over his head, pulling the thin cotton with a furious rush. "And besides, I still managed to make you come a few times!"

"They need to patent that tongue of yours," she agreed.

"Can we stop talking about the one time I couldn't perform to your satisfaction?"

"It's not that you didn't—" she protested.

"Or shall I bring up the time you fell asleep during sex?"

"Hey! Not fair! I was on painkillers after that dental surgery and—" The look on his face made her shut up. He was right. Not fair. "Fine. Truce." The quick kiss they shared righted the world. The steamy gurgle from the kitchen made it all even better.

Sitting at her—*their*—kitchen table, sipping from breast-shaped mugs Darla had given Josie as a gag birthday gift (*"Mama won them in an online sweepstakes contest. You should have seen the molded chocolates that came with them!"*), she sighed with contentment. And then she ruined the moment.

"I need your help in convincing Mike and Dylan to sit down and talk with Trevor and Joe."

Alex's surprised look quickly turned to confusion. "What the hell would those four have in common?

Oh..." His voice went low and his eyes registered suspicion. "What are you up to? Is this some stunt for Good Things Come in Threes?"

"No! It's not a stunt. It's more that Laura's so lost lately, and even though she's happy and life is better now that Jillian's out of the infant phase, it seems like she needs to talk to someone who's in the same kind of unique relationship."

"I'm not connecting the dots."

"She and Darla are getting together for lunch at Jeddy's."

"And you want Mike and Dylan to have lunch with Trevor and Joe? Joe? The kid is an inscrutable blowhard asshole—"

"You still can't let go of the fact that you smashed your face into a parking sign because you saw me touching him."

She expected protest, not: "Damn right I can't. Fucker."

"Alex! You're still jealous? I was touching his heart surgery scar at Darla's insistence! He was shirtless and we were on the porch and you and I were broken up and—"

His face had gone bright red and his fingers floated up to the tiny scar along his eye. It had been nearly a year and yet...

"It's not jealousy in the traditional sense. You never dated him, never kissed him, never...but in that moment I was so lost without you, and running past your house—no matter how juvenile—was a way to connect with you. And then to run past and see you touching another man just destroyed my world."

She gave him a look of sympathy and pain. He took a long drink of his coffee and continued. "Yeah. The guy bugs me. And even if you'd never touched him and I didn't have that imprinted in my mind on top of my emotional state at the time, he's a judgmental, condescending prick anyhow. The kind of guy I couldn't stand in high school and college.'

"He's twenty-three! Half the guys I knew at that age were like that."

"Doesn't mean I like him."

Josie finished her cup of coffee and just watched Alex. His wet brown hair was close cut right now, his haircut more a function of efficiency than of fashion. Being deep into his residency as an OB-GYN and working extra shifts in the emergency room on rotation meant that any part of his life that could be simplified needed to be.

In recent months he'd taken to this principle of optimization with great zeal, and living with Josie was part of his larger plan. Then again, perhaps it was the other way around: simplifying his life was just a convenient excuse for getting her to agree to share an apartment together.

Deep brown eyes framed with impossibly long lashes turned to meet hers, troubled and smiling at the same time. Alex could do that—inhabit two distinct emotional states at the same time with comfort, okay with the ambiguity. He didn't see the world in black or white like she did. Being with him taught her, slowly, that there were shades of gray.

And not the *Fifty Shades* kind.

"Hold on, though—you still haven't explained why you want all the guys to meet."

"And for you to be there," she said with a breathy, breezy tone meant to sound so offhand, so casual that it was nothing, no big deal, just a—

"*What?*" he roared. "Why do *I* need to be there? I'm not in a threesome relationship!"

Silence.

"Is this your way of saying you want to add a man to"—his hands waved in the air like giant, muscled butterflies—"*this*? Us?"

Coffee sprayed in a fine mist out through her lips, covering the tidy kitchen table top, onto the floor, and all over poor Crackhead, who had chosen that exact moment to leave the sanctuary of his spot under the bed to make a quick foray to the food bowl.

The cat hissed and sprinted into the tiny utility closet behind where Alex sat, the door of which was open a wedge. All the brooms and mops were stored in there, and when Crackhead shot into it, a broom came out of the closet, handle first, and in slow motion Josie watched it crash into the back of Alex's head.

"Yeow! *Fitz!*" Crackhead's howls of outrage matched Alex's as Josie watched him leap up and hold his head. She choked on coffee and laughter.

"Crackhead!" Alex shouted, which only made the cat yowl more.

"Welcome to domestic bliss with Josie and her cat," she said quietly, putting the broom in place and carefully stepping up on Alex's abandoned chair to kiss the top of his head. "And *only* Josie and her cat. Crackhead is the only third party in this house, thank you."

He looked up at her, rubbing his injured spot, eyebrows high. Standing on tiptoes, he reached for a kiss.

"That's a threesome I'll take. Me and two pussies. Isn't that every man's dream?"

She swatted him on the back of his head.

"Hey! Injured party here!"

"Now you're definitely going to lunch with Mike and Dylan and Trevor and Joe."

241

"I think you need more men in there. Four more and we have a baseball team."

"Consider yourself the moderator."

"Of what?"

"Of relationships we'll never understand."

"I'm an expert on that one." He stepped away before she could swat him again.

TREVOR

Joe was being a prick all the time these days, and Trevor was struggling to understand why. The two of them had met Darla more than a year ago, when he'd gotten high on peyote and found himself more than six hundred miles from home, naked and carrying a guitar, a lonely hitchhiker on an Ohio highway.

And Darla had been crazy enough to offer him a ride.

Right now? She was riding *him*. The three were one hot, sweaty mess of arms and fingers, sighs and moans, the slow, deep friction of sharing Darla like a slow song you dance to by rocking your hips in tune to a sultry beat that never hurries, that takes its time.

That *savors*.

But Joe was being a jerk.

Home from law school and working on the band, he was surly with Darla and only seemed to chill when they were having sex. All three of them.

Which was right now.

God, Darla was so hot. Lush and sweet and ripe, with eyes that invited you to come and play. Come have fun. Come let loose.

Just...*come*. He had a permanent hard-on whenever he was around her, and no amount of sex satisfied it.

Joe seemed to be the same way, except he resented the fact that Trevor lived in the same city as Darla. *Tough shit, dude. You chose to go to law school in*

Philadelphia. Not my fault I live closer to her and get the benefit of all her pent-up need for you.

How could you have a girlfriend like that and still be an uptight asshole? Joe managed to do it somehow, and while Trevor had been easygoing about plenty of things in his long-running friendship and now, er... whateverthefuck you called this "relationship," he was sick and tired of Joe's bullshit. Calling him on it was well past being overdue.

But not right now when they were both, quite literally, inside Darla. You couldn't share a body in that kind of close proximity and—

"Oh, Trev, right there," she moaned. How she knew which man was in which place was a mystery to him, but one he didn't spend many brain cells on, at least right now, because if he had any brain cells they were all congregated in the tip of his dick, and the rest were inside his balls, ready to rocket-ship out of his body and into hers.

Darla's fevered face was over him, completely absorbed in her own pleasure. He stared, transfixed, always turned on by watching her enjoy herself. It was a feeling he didn't know existed, or at least hadn't experienced, until he'd met her. Touched her. Teased and tasted her, and gotten intimate with her. You could have plenty of sex without intimacy, he'd realized recently. But the letting someone inside your head and heart was so much better than just letting them touch your body.

And when you could do all three, it was fucking awesome.

His back arched as he slid slowly in and out of her, Joe behind Darla, their bodies mingled together, sweat making them slippery. Darla clenched so hard around his cock that he couldn't move even if he wanted to, and his body surged, knowing she was close. Red fire shot through him and his thoughts dissipated, her soft flesh in his anxious palms, hands needing to touch whatever he could of her to cling as they both—all three, actually—fell off the cliff into the cavern of climactic bliss.

This was what it felt like to be complete.

He needed them both right here, right now, and especially Darla right fucking *there*.

She cried out both their names. The sound of her hoarse, uncontrolled release made him come, the three of them turning into nothing but surging muscle and spasming need, thrusts and friction and joy in one tangled bunch of limbs, curves and hard lines like a relief map of fucking amazing sex, and as Trevor rooted himself inside Darla and she crashed and crashed and crashed like waves hitting a breaker wall, a series of thoughts shot through his mind:

This is what love feels like. Not inside your heart or mind, but on your skin, musky and slick with fibers buzzing and grasping.

This is what love tastes like. Salty and free, sweet and sassy, like an orgasm on the tongue.

This is what love sounds like. His name, shattering the huffing cloud of sighs and groans, called out by a throat so perfect he could only answer Darla's calls with a kiss to that soft spot on her neck.

This is what love *is*.

Everything was more complete with Joe there, but they didn't talk about that, either. *Love* and *Joe* occupied two very distinct parts of Trevor's brain, like the two elements were radioactive when they got anywhere near each other, so he kept them in lead-lined box inside his head.

He couldn't deny it, though. Had stopped fighting it, mostly. Feeling whole left him with a kind of bliss that made the three of them a force of nature that no one defined except them. And that was good enough for Trevor.

Darla began to fidget, his clue that she was done and ready to cuddle. Sliding out of her made him shudder, just once, the final impulses of electrical power elicited by sex crawling out of his dick.

Now he was done, and as Joe took his place on her left side, Trevor on her right, the three settled into what he'd come to think of as The Movie Shot. Imagining them from above, suspended in space, he figured they looked like a group of twenty-somethings who were well fucked and damn pleased with themselves.

As they should be.

And yet Joe never was.

"That was amazing," Trevor said preemptively, as if he could control the mood by saying something first that would be positive. Like starting conversation on a good note would neutralize anything negative that Joe might say.

Didn't work.

"That's what you get all the time while I'm in Philly." The words felt like a cold bucket of ice water all over Trevor's body, and he hadn't signed up to take the ALS Ice Bucket Challenge.

Darla squeezed Trevor's thigh with a warning, but also a tacit statement of agreement that Joe was being an asshole.

"Whenever you come home, we're here," she whispered in Joe's ear, loud enough for Trevor to hear, but it was too late. His entire body had gone rigid with suppressed rage. *Way to ruin a nice moment*, he thought. Then again, Joe was good at that.

He was pretty much the expert, in fact.

"'Home'? This shithole is home?"

"You lived in this shithole before, so what happened? It doesn't meet your new, snooty Philly standards?" The words ripped out of Trevor's mouth before he could help it. And Darla's hand on his thigh couldn't stop him, either.

Joe just snorted and snuggled in with Darla more. Trevor didn't feel jealousy the way Joe seemed to, but the combination of the sneering words and taking casual advantage of her nice, wet, warm body made Trevor sit up and slice the air with quick movement, eyes burning a hole through Joe's head.

"C'mon. You can't take a joke?" Joe's taunt raised Trevor's anger level from rage to explosive, and he didn't *do* explosive. Darla could sense it, too—he knew from the way the corners of her mouth turned down, and how her green eyes went stormy, that this was as bad as he thought.

He couldn't calm down. Couldn't chill, couldn't back off, either. Always the appeaser, and generally willing to give himself a few seconds of distance between hearing one of Joe's wisecracks and reacting to it, he was out of patience.

Finally.

"Fuck you, Joe," Trevor ground out like he was chewing rusty nails. There went the shine off the afterglow. *Pfft*. Gone in one quick sentence.

"Nope. Sorry. All fucked out. Darla took care of that."

Trevor's breathing was labored, the whoosh of air being pushed in and out by fury as loud as a tornado rushing through his ears. Darla peeled Joe off her and sat up, eyes wide with alarm. He could feel the hair on his body stand on end, as if that same electrical current that had just fueled so much passion moments ago had gone rogue, now turning dangerous. Destructive.

Lethal.

He wasn't going to *really* kill Joe, of course. But if he could murder that fucker's sense of entitlement, self-importance, and most of all, the little troll of extraordinary negativity that inhabited Joe like a parasite, then maybe he'd get somewhere.

Because he just couldn't take it anymore.

"How in the hell are you so jealous?" he spat out, knowing it would make Joe take the bait. "We share. We're a threesome. That comes with the territory of what we are, together. You're not supposed to be like this when you choose to be with me and Darla, you asshole."

A few beats of silence. Trevor stared, hard, at Joe's face, searching for a crack. A fissure. Some hint that Joe felt *something*.

"Not jealous. Just stating the facts," Joe said, calmly stretching his carved abs, arms reaching up for the pillow beneath his head, Darla involuntarily turning to watch. Joe was dark and tanned, compact and marbled, while Trevor was tall and blond, with more bulk on him. Darla said she loved having her yin and yang, her men as different as could be, giving her everything she needed.

And Trevor had to agree that the three of them worked well together, like puzzle pieces that fit perfectly, but there was a fourth person in the room right now. Joe's negativity was an unwanted, interfering stalker, like an ex who can't let go.

The blasé attitude Joe exuded was completely manufactured, Trevor knew. He was faking it.

Joe faked lots of things.

Trevor knew how to make him be real, though. And that was the most dangerous thing he could do right now—make Joe emotionally vulnerable. Being in an intimate relationship with someone meant you knew every single one of their soft spots, and there was a tacit agreement that you just do not—ever—poke those spots with anything sharp.

Joe had broken that agreement, except the sharp thing he poked with was his tongue. And not in the good kind of way.

"Hey, guys, don't do this," Darla pleaded. Her voice held a gentle tone that made two layers of anger melt off Trevor's body. Unfortunately, Joe had made seventeen more appear.

"Don't do what? I'm not doing anything," Joe replied. "Trevor's the one doing it. I'm sitting here enjoying my first weekend with you guys in three weeks and he's being an asshole."

"*I'm* the asshole?" Trevor shouted, arms flying forward, hands clenched, an instinctive response. Joe just stretched again, the gesture a little too practiced. Trevor knew Joe was just as on alert, as primed for a ripping fight, and that knowledge made him unleash.

"Yep," Joe said.

Darla put one hot, dry palm on Trevor's chest, her sweet pressure making him tingle all over, but it wasn't enough. "Let's go out for coffee and talk," she declared, as if it were a done deal, as if she could paper over the fact that—

"You want out?" Trevor challenged. "You want to break this up?"

The room turned to ice. Darla's jaw dropped and her mouth made a little O of shock that made Trevor's balls crawl up into his groin.

Shit. He'd said it.

He'd finally fucking *said* it.

And man, did he wish he could take it back.

Because Joe suddenly wasn't so casual anymore. All the color had drained from Joe's face, and it gave him a sickly, nothing-to-lose look, his face all hard angles and his lips tight with steely fury.

Whatever came out of his mouth next would change life as they knew it.

Leave it to Darla to interrupt, of course. "Don't you dare say one word, Joe!" she said in a harsh voice, her tone high and thin, panicked and desperate. "You two are insufferable, and I won't let you keep doing this. You're going with me to lunch tomorrow and talking to Mike and Dylan about—"

"*What?*" he and Joe shouted in unison, the first time they'd had the same reaction to anything since, well...since they'd met Darla.

She wasn't backing down, though. Her breasts bobbed hypnotically as she gestured wildly, and all Trevor could think about, suddenly, was how those nipples tightened with the lightest whisper of touches, how the heft of those globes filled his hands—overfilled them—as if they were made for holding. Like an ornament, but one that was warm and willing. An image of a baby snuggled up tight against her chest flashed through his mind, and he shook his head like a dog that got wet, banishing the unexpected intrusion.

What the fuck? Where did *that* thought come from?

"You two are like old Boyd and Jersey back home," she spat out with disgust. Trevor was only half paying attention, his brain buzzing from what he'd just been thinking.

"Oh, great," Joe drawled in a fake Southern accent that sounded more like a drunk German pretending to speak Chinese. "We git ourselves zome hometown good-ole-boy ztories!"

Darla's face fell into a mask of cold anger. "You sound like Hitler on acid when you do that. I do *not* sound like that."

"You sound close enough."

"No, she doesn't," Trevor added, coming to her defense. Her accent was slight. Not as broad as it had been when she'd moved to Boston to join them. It wasn't even that there was a strong difference in how they pronounced words, but more her lazy use of grammar, her little colloquial sayings, and the tendency to drop the "g" at the ends of words when she got excited or upset.

As her voice became more cultured he found himself wistful for the broad, open mouth she'd had when they met.

Except right now that mouth was aimed at him and Joe, and boy was she letting 'er rip.

"Yes, she does." Joe stood abruptly and threw on a pair of jeans, tucking his junk down so he didn't pull a *There's Something About Mary* moment and zip himself in pain.

"No, she—wait!" Trevor barked, eyes on Darla's face this time, tempting as her tits were. "We're not sitting at a table across from Thor and Angry Firefighter and pouring out our feelings and shit."

"I never said that's what you'd—"

Joe and Trevor snorted at the same time, the sound like melody and harmony, in perfect tune. Darla was outnumbered here. Whatever plan she was hatching was so outrageous that Trevor couldn't even fathom why she'd want him and Joe to get together with—

Ah. Got it.

"You think because they're in a threesome we need to have a therapy session with some old dudes who have been there, done that, fallen off the bed during DP and have the scars to prove it?"

This time Joe snorted alone.

"Because I am not talking about what we do with anyone. This is *us*. This is private. This is"—Trevor's hands twitched and curled into questioning fists—"this is whatever it is, but it's not something anyone else has. It doesn't need to be analyzed or dissected or picked apart, damn it." His voice went low. "And besides, why the hell would two billionaires give a fucking shit about what their employee's boyfriends do?"

He expected Darla to pause, to be shocked into silence, to do anything but what she did next. "See? See there? Right there? Boyfriends. Zzzzz. With an 's.' Who in the ever-loving hell has boyfriend*s*? And I don't mean the women who fuck two men in serial—I mean who fucks men in parallel and has a relationship that's all about balance and meeting two men's needs while—" Her voice hitched and she stopped, eyes shining with unspilled tears, and Trevor's heart folded in on itself in that moment.

Fuck.

"So"—she sniffed, a sob in her throat so loud it made Joe and Trevor share a look of worry—"forgive me for wanting you to talk to the only two fucking human beings on the planet who might have a goddamned clue what to do and how to be like this. It ain't working right now with Joe's jealousy."

"I'm not—"

"And quit denying you're jealous, because you walk around like a puckered butthole that just got bleached and treated to road rash," she added.

252

Trevor's anus clenched involuntarily at her words. The woman could use vocabulary the way martial artists used nunchucks—with great skill, well-honed instinct, and ruthless efficiency.

Joe's look almost made Trevor laugh, and he would have if he weren't filled with a swirl of emotion. Too many things were being thrown out there like emotional debris after a wrecking ball hit the wrong building, and being naked and watching Darla's lush, creamy nude body in the middle of the chaos didn't help either. Trevor had a limit, and it had been reached in every possible way—emotionally, sexually, physically.

Joe spoke. "You can be such a—" The room turned to a freezer. Joe was about to call Darla a name, and Trevor jumped in front of her as if he needed to physically shield her, protect her from the B-word, as if he could take it into his own chest and let his body act as armor against what he knew Joe was about to unleash and could never, ever take back.

"—busybody!" Joe ground out. He flinched as Trevor appeared in front of him, and Darla's hand on Trevor's back was shaking. She squeezed. Did she expect it, too? When had the world become so charged, so unsafe? They were each other's sanctuary, the three of them, and somehow everything spiraled out of control within minutes of sharing their bodies and hearts.

Weren't you supposed to be able to share until the outer limits of what defined you were stretched beyond recognition, yet still come back more whole than ever before? Wasn't that the entire point of love?

"Why are you jumping in front of her like a spider monkey on crack?" Joe snapped. "You're acting like I'm some sort of...like I was going to..." His brows knitted in confusion and pain. "What the fuck did you think I was about to do, Trev?" He planted his hands on his hips and took a deep breath, the power of his chest expanding in a way that felt threatening suddenly.

Trevor moved closer, eyes boring into Joe's. "I thought you were about to lash out at her and do something you'd regret."

All the anger in Joe drained out of him, leaving eyes that were bleak and vulnerable. It made Trevor go cold with regret.

"Darla," Joe said softly, "do you think I'd...do that? Hurt you?"

"God, no. Not physically! No!" Trevor rushed to explain. "You just look like—"

"No." Darla's single word thundered through the room, the declaration a thunderclap of certainty that Trevor welcomed. He and Joe shuddered, as if her word recalibrated them, and Trevor felt his body tense in one big, long chain of muscles, like an orgasm without sex, as if he clenched and realigned every bone, every muscle, each tendon and fiber now back in place.

She had that effect on them.

And only Darla could do that.

"You can make fun of me for being a hick," she said, holding up a hand to stem the inevitable protest that Joe started to put up, "and you can be a crabby jerk because you're too uptight to admit that you hate law school and hate the life you've chosen at Penn, but don't know how to find your way out of the straightjacket of your parents' expectations for you," she said to Joe in a calm, slow, deliberate voice that made her seem timeless and wizened, mature and all-knowing. It made Trevor relaxed and self-conscious at the same time.

"But," she added, eyes combing over Joe, then Trevor, then back to Joe. The gooseflesh she left on Trevor's body came from the timbre of her voice, the cadence of a rock-hard declaration that neither of them dared challenge. "But—you do not get to ruin what we have just because you're afraid of what you don't know." Her eyes flashed and flicked between the two of them. *I mean you too*, she was saying to Trevor.

And he knew it.

"We're going to Jeddy's tomorrow," she said, pulling on Harvard-logo yoga pants and one of Trevor's oversized flannel shirts, eyes locked on Joe while she did the buttons. "And you'll sit across the table from Mike and Dylan and ask them how the fuck they figured this shit out ten years ago when they met their first woman. Because those two know something. They know something you two don't."

"What's that?" Joe croaked out. It made Trevor cringe.

"They know what it's like to fall in love in all the weird ways love gives you, and they know what it's like to have it all taken away not by someone's stupidity, but by the cruel randomness of cancer."

Trevor just blinked.

"They lost Jill and didn't have a choice. And then they got a second chance with Laura. Look at 'em. A happy family."

Trevor flashed back to the image of a baby at Darla's breast, and he held his breath. Her green eyes caught his, one corner of her mouth crooking up as if she read his mind.

"You want...*that*?" Joe choked out.

Trevor and Darla both looked at him. Trevor's mind seized up.

Darla took two, three, four measured breaths, unhurried and unworried, her placid outer self scaring Trevor more than anything she was about to say.

And then:

"I don't want...this. Which means you two had better go talk with Mike and Dylan and figure out how they manage to have a strong threesome relationship without making everyone feel like an obstacle. Going through life feeling like you're doing something wrong all the time with the people you're supposed to be most attached to isn't my idea of living."

And with that, she shut the door quietly, leaving Trevor and Joe in complete silence.

They were both holding their breath.

ALEX

How Josie talked him into this one would remain a mystery. Jeddy's was Jeddy's, the cracked red vinyl seats and the veneer-topped Formica tables still the same. Alex knew that Madge was fighting her grandson, Caleb, tooth and nail over every change he tried to make, because during the dinners he had with his grandpa and Madge, he heard about it.

Ad infinitum. She was eighty-four years old, had just weathered a heart attack this year, and kept his grandfather, Ed, busy with a sex life that Alex preferred not to know about. She also cared for Ed with such grace and tenderness that it made Alex tear up—in an entirely manly way, of course—to see how love could extend into the outer decades of life with a depth and authenticity that he hoped to have one day with Josie.

Who was currently grousing about his taking more room in her pantry than was fair.

"It's not like your food is *bigger* than mine," she hissed as they picked a booth. "It's just that you buy more and are hogging the space. I have to keep cereal on top of the fridge now, and I hate that. It's a little too Seinfeld for me," she added as Madge approached them with what passed for a smile these days.

"How are my two favorite lovebirds?" Madge asked. Alex stood and folded in half to give her a hug, his hands pressing into her back and measuring the change. Madge had lost weight since her cardiac episode, and Ed had asked Alex if he could recommend the absolute best cardiologist in Boston to make sure "his Madge" was around at least for the rest of Ed's life.

At least.

Alex had assured his grandpa that Madge already had the best of the best, but the fear in Ed's eyes had been so haunting it kept him up at night, staring at the ceiling fan in Josie's—now *their*—bedroom on the rare nights he wasn't stuck at the hospital.

Love might conquer all, but mortality was an interfering bitch.

And no matter how hard he tried, medical science couldn't beat death. But it could give it a run for its money.

"We're roommates now," Josie complained, standing slowly to give Madge a hug, too. She wasn't the affectionate type with anyone but him, and he always noticed the look in Josie's eyes when social niceties like hugs and handshakes were called for, as if she knew there was a protocol but couldn't quite nail the sequence. When his own mother, Meribeth, swept into a room with kisses and hugs, Josie looked like a helpless foreigner drop-shipped into a new country with an alphabet you couldn't even read.

Mom accepted it as she did everything—with equanimity and a tiny dose of worry for Alex.

"You're shacking up. Deal with it. Let yourself be happy. Your friend Laura manages it somehow, and she's got to please two men," Madge said after Josie gave her an anemic embrace. Alex watched Madge's swift movements, the coffee appearing before them as if conjured by a magic spell, a tiny tray of miniature deserts proffered before them.

"Yeah, but she's got two billionaires."

Alex pretended to be offended. "You want me to turn into a billionaire? I would think being a physician would be enough of a superpower."

"*Pffft*." The sound Josie made was distinctly unfeminine. "I've worked with hundreds of doctors over the years. You're all extremely human. Some are even subhuman. Give you a scalpel and you might be God for a few hours, but you all snore and drool and *hog cabinet space* like us mere mortals."

"I don't think you're quite human, Josie," Madge declared. "Look at that plate of delicious new desserts Caleb made. How can someone sit here and have that in front of their face and ignore it?"

Josie's eyes narrowed, making Alex laugh. She was so suspicious, and he knew her cranky outer shell just hid a soft, tender underbelly of vulnerability. "What are these? They look like little lobster cakes."

"They are!" Madge cracked in a South Boston accent, the words coming out sound like she'd said "They ah!"

"Red cake with…"

"It's pureed strawberries in a rich white cake, baked in little lobster molds, then filled with a vanilla amaretto cream." "Lobster" sounded like "lobstah" coming from her mouth.

"What's the glaze in the little cup next to it?" Alex asked. Each lobster cake had a little Boston Red Sox flag stabbed into the head.

"Toffee-caramel sauce—see how it looks like drawn butter?" Madge demonstrated for them, picking up a lobster and dunking its head in the sauce, then munching happily. The cake was headless, one claw hanging by a thin thread of confection.

Josie imitated Madge, and as her tongue poked out between her lips, mouth stretching into a smile of anticipation, Alex felt something in him harden and soften at the same time.

God, he loved her.

She moaned. "This is so good!" As she bit down, a rush of cream from the cake's center coated her lip, making the hard part of him even harder as she licked it away.

God, he *wanted* her.

Instead of reaching across the table and fucking her right there next to the little jukebox screwed into the wall above the salt and pepper shakers, he grabbed a cake, dipped the entire damn thing in sauce, and shoved it into his mouth, chewing furiously, hoping the blood that would be diverted to his digestive tract would lessen his raging erection.

Then his taste buds kicked in. The combination of thick, lush cake, the almond flavor of the amaretto, and the viscous toffee assaulted the pleasure centers in his brain, stomach engaged, salivary enzymes kicked into overdrive, the groan of gustatory ecstasy as involuntary as his hard-on.

"Jesus, tell Caleb he's outdone himself," Alex muttered as he and Josie both reached for the only remaining lobster on the plate.

Oh, no.

This would not end well. He normally deferred to her, but this was primal. His stomach growled; he'd come to the diner hungry and ready for lunch, and, unlike Josie, he couldn't eat a few bites of something and be temporarily sated. Once his stomach had a single bite of food in it he needed to have enough for a full meal immediately.

There was no turning back. Her eyes flashed as she reached for the lobster, but he beat her to it.

And then she snatched the ramekin of toffee-caramel sauce.

They were at an impasse.

And neither would back down.

Madge cackled. "He's got another tray of them in the back, you two. No need to launch World War III over a stupid piece of cake." She popped the other half of her piece into her mouth and munched happily.

"We'd like a dozen for here, and a dozen to go," Alex said, not moving, eyes tracking Josie, who lifted the cup of sauce to her lips and pretended to suck at it. She became increasingly X-rated in her movements and he shifted uncomfortably in his seat, his blood obviously tormenting him. It did not cooperate and flee his groin for his stomach, but instead filed in an orderly fashion from root to tip, making his shaft throb with unmet need.

Two nights now of overnight shifts at the hospital. This was the first time he'd seen Josie for nearly three days.

And they had to spend it talking with other people about their sex lives. Threesome sex lives. Josie had spelled it out clearly: he would "facilitate" the conversation between Mike, Dylan, Trevor, and Asshole.

Er, *Joe*.

A tray of these cakes would make it easier. Maybe if he sank into a sugar coma he could get through it. He didn't relish being shoved into the role of group therapy leader for a bunch of guys who were about as interested in being there as Josie was in becoming a submissive wife some day.

But he would do it because she had asked him—pleaded and cajoled—and sweetly explained that she was so worried about Laura and Darla that this was the

261

only option she could think of. It was a rare flash of emotional intimacy that he craved, and as she'd unfolded before him, pure and true, he couldn't say no.

The front door creaked open, and in walked the only man he knew who was as tall as himself, followed by a flash of blond hair at his armpit, then a darker man in between their heights. The first threesome was here, and he let out a huge sigh of relief, surprised by his own reaction. For whatever reason, it was easier to talk first to Mike, Dylan, and Laura than to the younger group.

"Younger" made him cringe inside, because they were only seven years his junior, and yet Trevor, Darla and Ass—er, Joe—were a generation away, it seemed sometimes.

"Hey," Mike said in that casual, nearly stoic way he had, wearing the Zen of calmness so well.

Alex stood up to shake hands and realized he was still holding the lobster cake. Josie plucked it from his fingers in the split second he was distracted, then shoved it down the front of her shirt.

"Hah! Mine now."

He leaned down and murmured in her ear, "If we weren't in public I'd retrieve that with my teeth."

"Oh, really?" She took the cake out of her shirt and pretended to slip it in the front of her pants, making him belly-laugh.

Laura looked at them with an expression of curiosity and pure happiness, so pleased, he knew, that her best friend had found what he hoped was enough. Sometimes the relationship seemed a little too easy. He liked all of her friends, got along well with Darla, and Josie didn't mind living the life of a partner to a doctor who was gone most of the time.

Other than her asking him to play Dr. Phil to a group of men who didn't want to be there, his life with Josie was pretty damn perfect these days. The moving-in-together business had a few bumps—mostly Josie's ego and her weird wall of fear that he would somehow smother her with love—but otherwise it was just fine.

Better than fine.

He thought that was how Laura, Mike, and Dylan lived. Fine. Better than fine. If he and Josie had an annual income bigger than that of the starting lineup for the Boston Celtics, they'd be waaaay better than fine. Aside from a mountain of student loan debt, though, their financial future looked solid enough, and he wasn't complaining.

Dylan's hand shot out, fast and strong, his grip like a vise made from titanium. Damn. Alex squared his shoulders during the handshake, drawing on core strength to match the ex-firefighter's tight clasp. Both men smiled, and Dylan's eyes flitted away, fast, as if he weren't quite convinced this meeting was a good idea.

Alex had to agree with him.

Laura gave him a warm hug that reminded him of his own mother's embraces, sweet and confident, caring and pure. You knew where you stood with them both, knew you were welcomed and appreciated exactly as you were. No pretense, no airs, no affect.

That was refreshing.

Josie was a skittish little dog by comparison when he watched her give out hugs and handshakes, her body trembling a bit, as if all the kinetic energy drained her muscles and bones to the point of the shakes, removing some essence that made her come unglued. Time would improve it, he hoped, but it pained him to watch her struggle with something so casual and social, a little bit of protocol that he didn't think twice about.

Someone's arms opened and you went in for the brief connection. A kiss on the cheek was a nice gesture. A handshake was a hello.

But for her, it all seemed to be land mines. When they were done, he would take her back to her—*their*—apartment and fix her a drink, and they would succumb to a few episodes of whatever new season of television she'd discovered, binge watching on the couch until their imaginations were full of someone else's life, one easier to digest and analyze. Her nervousness would be purged and he would touch her in ways that charged her batteries, deepened their intimacy, and made life more comfortable for her.

An island of two.

That was for later, though. Right now, he had reluctant alpha men he was supposed to corral into some sort of pseudo-therapy masquerading as lunch. And he had to act like he liked it. One cheesy grin coming up.

"You having a stroke, Alex?" Madge cracked as she settled Mike, Laura, and Dylan in the booth next to him and Josie. "You look like an altar boy who just drank all the communion wine."

The group laughed and he let them, though Josie gave him the side eye. "Just smiling," he said in as bland a tone as possible. The tip of Josie's toe bounced against his shin. She fidgeted like this when she got nervous, and mistook his leg for part of the table.

"Cut it out, then," Madge said. "You look creepy."

"I look creepy when I smile?"

"When you smile like that."

The grin faded all too quickly as the front door jingled, opened by three people, two of whom he liked and one he could do without.

"Josie!" Darla squealed as she rushed in and took over the room. Her eyes were big and wide as she looked around Jeddy's.

"You act like you've never been here," Josie said, taking in Darla.

"Not in the daylight, and not sober. Is the food good? Last time we were here I was so drunk I thought I ordered deep-fried Kit Kats dipped in tartar sauce."

"You did," Madge said dryly.

"And you *let* her?" Alex asked.

Madge shrugged. "Can't stop stupid. If I did, we wouldn't have two-thirds of our customers." She gave Dylan a hard look that made him do a double take.

"What does that look mean?" he asked.

"Whatever you want it to mean," she said sweetly. A little too sweetly, while patting Dylan gently on the cheek and then marching away to seat an eight-top group that had just come in.

Dylan gave everyone perplexed looks. "Why does she pick on me?"

Darla scooched in next to Josie and flashed Dylan a grin. "I've heard she only does that if she secretly likes you."

"Or is preparing to use you in a ritual druidic ceremony as a blood sacrifice," Mike deadpanned.

"Not sure which is worse," Dylan mumbled.

Laura elbowed him playfully in the ribs. "Hi, Darla!" she said with a chirp that was a little too friendly. Alex gave Trevor a nod and a wave, then extended the same courtesy to Joe, who hovered above the group, stiff as a board and with a face you could turn into a kitchen counter. It was polished granite, without a trace of personality, and hard as could be.

And where all the worst messes took place.

Trevor, on the other hand, was all friendly smiles and handshakes, though Alex sensed a bit of apprehension in him as well. Darla's voice was just a notch too loud, half a standard deviation off center, just nervous enough to make him wonder what in the hell these six (seven, including Josie) expected from today's talks.

He knew one thing, though: they expected great food. And would get it.

Madge cruised by. "No need for menus. I have Caleb cooking up a collection of everything."

"Everything?" the group intoned together, then laughed. All except Joe, who just stood there, bugging Alex more and more by the second.

"Everything you could want," Madge added. "Coconut shrimp, our new strawberry lobsters, the toffee pistachio crepes..."

Laura pretended to wipe drool from her mouth. "Yum."

"And the same old crappy coffee." Madge slid a series of carafes and white mugs their way, followed by a practiced swish of the hand as she sailed two pitchers of cream on the tables like a champion shuffleboard player.

"How do you do that?" Laura asked. Alex dug into his coffee, needing whatever fortification he could have for what was coming.

"Do what?"

"Slide it down the table so not one drop of cream is wasted."

"Practice. Lots of practice." Madge winked and disappeared. The scent of something garlicky wafted through the restaurant, followed by a distinct fryolater sound, like hot oil being breached by an ascending whale.

"That woman is a machine," Mike said in admiration.

Alex frowned slightly, then tried to shake it off, but Laura—always perceptive—caught the micro-change in him. She reached for his hand and frowned. "What? I know she had a heart attack recently…"

He didn't want to violate Madge's privacy, so he played it simple. "She's fine." His shaky smile must have been as bad as Madge had thought, because Laura's look of alarm didn't make matters any better.

"Is she in bad shape?" Laura asked, persistent. The tone of their private conversation must have been such that it set everyone on edge, because suddenly more sets of eyes were on him. Darla sat next to Josie across from him, and Trevor next to her. Joe stood at the end of the booth, while Mike had sat next to Alex. Laura and Dylan were right behind them, in the low booths, her neck twisted.

"Nothing more than simple age. She isn't immortal. None of us is."

"That old bat will outlive Jillian," Dylan said, clear as a bell. Darla snickered and Trevor looked a bit confused, picking up a sweetener packet and worrying it with thickly calloused fingers.

Joe looked like a giant slab of polished iron.

"She might," Alex agreed. "I think my grandfather will have something to say about that, though. The two of them have plans for how they want to die."

Josie went a bit pale at Alex's words and buried her face in her coffee cup.

Laura picked up on that, too, her head ping-ponging between him and Josie. "What? Say it." She bore down on Josie, who looked like she wanted to turn into a million tiny pieces and disappear on the wind. She kicked but missed his ankle.

"Ow!" Mike yelped, reaching down. "Wrong leg."

"Sorry. You both feel like you're part of the table underneath."

"That's what she said," Dylan drawled.

Everyone groaned.

Except Joe.

JOE

Five more minutes. Joe would give this farce five more minutes and then he'd march right out of here and go to the Thai place he loved down the street, stuff his face with noodles and chicken, and go back to the apartment to play with his bass and master the newest song in the Random Acts of Crazy set.

Not stare at Dr. Perfect Who Hated His Guts, the Secret Billionaires and their hot blonde, and Darla and Josie, yammering at each other like litter mates.

With big old surfer boy Trevor acting like some dopey teen out of a bad '80s sitcom they laughed at in reruns on Nickelodeon.

"Well," Josie said, stretching the word out. *Why didn't she have the same accent as Darla?* Joe wondered. "Ed told us that he and Madge plan to jump out of a plane and—I believe his exact words were—"

"Fuck like bunnies," Alex said, miserable as the table exploded with laughter.

"Without parachutes," Josie concluded. Joe gave a weak smile. Ha ha. How cute. Whatever. Old people smelled like rose-water and grease, and he avoided them as much as possible. Both sets of his grandparents had died when he was a toddler, so Madge was the equivalent of an alien life form to him.

Though naked fucking stunt diving sounded pretty rad. Add in a camera and a Twitch.tv streaming channel and it might be cool.

Darla had dragged them all here to talk with Mike and Dylan, and aside from thinking maybe—just maybe—he could salvage his time by being able to name-drop in a law clerk interview, or talk about scandal on a golf course, this afternoon was a complete time-sucking waste of air and thought.

At least he would get a piece of Jeddy's Boston cream pie. That was his only solace.

Happy fucking weekend break. These people were about as interesting as reading case law on transportation codes. In German.

Every single emotion he was capable of feeling had become unwoven, like a thick tapestry that turned into each individual thread, held in place by the memory of once having been intertwined with the others, but now free and unmoored. He carried inside himself a vague sense of once being able to live, day in and day out, within the chosen borders of this relationship with Darla and Trevor, but now...

He was just a pile of thread. A loose pile that added up to nothing solid.

Not that anyone could know that, though. These fuckers wouldn't make him talk about his pussified feelings, or—God forbid—get him to talk about how he felt so misunderstood, or make him into some new-agey confessional star like those dumbass television shows his mother adored. No way.

Somewhere in the Century of Selfies, society had gone off the rails, and Darla went right along for the ride, insisting he and Trevor join her in this lunch date, where she expected them to sit across from the human equivalent of a redwood and an Italian boxer dude who was half Rocky, half Joe Manganiello.

Was this how it would go? The three women would sit in one booth and breathlessly talk and joke about the five men in the other booth, segregated by gender like sixth-grade health class?

Not his idea of how he wanted to spend a precious weekend afternoon. In fact, he'd rather listen to his mother drone on about the latest research in medical genomics and how it related to his heart condition. His fingers involuntarily reached up and stroked the barest line of scar that he could feel through one layer of cotton. Most of the time he forgot about it, only three months old when the open-heart surgery took place.

His mom lived with it on the surface, as if she had been ripped open then, too. Except she'd never formed a scar. It was a sucking chest wound that lived outside her body. But that wasn't Joe's fault.

Why was he even thinking about this? His eyebrows twitched, and he felt the frown contract his muscles before he could control it. Darla picked up on the tiny change in his expression and tilted her head, trying to read him like tea leaves in the bottom of a cup.

"You okay?" she asked. He let his eyes close halfway, his only public reaction to the rush of *oh, shit* inside him, because all conversation ground to a halt, seven sets of eyes on him suddenly.

A whoosh of air behind him and there was that old waitress, delivering an impossibly large tray of food that made his salivary glands kick in.

Make that eight.

"You're the only thing standing between a plate or ten of coconut shrimp and that table, bud," Madge said. He moved swiftly, hands in his pockets, feeling like an obstacle. An obstruction.

An outsider.

The tray landed on the edge of the booth where Darla, Trevor, Josie, Alex, and Mike sat, and he watched as the old lady unloaded that food with such efficiency she might as well be a robot. Too bad his stomach had become a grinding mass of crushed glass and rusty nails, all churning in the flesh equivalent of a cement mixer.

"I'm fine," he said pointedly to Darla, answering her earlier question, as the waitress disappeared so fast she might as well have teleported herself across the restaurant. Darla, though, ignored him, her mouth hanging open, one hand waving air into it as she bit into a steaming piece of coconut shrimp that was obviously burning her mouth.

Joe reached for Trevor's wet glass of ice water and held it out to her. Grateful eyes met his as she gulped it down.

"Danks," she said. "I dink I burd my tug."

Dylan's laughter from the other booth was so loud, so raucous and unfiltered, that it seemed to help Joe's stomach unclench just enough to feel a moment of amusement, too. "That happens here," Dylan said, turning to look at Darla, who made a pouty face. "Occupational hazard."

"Occupational?" His voice surprised him. His smile surprised him more as he and Dylan looked at each other. "You guys professional diners now?"

"Something like that," Laura said, interrupting the flow while waving a fork that had what appeared to be a cheese-stuffed mushroom on it. "If I could do this for a living, I would."

But you can, Joe thought, but didn't say. Two billionaires and she couldn't just sit around and eat whatever she wanted, sampling the finest Boston—hell, the *world*—had to offer? Instead of doing that, she chose to run a threesome dating service where Darla and Josie worked?

Women. More complicated than, well... transportation code case law.

But infinitely more interesting. When he looked at Darla, that grinding cesspool inside his gut loosened just a little. Some day, he'd give her everything she wanted.

Unless it involved sitting at a booth and talking about his feelings with these men.

"How about we reconfigure?" Laura said in a voice that was both sweetness and light, and honed steel. There was no arguing with her, and the men stood, shuffling over to where Dylan sat, Laura picking up her plate and moving next to Josie, across from Darla. The other booth was bigger, U-shaped, and he waited until all the other guys were in place—Mike and Dylan in the middle, Trevor to Dylan's left, Alex to Mike's right—before grabbing a chair and turning it backwards, straddling it.

If he were just a tinge more paranoid he'd check the exits so he'd know where to bolt in the event of a true emotional meltdown.

And then his eyes did it.

Telling Darla he loved her, sexting and coming back for long weekends where the three of them went into the world they created, jamming with the band and coming back on long train rides for performances —those were part of the flow of life.

He didn't want to scrutinize who they were, what they were, too much, because then you had to pop that dome of perfection, where the three of them lived as if everything they did were right and okay.

As if society didn't exist.

His stomach betrayed him and growled. Alex pushed a plate of deep-fried cauliflower his way. "Try some. It's really good when you dip it in the aioli."

273

"Thanks." He did as suggested, and his mouth came to life. Damn. Jeddy's was a shithole he remembered from college years, and the food had been standard gut-rot back then. Cheese fries and shakes and bad coffee. Looking around as he munched, he took in the torn seats, the shabby, threadbare carpet, the stained ceiling tiles, the scuffed stainless steel edges of the main counter. The place looked like something he wouldn't set foot in. Too worn and broken for him. Too working class, too—

Authentic.

But you couldn't deny the nuanced skill of the cook in the kitchen, how the richness of what was offered contrasted with the run-down outer shell.

"This is amazing," he said as Trevor grunted in assent and shoved what must have been his fourth or fifth coconut shrimp in his mouth.

"I always forget about this place," Trev mumbled around chipmunk cheeks, then swallowed. Did the man chew?

"We practically live here," Dylan said pleasantly. "It was Laura's favorite restaurant when she was pregnant."

"And after," Mike added.

"And forever," she said from across the booth, sighing with satisfaction as the old waitress delivered a tray of what looked like tiny cannoli covered in what smelled like a maple glaze. "Thanks, Madge," she uttered through a mouthful to the old waitress.

Madge. He did a double take. The same Madge his mom talked about being here when *she* went to Radcliffe? That old lady must be a vampire. A second tray covered in tiny cannoli appeared like magic on their table. Trevor grabbed two and shoveled them in while the other guys took a more leisurely approach.

Joe wished his stomach would stop being so uncooperative.

Like you.

He was only doing this for Darla. She'd insisted, so angry at his jealousy. That, plus Laura was her boss. You do what the boss wants, even if you sneer behind her back while you do it. Not that Darla was like that —she really liked Laura. And so did he.

This entire lunch was the stupidest stunt he had been part of since they went to the island of Eden, though. And that place had been the epitome of stupid. And crazy.

The "I love yous" had been wonderful, and he'd thought he would come home and feel different, but instead he'd just been more forlorn. More torn.

Missed them more.

"We're supposed to talk about something," Mike said slowly, wiping his hands on a napkin and setting it neatly under his clean plate.

Joe rested his chin on his hands on the back of the chair and watched. He wasn't about to say a damn word. Not now. Not in that vast danger zone of being the first to crack. You couldn't shove a genie back in a bottle, no matter how hard you tried. His heart rubbed against one of the rods of the chair's back, a gentle pressure that grounded him.

"Sex," Dylan said as he finished off one of those cannoli.

"Sex?" Trevor choked on something, the painful sound of air being blocked triggering a weird wheeze that made Joe sit up, ramrod straight. Alex whacked him on the back and went blank, his face neutral, on complete alert in the way only a well-trained doctor could be.

Trevor made a strangled sound and then took in a huge whoop of air, eyes watering so badly Joe could see the tears run down his face as Trev dipped his head and reached for a glass of water—anyone's water—and drank it greedily, stopping only to breathe in hitched gulps.

"I'm okay," he rasped, holding up one hand to stem the expressions of concern, then hacking furiously.

"What's wrong?" Darla called out from the table next to them.

"We started to talk about sex and it made Trevor gag," Joe said quietly.

The entire group burst into laughter, making one side of Joe's mouth tip up in a reluctant grin. His heart hammered in his chest, skipping a beat here and there, otherwise pattering along at a healthy clip, his worry for Trevor fading as everything normalized into what passed for "normal" on this day.

Sex? They were going to talk about sex? He let out a huge sigh of relief. He thought they were going to talk about *feelings*.

MIKE

Poor kids. That was all Mike could think as he looked around the horseshoe table at Trevor and Joe. No, they weren't kids, and he remembered being twenty-three and hating being referred to as a kid. But now that he was ten-plus years out of that early adulthood phase, he couldn't help but view them as just that—kids.

Was it fair? No. Did he feel bad? Yes. He remembered that first year with Jill and Dylan, the tension between him and the cocky sonofabitch, how they were fluid and graceful, yet teeming with a swarm of emotion that didn't really settle until their third or fourth year together.

He didn't often let himself think about Jill these days, and the pang of pain that stabbed his heart was all too real. Jillian may have been her namesake, and he said the J word hundreds of times a day, but Jill was not Jillian.

And Laura was not Jill.

He had lived two different lives, truly. Before Jill. After Jill. Except it seemed unfair to Laura to call her something as simplistic as "After Jill," as if Jill were the standard by which time was marked.

Perhaps he should train his mind to think differently.

Before Laura.

After Laura.

Some part of him eased a little, a tiny obstacle removed, as the thought poured through and over him, providing a balm for a discomfort he didn't recognize, but that nonetheless had been in him, all-pervasive and omnipresent. Time was an elusive commodity these days, but even more elusive was time alone. With his thoughts. On the road, pounding out the confusion.

He hadn't gone for a run in four days, and that might as well have been an eternity for him. Coming here meant sacrificing what could have been ten miles of therapy, each footstep a confession, each stride a release.

Trevor's breathing went even just as Madge appeared with a tray of tiny red cakes shaped like lobsters, and a sundae bigger than his one-year-old daughter.

"What the hell is that?" Joe's exclamation made Mike smile. The Beefeater had cracked. Poor kid was wound tighter than a fishing line.

"It's The Orgy." Madge winked at Dylan, then dropped the grin for the two younger men. "Of all the tables to bring this to, I figured you guys would enjoy it."

Joe went pale as her words hit him. Alex tried not to laugh, while Dylan just picked up a spoon and stabbed at some kind of ice cream with peanut butter cups in it.

"Do we get an Orgy, too?" called out a voice from the other table. Darla. All five men turned in unison to find her eying Trevor and Joe with a coy innocence that made Mike, Dylan, and Alex chuckle.

Trevor and Joe just stared at her, and Mike felt less pity for him and Joe. A kindling of admiration began to form inside him. The way the three of them looked at each other gave him pause.

With no one else—*ever*—to talk about what he, Jill, and Dylan had created twelve years ago, he didn't have a roadmap. A pattern. A plan. They'd quite simply invented it all, from soup to nuts, those many years ago. He'd lost his parents—emotionally, for they'd cut him off when he'd finally told them the real nature of their relationship—and being left adrift like that from his family of origin had meant Dylan and Jill unfairly had to play two roles in his life, instead of the already single, complicated role they'd all chosen.

He watched Trevor return to his food, but Joe's eyes remained on Darla, the flicker of his upper lids moving, widening slightly, the only way to measure the guy's emotions. He was such a pressure cooker. Mike saw a little of himself in Joe—the self he'd been in college, a bundle of negativity stewing in itself, trying to break free but chained by his own expectations.

While Joe could easily pass for Dylan's younger brother, and Trevor was a shorter version of Mike (and that, alone, was disquieting), the personalities were swapped. Trevor was more like Dylan had been years ago, and Mike saw his former self in Joe.

God help him. The awakening that was coming—if Joe had the courage to go inward and explore the richness that the intimacy with Trevor and Darla could bring—would be a supernova. Cataclysmic and soul churning. Would Joe, Darla, and Trevor make it through to the other side?

Who knew?

Suddenly, he realized why this meeting was so important to Laura. And Darla. And especially Josie.

And it filled him with a resonating grief and comfort that made him fight back tears.

"I count twelve scoops of ice cream in there, seven sauces, four different kinds of cookies, and a bunch of

Thin Mints," Darla called out as Madge shot past. "Where's my Orgy?"

Mike coughed hard, clearing his throat and covering the massive wave of emotion that threatened to render him useless today. This was harder than he'd thought. The relationship between him, Dylan, and Laura was stronger than ever, and the addition of Cyndi as a nanny had opened up time for the three of them to reconnect consistently, to get a sense of equanimity, to revel in the joy of intimacy and laughter, of sensuality and bonds that made their family so much stronger.

He never imagined he could have this back in those early days when just wanting Jill and Dylan, wanting what he *wanted*, was considered so subversive that, in the end, it cost him his parents.

Being true to himself had meant losing the very people who created him.

Which was a bit like losing God.

Over the years he'd tracked his parents through understanding and loving family members who either didn't know the truth about the rift, or knew and didn't care. Mom was still working and Dad had retired. Did they know about his life at all? Had the news channel stories and the newspaper articles trickled out to them?

They'd never reached out. Not once. After being raised in such a conservative, religious household he'd been frightened to tell the truth, and it turned out he'd been right.

All too right.

For them, their beliefs and faith formed a core so solid they couldn't let him be himself without it shattering their view of the world. When the two came into conflict, they'd chosen—

Not him.

Joe was going through the same thing. Mike softened, watching the younger man, knowing that the anger that simmered inside came from a deep fear of rejection. Of not meeting expectations. Of not being good enough.

Of never, *ever* being good enough.

Dylan hadn't been that way. Some part of him had always been casual, letting problems roll off his back, remaining more centered, more stable in the face of challenge. And Dylan's parents—as staunchly Catholic as they were—had been more understanding of the truth about Dylan, Mike, and Jill. While they hadn't been unconditionally accepting, they'd been bemused, a bit awkward, but never seeming to invalidate their son for simply loving a different way.

The hum of fear that radiated off Joe touched Mike on a new frequency, and he slid the sundae toward him with a smile. "Dig in."

"I'm not really that hungry," Joe answered, though he smiled back.

"Not a fan of orgies?" Trevor joked.

"Ha ha. I *did* go to Eden," Joe shot back, grabbing a chocolate wafer cookie and absent-mindedly gnawing on it.

Dylan nudged Mike and pulled him over to whisper, "What's Eden? And what's up with Joe?"

"No clue about Eden," Mike whispered. "But remember me in college?"

Dylan stiffened. "Yeah. That bad?"

Mike held back a snort. "That bad."

"That why Laura wants us here? To try to help?"

Mike sighed. "I don't know, but I think it's a fool's game. I wouldn't have talked to anyone back then. Only you and Jill."

281

Dylan nodded. "And even then, you were a fucking asshole."

"We've gone over this before," Mike said tightly. He didn't need his nose rubbed in it.

"That time you told us we were abominations and that there was something wrong with Jill for wanting us both at the same time was a blast," Dylan threw out there, making Mike cringe.

"You really want to run through an inventory of stupid things we've done over time? Because I have a list with your name on it, too."

Mike sensed a change at the table and broke away from his whispered talk with Dylan to find Alex, Joe, and Trevor all licking ice cream-covered spoons and watching them carefully.

They both stared back.

Alex broke the silence, poking his thumb toward the tri-headed, huddled mass at the booth next to them. It was clear to Mike that Josie, Darla, and Laura were not bonding *only* over ice cream and caramel sauce. The whispered gasps made him extra curious, but he knew how this worked.

While Laura might share intimate details with her friends, she'd never share *what* she shared with him and Dylan.

And that was that.

He hadn't talked with any man other than Dylan about what he did in the bedroom—or in his heart—in...

Ever.

Never, once, had he been the guy who talked about conquests. In college he'd kept his damn mouth shut about sex, because what he wanted and what everyone else wanted diverged wildly. Better to act like he was one of them than to risk being labeled a deviant.

At least with Dylan and Jill they'd been deviants together.

Safety in numbers.

A decade of adjustment and two years with Laura now meant his headspace was a lot clearer, and he could talk more openly if pressed, but as Joe folded in on himself with Alex's words, and as the food dwindled down to table scraps (mostly from Trevor, who had the appetite of a thirteen-year-old boy with hollow legs and a tapeworm), the anticipation of what was coming made all the men seem disturbed. Rattled.

Deeply uncomfortable.

Mike included.

Dylan, on the other hand, stretched his arms wide with a yawn, muscles bulging, and then kept his arms high, though never touching Mike or Trevor.

"Who wants to talk about dicks and holes? Lube? Sex toys? How about swings that don't have cheap clamps that break while you're in the middle of—"

Madge walked right up behind Joe with eyebrows high. Alex turned bright red at her appearance, and Mike bit the inside of his cheek to avoid laughing. Trevor was flushed, like an errant schoolboy.

Dylan just stared her down.

"You need to get a good quality beam clamp. One that can hold..." Her eyes catalogued Mike, then Dylan, and finally flitted over to Laura. "Can hold a good seven hundred pounds or more. Not hard. Just go to White's Hardware and explain that you need one that can handle lots of wear and tear and that kind of weight load. If Dmitri's there, tell him Madge sent you." She winked. "He'll know exactly why you're there."

Joe pushed his plate away from the table and kept his head low, as if the old woman would smack him upside the head if he brought any attention to himself.

Dylan wasn't cowed. "Seven hundred pounds? How big is your grandpa?" he asked Alex with a giant, shit-eating grin on his face.

"Oh, not from Eddie," she answered, laughing and placing a friendly hand on Alex's shoulder. "From... before him." Her voice went low, and Dylan just laughed.

Alex looked like a statue. A closed-eyed, post-apocalyptic statue who remained stoic in the face of complete, soul-sucking destruction. Mike imagined that thinking about his grandfather's sex life was about as appetizing as tea-bagging the old Warlock Waitress cardboard cutout.

"Madge, could you please not talk about my grandfather and sex in front of me? We've talked about this before," Alex said in a voice that sounded like broken guitar strings. He let out a long, hot sigh, and Mike was surprised by Madge's reaction.

She looked *chastened*.

Dylan sat straight up and folded his hands in his lap, staring at Alex like he was a god.

Someone had made Madge *behave*?

"For you, sweet Alex, I'll stop." She touched his cheek and strode into the kitchen, then shouted, "Caleb, get out those penis molds! We need to make more lobster cakes!"

"Your grandfather is a lucky man," Mike joked, ribbing Alex. He got an anemic smile in return.

"Your grandpa is Madge's boyfriend?" Trevor asked.

Alex just nodded.

"Holidays must be really fun. The dinner conversation. Does she bring a strap-on to the table?" Dylan asked.

Alex threw a sugar packet at him.

The atmosphere had changed just enough to make everyone relax slightly, an odd reaction to geriatric sex toy jokes, but hey—they'd take what they could get. That locker-room jocularity that Mike never understood descended over the group, Dylan and Trevor most comfortable with it, Alex somewhere in the middle, and Mike and Joe bewildered, it seemed, if Mike was reading the younger man right.

"You ever been in a threesome relationship before?" Dylan asked Joe directly.

Joe's mouth dropped open, and Mike was sure pea soup was about to pour out of it.

"First time. We're cherries," Trevor said as he dragged half a red lobster cake through a congealed mass of melted ice cream and marshmallow sauce, then shoved it in his mouth. The guy must have the metabolism of a hummingbird.

"Cherries," Joe echoed.

"And so far, so good?"

Joe just nodded. Mike resisted the urge to roll his eyes. Dylan was being cagey and coy on purpose, making a mockery of the entire scene. What was next? Talk about the weather?

"Look," Mike said, leaning forward. All four men leaned with him. "This isn't exactly the easiest conversation to have," he added in a hushed tone. Out of the corner of his eye he saw Madge gently push on Darla's shoulder, the younger woman giving her a WTF? look, but sliding in, turning their three-top into a four-top. Mike's curiosity opened to full throttle, but he was trapped.

Had to deal with the drama in front of him, no matter how interesting the drama next door was.

"We can just pretend," Joe said in a voice full of contempt, the scoff so strong Mike could feel it scrape against his skin. "They don't have to know we didn't really talk about...you know..."

"Being in a threesome?" Dylan's voice made Joe flinch. That seemed to be Dylan's goal.

Mike was starting to see how this would all play out if they didn't take control.

"Yes," Trevor said in a long sigh. "Being in a threesome. But Joe doesn't like the fact that I'm around. He wants Darla to himself."

"Not true!" Joe hissed.

Trevor made a noise of disgust. "You're fucking jealous, dude, and you won't admit it."

"If I were the jealous type I wouldn't be in a—"

"Threesome." All four of them said it in unison. Joe's lips pursed, jaw clenched so hard his teeth could cut fiberoptic cable.

"Threesome," he mimicked back. "It's not like I can't say it."

"Have you said it to your parents?" Mike asked softly.

The haunted eyes that met his looked like the soul's mirror. He couldn't have been more different from Joe in physique, coloring, carriage, and mannerisms, but he was staring into the eyes of his emotional twin for that split second.

"No. Hell no."

DYLAN

ucky bastards. That was all he could think as he took good, long looks at Trevor and Joe. Ten or more years separated them, and an endless sea of experience. Trevor and Joe had youth and time on their side, and everything coming up would be new. Fresh. Exciting and unknown.

A cornucopia of opportunity awaited them, two young rock-star law students who had everything going for them.

He envied them deeply.

It wasn't that he would change one bit of his life right now. He adored Laura, and he and Mike were... well...they just *were*. That wouldn't change—not ever. Jillian was the light of his life, and now that they had a great nanny, Laura had relaxed. Chilled.

Warmed up, actually. Sex returned, the bright, brilliant spark of a really good fuck no longer something to count down for the rare moment, but a dependable source of fun and love. This was the phase of life he had signed up for, the rich, multilayered realm of settling down, barbecuing in the backyard, hanging with his (not quite) wife and kid and Mike, and it was everything he wanted.

Until he looked across the table and saw what youth could bring.

The entire lunch was a game to him, a silly joke that he'd indulged in because Laura asked him to be here, asked him and Mike to talk to these guys. Talk?

About what? Trevor was an overeager puppy and Joe was like Mike back in college, an unstable rageball who seemed to think that a hard edge on his own skin would keep him from getting hurt. Mike had made the same mistake when they'd met years ago, and it had been Jill who had softened him, working inside, worming her way into his heart.

Dylan had been along for the ride back then, breezy and fun, all about the party. He could sniff one out, or create a wild, fun scene with two people and enough beer and ganja. While Mike had needed someone to crack him open, Dylan had needed gravity. Someone to tether him.

Jill had been their touchstone, the keeper of truths and saver of souls.

Did Darla serve that purpose—that mission, really —for these two young fools in front of him? Who knew. None of his business, right? Laura was making it *her* business, though, to stick her nose into the younger threesome's business, prodded by Josie.

Josie. Don't even get him started. Bane of his existence and, somehow, also one of the best things to happen to Laura. Their friendship kept her going in ways he and Mike would never understand, so while he was grateful to Laura's friend, did she have to be such an interfering pain in the ass?

"You afraid?" Dylan asked as silence reigned after Joe's declaration that hell no, he hadn't told his parents about his threesome.

"Yes." The answer was instantaneous, almost involuntary, and Trevor jolted. Dylan bit back a wry grin. He knew that feeling, too. Partnering with someone who was so cagey and confusing, hard to read yet teeming with anger, and at the same time so...right for you...meant accepting that you were going to be shocked.

A lot.

Because you never knew what was coming next, and you expected negativity. The vulnerable moments were the ones you lived for, though—because that was where the other person's heart showed itself.

And why you stayed.

"Good." Mike's voice was flat and even, warm and tempered. Like he knew he was talking to a spooked animal. That's all Joe was. A spooked, naïve kid who was in way over his head for the first time in his life.

Same as he and Mike had been back when they'd come together with Jill.

"Good?" Joe scoffed, the mask descending like a trapdoor. "What do you mean, 'good'? It's good to be afraid of my own parents?"

"No, it's not," Mike said, pouring himself another coffee. His deliberate, steady motions were part of a general approach he was taking. "But it's good to be realistic." Anyone else wouldn't catch the meaning behind Mike's words, but Dylan did. On the surface, what he said was what he meant.

Underneath? He had experienced that fear, faced it, anyway, and his fears had come true.

"Why?" Joe's single-word question shot out toward Mike like a bullet. Part challenge, part insistence, part threat, it made Dylan clench his hands instinctively, as if he needed to prepare for a fight.

"Why?" Mike pitched forward on his elbows, face tipped up and across the table, ocean eyes stormy and more blue than green, like a darkening epicenter in a Category 5 hurricane. "Because they may love you, but they also may turn you away if they can't handle the truth of who you are."

Joe slumped forward, chest heaving with the effort of continuing to breathe through Mike's words. Dylan's stomach dropped, half from watching Joe's reaction and half from the memory of Mike's dad and mom the day he told them the truth.

"It's your biggest fear. Being rejected by your parents. The very people who set all the expectations inside you for how you conduct yourself through time and space as a human being." Mike's eyes softened. "I can see it now as we raise our daughter." He gave Dylan a split second of eye contact, then rubbed his chin slowly with a sheepish look. "It's so easy to plant in them the great paradox of parenting."

"Which is?" Trevor asked quietly.

"That you love them unconditionally but want them to be exactly what you imagine in your mind. That when they stray from your own set viewpoint of how the world should work, it's like you've failed. You're a little bit like God when you have a child, and when the child doesn't do what you want, it's easy to think it's a reflection on the job you've done. Like it's all about you."

Joe nodded slowly, mesmerized. Dylan leaned in, wishing he could make Mike's very real pain and Joe's imagined future pain disappear.

"You told your mom and dad?" Joe asked, blinking hard but otherwise immutable. "I take it that didn't go well?"

Dylan and Mike exchanged a look that gave Mike permission to sigh, the slow hiss of release making Dylan glad he was here. Laura was of great comfort to Mike as they'd navigated time and family. She hadn't understood how his parents could choose not only to shun him but also baby Jillian, but Dylan got it. All too well. Not because he agreed, for fuck's sake.

Because he'd been there. Right there when it had all gone down.

His heart raged for Mike, and already just a little for Joe, if that was what Joe was afraid he might face.

"It was the biggest mistake of my life." Mike's words echoed through a lull in the restaurant's busy background noise, giving them a dramatic weight that shook Dylan a bit. Laura looked over at them with an expression of unease and mouthed, *You okay?*

Dylan just shrugged. She closed her eyes, nodded, then looked away, huddling once again with Josie and Darla. Whatever conversation they were having looked leaps and bounds better than *this*.

"The threesome?" Trevor asked in surprise, his voice up half an octave.

"The telling. The threesome was the best fucking thing of my life up to that point. I felt whole. Full. Complete." Mike swallowed hard. "Real."

"And your parents…" Joe said, obviously not wanting to the know the answer, but Dylan saw he had to ask. *Had* to.

"My dad nearly beat the shit out of me. Dylan had to stop him."

"You're the size of a fucking redwood out of Muir Woods. How could your dad—?"

Mike's sad grin made him look so forlorn it caught Laura's attention again. Dylan reached up and scratched an eyebrow, finding the skin of his brow knitted so tightly it hurt.

"You think I'm tall? You should see Big Mike. I'm *Little* Mike."

"It's like Sam." Trevor's voice trembled just enough to make them all turn and stare at him. Alex had stayed quiet during all this.

291

"Sam? Your drummer?" Dylan had been to one of their concerts a few months ago with Laura and Mike.

Trevor nodded. Joe just gave him a thousand-mile stare and looked at Mike. "Sam's not in a threesome or anything. I just mean he has a dad who rejected him. Beat him up. Sent him away."

"Ouch," was all Dylan could think to say.

"What about Laura's parents?" Joe asked.

"Dead," Mike said. "She just has this one crazy uncle left, and no one's heard from him since her mother died."

"And yours?" Joe's eyes lasered on Dylan.

The question gave Dylan a chance to shake his shoulders, to unburden the tension that lingered there like the weight of a human on his back in a fire, like the responsibility of a person's life.

"Mine? Mine tolerate it. I think my mom doesn't know what it means, and Dad just pretends Mike's my roommate. They create their own false sense of reality and go with it." Shrug. He wasn't about to get touchy-feely with these two. For so long the only lifeboat they had were Dylan's parents and Jill's mom. Her dad had tried to have her disinherited after her death, but her mom had put a full stop to that.

And now he and Mike were the beneficiaries of $2.2 billion that Jill's dad had tried to deny them. Couldn't blame the guy, really.

Would Dylan or Mike have done the same?

"They accept Laura and Mike?" Trevor asked.

"They *love* Laura." Dylan smiled as Mike groaned. "And they really like Mike. They just don't know what to do with Mike *and* Laura. They're binary. They think relationships are in serial. Not parallel."

Joe barked out a laugh that made the table chuckle. "But…" His voice held a pleading tone, as if begging for the answer he wanted. Dylan steeled himself. He doubted he could give that. "But did they freak on you when you told them? Kick you out? Cut you off?"

"Cut me off from what?"

"Money."

Dylan made a dismissive noise. "What money? I had a paper route at twelve. A part-time job unloading trucks at fifteen. Mom and Dad did fine, but we weren't rolling in it. It's not like I got a shiny new BMW in the driveway with a ribbon on it for my sixteenth birthday."

As the last sentence came out of his mouth Dylan realized it was the worst thing he could have said in that moment, because apparently that was the life Joe *did* live. And he'd just alienated him by making fun of it.

Too bad. His own truth wasn't worth sacrificing so he could help some entitled kid.

"It works that way with your parents? They still give you money? Paying for law school?" he asked.

Joe didn't respond, but Trevor jumped in. "They do. Different worlds." He gave a one-shouldered shrug. "And when you're used to all that, you don't know what to do."

"You go out and hustle and get a job," Dylan muttered.

"It's not that simple," Joe said. "The money isn't just love."

Mike startled, touching Dylan's forearm. "They're right. It's not just about the money. The money *is* love, though, in its own way."

"Bullshit. Just because you don't have money doesn't mean you love your kids any less," Dylan snapped.

293

"No, not like that," Mike said, shaking his head. "It's more like cutting off money for not choosing a life someone else told you to live."

Joe just blinked.

And then Madge got up from her spot at the booth with Laura, Darla, and Josie and began clearing plates.

"Want more?"

"Whatcha got?" Trevor asked.

"Fried green tomatoes covered in parmesan with sauce?"

"Sure."

She sized up the table. "I'll bring three orders."

"How many tapeworms do you have?" Dylan asked Trevor, giving him a friendly elbow shove.

"Enough to keep eating."

"Oh, to be young and have that metabolism again."

"Sucks growing old."

Old. Ouch. "Who's old? We're thirty-four!" Dylan's cry of protest was met with smirks from the two younger men.

"Speak for yourself! Thirty over here," Alex added.

"I don't mind growing old, as long as it's with Laura," Mike said in a voice designed for the women at the next table to hear it.

"Sure, Mr. Zen. And the first time you find a gray pube on your balls, you'll be bitching about it like the rest of us," Dylan challenged.

"You found a gray pube already? Dude." Trevor spoke in a voice filled with alarmed sadness. "I'm so sorry. Time for Viagra, huh?"

What. The. Fuck.

"I do not have gray pubes on my nads!" Dylan shouted. "And I don't need Viagra! In fact, I have a refractory period that would put you to shame. Four times in five hours. Just tested it last week!"

"That Viagra can really let you pump 'em out, huh?" Joe commented.

"I do not take Viagra!"

"Okay. Whatever. We believe you." Those two little assholes snickered away. Even Alex and Mike tried not to laugh. How the hell did the conversation go from a deep, painful reflection on how their families handled the revelation of their threesome to gray pubes and Viagra? In ten seconds flat?

"You damn well better believe me. Mike can vouch for it."

That made Trevor and Joe turn beet red. Huh.

"Not so comfortable with each other, are you?" Dylan's turn to put them in the squirmy position of being under the spotlight. "Can't admit that you like it."

"Like what?" Alex asked, surprising everyone.

"Like being with each other."

"We're not *with* each other. We don't...you know."

"You don't touch." Dylan's statement made Joe's face lose a little of the flush.

"Right."

"But you're still together."

"Huh?"

"You're together. You wouldn't be with Darla—both of you—if you didn't feel better having him there than you do *not* having him there," Dylan pointed out.

"No, it's not like that. It's more like..." Trevor frowned, then made a face of acquiescence. "Um, I guess it *is* like that."

"We're perverts," Joe said, sighing, banging his head slowly against the back of his chair. "Might not even be able to get an attorney's license if someone knew."

"Not true. No one can strip you of that right," Mike said. "Don't overthink like that. You'll drive yourself crazy."

Trevor shoved Joe's leg, hard. "See? Told you."

"Someone in law school told me they used to deny licenses to gay attorneys in some states." His face changed to a look of horror. "Not that we're gay!"

"Okay. Whatever. I believe you," Dylan said, nodding with glee.

Joe and Trevor gave him sour looks while Mike and Alex just laughed.

"Fair point," Trevor finally said. "Sorry about your gray nads."

Joe snorted.

"But you can admit that the entire reason you're in a threesome is because you like it better than being in a twosome."

"Isn't that the whole point?" Alex asked. "You make it a triad instead of a dyad because it's..." He shot Dylan a helpless look.

"It's what?" Trevor asked, looking to Mike and Dylan for guidance. "What the hell *is* this? Because we didn't choose it. Didn't want it, even. We don't fight it."

"We fight with each other," Joe pointed out.

"But we don't fight *this*. We don't argue over *this*. You get jealous because I'm with Darla and you're not, but you don't get jealous of the fact that I'm here when all three of us are together. It's confusing. It makes no sense because it defies logic!"

Trevor looked at Dylan dead on. "Do you guys have that? Jealousy that isn't jealousy. It's— whatthefuckever it is, it's driving me insane. He won't stop it. He just gets pissed all the time and takes it out on us."

"Fuck off, I do not!" Joe shouted.

Darla gave a nervous look at the group. Dylan winked at her. *Hey, this is what you and Laura wanted...we're talking.*

"Yes, you do!" Trevor pounded the table with his fist. Just once, but enough to make Mike and Alex exchange looks with him.

"It's not my fault. You're trying to make her like you more."

"What?" Trevor yelped.

Mike shot Dylan a look that made both men burst aloud and say, in unison, "Been there, done that."

Alex stood, looking nervous and uncomfortable. "I'm being paged, dammit. Just when this gets good." He pulled a buzzing phone from his pocket.

"We'll save the sex talk for after you've gone."

His face fell, and Dylan laughed. "You mean I hung on for all the crap talk and now I have to go before it gets kinky?"

"You want to learn about threesomes, just go on YouPorn," Josie said from behind him, pinching his hip. Dylan looked at the women's booth and saw Darla and Laura in deep conversation.

"Or ask Josie about hers," Darla piped up.

Alex gave her a blank look that made Dylan's balls crawl up his thigh a few inches. "Your *what*?"

"Bye! See ya!" Josie called out as she dragged Alex through the front door, the two in a heated discussion that made Dylan grin with an evil chaos.

"Josie had a threesome," Mike said drolly, cocking one eyebrow at Dylan. "Did we know that?"

"How the hell would I know? She chatters so much it's like one of those old dolls. Pull the string and the Real Baby talks!"

"You seriously don't get jealous, though?" Trevor asked, giving Joe a hard look as his words were directed at Dylan and Mike. "At all?"

"Not jealous of each other. No. But jealous of one of us having more time than the other with Jill or, now, Laura?" Dylan's turn to give Mike a hard look. "I think Mike should answer that."

"You two had sex on my day!" Mike exploded. "We had a schedule!"

Aha.

Now they were getting real.

"You *do* get jealous!" Joe said with an excitement that made Dylan uneasy. "See?" He gave Trevor a hot look. Angry look. A look of triumph. Of being right.

"Even after this long?" Trevor seemed defeated. "I don't have it in me to put up with his shit forever."

"It'll change when you live together," Dylan said. Both younger men gave him skeptical looks. "No, really. When we moved in with Jill it got better, and now that we're with Laura, Mike's the one who gets jealous. I don't."

"He really doesn't. It's weird," Mike added.

"Weird," Joe muttered.

"Why is it weird?" Trevor asked. "I think it's a sign of maturity."

Dylan reached across the table to high-five him and did a double take. If Mike were even five years older he could be Trevor's very young dad.

Old. Dylan felt so fucking old. Next time he took a piss he'd need to check for gray pubes after all, because this entire conversation had aged him by five or ten years.

"It's weird," Joe said tightly, "because it's natural to feel jealous."

"No, it's not," Dylan and Trevor said together.

"Yes, it is," Joe insisted. "It's part of human nature."

"Nope," Dylan declared. "I used to think that, too, but you spend enough time following your own drummer inside you and you realize that all the things people call 'human nature' are made-up shit they create to justify their own feelings and behaviors."

Joe frowned. "From an evolutionary biology standpoint, that seems wrong."

"But from a real-life, daily-life perspective, I'm right. Live with Darla for a year. All three of you. Together. And then see what happens to the jealousy."

Both of the younger men's eyes widened. Ah. They weren't there yet. Too much commitment. Dylan understood. He and Mike had been terrified to move in with Jill. It was as close to marriage as they would ever, legally, be allowed to come, so it had more gravity to it. Felt bigger.

Seemed enormous at the time.

"And I don't think you're jealous," Mike said to Joe. "I think you're pissed at yourself. Not Trevor."

Trevor's eyebrows shot up while Joe's forehead furrowed with fury. "What?"

"You made a choice to live far away. You shouldn't be punishing Darla and Trevor because you're unhappy with your decision."

"Oh, great. Here comes the therapy. Where's your couch, Dr. Freud?"

Mike shrugged. "Take it or leave it. But it's obvious to everyone else. You're unhappy and don't want to be away but won't make a change. It's all on you. You are making yourself miserable. You're not jealous of Trevor's time with Darla. You're jealous of something else."

"What?"

"That they are living their own lives and doing what they want."

"I'm at fucking Penn! Ivy League law!"

"And look at how happy that makes you."

DARLA

"Joe looks like Trevor just shoved Mavis up his ass and did the Funky Chicken dance with her," Darla said as Laura giggled. They'd spent the better part of the past twenty minutes talking shop, mostly comparing notes on Good Things Come in Threes clients.

Between Dylan shouting about his erectile dysfunction and Joe yammering on about yet another thing he was pissed about, it sounded like the men were having a more contentious time than the women.

And Alex looked kinda sick over there before they left. She wondered what on earth the other four men had told him to make him so...green. The man delivered babies for a living, for goodness' sake. He saw hoohaws ripped open, women who birthed babies from their vaginas, and giant alien placentas and whatever else gushed forth as you pushed those muscles down there, and he did all that with a soothing, calm demeanor and a smile.

Really—what had those men said to unsettle a guy who took needle and thread to labia? She frowned and gave Trevor a look that was designed to cut glass, but he was oblivious. Typical.

"I wish I were a fly on the wall over there," Laura said, turning to flash Dylan a smile that Darla couldn't help but admire. He winked back at Laura, and a part of Darla swooned. She got it. Joe and Trevor made her feel that way times a million. Glad to see Laura had the same thing with her guys.

Or did she?

"When are we going to talk about your threesomes?" Josie asked, rubbing her hands like a blackjack dealer with a super-drunk millionaire in front of her. "I want some good gossip."

"You have no friends other than us," Darla said. "Who the hell you gonna gossip to? Your cat, Crackhead?"

"He listens," Josie said, pouting. "And Alex."

"Alex is a steel trap. Won't say a word," Darla said.

"How do you know?" Josie eyed her with suspicion, and Laura joined in, curious. Darla wished she'd kept her mouth shut. Once Josie was on your case, you were doomed. She'd still managed not to spill the truth about her friend Amy getting her cell phone caught in her vagina (*vibrator apps. Who knew?*), and how Alex had come to the rescue.

Some stories are best left untold.

Unshared.

Buried.

"He's just so dreamy," she said, trying to throw Josie off the scent.

But it made Josie even more suspicious. "What are you up to, Darla?"

"I'm up to talking about the best lube for getting one man in your back door when another one is nicely nestled in your pink tunnel," Darla shot back, desperate to talk about anything but the secret she and Alex shared.

Laura turned the color of roses and picked up a stray menu, fanning herself. "Is it hot in here, or is it just me?"

Josie snorted. "She's just deflecting."

"Or those tunnel butt plugs. Let me tell you, whoever invented those deserves a goddamn Nobel Peace Prize for saving anuses worldwide," Darla said.

Madge happened to walk past at that exact moment, stop cold, and give Darla a long, contemplative stare.

"Contoured, or straight? Because the contoured ones make it so much more comfortable to use between the two of us," Madge asked.

Alex was the closest man to the women's booth and, if the grimace that crossed his mouth were a measure, he had heard Madge's declaration.

"They make 'em contoured?" Darla asked sweetly, like they were talking about press-on nails. "I'll have to try one. What about lube? You found one that helps everything fit in there?"

"Fit?" Madge asked, eyes gleaming.

"When you have them both in. You know."

"Both—oh! No, no. I just have Eddie." Madge tittered. Her face changed suddenly, and she nudged Darla, who followed the old woman's lead and scooched in.

"But," Madge said in a conspirator's voice, "I do have a question. I have a granddaughter who is in this weird relationship."

"Weird?"

"Like you two," Madge said, pointing to Laura and Darla.

"We're not in a relationship." Laura giggled.

"I mean how you two are each with two men. Lydia's got that now. Two men." Madge paused and looked Laura over. "Two billionaires, actually."

Laura looked like she'd been slapped. Slowly, like an interrogator who is receiving a confession from a serial killer and can't quite believe the turn of events,

Laura leaned across the table and grasped Madge's weathered, bony hand.

"You have a granddaughter," she said quietly, "who is in a threesome relationship with two billionaires?"

"Yes." Madge frowned. "At least, I think they're both billionaires. Their names are Mike and Dylan," Madge said dryly.

Darla and Josie couldn't help but laugh. Laura didn't.

"That's not funny. The Mike and Dylan part is, but lying about your granddaughter and making fun of me and Mike and Dylan isn't—"

"I'm not lying. Lydia's with Mike Bournham."

"*The* Michael Bournham?" All three of them gasped.

"*The*. Yes. And Jeremy. His best friend."

"And they're both billionaires? I mean, I know Michael Bournham came close, but who's this Jeremy guy?" Darla asked. The Bournham scandal was the talk of the town. The guy had been caught with his pants down—actually, *off*—on camera fucking some admin at his company and—

"Was she in the sex tape?" Josie asked. "The one who got her reality television show?"

Madge's face closed off in a marked manner, and Darla knew that look well. That was the look of a mama bear who wasn't letting no one mess with her cub. "No. Not her." Something about the way Madge's eyes turned to two dead stones made Darla stop moving, as if she needed to blend into the background before the world ended.

Because Madge could take a person *down*.

"Oh." Josie's simple answer said it all. Laura held her breath. Ribald laughter broke out at the table next to them. Darla wanted to look, to call out and ask what the joke was, but she didn't want Madge's eyes on her, as if Medusa might turn her to stone. Clearly, asking about the sex tape had been about as bad as asking a pregnant friend if she'd used protection.

You just didn't ask.

"She's traveling in Thailand with both of those boys right now," Madge explained, as if nothing had just happened, as if she hadn't sucked all the available oxygen out of the room and left them emotionally gasping for air. "Lydia's always been so independent. A feminist. And now she has no job and they're gallivanting all over Southeast Asia checking on Jeremy's 'investments.'"

"You sound skeptical," Laura said.

"I am skeptical. That boy's probably got a poppy farm and a string of opium dens. He's a bit of a free spirit." The skin around her eyes looked like a smiling elephant's. "But he does love her dearly. So does the other one." Madge waved one hand dismissively and tensed her whole body, her thigh connecting with Darla's, transferring energy in a very bad way.

Something about that phrase—"the other one"—thrown out so casually, and with a kind of dismissal that bordered on contempt, made Darla's hackles rise.

"That's like 'you people'?"

"What?"

"You throw it out there, like she has one real boyfriend and 'the other one.' Sounds like you disapprove. Here you are, Ms. Old Lady Dom with a butt plug fetish, tricking out with Alex's grandpa and being all badass, and you're judging your granddaughter for being in love with two men at the same time?" Darla could feel the curve of her neck extend, could taste the bile in the back of her throat, and as the air slid into her body slowly through her nose, inhaled like a battery charge, she knew that it was on.

Death Match at Jeddy's.

News at eleven.

Laura and Josie's eyes flew wide open in alarm as Madge turned slowly to her, a look of condescending disgust on her face, and said, "You're judging *me*? I shat pieces of corn this morning older than you."

"When you act like the life your granddaughter has chosen for herself out of a drive for love is something to sneer at, you bet your flat ass I'm judging you, lady."

Madge leapt to her feet. "Fat ass? *You* are calling *me* 'fat ass'?"

"I said flat. *Flat.* The Gravity Fairy done visited your backside plenty of times, huh? Looks like Kansas back there."

"And the Oreo Fairy visits you twice a day, it seems." Madge craned her neck ostentatiously to pointedly look at Darla's admittedly lush ass.

"I have a Knuckle Fairy who'd like to—"

"Enough!" Laura shouted. "Both of you! I'd expected it to come to fists today, but not at *this* table!" The women all looked over at the guys, who were huddled and laughing, looking like something out of a Polo Ralph Lauren ad.

"Jesus Christ," Madge muttered. "I break up enough fights. Don't need to flatten some pissant little shit like you and bring on more trouble here."

Darla's heart threatened to shatter her breastbone like the giant pitcher of Kool-Aid crashing through the fence.

"Then quit denigrating your granddaughter's relationship with her boyfriends while claiming to be nonjudgemental. Because all you're doing is shaming her behind her back."

Madge looked like Darla had just whacked her with a coffee pot.

Good.

Laura tilted her head, and Josie watched them with narrowed eyes, a look Darla knew all too well. She was ready for a throwdown if need be. Back home, Josie had her back. Not that Darla routinely got into catfights with eighty-year-old waitresses in dive bars.

Okay, maybe once or twice. And maybe she won.

Most of them.

Madge was a tough old bird, but a reasonable one. Her face sagged with sadness as she turned to Laura and asked, "Is that shaming? What I said?"

Laura's eyes filled with tears. Darla fought hers back, too, because the genuine befuddlement and caring in the old bat's voice made it clear she deeply loved her granddaughter.

Laura reached for her hand and looked at her. "Yes, Madge. When you call one of her boyfriends 'the other one,' it strips him of an identity. She has two boyfriends. Two. Both are as important as one."

"But I didn't mean it that way. It's just a joke." Maybe Darla had been to quick to anger.

"Just 'cause you think it's a joke doesn't make it funny," Darla fumed, conflicted inside.

Madge ignored her and focused on Laura. Darla's field of vision began to speckle, a furious cloud of rage taking over. If she wasn't careful, she'd end up charged with assault, hauled off in handcuffs, humiliated for beating down a woman old enough to be her great-grandma, and she'd lose her job.

Add a surprise pregnancy and a dead dog and she'd have a really boring country music song.

"I don't understand why you can't just be kinky and have one guy. Why two? Why does my granddaughter Lydia need two? Two at once, no less. I get wanting some variety, but that's not a buffet. It's an overloaded plate with all the different delights touching each other, blending into too many flavors in one bite."

The food metaphor went over Darla's head. "You're comparing threesomes to a buffet? I ain't all you can eat."

Josie broke out into a nervous, barky laugh at that one. Even Laura giggled.

"That's not what I meant!" Darla protested, though Madge started snickering, too. Alex gave them a weird look, and Darla's balloon of anger popped, a slow hiss deflating her.

"Madge," Laura finally said. "If Lydia could be happy with just one of them, she would be. It's not like we choose to love this way. It just is. Society turns it into some shameful thing, but not us. If we could be happy with just one of them, I think..." She shot Josie a helpless look.

"Why are you looking at me?" Josie squeaked. "I'm the one who's living with one man, and he's a pantry hog."

"I heard that," Alex said casually, then stood and looked at Darla. "You and Madge done? Because I've been here on the periphery ready to jump in and protect you."

"Me?" Darla exclaimed.

Josie and Laura gave her a sympathetic look as Alex said, "Yeah. You. Who do you think would win in a hair-pulling contest?"

Madge shot her a shit-eating grin.

"Aw, hell no," Darla drawled. "You come to central Ohio and meet Aunt Marlene sometime, Madge. That woman could take *him* down," she added, pointing to Alex.

Josie's turn to flush bright red at the mention of her mother and Alex.

His eyebrows shot up, and he looked at his girlfriend. "You've told me stories about your mom, but..."

"Mrs. Tucker, the town clerk, had to have plugs put in after she and Aunt Marlene got into a nasty fight over the plumber's son, and Marlene ripped half her hair out," Darla added helpfully, enjoying someone other than her experiencing the crippling humiliation of this entire conversation.

Josie stood. "You beeped?" Her words were aimed at Alex, who was looking at his phone.

"I did."

"Then let's go."

"He beeps and you need to go? You an obstetrics resident suddenly? Need to deliver a baby?"

"Not until it's our own," Alex said merrily.

Josie turned the shade of cream as Laura gave her a look. "Something you want to tell us, Josie?"

"He just moved in! Pantry hogger."

"My Eddie does that, too, sometimes. I find him wearing my panties, one pair around his hips, another one clenched in his fist while he's—"

"Pant*ry*, Madge! The woman said pant*ry*!" Alex choked out, grabbing Josie's hand. "Not panty!"

The four men at the other table gawked at them. "I want to talk about what *they're* talking about!" Dylan announced. Two people at a table across the way turned, all eyes suddenly on Madge, Darla and Laura.

"This is not going exactly how I thought it would," Laura groaned, picking through the remnants in the sundae dish and stuffing a chocolate chip cookie covered in caramel sauce in her mouth. Darla was jealous.

Madge had some weird sort of food radar, like a bat has echolocation, for she picked up on Darla's thought and raced away, shouting, "One more Orgy for the table, coming up!"

"Now I *really* want to sit over there," Dylan said, struggling to shove Trevor out of the booth. Trevor scrambled out, too, and came over to Darla, hands on her shoulders, kneading muscles made of stone.

He bent down and whispered, "You okay?"

All she could do was nod.

"And you could totally take her," he added with a raspy voice that made her grin.

Damn straight.

LAURA

As Madge returned with an enormous sundae that made Laura's stomach ache, her phone buzzed again. Alex and Josie disappeared, and the table was overrun by penises at the appearance of the delectable ice cream extravaganza.

"Ours wasn't nearly as good as this," Joe moaned as he bit into chunk of toffee brownie.

Worried it might be Cyndi, Laura reached into her purse and retrieved her phone. It was an email, but it looked like the second email from the same address. Weird. While the guys picked the sundae clean, and Darla relaxed with Trevor and Joe on either side of her, Laura figured this was as good a time as any to let everyone de-escalate and calm down.

She still wanted more of a talk with Darla—they'd talked about everything but their respective relationships—but the entire group could do with downtime.

The email turned out to be anything but relaxing for her, though. Whatever her face looked like as she read it must have triggered something inside Mike, because he came to her side and touched her arm.

"Something wrong?"

"An email. From my uncle."

"The one you haven't heard from in years?" Laura had told Mike about her Uncle Frank. She hadn't heard from him since her mom died. And even then, he'd only reached out to her for one thing: money.

"Yes. Him."

"Uh oh. That's really weird. I was just mentioning him..."

"You were?" she asked in surprise. Frank wasn't exactly a common topic for discussion.

"We were talking about how our parents handled learning about Jill." Laura reached out to touch him, knowing how painful that subject was. "And Joe asked about your parents. I just mentioned you had a crazy uncle."

Even Mike knew what this might mean. Frank was, in the kindest of terms, a ne'er-do-well. Her mother had kept him at arm's length after he'd ruined her credit rating when Laura was in high school.

"Yeah. Crazy uncle. I'd just ignore it, but..." She held up the telephone screen and let Mike read the email:

Dear Laura,
You haven't had any contact with me in so long, my dear, and so I thought I would reach out. I recently came across news footage about your new life and am so pleased to learn about your happy circumstances. And I have a great-niece, from what I've read! I should like very much to meet with you, your daughter, and your husbands. Your old uncle Frank doesn't have quite the exciting, luxurious life you now lead, but perhaps you can find time for me to see my only living niece and grand-niece. Family is so important, and as I age I realize that blood is all that matters.
Your loving uncle,
Frank

"Ah, shit," Dylan said from behind her. "Is he money grubbing?"

Because it had been so long since she'd seen him—since her mother's death, when he'd convinced her to hand over part of her mom's life insurance for his pain and suffering—she hadn't really talked much about Frank. A few conversations boiled down to the simple point that Frank used people. Mostly for money. And her mother had taught her to keep him at as much of a distance as possible.

And now he was back, with more knowledge about her life than she was comfortable with him having. A cold chill began at the base of her spine and spread up as she reread his words. The thought of him being part of her life, of Jillian's life, left her with an unsettled, mildly frantic feeling that he knew would reverberate through her, pinging and ricocheting endlessly until this was resolved.

Dylan and Mike could feel it, too. They crowded around her, safe and solid, a big, impenetrable wall of protection.

The threat, though, was so much more than physical.

"Ignore it," Dylan and Mike said at the same time.

"Delete it," Dylan whispered. "You don't have any obligation to him."

"I know," she whispered back. Mike set his chin on the top of her head, arm wrapping around her, the warmth a comfort. She was suddenly cold.

And just as instantly, she needed to hold Jillian. Touch her. Embrace her. Be with her.

Protect her.

Frank's words looped through her head. "Happy circumstances" and "luxurious life" and "blood is all that matters" all set off alarm bells in her head.

Why now? Why was he appearing *now*? She'd been with Mike and Dylan for two years. They'd been all over the news in the early stage of their relationship, though more the guys than her. Nowadays she was featured in small news articles on blog sites, mostly, talking about alternative lifestyles. No one ever photographed Jillian—all three of them were fierce about her privacy in that respect—so Frank couldn't know that much about her.

But she bet he knew 2.2 billion reasons why he wanted to reconnect with his niece and grand-niece, dammit.

Laura stood abruptly, Mike and Dylan on their feet in seconds, the three a unit. "Darla," Laura said, her own words breathless, the panic coming out in her voice. "I'm so sorry, but I have to go. There's an emergency."

"Is the baby okay?" Joe asked. Trevor and Darla gave Laura a look of such concern that it made her feel instantly overwrought. What was she so anxious about? It didn't make sense, but the feeling fluttered inside her. She couldn't deny it. All she could do was get home and hold her daughter. Then she'd be able to think and act clearly.

Until then? Everything she did was pointless.

"Jillian is fine," Laura said, more to calm herself than anyone else. That seemed to allay the younger group's fears. "It's just, something else has come up, and I need to cut this short."

She reached for Darla, who stood, and the two shared a deep, long hug. "Let's do this again, but only the two of us."

"Yes!" said the men in unison.

Laura and Josie shot them dark looks. All four of them shrugged. It was like a human wave of flesh relief. If Laura weren't on high alert, so triggered by her uncle's email as to be in a different plane of mental existence, she would have laughed.

Jillian.

All she could think about was wrapping her arms around that sweet little toddler and taking a long, deep breath.

Mike and Dylan saw the unease in her, and within seconds they were out the door, headed for the parking garage, where Mike's Jeep would take her to sanctuary.

"You're shaking," Dylan said in a clenched voice, his jaw muscles tight, eyes like a hawk's. "Did your uncle do something else? Threaten you?" They climbed in the car, and Mike peeled out of the parking structure, the squeal of tire on painted concrete making her feel like they were moving faster than they really were.

"No! Oh, no. Nothing like that. I just need her." Laura's throat began to close with tears, eyes joining in waterworks. "It seems so silly, I know..."

"Not silly," Dylan said evenly. He was in the back seat with her, arms enveloping her as Mike drove. "You feel what you feel. And no one can hurt you."

"Or Jillian." Mike's words came out like a growl.

"Or any of us," Dylan assured her. She felt so safe with them both. Secure.

Fine.

A deep breath helped. Dylan's warm hands on her hip made his words sink in. This was fine. An email out of the blue could be ignored. Frank wasn't any sort of threat. In fact, she'd just let a stupid email interrupt a very important lunch date.

"What am I thinking?" she blurted out. Mike was weaving through traffic to snake through Arlington and get to Route 2 and home. "This is silly. We don't

315

need to rush. Maybe we should go back so I can talk to Darla some more."

Mike caught her eye in the rearview mirror. "Don't do that."

She startled. "Do what?" Dylan was so warm, so hard and secure, like being hugged by a muscled teddy bear. The afternoon's conversation, the sparring between Madge and Darla, the talks about threesomes as if they were normal and just another way to love, all pinged through her mind.

Overwhelm.

She was living in overwhelm. And that was why Frank's email was sending her home.

"Don't try to convince yourself that your first instinct is wrong," Mike elaborated, driving with his eyes on her through the tiny mirror. "You're doing that female thing. Don't invalidate yourself. Believe in whatever's driving you to get home to Jillian. It's important. It's worthy. You're valid for believing whatever's in your gut."

That made her tear up even more.

Traffic was backed up—no surprise given that it was already nearly five o'clock. By the time they got home it was well past six, and Cyndi was fine with their lateness, always reasonable and understanding. Closing her arms around little Jillian's chubby body, legs like chunks of soft dough, cheeks the color of freshly picked cider apples in late October, made Laura feel like her heart was safely behind her ribs again.

It really was okay.

"I gave her a bath when you texted, and she already ate dinner. Given the time"—Laura knew it was 6:45 p.m.—"she's probably ready for bed soon enough," Cyndi declared. Short and thick, with steel-gray hair, the nanny's piercing blue eyes were troubled,

316

if no-nonsense. "And it looks like you could use a good night's sleep as well, Laura."

All Laura could do was bury her face in Jillian's neck.

"Mama seepy," the little girl said. "Zzzzzz." It was a game Mike and Dylan played with her, and Laura laughed that her daughter had made the connection between Cyndi's words and the dads' game. Every day, little changes like this made her marvel. She hadn't given birth to a baby.

She'd brought a little whole human being into the world.

Now *that's* a superpower.

"Mama's sleepy, yes," Laura repeated as Jillian rested her brown curls on Laura's shoulder, snuggling in like she was molded to live there. Which she was.

"Is everything okay?" Cyndi asked quietly. "You seem anxious. Did something happen?"

"No," Laura rushed to say, not wanting to deal with anyone else's emotional state right now. A dawning realization made her elaborate.

More than she wanted to.

"Did anyone call the house while we were gone?"

Cyndi's face lit up. "Oh, yes!"

Oh, no.

"Your Uncle Frank called. I didn't know you had an uncle!" Cyndi hurried over to the counter that separated the large, open-concept kitchen from the living room and picked up a slip of paper. "Here. He asked that you call him as soon as possible. Said he might swing into town for a few days and would love to see his favorite niece."

His *only* niece.

Laura's stomach dropped through the earth's crust and into the magma layer. "Thanks," she gasped.

Cyndi frowned, then her eyes changed to a wary look. "Oh dear. He was so charming on the phone, and I just assumed..." She touched Laura's hand. "He's not someone you want in your life, is he? I hope I didn't make a mistake."

"You didn't do anything wrong," Laura answered, but she reached for Cyndi's hand and clasped it like it was a lifeline. Kind, wrinkled eyes, intelligent and perceptive, yet so compassionate, met hers.

Jillian's weight on her shoulder shifted just enough for Laura to realize that the baby had fallen asleep, her breathing suddenly even, her little lips nuzzled against Laura's ear.

"She wanted her mama," Cyndi said with a squeeze of the hand.

Laura swallowed hard as Mike and Dylan came into the room, brows furrowed, worried and ready to talk.

"Her mama," Laura said through a voice full of worry over the unknown, "wanted her."

"Something more happen?" Mike asked, crossing the room, his sheer size a comfort to Laura. Cyndi looked up to meet his eyes, and it was like she was watching Superman fly overhead.

"Uncle Frank called," Laura whispered.

"*Here?*" Dylan asked, incredulous. "The house phone? It's unlisted."

"I hadn't thought of that," Cyndi said in an apologetic tone. "I just assumed he was a family member and it was okay to talk to him. To tell him."

Laura's extremities went cold. "Tell him *what?*"

Cyndi dropped her hand and gave Mike and Dylan beseeching looks. "He asked about Jillian. How she was doing, what she was like, and how Laura was.

Asked about you two as well. Whether you treated 'his girls' right."

Laura's eyes bugged out of her head. Mike and Dylan exchanged angry looks.

"I'm so sorry!" Cyndi gushed. "I'll never make that mistake again."

Laura shook her head, as if trying to get rid of a bad thought. Which she was. The movement made Jillian rub her face against Laura's neck. The toddler's body heat was the only reason Laura wasn't chilled to the bone with dread.

"Cyndi," Mike said, "you haven't done a thing wrong. We're not certain why Laura's uncle has suddenly come out of the woodwork, but Laura's worried, and that's good enough for us. From now on, screen his calls."

"And if he shows up here," Dylan added, lips tight, anger morphing his features, "don't let him in. Call us right away, and worst case, call the police."

"The police!" Laura cried out. Jillian smacked her lips in her sleep, and Laura lowered her voice. "Guys, I think I'm making you overreact. Frank's not harmful. He's never hurt me or threatened me before. It's not like that at all."

"You're freaked, though. I can smell it on you." Mike's words made Cyndi do a double take, but he was dead serious.

"I'm freaked out because it's just weird. And having him call here..."

"Why would he?" Dylan asked, but it was quickly clear his question was rhetorical, for he answered it himself, Mike and Laura all saying the word at the same time.

"Money."

Cyndi made a clucking sound. "People come out of the woodwork when it comes to big money," she said. "Not that I would know." Her rueful grin made Laura feel sheepish.

"We didn't live with money either, until a few years ago," Dylan said. "You know I was a firefighter and Mike was a ski instructor."

"We weren't exactly rich," Mike added.

"But you are now," Laura pointed out.

"*We* are," Dylan said. Everyone went quiet. Cyndi looked a bit embarrassed. Truth be told, the guys and Laura were, too. It was one thing to have money—their daily life made it clear that they did, because they had the freedom to spend their time as they pleased, a luxury more valuable than coin—but it was quite another to talk openly about it.

Which they didn't. Not generally.

Then again, the news channels had covered Mike and Dylan's inheritance after Jill died, so it was public knowledge.

Knowledge her Uncle Frank now had.

What on earth had happened to the pioneering lunch Laura had planned with Darla? The exchange of thoughts and feelings and ideas no one else experienced? Wasn't she supposed to be dealing with the emotional aftermath of that right now—and not of Frank?

Life changed on a dime, didn't it?

"I'm going to put her to sleep," Laura said in dulcet tones, as Mike huddled with Cyndi, sounds of reassurance telling Laura he was making sure the amazing nanny understood all was well. Dylan followed her into the bedroom, where she settled Jillian on the enormous California king bed that Mike, Dylan, and Laura shared.

He cocked an eyebrow.

"I know we're not co-sleeping with her anymore, but for tonight, I just want her there. I don't know why I'm so worried suddenly. It doesn't make sense, I know, but I don't care. I want to have her near me."

He pulled her into a warm embrace with arms like steel. "I understand, honey," he murmured against her cheek. "And besides, trying to squeeze into her crib isn't practical."

"You'd know," she said with a chuckle. "Remember that time it was the only way to get her to sleep? You took one for the team climbing in there with her."

"And Mike has the pictures to prove it," Dylan said with a pseudo-sour tone.

"You rang?" Mike appeared in the doorway. "My ears are burning. You guys talking about me?" His eyes lit on Jillian, a tiny cherub curled up in the center of the enormous bed, and he smiled.

"I see I'm going to get kicked in the kidneys all night," he said.

"And not from me this time," Dylan joked. Kind of. Dylan was the bed hog now that Laura wasn't pregnant.

Mike joined the embrace, covering the side of Laura that Dylan wasn't on. He kissed the top of her head and declared, "It'll all be fine. I'm sure this whole Frank business will turn out to be nothing."

Oh, how Laura wished he were right.

Oh, how wrong he turned out to be.

COMPLETE WE

Chapter One

Josie

Josie was at the reception desk for Good Things Come in Threes when the most irresistibly pleasant older gentleman knocked lightly on the main door and entered. Well into his fifties, but preserved with a self-effacing confidence that was charming, the man looked like a cross between Robert Redford and Harrison Ford. Smart. Clued in.

Almost *courtly*.

"Excuse me," he said in a voice that reminded her of *Mad Men*, as if he were enjoying two fingers of brandy in a square highball glass, sitting in a leather-covered chair at a steakhouse, smoke trickling up in willowy lines from a manicured man's hand. None of that was true, of course, but the sense of that impression was so strong, just from that opening phrase.

"Is this the threesome dating service?" he finished, using a lower register in his voice, not out of shame but from a sense of privacy. His eyes were whisky dipped in moss, an unsettling shade of green against hair the color of wet sand. A little grey was interspersed above his ears, and he had those deep wrinkles that people who smile—a lot—get on their face, from forehead to cheeks.

An appealing man.

"Yes, it is." Josie stood, came around to the front of her desk, and stuck out her hand, a bit wary. He could be a reporter. Or a warrant processor. Or someone from the property management company, concerned about parking spots again. A thousand scenarios flashed through her mind, but number one was:

Why did I have to give Darla the rest of the day off?

They didn't get many walk-ins, and the ones who did come in tended to be the slimiest of the slimes, members of the media or part of a fundamentalist Christian group that was closely associated with the Westboro Baptist clan.

So Mr. Suave was already pinging her subconscious radar, no matter how sophisticated and nice he seemed to be.

"My name is Frank Stedman." His grip was warm and friendly, the handshake of a man accustomed to pressing the flesh a great deal. His cultured voice was like liquid laughter, and against her better judgment she found herself melting into his niceness.

"Josie. Josie Mendham. Nice to meet you, Frank. You here for business?"

"I'm here to learn as much as I can."

The hair on her upper shoulders went tingly. "Learn? Are you doing an investigative piece?" Two months ago a journalist had come in and claimed to be an intern at a local college newspaper. He had asked a million questions and then wrote up a three-thousand-word exposé for a major newspaper, the web link making its rounds. The nasty comments on the web had led her to ban her friends from reading the articles, not that she had any sway.

Laura had read them, as had Darla. The former was worried for Jillian, the latter that she'd lose her job.

Twenty-seven new clients had signed as a direct result, so *hooray* for unintended consequences, but the stress of the negative wasn't worth it. They were getting closer to making matches, and another biased news article could threaten that. Then again, maybe it would get the right person's attention...

"No," he said, shaking his head slightly, clearly perplexed. "I'm here to find the right people so I can live in perfect threesome harmony."

Those words sounded so fake, so scripted, that Josie laughed in his face. C'mon. This guy wasn't for real. And he wasn't even a good actor.

"Frank," she said matter-of-factly, positioning herself closer to the door in case he gave her trouble. The UPS guy Darla slobbered over was due to deliver packages soon, and she also knew that the weekly staff meeting for the CPA firm next door would end any minute now. The more company, the more eyeballs and ears she could get if needed, the better. "I don't think we have what you're looking for."

He fixed her with a hard, solid look, no negativity. Just a cold calculation, measuring her as surely as if he'd pulled out a yardstick. What he was measuring was a mystery to Josie, though.

The two sat in silence. She sure as hell wouldn't crack first.

He did. "Josie," he said with that warmth in the back of his throat, as if he could translate caring with his vocal cords, "I'm here because I lost someone very important in my life years ago, and I want to find my way forward. Your dating service is the only way I can do that. I absolutely need your help."

Frowning, she took him in. Plenty of perverts cajoled and begged and asked for every erotic encounter you could imagine—but as she told them, she wasn't a madam in a brothel, so if all they wanted was a kinky fuck, go on Craigslist and post a Casual Encounter Wanted ad.

Frank Stedman wasn't looking for that, though. "We're your only hope?" Josie joked. "Who are you, Princess Leia? Sorry. I'm no Ben Kenobi."

His face lit up with a smile. "I don't look good in that bikini, and being chained to Jabba the Hut goes a little too far for my kink comfort zone," he replied.

Josie's turn to laugh, but she didn't take her eyes off him, especially his hands. "Fair enough. Are you here to become a client?"

He sidestepped the question, and it would take days for Josie to reflect back on this conversation and realize how skilled, how unctuous he'd been in choosing his words very, very carefully.

"I'm here to learn more about your service," he answered, nodding. "And to see how I can benefit from it."

Josie's eyes narrowed, her heart beating a few steps faster than its normal pace, her mind struggling to assess the situation and act accordingly. A gut check told her he was fine overall, but something didn't sit quite right.

"How did you learn about Good Things Come in Threes?" she asked, gesturing for him to take a seat. With great skill she maneuvered so she was closest to the door.

"On the internet. Google, of course. The great replacer of the neighborhood fence chat. Can't ask your neighbor Agnes anymore which threesome dating site she recommends, so…"

She smiled without showing teeth. It seemed to rattle him in the tiniest of ways, for he hesitated, eyes reading her. He was evaluating her as much as she was studying him, and it had nothing to do with sex or love or kink.

This was primal threat assessment.

"We don't get too many walk-ins, Frank, so forgive me. Just making sure you're not here for the wrong reasons."

Something in his eyes flickered, the skin around them widening slightly, making an inner alarm start to ding in her chest. But he tilted his head, that brown-silver hair parted loosely on one side, the bangs falling in light waves across his forehead. God, if he were twenty years younger she'd be squirming in her seat right now, flushed with unwelcome desire for a man who by all rights she shouldn't—*couldn't*—have naughty thoughts about, because that man was supposed to be Alex.

Was Alex.

Is Alex.

Frank's age had little to do with her ability to keep her clit in check. It was something else, an instinct that freaked her out, because it made no sense.

She had learned to listen to it, though. It was the same feeling she got when her mother went on a bender and brought someone home to fuck.

Preservation.

"What would be a wrong reason, if I may ask?" He saw her eyes blip over to the door and his face morphed to a look of alarm. "If you feel unsafe with me, Josie, by all means we can take our discussion to the coffee shop downstairs, or you can open the door." His face softened, eyes appearing to reflect her own worry back to her. "I would never want you to feel

329

uncomfortable around me, and your personal safety is of utmost importance." The smile he gave her was meant to offer solace, but instead made her feel ashamed.

Where was *that* coming from?

"No, no," she said, backing down even as an inner voice screamed for her to be bold, to stand and go to that coffee shop, to do exactly what he had offered. That was the problem: doing what he suggested felt like a failure, a defeat, like she was giving in to his belief that she was overreacting. This was crazy-making. How could she have been bent over business expense spreadsheets just minutes ago and now she was second-guessing her emotional reaction to this man?

"If it would be better for me to return when you have a coworker here—" Frank started.

"Darla will be back shortly," she said primly, remembering her self-defense training classes. Never let a potential predator know you were alone. The lie lived on her tongue quite happily.

"Do you have other coworkers? I'd imagine a business like this must be bustling. You've practically cornered the market." He winked. "And it's an important market. I read the write-up you got from that national sex columnist."

Half of Josie's mouth went up in a reluctant smile. Charmer. But it was working. She was damn proud of getting such positive coverage for that interview. Laura had stayed behind the scenes, as usual, but Josie embraced her work now.

"We're a small operation," she replied. "Just the owner, me, and some clerical workers."

"And the owner—I believe she's in a loving, stable threesome relationship with two men herself?" He kept his face impassive, eyebrows raised, the corners of his lips turned up just enough to convey friendliness, but those eyes.

Hawk eyes.

Laura's story was one that they worked hard to manage and protect. Potential clients were always eager for details; knowing that their dream was a reality for at least one group was the best promotion the service could possibly get.

Yet maintaining Laura, Mike, Dylan, and baby Jillian's privacy was far more important, to Josie, than hawking the service's wares by whoring out details on Laura's life.

Walking that tightrope was *hard*.

"Yes." Josie gave a tight smile. "She is. The owner lives the life."

"And do you?"

Her smile fell. "I don't talk about my personal life with clients, Frank."

"I'm not a client, Josie."

Ice water ran through her as those hawk eyes zeroed in on her as if they'd telescoped, prey spotted, target isolated.

Attack imminent.

He chuckled. "I'm so intrigued by this company, by the lifestyle. You find a way to help people achieve a kind of love that mass society considers a sin."

The alarm bell migrated from her chest to her head, ringing in duplicate.

Muted voices next door, plus the shuffling sounds of chairs being pushed around, told her the CPA meeting was over. One of the accountants, Janet, might stop by and ask Josie if she wanted a latte from the very coffee shop Frank had suggested they move to.

Please stop by, Josie thought.

331

Frank looked at his watch, an expensive Movado or a cheap knockoff. Josie couldn't tell the difference. "Oh, dear. Time for me to go. Do you have an application I might take with me? A brochure? I'm very interested in learning more about how this lifestyle works."

Sin. Lifestyle. Code words? Was he with the religious protestors?

She added another deadly sin to the conversation: lying. "I'm so sorry, Frank," she said, handing him her business card, "but we're revamping all our sales materials right now. We're completely out of print brochures. But if you give me your telephone number and mailing address, we can be sure to reach out and give you whatever you need."

"Whatever I need? Sounds good to me," he replied, scribbling on the back of a card he pulled out of his breast pocket. He handed it to Josie and she took it, not looking at it.

"We'll be in touch," she said as he slipped out of the door. Janet was in the hallway and caught Josie's eye. Josie gave her an index finger to ask her to wait.

"Oh, yes, Josie," Frank said with great affect as he pumped her arm silly with an overly enthusiastic handshake, "you most definitely have not seen the last of me."

Josie's phone buzzed, trapped in her purse in a desk drawer. She ignored the sound as Frank walked away, whistling some tune she couldn't name, the echo following him.

Janet craned her neck and let out a low whistle of her own. "Who's the silver fox? Meow." Janet was about the same age as Frank, Josie guessed, and was happily married to her high school sweetheart, a marathon runner who cracked chests as a cardiac surgeon in his spare time. Talk about a power couple.

"Someone who wants to be a client," Josie said absentmindedly, fingering the card he'd given her. The handwritten phone number and mailing address were barely legible, but indicated a Boston address. No surprise there. Most people who became clients were local, though an increasing number were signing on via internet.

"Huh. If I could get Herb on board, and if that's the kind of man you're getting as a client," Janet muttered as she watched Frank's ass turn a corner, "then maybe I need to come in for a free information session."

Josie rolled her eyes and snorted. Janet's husband, Herb, had the personality of Mr. Rogers. The man served homeless guys on the street in downtown Boston, handing out wool blankets in subzero temperatures in the winter.

"That's enough. You're buying," Josie choked out.

"Why am I buying?"

"Because now I need coffee to bleach out the vision of you and Herb and...that guy..." She shuddered.

"I can't believe you're such a prude and you run a threesome dating service!" Janet's eyes twinkled and she said the words quietly, leaning in as though sharing a salacious secret. Which, actually, she was. While most of the accountants knew what Good Things Come in Threes was, they didn't talk about it publicly.

"Not a prude. Just don't want to know about your fantasies. Or Herb's." Josie shuddered again.

"Hey, I do commit double entry all the time." Janet cocked one eyebrow. "In a strictly professional sense."

Josie's groan filled the staircase as they made their way down to latte central.

Even a cup of great coffee, though, wouldn't drown out the voice of warning that wouldn't stop yammering inside Josie.

She needed to talk to someone, and Janet wouldn't do.

"Shit!" she barked as they made their way down the stairs. Janet always took the stairs, both up and down; she said working at a desk meant she needed to move her body whenever she could. "I left my purse back in the office."

"I'm buying," Janet said with great sarcasm. "Remember?"

Josie perked up. "Oh. That's right. Never mind. It's locked in the office. Thanks!"

By the time she read the nine text messages from Laura later that afternoon, the coffee's buzz had long worn off, but the bitter taste in her mouth remained.

* * *

As Mike and Dylan walked into her East Cambridge apartment, Jillian perched on Mike's hip, it occurred to Josie that the men had never been here. Laura had come over with Jillian plenty of times, for business meetings or "business meetings" which were thinly disguised coffee chats that Laura needed, but Mike and Dylan had never been over.

For a split second she felt self-conscious. The place was neat and tidy, so no worries there, but it certainly didn't hold a candle to Mike's lodge-like cabin in the woods, a fortress buried in the middle of nature, where the sounds of the city were as distant as the heavens. Her place was small and a bit shabby, with baseboards that hadn't been painted since the late 1990s, old radiators that hissed and groaned when called to action during New England winters, and her cat, Crackhead, who stared at the now-toddling Jillian with a look of horror so pronounced it made Josie burst into giggles.

The cat shot under the television cabinet in the living room and probably would be there for the next three days.

"Kiht," Jillian said with glee, practically running to the cabinet, swiping her hand to grab at the disappeared cat and knocking over a stack of DVDs.

Shit. Her (and Alex's) apartment was about as childproofed as Jennifer Lawrence's cell phone was secure from hackers.

Which was to say: *not.*

"Sorry," Dylan muttered, bending down to pick up the DVDs. He grabbed a small stained-glass candle holder from a lower shelf and handed it to her. "Jillie will destroy this, so you might want to put it high."

"And secure your car keys," Mike said pleasantly, sitting in one of her chairs, legs stretched out. He was just a tiny bit taller than Alex, and his legs nearly touched the TV cabinet. When Josie sat in that chair, *her* legs barely touched the ground.

"Yeah," Dylan said, laughing. "She threw mine down the vent again."

"No vents here," she said, pointing to the silver-painted radiators. "Just those."

"Good thing it's summer, then," Laura added, walking in behind them, carrying a diaper bag the size of an Appalachian backpacker's supply pack. "We wouldn't want her to burn herself."

"Geez, I'd never thought of that!" Josie exclaimed, looking at her apartment through what felt like new eyes. Childproofing? Kids losing car keys? Tiny toddlers getting burned by parts of her everyday life that seemed perfectly benign?

Parenting sure wasn't for wimps.

And Alex, she knew, wanted kids. Her heart started to spin in circles and she changed the subject. "Coffee, anyone?"

Three "yeses" later and she found herself gratefully making brews for the group. Jillian was drinking from the tap when Josie returned with the coffee, Laura settled on the couch next to Dylan, shirt pulled up.

"You're still nursing?" she asked, regretting the words instantly.

"You're still breathing?" Dylan asked.

"I wasn't being judgmental. Just...you don't see too many people nursing a thirteen-month-old. Not where I'm from, at least." She frowned. "Then again, I never paid much attention. Maybe they did and I didn't notice."

"You ever see thirteen-month-olds drinking from bottles and using pacifiers?" Mike asked evenly.

"Yes."

"Same thing, right?" He had a point.

"How about we switch topics and talk about Laura's uncle. You said he came to the office?" Dylan's voice was flat and chilling, making Josie's heart return to that spinning sensation, like she had a wound top inside her chest that had been released. She'd read Laura's texts after coming back from coffee with Janet and had texted right back, rushing home.

To her surprise, Laura had wanted to meet *here*.

She recounted the story with as much detail as possible, careful to convey every subtle gesture, every calculation Frank had seemed to make during their encounter. Laura was, by turns, upset, shocked, chagrined, dismissive, and worried, and it hurt Josie to think that she might have contributed to some sort of growing issue.

"Why now?" she asked. The looks on all three faces told her it was a question they'd been pondering, too.

"Money," Laura said with a sigh. Jillian popped off Laura's breast and shouted the word, making them all laugh.

"Wan Bub Gup," she said, pointing to the television.

Josie gave Laura a perplexed look. "Bub Gup?"

"The only television show she watches. We put on Bubble Guppies once a day." Laura seemed guilty. Josie couldn't fathom why. Television had been her babysitter as a kid.

"I don't know what that is. Is it on PBS?"

Dylan named a different channel.

"Oh," Josie said apologetically. "Sorry. We don't have cable." When Alex had moved in, they'd gone over every single bill each had, an exercise in financial nudity that still left her feeling weirdly vulnerable. Sharing expenses but also revealing debt loads made her woozy. It was one thing to know he had enormous student loans from medical school, but quite another to admit how much she spent on coffee at little shops, or to show him her Victoria's Secret credit card balance.

They'd cut a bunch of expenses to tighten their budget, and cable had been one of the items to go. As long as they had Netflix, she was fine.

"Ow tide?" Jillian asked Dylan, rolling off Laura's lap and sinking a chubby shoe into Laura's midsection as Laura gasped but took the kick in stride. "Ow tide?"

"You want to go outside?" Dylan asked, holding the baby now, who started to bounce with anticipation.

"OW TIDE!" she screeched, making Josie's eardrum buzz like a sonic boom. Holy hell. The kid had chops.

"I guess we're going outside." Mike snickered, grabbing his coffee cup. "Is that a park across the street?"

"Yep. With a baseball field."

Mike's brow furrowed. "A playground, though? With swings?"

Josie had to think for a second. She didn't really go over to that section, but yes—there was a playground. "Let's go over and I'll show you," she said with a nod. The past few minutes had unnerved her. The sudden appearance of Laura's uncle Frank was unsettling enough, but more than that was the paradigm shift in everything.

Laura, Mike, and Dylan lived their life through the lens of Jillian. She was watching it in slow motion, rolled out second by second, from the layout of her apartment, to how Laura used her body, to where they talked. Parenthood hadn't just given them a human being to raise, nurture, and love.

It had literally changed how they viewed the entire world.

And Josie didn't have that.

Yet.

She felt like they breathed a different air, spoke the same language but did so with different meanings. Like they were living in the same physical space but in a slightly altered dimension. It felt weird. Alienating. So jarring that Josie's brain split into a thousand little pieces of ribbon that started floating aimlessly, blown by a growing wind of discontent.

Dylan carried Jillian as they crossed the street, while Laura managed two coffee mugs, her shirt and

338

bra back in place after the nursing. Mike tagged along, ambling slowly, enjoying sips of coffee as they passed the famous No Parking sign where Alex had hurt himself.

Laura giggled as she read it. "Dr. Perfect recovered from his wound?" It was a rhetorical question, because that had happened ages ago. Eight months or so, but still... She and Alex had been broken up and Darla, Trevor, and Joe had been on the porch with her, drinking coffee and talking. Alex's apartment had been a few blocks away and—he later confessed—he had taken to going for runs around the park in hopes of catching a glimpse of her.

On that fateful morning he'd caught a glimpse, all right. Of her touching Darla's boyfriend's bare chest, a heart surgery scar Darla insisted Josie check out.

Slam! Alex had been so distracted he'd run full force into a parking sign.

That damn sign was responsible for a wicked daring scar on his eyebrow and their reunion.

Thank God for glimpses.

"Ha ha, Laura, you know he is."

"You recovered from having him move in?"

Josie opened her mouth to answer back with a wisecrack and found herself wordless. The correct answer was "no."

"Ummm..."

Laura nodded as they reached a set of baby swings Dylan had rooted out as if powered by parent echolocation. He was lowering a squealing Jillian into the little seat.

"Ting! Ting!" she crowed. *Swing!*

Josie couldn't help but smile. Dylan, her ever-faithful servant, did as ordered.

It must be good to be the queen. And Queen Jillian grinned and giggled, shouting, "Mo! Mo!" with the assurance that her daddy would, indeed, give her more.

Josie couldn't help but tear up, suddenly.

Laura's reassuring hand was on her shoulder, rubbing her back lightly. "You okay?"

Josie nodded and gulped hot coffee quickly, doing anything to break through this strange emotional state she floated in. "Yeah. Fine."

Eyes bouncing between her daughter and Josie, Laura looked at her friend, settling on an expression of compassion. "You guys talking about kids yet?" Before Josie could answer, Laura interrupted, "No. Wait. Let me guess. *Alex* is talking about kids and you are still hyperventilating because he uses your towels to shower."

"Something like that." Josie stared glumly at the bottom of her empty coffee cup. A change of subject was desperately in order. "Let's talk about Frank."

"Let's not." Mike walked up behind Laura and placed a long, strong, protective arm around her shoulders, careful not to jostle her and spill the coffee she carried.

"Let's not what?"

"Talk about Frank."

Mike's jaw tightened and his face turned worried. For no clear reason, Josie's heart squeezed and she wished Alex were here. He'd called earlier—a birth had turned into a messy surgical case—and there was no hope of seeing him for at least eight hours. Which normally was fine and no big deal, but this Frank business was turning *into* a big deal.

"Why would he come and see you, Josie, and not Laura?" Mike asked. She knew he already had his own ideas, but was trying to tease it out. They could analyze Frank's actions all they wanted, but answers were fleeting.

She shrugged. "No idea. But when I go over that conversation, he was clearly fishing for information on Laura."

Laura's grip on one of the coffee mugs tightened, and her hand was shaking as she lifted it to drink. Mike unwrapped his arm from her shoulders and wordlessly took Dylan's mug out of her hands. She gave him a grateful look.

Laura sighed. "He wants money, just like he did after my mom died. Mom told me he did the same thing after my grandparents died. He just does this."

Mike seemed to struggle with whether to say anything. Josie felt for him. A million questions swirled through her disjointed brain, but she couldn't find a tactful way to ask any of them.

Fortunately, Mike did. "And did anyone give him money?"

Nodding as she sipped more of her now-lukewarm coffee, Laura answered, "Sure. Mom and Frank split everything after Grandma and Grandpa died. Fifty-fifty, even though my grandparents left more to Mom. Mom said it was easier and more ethical that way." A pained expression clouded her face. "But a bunch of family heirlooms went missing. Mom always wondered…"

"You think he stole them?" Josie asked.

Laura gave her a tiny shrug, tentative but clear.

"And after your mom died, he put the thumbscrews on you," Mike said in an angry voice.

Josie just looked at Laura with as much compassion as she could. "Really? You never talked much about it."

Laura's face reddened. "I wasn't sure *how* to talk about it. Mom died and between insurance and whatever assets she had, there was a small amount. A little more than five figures. But Frank came along and pushed for me to sue for pain and suffering and a bunch of issues related to her asthma attack and the car accident."

"But you didn't. I would have heard about it," Josie said, frowning.

This time, Laura's red face came from anger. "Frank...well, *bullied* is the wrong word, though it's the first one that comes to mind. He *shamed* me. I can see that now, but I couldn't understand it then. He told me this was private, a family affair, and I shouldn't talk about it with anyone. That there could be legal ramifications." She gave Josie a pleading look. "So I didn't. Not even with you."

A big lump formed in Josie's throat. "Laura, I'm so sorry."

"No, *I'm* sorry. I should have shared."

A ragged breath escaped Josie. "No! No! I understand why you didn't talk about it, and I'm not hurt or offended or whatever. I mean, I'm sorry Frank did that to you. Your mother's death was hard enough on you, but to have him do that to you on top of it all is so disgusting!"

Mike and Josie shared a look of well-defined righteous anger on Laura's behalf.

At that exact moment, Dylan called out to the group, "Help? Can I have someone take over? My arm's about to fall off and I am in need of a caffeine injection!"

The three of them walked over, Mike taking on the onerous task of pushing Queen Jillian over and over as she leaned forward in the baby swing and chomped happily on the black plastic edge.

"Oooooh, gross," Josie exclaimed, unable to help herself.

All three parents didn't react. "Whatever. She teethes on anything. At least it's not the toilet brush handle," Dylan said casually. *Too* casually.

"What?" Mike and Laura said in horror. Josie couldn't even speak.

"That was a joke," Dylan hastily replied.

"Better be," Laura muttered under her breath.

"Speaking of things that live in toilets, are you guys talking about Frank?" Dylan asked, then gulped the entire mug of coffee down in an impressive display of throat muscles and desperation. "Ah...coffee. My mistress," he added with a wink to Laura.

She gave him a wan smile. "Just telling Josie about how Frank convinced me to give him money after Mom died."

His face contorted. "That bastard. I wish I'd been there. Wish I'd been part of your life..."

"*I* was part of her life, and it sounds like he manipulated her so badly," Josie declared.

"I'm not the same person I was back then," Laura said softly. "I made mistakes. I undervalued myself." She pulled herself up to her full height. "I let myself think I was lesser than other people, that I was inferior."

Dylan pulled her in for an embrace, kissing her cheek. "You're anything but."

"I know that *now*. But I didn't know it then, and Frank has this...way about him. A charm. A manipulation or, like, a—"

Josie nodded. "A pull. Like he's your friend. Like he's the—"

343

"Nicest guy in the world," Laura and Josie said simultaneously.

Laura shot Josie a shocked look. "You felt it, too?"

"Yep. He's smooth. *Too* smooth. But even a jaded old bitch like me started to find him intriguing. Alluring. Like he made me feel important even as he picked my pocket. He's one hell of a *something*."

Laura just nodded.

"What did you give him? And did you sue?" Josie asked.

Laura's shoulders slumped at Josie's question. Peals of laughter came from Mike and Jillian, and an involuntary smile spilled over Josie's face. A flash of a tiny, dark-haired little girl, a blend of her and Alex, hit her be-ribboned brain like a lightning strike.

That made her smile even more.

Set her heart a'spinnin', too.

"I looked into suing. Took Frank with me to a few attorney consults, but they were clear: I could sue, but there really wasn't cause for wrongful death. She had an asthma attack and lost control of the car. It really was that basic. And Frank spent most of the time trying to find a way to get the attorney to tell him how he could sue."

"Why would you sue, though?" Dylan asked. "I'm no lawyer, but I testified sometimes as a paramedic for some nasty car crashes. And the only way a family member can sue is, well…" His brows knitted. "I don't remember the details, but you can't just sue. You have to have a good reason."

"That's what the lawyers all told him. He got more and more upset, less and less smooth as each appointment led to more of the same."

"And then…" Josie said.

"And then it's like he just stopped. Not so much gave up, but pivoted. Changed his mind. He told me he'd been secretly helping Mom financially for years, and asked for some—later, *half*—of her estate."

"You gave it to him?" It took everything inside Josie not to scream the words with incredulity. Only respect for Laura and love for the woman who'd been is no much pain held her back.

"Yes." Forlorn and embarrassed, Laura gave Josie a look that begged her to stop judging. "I just wanted him to go away."

"And now he's back." Josie sighed. What a mess.

"He's back, and you have *us* to make sure he never takes advantage of you again," Dylan said.

Laura's eyes filled with tears. "Don't you see, Dyl? That's the problem. You two and Jillian, I mean."

Dylan flinched. "We're *problems*?"

"You and Mike have trust funds totaling $2.2 billion. Maybe even more now. Back then I had a little over $11,000. He went away after a while."

"And you don't think he's going away this time?" Dylan swelled, his thick chest seeming to grow with a long, deep breath of anger and protectiveness that made Josie feel secure, and she wasn't even his partner.

Laura's words punctured that security.

"Not easily."

CHAPTER TWO

LAURA

"**T**hree plates of fried food?" Madge asked with skepticism, but scribbled the order on her electronic device. "And three pieces of cheesecake? Or more? How many of you are coming?"

"Just me and Darla," Laura peeped.

Madge's mouth twisted into an apprising frown, as if she were impressed. "That'll do. You need to talk about your threesomes, huh?" Sunlight flashed on a small ring on Madge's hand as she placed the order on her handheld electronic device, making Laura blink.

"Excuse me?" Laura choked.

Madge thumbed toward the door, as if there were some meaning Laura was supposed to get from the gesture. "You two didn't get a chance to really talk when you had that posse of men in here, stumbling over themselves to prove how cool they all were."

"Right." Laura's body went hot and cold, and she froze. Now she was talking about her personal life with Madge?

"We have a new specialty. Maple jalapeño—"

"You can stop right there and just bring us a plate," said a voice Laura recognized, bushy blonde frizz invading the space between her and Madge. Bright green eyes, same color as Laura's but so different, perfectly round and constantly evaluating everything she saw, sharp and calculated, met Laura's.

Darla.

"Howzitgoin'?" she said to no one in particular and yet to both Laura and Madge at the same time. It was a neat trick. Making people feel comfortable seemed to be embedded in Darla's DNA.

And that was exactly why Josie had hired her. Laura understood now that it wasn't just that Josie wanted to help her niece—which was perfectly understandable if that were the only reason to hire her. It went deeper. Not only was Darla in a permanent threesome, like Laura, she also possessed a gift of being so real. A little too real sometimes, but if you had to err in a direction, it was always better to tip toward the awkward than to be aloof.

Darla reached around behind Madge and began to fill a carafe with coffee, plunked it on the table, and snagged two mugs.

"You want a job as a waitress?" Madge asked with arched eyebrows.

"That can be my fallback," Darla said with a wink.

"I said that too, honey. Sixty-six years ago..." Madge's cackle sprinkled the air with something that made Laura smile as the old woman put in their order, yelling something to the cook in the back.

"We finally meet. Alone," Laura said as Darla poured herself a cup of coffee and dumped enough sugar in it to turn the mug into a pile of rock candy.

"No Josie. That means actual words will be exchanged between us," Darla cracked. Sizzling sounds of a deep fryer percolated through the nearly empty restaurant as Laura took a tentative sip of her own java.

"So." Darla's word came with a sigh. Her eyes were bright with repressed eagerness. "Time to talk threesomes."

"Yes."

How do I do this? Laura wondered. Darla made it easy.

"You wanna talk about sex? Or emotions? Or what to do when one of 'em is jealous? Or how—"

"How about we ask each other questions and just take it from there?" Laura said, struggling to find a way to make sense of this. Maybe she was being silly. Josie had strongly urged her to schedule this follow-up meeting, but now she was beginning to regret it.

"You go first." Darla dumped half the cream pitcher in her coffee and looked nervously around the room.

"Sure. So...does your mom know about you and Trevor and Joe?"

Darla began to choke, barely holding in what looked like a big swallow of coffee. As her throat spasms kicked in, Laura felt guilty. Wrong question to start with.

"Ah. No," Darla coughed out. "She wouldn't understand. She just thinks I moved out here for the job Josie got me."

"She doesn't know anything about Joe and Trevor?"

Darla shook her head slowly. "She kinda thinks I'm dating Trevor."

Laura shot one eyebrow up. "Kinda?"

Darla's shoulders slumped. "Uncle Mike saw me on the side of the road with Trevor and Joe, and then he gave me a ride to move out here, and it's like damage control, you know? Like politicians do. I had to give a tiny *sliver* of the truth to cover up the big fucking *whopper* of a truth so dangerous it couldn't be said."

Laura just blinked, taking that in. "Your turn," she said, dipping her head to drink more coffee.

"You three do a lot of DP?"

Laura's throat closed up and seized, tears pouring down the sides of her face as she set down her mug, hands flapping, cold water not helping. "What?" she croaked.

"DP. Double penetration," Darla clarified.

I know what it is! Laura thought, just as Madge delivered the food.

"I wish I had time to crash this talk," she said with a leer, disappearing as she shouted something about a truck delivery to the kitchen staff.

"You do that much? Because me and Trevor and Joe don't. I mean, once in a while, but everyone seems to think that's what threesomes do—and I—"

"Everyone? Who's everyone? How many people do you talk about your sex life with?" Laura marveled.

Darla started counting on her hand. "Two. Amy and Charlotte. And sometimes Josie, but the problem with Josie is she—"

"Overshares about her sex life," Darla and Laura said in unison as Laura dipped a fried green tomato into horseradish sauce.

They both laughed.

"And to answer your question—sometimes we do. But it's not like that's the main focus. It's a mixture. Me with Mike alone, me with Dylan alone, me doing something for one of them, all of us together…we mix it up. Like anyone in a one-on-one relationship, it's not like 'sex' means penis-in-vagina intercourse all the time. Same with us. It's not like 'sex' means DP every single time."

Darla picked up a fried mozzarella triangle and took half of it in one bite into her mouth. She looked relieved. "Same here."

Darla's phone buzzed and she checked it, chuckling as she read.

"Something funny?"

"Just Joe." Her cheeks turned pink as she shoved the phone back in her pocket. "Sexting."

Laura's face went a bit warm and she just said, "Oh." Dylan and Mike didn't do that with her. Was it generational? Texts from them tended to be along the lines of *We need milk* and *Where are the spare car keys?*

Maybe she could spice things up with suggestive Snapchat photos. Hmmm...

"How do you handle jealousy?" Darla asked, her face twisted with a sincere yearning for an answer Laura suspected she couldn't provide.

"What jealousy?"

Darla's face fell. Oh, shoot.

"You don't have that problem?"

Laura shook her head helplessly. "But I live with them both. I know you said Joe is so far away and he gets upset—"

Darla snorted, green eyes troubled. Madge dropped three sundaes off and Darla looked surprised.

"*Three?* Is someone else coming?"

"No. I couldn't choose just one," Laura explained guiltily.

Whoops of laughter poured out of Darla. "Neither can I. Guess that's why we're both with *two* men."

Laura's laugh burbled out of her before she could think.

"You're a woman after my own heart, Laura." Digging in, Darla spooned chocolate-espresso ice cream into her mouth. "And stomach."

351

They ate in silence. It was comfortable.

"What about marriage?" Darla asked.

Laura frowned, scraping the bottom of her dip cruet with a fried coconut shrimp. "What about it?"

"You ever wish you could get married? Like normal people? Like Josie and Alex?"

Laura gagged from the laughter that exploded out of her. "'Normal' and 'Josie' in the same sentence. How did you say that without laughing?"

Darla's shit-eating grin split her face into a glowing sun. "I *really* like you, Laura."

After she'd centered herself, Laura got serious. "I've thought about it. A lot. Especially since we had Jillian. But I can't choose just one of them." She gestured toward the ice cream dishes. "I can't choose a single *sundae* flavor. How am I supposed to pick Mike or Dylan?"

Darla swallowed, hard, but said nothing.

This time the silence between them was more contemplative. Laura's stomach flipped as she struggled internally with Darla's question. Marriage. Out of the question for her, Mike and Dylan. The law made that a reality.

Didn't make it any easier emotionally, though.

"What about your family?" Darla finally asked, breaking the quiet as they pinged between appetizers and ice cream.

"I don't have any," Laura said.

"You have that sneaky uncle, right?"

Josie and her big mouth. Laura frowned. "You know about that?"

Alarm filled Darla's eyes. "Josie told me about it because he came to work. Wanted me to know in case he showed up at the office." Her hands flew up in the air in a gesture of surrender. "I swear that's all I know and she didn't tell me nothin' personal." Darla's mild accent always came out when she was scared, and Laura reacted by trying to put her at ease.

"It's okay." Laura sighed. "Yes, crazy uncle." She laughed bitterly. "Crazy like a fox."

"He blackmailing you?" Darla's question was completely understandable, and if roles were reversed Laura certainly would be wondering the same thing. The boldness of the act of asking it was what made Laura's mouth drop open in shock.

Darla just blinked at her, clearly expecting an answer. If only Laura had been so confident when she was younger. So direct. So clear. Darla seemed to know herself and not take shit from anyone. Maybe she could teach Laura a thing or two.

"Not...no. Not that." *Not yet*, she half thought, brow frowning in consternation. "He's just skulking around and being creepy."

"Money," Darla declared. "You have it. Bet he wants it." Darla took an enormous spoonful of creme de menthe sundae, shoving the little dark chocolate peppermint in her mouth, mumbling around it. "Might be better to pay a weasel like that off."

Well now, wasn't she *blunt*?

"Won't that make him come back for more?" Laura asked.

"Can't stop a weasel from coming back to a henhouse full of chickens," Darla observed, mouth pursed and twisted up to one side as she clearly thought something through.

Then she pointed her long sundae spoon at Laura and added, "But you know how you handle a weasel?"

Laura leaned forward eagerly. "How?" This was better than talking about threesomes, or having a "girlfriend" chat about relationships. She didn't need that the way Josie thought she did. Knowing that she was secure in her own triad was good enough for Laura.

What she needed was this. Someone to talk to about Frank. Someone other than Dylan and Mike.

A slow, evil smile spread across Darla's face, making the skin on Laura's neck tingle.

"You find the weasel's predator. And you unleash it."

DYLAN

"**I** know it's not much to go on, Murph, but any help your brother can give me would be great," Dylan added, managing his phone while cutting strawberries for Jillian to chow down on. The meeting with Josie in Cambridge last week had made him feel like he was spinning his wheels, helpless and disemboweled. Unable to sleep last night, he'd come upon an idea in the deep, dark hours of the restless night.

A private investigator. The only person he knew who might know someone was his old buddy Murphy, and now he smiled a tight grin as his old friend turned out to be the right choice.

"Man, that's one hell of a mess, Dylan," Murph said, the sympathy oozing through the guy's voice. Murphy had been Dylan's fellow firefighter at the station, back when Dylan worked for a living, and they stayed in touch even as Dylan had stopped taking on volunteer shifts. Murphy's wife had weathered breast cancer and was doing very well—in part, Murphy constantly reminded him, because of well-timed financial help Dylan had been very glad to offer.

"Yeah, right? Bastard comes sniffing around wanting more."

"Can't say I'm surprised. People can be real assholes when it comes to money. Especially big money. Not everyone's like you," Murphy added. A few beats of silence made the air go tense as Dylan struggled with how to answer that. Guys at the station didn't do feelings, so this was...weird.

"Uh, thanks."

Murphy felt it, too, and his next words came out in a gruff tone. "No matter what, my brother Nick can find out anything about anybody. He was a cop for twenty-three years and just got his private investigator's license. He'll be fucking happy to get a referral." Murphy paused and let out a garbled laugh. "Fucking *shocked* is more like it. The last thing he'd expect me to do is send someone his way. I'm the clean one in the family."

That made Dylan smile. Man, he missed his old friends.

"You, *clean*? Hah."

"Hey, my mom had five kids. Two are in jail, one's dead, and there's just me and Nick left. A cop and a firefighter. Too bad Mom isn't alive to see us." Dylan could hear the sound of stubble being scratched. "Then again, maybe it's good she never saw Sarah and Joey's trials."

"What they in for?" Dylan was surprised to learn all this. Murph had been pretty closed-lipped when they'd worked together. Talked about his wife, his kids, that kind of thing, but he'd never really gone into specifics about his family of origin. Then again, neither had Dylan.

Murph snorted. "What else? Drugs and assault. Stupid kids. Sarah got her physical therapy assistant license and then she started stealing painkillers. Got caught. The DA made an example out of her. Joey got into a gang fight that left another guy half paralyzed. God love my little brother and sister, but they never had much sense."

Dylan knew the casual tone hid the pain of what he'd really gone through. You couldn't stop someone from a path of self-destruction. All you could do was make sure you weren't a casualty or collateral damage.

"Sorry, man. I had no idea." He wondered about Murph's dead sibling but didn't ask. Some lines you don't cross.

"And we had no idea you were going through all the shit you were going through, Dyl. We keep our shit to ourselves because sharing it makes you feel like a freak."

Dylan burst out into relieved laughter. "Isn't that the truth."

"Only truth I know, man. The only truth I know. Take care and Nick will be in touch." *Click.*

Dylan stared at Jillian's little red face, lips covered with strawberry juice, pale green eyes gleaming with joy. She was so little, so much work, and yet really simple when you thought about it. Feed her. Love her. Keep her clean. Keep her occupied. Move her when she needed to be moved. Leave her alone when she needed peace. Soothe her when she was upset.

Why couldn't everyone be so simple?

Her face split into a grin that touched his heart.

And so cute.

"Wah tees?" she asked.

"Cheese?" he clarified.

"Tees! Tees!" she said, eyes on the fridge. Her language acquisition was frighteningly swift. And if he wasn't careful, she'd imitate every word he said. The'd already learned that the hard way a few weeks ago when he'd hurt himself fixing a leak in the bathroom and shouted, "Shit!"

Little Miss Imitation had cried out "tit!" for the next week. Laura's glares had lasted far longer.

Parenthood. Can't win.

Mike walked into the kitchen, hair wet from a shower, and started making coffee. "Was that Murphy you were talking to? How's his wife?"

"Good. Still cancer free. And yeah, I called him. His brother, Nick, is an ex-cop and just got his private investigator's license. Murph gave me his number."

Mike nodded slowly. "You think this is the right path?" It wasn't much of a question, though, as Mike's jaw clenched.

"I think it's the only path. Whatever Dear Old Uncle Frank is up to isn't anything good."

"What Josie told us..." Mike's voice dropped two octaves. "Sniffing around like that. And now poor Laura can't sleep."

"You noticed, too?"

Mike gave him a very rare eye roll. "I'm next to her too, Dylan."

"No, man, I know. It's just you normally sleep like the dead."

"I do?" Mike seemed genuinely surprised. "How do I master that in my six inches of bed?"

Jillian called out, "Tees! Tees!" before Dylan could come back with a wisecrack. Mike's coffee finished its steamy sputtering just as Laura walked into the kitchen, frumpled and sleepy.

She reached for the mug and cradled it to her chest, sipping slowly. "Ahhh, thank you so much. You're the best." Standing on tiptoes, she kissed Mike's cheek, then walked over to Jillian for a quick smooch. Dylan burst into laughter at the look of pure confusion on Mike's face.

"She totally sniped your brew," Dylan declared. Laura walked out of the kitchen with that sleepy shuffle he knew so well.

"And on one of the few mornings when I'm in a rush," Mike added, starting the whole coffee process over again, bemused but not upset.

"It'll take two more cups of coffee before she realizes what she did, and then she'll feel sorry," Dylan said.

Mike nodded, the curved ends of his overgrown blonde hair making the collar of his business shirt wet. "Yeah. I know. She didn't mean it."

Dylan stopped for a moment and took a good, long look at Mike. Shined black leather shoes with laces. Wool pants perfectly pressed, with a crease that could cut you if you brushed up against it. White business shirt with cuff links, the gold ones Laura gave him for his birthday last year. A loose tie around his neck, red with little white, stippled dots through it. Whatever Mike was dressed for, it was the big time.

In contrast, Dylan looked down at his own body. Gym shorts he'd played basketball in so many times they might as well dribble on their own. Commando underneath.

And…he wore nothing else.

"Where you going, Christian Grey?" he asked as he put little cubes of cheese on Jillian's high-chair tray. She scarfed them down like they were chocolate, grinning madly.

Mike chuckled and poured himself a bowl of coconut flake cereal, covering it with almond milk. He was on some paleo diet kick these days. Dylan humored him. "Meeting with some commercial real estate folks."

"Real estate? You buying something?"

"No," Mike said through a mouth full of cereal. "They're the buyers."

Dylan frowned. "You're selling the resort?" Their cabin was on the resort, and it was their home now. If Mike were making a decision that enormous, he should have clued Dylan and Laura in a long time ago.

"No, no. Not—it's not what you think." Milk spilled from Mike's spoon onto his shirt. "Damn it!" he exclaimed.

"Jammit!" Jillian echoed. "Jammit, jammit, jammit."

Mike and Dylan shared a look of horror.

"Shit," Dylan muttered without thinking.

"Tit! Tit!"

Laura, of course, picked that exact moment to shuffle back in for her second cup of coffee. How that woman managed to drink it that hot and that fast made Dylan's mind reel.

"Great!" she said with abundant sarcasm. "Just great!"

"Tit mama. Tit mama!"

"She's got *that* right," Dylan said, staring at Laura's lush, untamed breasts. His favorite time of day was morning, when she awoke braless, letting the girls hang out as they should. He hardened under his all-too-thin shorts, and it was painfully obvious.

And painful.

"Jillie, don't say...you know..." They'd learned the hard way that a toddler would just keep repeating the very thing you try to tell her not to. Toddler Logic 101.

"Tit! Jammit tit!"

"Damn tits making me hard," Dylan said in a voice meant for Mike. But he was a little too loud.

"I heard that!" Laura exclaimed. Her eyes traveled down his shirtless chest to his raging cock. "And I can see it, too."

"You gonna do something about it, lady?" he asked in a teasing voice.

Mike made a dismissive sound. "Get a room."

"You offering to watch the baby?"

Mike looked at the clock on the stove. "You two serious?" He looked at Laura, who arched one eyebrow.

Ah, God, she was so ripe this morning. Dylan could taste her, thinking of her thighs pressing against his cheekbones...

And his cock made his shorts rise like an eight-person dome tent.

But he only needed one person right now...

Mike smiled. "You do the same for me tomorrow?" he asked Dylan. "I gotta leave in fifteen minutes, though."

Laura laughed and pointedly looked at Dylan's crotch, which only made him harder. "I think three minutes will do it," she teased.

"Three? Only three?" He gave a look of concession. "Okay, to come inside you." He grabbed her hand and pulled her toward the bedroom. "That gives us twelve minutes for everything else."

She followed him, jogging a little, which made her tits bounce and his body tense with growing arousal. Jesus. She was serious. He had been joking about sex and now—

360

Man, he loved his life.

Throwing her on the bed, he stripped her out of her pajamas in seconds, throwing his own shorts so far across the room he'd find them later in a spider plant that was perched on a shelf above the bathroom doorway. Their mouths pressed together, hot and wet, tongues dancing at the rush of decidedly illicit pleasure they were both stealing. Technically, nothing was stolen except for time.

And time was a precious commodity these days.

"Cyndi's coming tomorrow," she whispered as he took one nipple in her mouth.

"And you're coming right now," he answered, fingers on her hot red nub already, the combination of sucking and touching normally enough to drive her to her first orgasm.

"I meant," she gasped, "we could go to the sex cabin when she watched Jillie." She frowned, her body tensing. He stopped and pulled up, looking at her obviously in distress.

"What?" he asked, desperate to make her happy again.

"I just...maybe we shouldn't. Not with Frank coming around suddenly."

Motherfucker. A flash of hot rage filled him, making him soften. "When you're with me or Mike, you're safe. Period." His head buzzed like a hive full of disturbed yellow jackets, ready to plunge their stingers into the source of the problem. Laura most certainly was not the cause of any of his issues, but the urge to sink into *something* needed to be appeased. Preferably his cock sinking into her warm, loving core versus his fist into her uncle's face.

"But I—"

"How about we focus on the present and worry about the rest later?" he said, nuzzling her neck. He was taming her and gentling her all at once, her body tense and eager, aroused and suspicious, centered on the edge of some kind of yawning chasm of anxiety and dread.

She relaxed, but he could feel the difference.

Frank needed to be dealt with. *Now*.

"You're right. I love you so much. And I love *this* so much," she said with a gasp. Her touch on his shaft made him hard again. He was a simple man with simple pleasures, caught in a complicated web. Later, after he made her head and body explode, he'd simplify this Frank mess.

Simplify the *fuck* out of it.

"Ah," he said, words already falling from his mind like dying leaves. Inarticulate half-thoughts fluttered through the cavernous space where linear thinking was supposed to take place inside him. Replacing it was a singular throbbing need to get inside her. Now.

Now now now.

Her eyes were unfocused, mind a million miles away, even his touch unable to ground her. A wellspring of aroused madness bubbled up inside him, making his blood rush to the surface of his body, turning him into a throbbing mass. Maybe he didn't need to ground her.

Pinning her in place with his cock would do.

He prowled over her prone body, one hand doing the swift job of parting her legs, mouth on her before she could protest—but she didn't even try. Her hips thrust up in grateful acceptance of what he gave, and it was his own gratitude and grinding need that met her in his mind.

She pulled his head away, though, squirming under his tongue. "No. Not this. I want you to fuck me. Hard. Now."

That was an order he'd gladly obey.

Pulling himself up in a swift, flowing movement, he belied the laws of physics, his shaft filling her, meeting wet, slippery silk as he groaned, neck muscles tightening with the surprising pleasure of how good this moment always felt. *Always*. His power over her was matched by Laura's own intensity, eyes wide open and meeting his, the challenge met by paired flesh that sought one conclusion.

Her hands were rough, hard fingers digging into the corded muscles of his shoulders, his back, and when her fingernails sank into his ass he pulled out, plunging deep, the change in pace calibrated to make her gasp.

"Oh!" she moaned, the sound clipped by another thrust, then another, the lovemaking intense and hard, fevered and not gentle, as if he were driving out all her insecurity and fears by pushing her body to the limit. Maybe the mind would follow, vanquishing the confusion and overwhelm, but Dylan had no control over that. Her mind was hers. She had to find her own way.

Her body was a completely different subject, and as he pressed his fists into the mattress, curved his hips up and in, he pierced her with a final push that made her gasp turn ragged, the sweet pink of her cheeks matching the soft walls below that he played so well to elicit her explosive climax.

She shuddered and he followed, eyes now closed and body tightening, his worship of her soft, lush landscape the only thought he was capable of clinging to, sweat sprinkling his back, the hot push of abs against abs, her legs cordoned around his waist like he was rescuing her making him feel like a god.

Laura did this to him. Made him feel omnipotent. Made him feel like he could do anything when he was inside her, as she wriggled and groaned, shimmered and panted—because he did that to her.

He did.

His muscles twitched, hot seed pouring out of him, draining him, his mouth sucking one pert nipple in as she convulsed in an aftershock of sensual glory. And then it all faded, the red lights of the clock's numbers telescoping into focus, his mind back in the real world even as his flesh was encased by her.

Slipping out, he separated himself from her, heartbeat normalizing, the transition from sex world to practical life always fragile. He grinned at the ceiling, willing his body to go back to baseline.

"Thank you for that," she said with a sultry voice, the sound of sex in the cadence of her words. It was a full-throated sound that hinted at a landscape of lust and more. He was hard again.

She noticed.

"Nice refractory period," she said, nodding with approval. That made him laugh, and the two dissolved into giggles.

"One minute!" Mike's voice barreled down the hallway. "I really do have to go!"

Dylan jumped up and searched for his shorts, finding them dangling over his head, making him laugh. Laura mimicked him, jabbing her legs into her pajama pants.

"I got this," she said, pulling him in for a kiss, the press of his naked body against her flannel-covered hips and legs making him inhale slowly. Sensation receded, replaced by thought as the day's tasks spread out before him.

Rather have *her* spread out before him, but hey—duty called.

As she sashayed out of the bedroom and she heard Jillian shout, "Mama! Mama!" his eyes lit on his phone. Naked and distracted, he grabbed it, searching for Nicholas Murphy, private investigator. Mike walked in as he searched the Google listings.

"Hey." Mike opened the closet door and pulled out another white shirt, undoing his cuff links. "You mind covering your junk?"

Dylan looked down and shrugged. "You've seen it before. Don't look if you don't like it."

Mike snorted, peeled out of his dirty shirt, grabbed the new one, and marched out down the hall, shouting, "Laura? Can you tie my tie for me? You do the knot just right."

Within three minutes he had the number. And just as he heard Mike's Jeep roar out of the driveway, a voice rougher and more jaded than any he'd ever heard in his life answered the phone.

That was a big fucking comfort, because rough and jaded got shit *done*.

CHAPTER THREE

MIKE

Leaving Laura, Jillian, and Dylan wasn't hard—Mike knew Dylan would keep them safe if something happened, and the chances that this Frank character would cause problems were remote. While Laura was clinging to Jillian like she was a life preserver, Mike looked at this from a different angle.

Frank wanted money.

What was his price?

A five-figure check could make this all go away. Maybe. If Frank knew how deep their pockets were, he would want more. And if they gave him money, he might come back again. Knowing the tap was as big as it was—and the $2.2 billion trust fund was public knowledge—would Frank's interference never stop?

Then again, this was shadowboxing right now. The guy didn't have the balls to approach Laura directly. Josie—in person. Laura—by email.

He was cagey, all right.

And Mike had no problem writing a check to make this all disappear.

His call to his lawyer had been revealing, and when all was said and done they'd scheduled a meeting for later today to discuss the implications of possibly giving Frank money to go away. First, though, he had this real estate buyer's meeting.

While he wasn't planning to sell the resort, he was prepared to sell off enormous tracts of land for a singular purpose:

To preserve them.

A real estate developer had recently made plans to put in more than one hundred new homes on land that had come available earlier in the year, along with strip malls that could drive small local businesses into the ground.

He was too stretched to buy it then—even a $2.2 billion trust fund had its limits when you split it with another person and only could use the income each year. No complaints. That amount was a small fortune, but in terms of running a complex business like his ski resort, with more than a hundred employees, loads of heavy machinery, high liability costs in cases of injury, and myriad issues that plagued small ski resorts, it wasn't as much money as he'd thought.

But he was fine.

A conservation group's attorney had approached him last week to discuss buying ski resort land that abutted the proposed development for a simple purpose: protection. If the land were environmentally protected, the developer wouldn't be able to put houses so close to the ski resort.

Locals were excited by the idea, and it could help the community.

A thought nagged at him, driven by comments from Laura:

When was enough *enough*? He didn't have to own the resort. He didn't have to run it. While he'd handed much of the workload over to Shelly, his now-operations manager, he still worked too many hours.

Work invaded his mind constantly, and he never, ever felt like he could turn it off. Never felt like he could relax.

Never could let his guard down.

And now Frank came along and made his guard go way, way up. Unlike Dylan, he wasn't hyped up. Unlike Laura, he wasn't scared.

Mike's view of this was more tactical. Figure out the guy's weakness. Figure out what he wanted most. Manipulate those two pieces of information to strategic advantage. Develop a plan. Execute it.

And then walk away from the entire mess.

If it could be so easy, though, it would be. Nothing was ever that simple. As he picked up Route 2 to head into the city, his mind was everywhere but where it should have been.

Home.

With the people he loved most.

* * *

The meetings in Boston had gone well enough that he drove back to the ski resort's corporate offices with a much lighter heart. The conservation group advocates were well informed and pleasant to work with, and his lawyer had given him the most basic of advice regarding Frank, which boiled down to one simple word:

Delay.

Whatever Frank hinted at wanting, assuming it was money, just buy time. The lawyer also recommended hiring a private investigator (off the record) to learn more about Frank's past. Dylan was already on that one, and Mike felt like they had this. Frank could be managed out of being any sort of a threat. Or even a bother.

Feeling like a nine-hundred-pound weight had been lifted from his shoulders, Mike found himself practically whistling as he walked into the resort's offices, his pleasant mood cut short by the look on Shelly's face when he walked in.

She looked a bit sick.

Her fingers dug into the wool of his suit jacket, slipping on the soft material, then tight again as she yanked hard to get him to walk into a small, unused office. Considering their size difference, her efforts were futile. It was like watching an ant try to move a brick.

Nice of you to try, but good luck.

"Sorry. Did that hurt?" she hissed as her fingers dug into his arm and she tried to make him move. He took pity on her and followed, giving her the impression her efforts had any effect.

"No. Not a bit. What's going on?"

"You know some guy named Frank?"

He went cold. His entire body went frozen and numb, from scalp to toes, and when you're six and a half feet, that's a lot of frozen tundra.

"Is he here?" The look on Shelly's face told him just how deadly his voice sounded.

Which meant it reflected exactly how he felt.

"Yes. Been waiting for an hour. Says it's important and he's your uncle."

"My *what*?"

Shelly gave him a sour look. "I knew you'd never mentioned an uncle, so...I stalled."

"You've been wasting the past hour just hanging out here?"

She looked nervously toward the reception area. "I don't trust him."

"Hackles up that fast?"

She nodded, auburn hair spilling over intelligent eyes that nothing got past. "Right away. He's too smooth. Too oily. Someone like that will talk you out of your pants while draining your bank account, and expect you to make scrambled eggs and coffee in the morning for them."

Mike wanted to laugh. Really. It was funny, and he knew she made the joke to add some levity here, but it wasn't funny.

And Shelly knew it, too. Because she was serious.

Dead serious.

He pulled out his phone and tried to call Dylan. No answer. Laura. No answer. Machines both times, damn it.

He sent a group text, cringing at the thought of Laura's reaction:

Frank's here at my office.

And with that he squared his shoulders, tucked his phone in his breast pocket, and quietly thanked whatever deity watched over him that of all the days, today he'd dressed in his best Christian Grey imitation.

He would need all the power-tripping domination skills he possessed to get through this.

Bzzzz.

Before he could take ten steps, his phone jumped like a scared rabbit in his pocket. He took a long, deep breath and checked it.

WHAT? Laura's text only needed one word.

Then his phone rang. The second he answered it, the panicked stream of words just didn't stop.

"What do you mean he's there? At your office? At the ski resort? Why is he there and not here, visiting with me? What am I supposed to do now? I should answer his email, shouldn't I? Stupid, stupid, stupid of me to ignore it! Maybe if I'd answered it he would have said whatever he needed to say and none of this would be happening. I don't know why he's doing this! Why is he at your office? Why did he visit Good Things Come in Threes and talk to Josie and not—"

Dylan's voice suddenly cut through her rapid speech. "Hey, Mike. She's freaking out."

"You *think*?" Mike said with an arch in his voice.

"You need me there?"

"I think Laura needs you way more than I do. I don't know the man. Have nothing against him except for the impact this is all having on Laura."

"Plus you have Shelly. I'd want her to have my back in a brawl."

Mike smiled and laughed, the sound loose and shaky. He'd summoned all his reserves to deal with Frank and hadn't expected he'd need to talk with Laura and Dylan, too. Not like this. Laura's panic was a wee bit contagious, and he drew on his inner self to set himself back to center. Whatever he was about to face in his office wasn't going to control his entire family.

No fucking way.

Not normally the type to exert that alpha-male bullshit when confronting another man, Mike had to take a moment to collect himself. Channeling Dylan, he thought about which part of himself to tap into. Frank hadn't done a single threatening thing yet. His mere reappearance and presence unsettled Laura, but one fact remained:

Frank hadn't *done* anything.

Mike clued in on that for a moment. If this meeting was a blank slate, and technically there was no history between the two of them, then this was a pure and simple case of sniffing asses.

He frowned. In man-to-man terms, they were establishing dominance and submission in this first meeting. His lawyer had advised him to keep control over all conversations and to delay. Don't act. Just wait.

That didn't mean he had to roll over and beg to have his tummy scratched, either.

One of the advantages of being the size of a redwood tree was that other men tended to defer to him, even if Mike didn't know what to do with that power.

Right now, though, he knew damn well what to do with it, and as he opened the door to find Frank sitting in the chair across from his massive desk, he braced himself.

Alpha male engaged.

As Mike grasped the doorknob and entered the room with a confidence he found surprisingly easy to fake, he saw the back of the head of a man whom he presumed to be Frank. The man paused, not standing at first, seconds ticking by.

Half of Mike's mouth lifted up in a sardonic smile.

I was right, he thought. Already, the non-verbal power play began. Mike could play this game, too. After all, he had more than a decade of watching Dylan master it in a different setting, with jocks and firefighters and models. If anyone could provide him with lessons, it was Dylan. Funny how it hadn't occurred to Mike to do just that.

Get instruction from the master.

It was just as well, for Dylan had other issues he was working on. Hiring a private investigator to understand the inner workings of the man who was in front of Mike, now slowly standing and turning, giving Mike a friendly grin, was just as important.

"Michael Pine. It's a pleasure finally to meet you." Frank strode across the room with large steps, as if he owned the office. Mike stood still, knowing that being calm, centered, focused, and—most important—*unflappable* was key here.

His eyes bored into Frank's as they gripped hands. What they engaged in was less a handshake than an arm wrestling, Mike's younger, stronger clench finally winning out as he felt Frank's bones crunch under his grip.

"Hello..." Mike gave Frank a puzzled look. "And you are...?"

Frank's eyes gleamed with cunning. *Ah, so that's how it is?* they seemed to say. Mike detached himself from any emotional reaction. One blink could throw him off. This guy needed to be treated like he was dangerous. For all Mike knew, he could be.

Laura's reactions lately seemed to make it a possibility.

"Frank Stedman, of course." He reached out and slapped Mike's shoulder with enough force to rattle a smaller man's teeth. "Surely Laura has mentioned me!" The look on Frank's face said he'd be offended if the answer was "no," and yet the man clearly knew he was on shaky ground.

"Laura has talked about a distant uncle, but said it's been years since you've had any contact..." Mike let the sentence hang in the air, his face neutral but eyes lasered in on Frank's.

No blinking.

"It isn't as if I haven't tried!" Frank protested, sweeping his arm out toward Mike's desk. "You know Laura," he said with a conspirator's chuckle that made

Mike's fists clench. His jaw followed, forcing him to inhale very, very slowly to keep his cool. How dare the man claim to know Laura intimately enough to be so blasé?

"Why don't we sit and chat?" Frank added, watching Mike carefully, clearly searching for ways to read him. Mike wasn't giving any quarter.

"I prefer to stand." Mike's voice came out cold and hard. It grated against his own ears, and yet he let his eyes go dead. This was how he had to play if Frank was going to lead the charge with lies.

Lying about Laura right to Mike's face put Frank in the dangerous category, all right.

But Mike had plenty of danger in him, too.

"Stand. Hmmm." Frank broke eye contact and turned toward the massive window, floor to ceiling, that looked out over the large mountain that made up the ski resort. "With a view like this," Frank said with a conspirator's chuckle, "I'd stand, too."

Ignoring the fact that his desk chair faced the same view, Mike clasped his hands together at his waist and said nothing, blinking evenly, forcing his throat muscles to relax. Silence could unnerve most people.

Mike was good at silence.

Frank was not.

Ten beats went by. Twenty. Frank began to cast nervous glances at Mike, which would have unnerved him on any other day, in any other setting, but instead —to Mike's pleasant surprise—the looks only fortified him. Intensified his resolve to get this man out of Laura's life and to bring her back to the equanimity she so desperately desired.

Frank was a threat to their happy little life, and that meant he needed to be managed.

One quiet second at a time.

Finally, Frank broke. Clearing his throat, he said, "I'm sure you are wondering why I am here."

Mike decided to up the ante, moving swiftly toward Frank, only needing five powered steps to come within close range. Frank stiffened but did not move.

"I am." Mike measured his words in centuries, not seconds. The slower he spoke, moved, thought—*felt*—the more control he could maintain. An inner fury spun in circles, building an energy within that threatened to burst out of him.

He did not like this man.

In fact, *hate* might be strong enough a word to apply, because Frank represented something that was rotten to the very core, as if a seed itself were defective.

Frank gave a practiced, tight smile, instantly alerting Mike to the fact that nothing that was about to be said was true. "I've lost touch with Laura these years, and I regret it. She hasn't responded to my emails and I've started talking to her friends out of desperation."

Desperation. Mike would use the word *manipulation*, but semantics weren't important right now. Narrowing his eyes, Mike said nothing. Let the man stew in his own soup of insincerity.

Frank was a little too comfortable simmering there, for he went on, seeming to think Mike was buying this.

"And so when she didn't answer my email, I went to her place of business." Frank picked up a framed photo Mike had on his desk, a shot of the four of them at a huge outdoor festival last month, Jillian on Dylan's shoulders, chubby fists buried in his hair, a four-tooth smile lighting up the photo. Laura's hair was windblown and her face ruddy from the spring chill, but the picture was a pretty accurate summary of their messy, authentic life.

He wanted to peel it out of Frank's hands and hide it. The man didn't deserve to touch a representation of Laura and Jillie, much less sit here and claim to be the poor uncle nobody would talk to.

"You spoke with Josie," Mike said in that same cold voice.

Frank's eyes lowered, his head nodding slightly, the whole thing so choreographed Mike wanted to laugh, a bitter sound that clogged his throat now as he held back.

"I did. Lovely young woman." He gave Mike a bit of a leer, the kind of look men shared quietly when they talked about women as if they were compilations of soft flesh and nothing more. "I can see why she would be shared by two men."

Snap.

The thin layer of restraint in Mike gave way.

"How much?" he spat out.

Frank pretended to be offended. *Frank pretends a lot*, Mike thought. Mike needed to pretend right now, too. Needed to pretend it was a bad idea to beat this man to death and hide his body in the office supply closet.

"Mike, I...this is about *family*, not money."

Mike snorted, heat pouring through his skin in waves, as if someone were dipping him in hot wax. The rage, the fury, the endless assault of everything out of control whipped up in him, rising to the top. If he didn't end this now, didn't run for so long he couldn't think, didn't get home to touch his woman and his daughter, he was going to explode.

And right now, that meant losing everything that was important to him.

So he offered up something that paled in comparison.

"How much 'family' do you want?" Mike kept the finger quotes tight and restrained. "We both know why you're here." Mike strode with purpose to his desk and yanked open a drawer, finding his personal checkbook quickly. Wishing he'd prepared for this, he pulled one check out of the book, the *tick-tick-tick* sound of the paper's perforated edge like a heartbeat that ended the second he tore the page loose.

"I'm...no, no, Mike, you have me all wrong. I'm not here for your money."

"You're here for Laura's." Mike didn't ask. He declared.

"I am here to get to know my niece and grand-niece!" Frank declared in a staged voice, as if there were an audience. Mike was a singular witness, though. Shelly was long gone.

"You're here to exact money from us, just like you forced poor Laura to cough up a bunch of her mother's estate," Mike said flatly. "Don't play games. We know."

"Is that what Laura told you?" A bitter, sad laugh followed. "I knew she was mentally fragile, but I didn't know she was...inventing like that."

Mike's heat flashed over to ice cold.

"Excuse me?" If he'd possessed a weapon of any kind, he wasn't certain he'd be able to stop his hands from using it. Shit. Dylan would know how to end this, how to make this guy leave, how to drive him out like a dog with his tail between his legs. Mike wasn't good at this, and his internal sense of how to structure his words, how to read Frank's nonverbal cues, was falling apart.

He was devolving into something primal, the instinct to protect Laura and Jillian at full throttle, and if he gave in to it Frank was going to get hurt.

Writing a check for more than he earned in a year just three years ago was less of a price to pay than a lawyer's defense fee on an assault charge.

A tiny voice inside him, the one that guided him through breathing deeply and not turning Frank into a pile of ground beef, couldn't fathom that he had the potential for such violence in him.

Apparently he did, and Laura and Jillian were the trigger.

Frank tilted his head as if he were struggling to say something distasteful, as if he were being modest and not wanting to speak ill of someone. A white and red cloud of rage made it hard to actually watch the man.

"Laura always had a flair for the dramatic," Frank said with a low chuckle, moving covertly toward the door. Perhaps Mike wasn't hiding his anger as well as he thought.

Perhaps that was a good thing.

"Dramatic." Mike repeated the word like he'd taken a bite of fresh cow shit.

"So you know?" Frank's smile twisted Mike's guts.

"I know what?"

"How she can make situations seem different from the facts."

Oh, no. Oh, no. The man did not just do *that*.

"Get out," Mike roared. The sound was so loud, so packed with sheer fight, that it made Mike's ribs vibrate. He half expected the window to shatter.

Frank jumped, his neck twisting with shock. "Excuse—"

"Get out of my office before I show you exactly how I handle someone who comes into our life and

379

accuses my woman of lying." Mike bore down on him, making Frank stumble. A warning voice told him not to touch the man, but there were about three seconds left between Mike's ability to hold himself back and the need for Frank to get the fuck out of his sight.

"Lying? No, I wasn't—" Frank froze. Whatever he saw in Mike's eyes made him shut up and walk to the door, as jittery as a man fleeing an uncaged game lion.

"You have exactly twenty seconds to be out of my building before I call security," Mike ground out from his door, grabbing the edge with a hand that left finger imprints in the soft wood.

Shelly came out of her office and looked at both men. "Can I—"

Slam!

Mike picked up the phone, stabbing the numbers with brutal efficiency. Dylan's voice cut through the oppressive cloud of everything.

"Mike?"

"He was here."

"And?"

"Get that PI on the case now. Right now."

"You okay?"

"No."

Dylan's long sigh made Mike wince. "Go for a run, man. Right now."

"Can't. I'm in a suit."

"You own the place. Just run. Do the stairs, go on the trails—just run. I don't want you driving like this."

"Like what?"

"Mike," Dylan said in a low voice. "You sound like you're about to murder someone."

Mike's hand holding the receiver began to shake. "I was."

"I know." The gentle tone his partner took made the mist clear, dropping like a fine dust all over Mike's soul. "And I know you. Run it out. Fuck the expensive suit and shoes. Pound it out before you come home. And for God's sake, don't go near that motherfucker. I don't want to bail you out of jail for assault."

"Hasn't happened yet," Mike barked.

"And I hope it never will."

"That guy comes near Laura or Jillie, so help me God—"

"He won't."

"But if he—"

"He *won't*. Just run."

Mike could feel his heart beat again, the slow adjustment back to a more aware state seeping in. Pure fury had taken over, mingling all his body functions into a cloud of noise. Now he could feel the hard plastic of the phone against his palm, how the receiver scratched against his chin, the way his blood pounded through his thighs, needing to be drained and wrung by a long run.

"Just run," Dylan repeated.

So Mike did.

CHAPTER FOUR

LAURA

The front door opened and in walked Mike, dripping wet from sweat, wearing the same gorgeous suit he'd worn this morning, battered black dress shoes flying across the floor as he kicked them off. His hair was absolutely drenched, so wet it curled up in little ringlets around his head, just like Jillian's did after a bath.

He was soaked through, suit jacket and all, a handful of dry patches here and there. Pants, too—sweat spots took over most of the clothing.

"Run into a sprinkler on your way home?" Laura joked. She caught a peek at the driveway outside before he closed the door behind him and stared in confusion. "Where's the Jeep?"

"Not here." Mike could barely talk as he peeled off his clothes in the foyer, dropping the fine cloth to the ground, where it hit with a strange thud, like a melon wrapped in a wet pillowcase.

"What do you mean not here? Did the Jeep break down?"

"No."

She felt Dylan's presence behind her and turned around to see an inscrutable look on his face. His eyes met Mike's, and something passed between them, some unspoken message that she knew she'd never know. They had this...*ability* to do that. It used to make her feel left out.

Right now, though, she was just glad that someone understood what on earth was going on with Mike, because it looked like he'd just—

"You ran home," Dylan said in an admiring tone.

"Yes."

"From where?" Laura asked. "And in dress shoes and a suit?" Why would he run home? Had there been a catastrophe? A flash of September 11, 2001 shot through her consciousness, making her eyes dart to the blank television screen, the set turned off. Had some world disaster struck?

"From work." Mike's two-word sentences were freaking her out.

"From the resort office?"

"Yes." Now he was down to one-word utterances and she was being driven absolutely mad.

"But that's miles!" Her own shrillness made her stop talking, swallow hard, and turn to look at Dylan, who was staring at Mike. She knew Frank had been in his office. How bad had it been?

"I run it all the time." Mike struggled to unbutton a cuff, and after the third failed attempt simply ripped at the fabric, a button pinging off a light fixture, landing an inch from her foot. Peeling his arm out of the wet cloth, he dropped the shirt on the floor. A part of Laura's mind did an inventory of buttons; Jillian would find one and swallow it if allowed. She bent down to get it, and her eyes found his shirt and mentally cataloged. All buttons accounted for.

Mike's sense of balance was remarkably absent. If only it were as easy to track as buttons...

"You run home, yes," she conceded. "But in proper running shoes and clothes! Not in tight wingtips and a business suit!"

Bright eyes met hers, feral and predatory. Dangerous. She shut up instantly.

Dylan's warm hand covered her shoulder and she took a few breaths, trying to understand what had happened. "It's cool. Go shower, Mike. I'll explain it all to Laura."

Mike was stripped down to his boxer briefs, which were as soaked with sweat as if he'd gone swimming in them. His body gleamed, muscles swollen with use, his legs strong and contoured. An urge to touch them, to run her hands along the hills and valleys they made on his thighs and calves, swept through her, her eyes drinking in the slopes of his glutes, how he looked like a tanned black diamond ski trail, all twists and turns and something she wanted to summit.

And go down.

Sex was the last thing on Mike's mind, Laura knew, as he shook his head curtly and marched past her. The hiss of a shower turning on echoed in the distance.

Laura turned to Dylan and asked, "What the hell is that all about?"

He reached for her hand, then nudged her toward the couch. Uh-oh. Something was *wrong*.

"Is this about Frank?" she asked in a voice so shaky she cringed, hating the neediness in her own tone. Not that she could help it. Her mind raced to locate Jillian in time and space. That's right. She sighed and turned around to find Little Miss Sweetie spread out on an activity blanket on the floor in front of the sofa, a set of stacking cups in front of her, spilled pell-mell all over the place.

385

Jillian was chewing on the edge of one of Dylan's tennis shoes.

"Yes," Dylan said, pulling her in for an embrace she didn't know she needed until his warmth covered her.

"Mama hug! Mama hug!" Jillian called out, clapping fat little hands. Abandoning her snack, she leaned forward, stuck her bum in the air, and pushed herself up to standing, toddling over to Dylan and Laura, inserting herself between. Tiny ringlet curls banged against Laura's knee.

She laughed, the sound tight and almost hysterical. Dylan wouldn't let her pull away. But she had to.

"I need to check on Mike," she said, and as if she'd hollered *Open, Sesame,* Dylan's arms parted, landing on her shoulders as his eyes locked with hers.

"Go to him," he said in a deep, calm voice. "He needs you right now more than anything."

"Dillie hug! Dillie hug!" Not quite mastering her Js yet, Jillie knew how to advocate for what she wanted, making Laura reach down and rub the light hair that covered the little girl's head.

Dylan picked her up like she was a bag of sugar and tipped her, ass over tea kettle, onto his shoulder, giggles pealing out like happiness in the form of sound. "Dillie, huh? Is that my nickname?"

"You dada!" Jillian shouted, pointing to herself. "Me Dillie!"

That's right, Laura thought. *You dada.* A sharp, bitter taste filled her mouth. If it had a color, it would be green. The same feeling, like a squeeze over her heart, had started when Jillian was tiny, just days old. Her own father took off long before Laura could form memories, and watching Dylan and Mike form a fortress of love around their daughter made Laura deeply jealous. Jealous. Not envious, because she certainly didn't want to take one drop of her fathers' love away from Jillie, but jealous? Yes.

Ferociously.

The only person she knew who she could even talk to about it was Josie, but right now Josie was so busy with the business and with Alex that Laura hadn't had two seconds to give her a call and bring it up. Besides, she thought with a sigh as she strode toward the bathroom where Mike showered, there were more pressing matters to attend to.

Franks's sudden appearance threw her entire life out of balance.

And rightly so.

The man was supposed to have filled the big hole left behind by having no father in her life, but instead he'd never been around. Grandma and Grandpa didn't talk about him much, but when he breezed into town every few years they'd made a to-do about him. The one Thanksgiving and two Christmases she remembered seeing Frank were etched in her mind, because they were the only holidays where she'd watched her mother drink to the point of being drunk. Slurred words and silly behavior from a woman who, generally speaking, was mild-mannered, a diligent worker, and a steady presence in Laura's life.

If a little boring.

Grandpa had better filled the father role in Laura's life, and he'd been good. Not enough, though. Not what Jillian had with Mike and Dylan.

Frank's weird appearance was triggering her emotionally, left, right, and upside down. Mike, too, it seemed.

Mike.

She shook her head slightly to clear her thoughts, eyes tracking Dylan as he carried Jillie into the kitchen to give her a snack. The two spoke to each other in rumbling laughter that faded as the sound of the shower grew sharper, filling Laura's ears.

A loud thumping alarmed her and she barged into the bathroom, shouting for Mike.

"You okay? What's that sound?" she called out through steam so thick it covered up the world.

"Fine. In here." The thumping stopped. A hand splayed across the shower door, peach skin against the white condensation. A thin pink licked at the edges.

"You're bleeding!" she gasped, opening the shower door. Rough hands pulled her in, clothed and all, the shock of being soaked through by hot needles of wetness making her breath come in hitched whoops, trying to re-establish normalcy. Mike's hands gripped her, palms so big he could wrap his fingers around her biceps, and as that registered, the dig of frantic flesh pressing against hers, all thought was obliterated by the crush of his mouth against hers, sucking all the air out of her lungs, the room, the world.

The slick movement of so much muscle and bone, desperate hands smashing her to him, the rub of a stray button between his abs and her belly made her hot. The feel of wet heat against her ankles, her inner thighs, the slow rise of temperature from warm to impossibly scorching across too many stretches of skin. As Laura disintegrated into the kiss and matched Mike's intensity was like a sensual violence, and she found the typical thoughts that would make her stray from the immediacy of him were gone.

Just...gone.

His urgency penetrated every cell, hands ripping at her clothes, the wet cloth flying off her as if helicopter blades shredded it, his thighs smashing into her knees as he bent to bite her breast, hands grabbing her naked ass, fingers digging in and pressing hard.

Any protests she might normally have vanquished instantly as his rock-hard cock nudged against her thighs, making her quiver with heat and urgency, his sensual rage contagious. She wanted to fuck her way out of this feeling that the world was crooked.

Maybe he could jar her back to center with the force of being taken.

As he entered her, the shower spray hit her full-on, making her gasp and gulp to find air, his teeth no longer gentle on her breasts, her shoulder, his hands cupping her ass and pulling her up along the tiled shower wall. As he lifted her, she wrapped her legs around his waist, strength matching his, daring him to try thrusting so hard.

He took the dare, bending slightly, making his thighs a platform for her invasion. She pulsed in place, his hammer strokes rough and violent, her mouth biting his shoulder now, fingers threading through wet hair as she could only cling with the barest of instinct.

Mike's eyes were closed as she looked at him, frantic and panicked, on the edge of a climax that felt too great, too much, too...everything. The power between them created by friction and desperation, intimacy and quake, became an impulse that felt out of bounds, as if giving in to it violated the laws of physics.

Of love.

Of—

Mike's mouth uttered a sound that vibrated from his hips on up, the rigid muscles of his neck and back a warning, the sudden force of his entry a slam into muscles inside her she could not name. The pain splintered her vision, making lightning bolts appear as

Laura perched on the precipice between pain and forbidden pleasure.

One finger slid to the puckered skin of her ass, wrenching its way in as she cried out against his chest, his motions too strong for her to fight, her dire need too compelling for her to stop.

She lost her senses in one stroke, the push of Mike and his primal shout like a portal into a place where she disappeared into pure essence, where even love was too little compared to the greatness they'd created in this moment.

Slowly, she became conscious of the weight of him, his chin on her neck, the pinpricks of hot water on her cheekbone, the raw burn of his finger that penetrated her still.

"Ah, God," he grunted, lifting her up and pulling out with a shaky sigh. "Did I hurt you?"

She couldn't lie. "Yes." But it was a cleansing pain, one she needed along with the intimacy and love.

"I'm sorry—"

She pressed her fingers against his lips. He would not meet her eyes. Rivers of water poured down his darkened hair, finding the path of least resistance on the planes of his face. Drops suspended on the ends of his eyelashes, like diamonds.

"Don't. Don't be sorry."

And then whatever came next—whatever might have evolved in that moment—was cut short by the sound of the doorbell.

Mike slowly dropped Laura down, helping her to stand on legs that quivered.

And then he punched the tile wall with his still-bleeding hand. Over and over, like thrusting into her again and again, a rhythm designed to make a very different kind of pain go away.

DYLAN

Ding!

"**D**ing!" Jillian called out, in pitch-perfect imitation of the doorbell. Dylan gawked at her; how did she do that? Even if he tried, he couldn't come close. Marveling at yet another discovery about the odd inner workings of tiny beings, he walked to the door, glancing at the clock. Cyndi was due in an hour, and—

He halted.

Wait. That was tomorrow. Cyndi came *tomorrow*.

Eyes narrowing by instinct, he cut to the right, avoiding being seen in the tall, narrow floor-to-ceiling windows that surrounded the front door. White sheers covered the glass, but anyone waiting outside could move an inch or two and see in.

Frank could, that is. Frank. Dylan had no doubt about who was out there.

"Dada!" Jillian called out from the kitchen, still in her high chair, fingers picking up little cereal Os with precision. The coffee machine burbled and he took careful breaths, as if five more steps to the front door would tip him into another dimension, like his life was divided by the living room carpet and how much of it he let stretch between him and his daughter.

Dylan had no reaction right now. None, other than the quick thoughts that sorted themselves like a triage nurse examining a bus crash to determine priority care. No raised heartbeat, no panic, no worry, no what-ifs like Laura.

This was the what-if come to life. Time to face it. Head-on.

With great purpose he crossed the room, flung open the door, and barked out, "We aren't buying it."

"Not buying what?" said a man's voice. Dylan looked straight ahead. The man standing before him looked nothing like Laura, and was the exact same height as Dylan, given the single step up into the cabin. After years of modeling, Dylan had an eye for what society considered "attractive" in men, and Frank was it. To a T.

The guy, in fact, could go out and get a fifty-plus modeling contract in three seconds or less, with a slight peppering of the temple hair against dirty-blonde looks, eyes that were two shades darker than Laura's, and that devil-may-care kind of personality that people in modeling circles love, but that always made Dylan's teeth grind.

People that casual were usually sociopaths.

And Dylan wasn't wrong this time.

"Whatever you're selling."

"I'm not selling anything." Frank spread his hands out in a gesture of supplication, like a preacher at a revival asking for God's grace.

Or for more money from the crowd.

"No solicitors," Dylan said, done with this game.

"Dada!" Jillie screeched, a thumping, skittery sound joining her little voice. Dylan abandoned the door, sprinting for the kitchen. When he arrived, he found her covered in cereal dust, the tiny bowl on her head, and she'd managed to grab a towel off the counter, and with it, pulled down the box of cereal.

As Dylan surveyed the mess, Frank appeared in his peripheral vision.

"Get out of my house," Dylan growled.

Frank's hands flew up in surrender. "I just wanted to make sure she's okay."

"Then quit scaring the fuck out of her mother."

Frank looked like he'd been slapped. "Laura? How on earth have I scared Laura? She hasn't replied to my emails. And by the way, I'm—"

"I know who you are," Dylan said, ignoring the proffered hand. "And I mean it. Leave. If you want to talk to Laura, this is not the way and now is *not* the time."

"Who was at the door—oh!" Laura said as she rounded the corner, hair soaking wet, wearing her bathrobe. Dylan cocked a mental eyebrow over that one, wondering what, exactly, Mike and Laura had just done. "Take care of Mike" meant something different to her, apparently.

"Laura." If Frank had dipped the word in oil and offered it on a silver platter it couldn't have sounded more slimy, his words melodic and freakish at the same time. Even Jillian did a double take, mouth open, a thin line of drool dripping over her little red bow-tie lips.

"Uncle Frank." Laura's words came out breathy, in a tone Dylan couldn't recall hearing from her since that very first date they'd had two years ago, back when Laura was always nervous, always insecure, always so unaware of how much power she really had.

His gut seized with a kind of pain he couldn't name as his fists curled with anger.

"Fang! Fang fang fang," Jillie called out. "Mama fang." Dylan absentmindedly picked her up as Frank's eyes went from Laura to Jillian, then to him, clearly trying to figure out paternity. The hot ball of nuclear waste burning through his gut got hotter. If Mike came in right now…

393

Laura's eyes locked with Dylan's, and all he saw was pure panic. Nothing else. *Shit.*

Brushing cereal dust off his little girl, he tried to communicate telepathically with Laura, but unfortunately that superpower appeared to be on hold right now. Frank didn't have the decency to be self-conscious. The guy didn't have a shred of any discomfort as he stood, uninvited, in their home while Laura shifted from foot to foot wearing wet hair and a short bathrobe.

"Why don't you get changed, hon, and I'll take care of Jillie?" Dylan said in a measured tone, eyes drawing Laura to him.

"Jillie?" Frank leaned forward and stroked the baby lightly on her chin, spilling a heart's worth of giggles out of her. Dylan caught Laura flinch when Frank touched the little girl, but Laura said nothing.

"Good idea," she said, looking in the general direction of Frank but not at him. "I'll be right back."

Frank took that as some sort of social apology on Laura's part and said, "Oh, it's fine, dear. I'm sure you're careful not to dress down like this for anyone but family." Her cheeks turned bright pink and her eyes widened. Motherfucker. Dylan was about to grab a cast-iron frying pan from the pot 'n pan rack in the kitchen and beat the guy senseless.

"Of course you're fine, Laura," he said, marching across the room to give her a gentle hug before she left. Laura stumbled slightly, clearly trying to hightail it out of there, but Dylan needed to make a point. A clear, don't-fuck-with-us point. "It's not as if you've seen your uncle in years, and there's no reason to expect you can't be comfortable in your own home."

Dylan gave Frank a very unambiguous look, his eyes finding the man's. "You're lucky I'm wearing underwear."

"Considering your past as a model, perhaps I'm not so lucky," Frank said, waggling his eyebrows.

Laura began to choke with surprise. If Dylan weren't so wired and pissed he would have laughed, too. This guy was complicated. At least he'd finally showed up, but now? Right now? Dylan took the opportunity while he could and shooed Laura into the bedroom, setting Jillie on the floor with some stacking blocks.

"Go ahead and change, and let Mike know we have a guest," Dylan said, hoping she took the hint.

"Right. Mike," Laura replied, the fleeting look between them transmitting a thousand words. Mike still hadn't debriefed them on what had happened today at the office, but Dylan assumed it was a doozy.

Laura left, but Franks's eyes were only for Jillian. "She looks so much like..." Frank's voice faded out as he gave Dylan a skeptical look, clearly comparing the dark hair, darker-toned skin, and Italian features with Jillian's light hair, hazel eyes, and coloring that made it seem impossible for Dylan to be her dad.

It wasn't like anyone else hadn't questioned it, too, but *this* guy? Dylan's flush of anger returned. Being judged by strangers was one thing. Being judged by an entitled asshole who seemed to think he could sweep into his niece's life and dictate the terms?

No fucking way.

"Like?" Dylan growled the word out.

"Like Laura," Frank said softly, taking the diplomatic way out.

Dylan snorted. "Little girls tend to do that."

"And Laura looks so much like my sister. Speaks like her as well. You never met Sharon, did you?"

"She died long before I met Laura." Dylan measured his words carefully, saying "I" instead of "we." Normally, he and Mike coded their words, trying to be as inclusive as possible. Even though he knew Frank knew about their permanent threesome, something made Dylan go into lockdown mode, giving away as little information as possible in an effort, however possibly misguided, to control what was going on here.

Where in the hell were Laura and Mike?

Jillian toddled over to Frank now that Dylan had put her down. She reached a grubby, gummy hand out to her great-uncle and said, "Dada?"

A hearty laugh poured out of Frank. "At this age they think every man is a daddy, hmm?"

Dylan had to give him that.

"And around here, it goes double!" Frank added.

Dylan could have done without the extra dig. He couldn't soften toward the guy, who stared at Jillian and pretended he hadn't said what he just said. Going against instinct, Dylan kept his mouth shut, hoping Mike and Laura would make an entrance soon. Not knowing what had happened between Mike and Frank earlier was killing him, though. He'd already ordered Frank to leave and that hadn't gone so well.

Hopefully, Mike was filling Laura in right now and that was why they were delayed.

"Fang," Jillian said as Frank let her play with his nose.

"Frank," he said, clearly amused.

"Fang."

"Uncle Fang it is, then." Frank made a quiet chuckle. "I'm sure your other daddy thinks that's about right." His lips twitched with a condescending amusement that made Dylan momentarily homicidal.

Dylan frowned. "Why would Mike think that?" If Frank thought he was being funny, he was wrong. If he thought he was a master of manipulation and that the comment would undermine Dylan, all it had done was to make him more suspicious. Frank fail.

Frank swallowed audibly. "I think we got off on the wrong foot earlier today. I went to see him at his office and he seemed very angry. I'm going to assume he's a hot-headed guy—"

"You assume wrong." Dylan's words sounded like a gong in a Buddhist monastery, ringing forth and permeating every cell with the vibration of the refusal to be ignored.

Frank cocked one eyebrow, refusing to back down, and yet... "Then perhaps I caught him on a bad day. He seemed abrupt."

"Perhaps he didn't like what you had to say."

"Had he allowed me to say it, I might think as much," Frank snapped back with a smile. "But he didn't."

"Why didn't you come straight to Laura? Why go to Josie, then Mike, and now here?"

"Jealous?" Frank asked.

"Of...?"

"That I didn't come to you first?" Frank shrugged, as if *that* were the problem here.

Letting the question hang in the air, Dylan took long, slow breaths through his nose, not rushing. Frank pretended to scan the room and bent down to pick up one of Jillian's stuffed animals, a caterpillar of different colors. Dylan knew damn well Frank was monitoring his every twitch, every sigh, each breath and each blink. The blasé attitude wasn't working.

Thank God Frank had decided to come when both he and Mike were home with Laura and the baby.

That gave Dylan pause, cracking his facade slightly. Why did Frank decide to come today, knowing full well they were here? Damn it, he wished he had time. Time to talk privately with Laura. Time to catch up with Mike and learn what happened. Time to get Jillie settled more.

Time to *think*.

Instead, he was being stared down now by Frank, who had made a calculated decision to change his entire demeanor, pinpointing Dylan in place and trying to mindfuck him.

Might work on Laura, but on him? Nope.

"I don't care who you came to first," Dylan said, his words belying his attitude. Because he didn't care— not one whit. What he cared about was—

"And you came to Josie first, Uncle Frank. Why?"

Laura's interruption jarred both men, Frank practically jumping an inch off the ground as her soft, feathery voice inserted itself between them. Dylan couldn't help but take in her appearance: hair wavy from being wet, skin flushed with the excitement and anxiety of this situation, body wrapped in a gorgeous maxi dress that covered her, neck to ankle, in curvaceous rapture. If Frank weren't here, he'd ogle and admire.

Protect and defend was more his approach in this instance.

"Because you ignored my emails," Frank said in a fake hurt voice. *Oh, please*, Dylan wanted to hiss, trying to catch Laura's eye. The guy was a walking phony.

She was looking at Frank so solemnly, chin down and eyes upturned, that he caught a glimpse of what she must have looked like as a chastened child.

Oh, hell no. No way she was falling for Frank's crap.

"You wrote her an email for the first time in years and waited two days before barging into her life!" Protectiveness rose up in him like the swell of a tsunami, taking over half a mile of inland beach as it destroyed everything in its path. Laura had done nothing wrong. Not one fucking thing. And yet this guy was dismantling her, emotional brick by emotional brick, right before Dylan's eyes.

"I should have replied," Laura said in a shaky voice.

Frank's eyes gleamed with victory, his mouth stretching into a facsimile of gentle caring. "You've been busy. I understand."

Dylan's head exploded. "Get *out*."

"These two really are a pair," Frank mumbled. Dylan had no idea what the hell that meant until Mike walked in the room, wet hair matching Laura's, angry face matching what Dylan imagined he himself looked like.

"I said the same words to him a short time ago," Mike said quietly. Too quietly. Dylan's alert level rose to flashing red. Mike was trying to say something without words, but all Dylan could sense was danger.

Laura's eyes jumped from Frank to Dylan to Mike, her emotions changing as she looked at each man. Then she said:

"Frank, you really need to see this from our perspective. You emailed me, waited less than two days, appeared at my place of business and questioned my work associate, then you went to Mike's workplace. Now you appear here, out of the blue, and you act as if you're the injured party." Laura took a slow, deep breath, eyes unwavering, staying on her uncle. Her voice shook. Her hands shook.

But damn if her essence wasn't ramrod straight. She was feeling the fear of saying what she needed to say and doing it anyway. *Attagirl.*

Dylan caught Mike stand a little taller, dip his chin a little lower, and fixate on Frank, as Laura finished her words. He wanted to cheer for her.

Frank's next words, though, made everyone shake.

"I do not see anything from your perspective, my dear, because your perspective is untenable." He took two steps closer toward the door, then paused to make eye contact with each of them. "I learned about your... *arrangement* from a business associate who remembered hearing about your dating company on talk radio. When I put two and two together and realized that the Laura Michaels they discussed on the radio was my little Laura, I was appalled."

So *that's* where this was going. Dylan didn't hold back rolling his eyes. Mike joined him. Frank had stainless-steel balls to come in here with a morality play. It wasn't just about the money.

It was all about shaming them.

Not gonna work, bud, Dylan thought. *Never in a million years.*

"You think I came here for money," Frank said with a jerk of his head toward Mike. "And you think I came here to scare you or creep you out," he said to Laura with such an even tone that Dylan felt like this was quickly turning into the monologue in a bad B-movie.

"But I came here because I am deeply concerned about the welfare of a poor, innocent child—" His eyes cut over to Jillian. "Who is the victim in this mess of a relationship you claim to have."

Of all the statements Frank could have made, this was the most incendiary he could possibly have spat out. The words whipped through the room like a wildfire on a windy day, igniting Mike, Dylan, and Laura.

She sprinted across the room and swooped down on Jillian, scooping the baby into her arms. "Leave now," she ordered. The look she gave Mike and Dylan made both move, instantly. Poke the Mama Bear and watch out.

Mike and Dylan were at Frank's sides in seconds, bookending him but not touching him. Yet.

"Are you threatening me?" he asked, clearly amused. Any normal man would have backed down, but this guy was a piece of work.

A piece of disordered, entitled work.

"We're not *anythinging* you," Laura snapped. "But if you think you have the right to waltz back into my life and judge me in my own home, critiquing how I choose to live my life, then you are wrong, Frank. Dead wrong."

He pulled his arms away from Mike and Dylan as if they'd touched him. Hands burning, wanting so much to grab the guy and shove his foot up the man's ass, Dylan held back.

And then Frank said: "Sharon would be so disappointed. And so would my mom and dad."

Tears pooled in Laura's eyes and Dylan's heart cracked in half. If he could have, he'd have yanked it out of his chest and beaten Frank to death with it, but instead he swelled with pride as Laura said in a cold, deadly voice:

"On the contrary. Grandma and Grandpa were disappointed in you. Did you know that Grandpa called you 'Shiftless Frank'? It was only when you came for family gatherings that they put on the whole fawning bit. When you were gone, Grandma cried into her pillow. When you wired Grandpa for money, he took it from their own funds and boasted to Grandma how your 'new investment' would pay off 'this time.'" Her fingers made air quotes, face twisted with mocking sarcasm.

Frank didn't respond. At all. His face was as blank and polished as a granite counter.

"And then when it didn't?" A shrill laugh filled the room. "They'd eat rice and beans for the next month. Grandma would take half her heart medication instead of the full dose, making it stretch." She handed Jillian off to Dylan and marched right up to Frank, finger in his face.

"You have a lot of nerve coming in here and judging me. Trying to shame me. It worked, though, didn't it? After Mom died?"

Frank's eyes narrowed, but he didn't look away.

"You shamed me and bullied me into giving you half of her estate, and I did. I really felt like you 'deserved' it. And now you think because I'm with two guys who have more money than you ever imagined, I'm some kind of mark you can pressure."

"I'm here because your daughter is being raised in depravity," Frank finally responded, chin jutting out. "And I'm certain child services would be very interested in...this."

Dylan broke out into a laugh he didn't know he had in him. "You're threatening to call child services because we...what? Have a clean, loving home for our daughter? Because Laura lives with two men? Good

402

luck, buddy. Not only will you be laughed off the phone for making a call like that, we'll countersue you so fast that judgmental chip on your shoulder will boomerang through the air and slice your head off before you can say 'boo.'"

Frank just snorted and ignored him, eyes on Laura. His face shifted to concern. "I know it was hard after your mom died, honey. But this? This isn't the kind of life you were raised to have. Not you, and certainly not my great-niece."

"I asked you back at the office how much you want to go away," Mike said. "You get one check, Frank. One. Make it a good number."

The room grew still, the only sounds Laura's ragged breath and Jillian's little baby noises.

A stillness filled the room, making baby Jillian pause and gawk, first at her mother, then at Frank. Her great-uncle's eyes narrowed, then flared, as if the muscle in his body were expanding and contracting on instinct, uncertain which way to move.

Dylan felt the same way.

Mike's challenge hung in the air, and as Frank's eyes moved to Laura, Dylan wanted to see genuine emotion in them. Something that tied her own flesh and blood to her, a deep-seated need inside Dylan to believe that family actually meant something to the man, and they'd all misjudged him.

"I'll be in touch," Frank said, cutting the entire conversation short by turning on his heel and heading toward the front door. Dylan looked at Laura, whose face was a mask of alarmed fury, and Mike—who was nothing but stone.

And then a parting shot from Frank. Of course.

"Remember, Laura—I tried." Frank's voice cracked as he stood with his hand on the doorknob, face consumed by an expression of grief. "I tried to see you. Tried to reconnect. Wanted to know Jillian. Wanted to..." As his voice trailed off he looked down, shaking his head, making a *tsking* sound that triggered a violent impulse in Dylan.

The man was playing her like a fucking violin.

"You're a grown woman now and can make your own choices. But Jillian—" He made a dismissive sound, not quite a sigh, not quite a gasp. "I cannot abide by watching my own flesh and blood, so innocent—"

Mike stormed across the room with a speed Dylan never imagined he possessed and ripped the door open. Although he didn't technically touch Frank, the force of the air moving around him seemed to push Laura's uncle out the door like a gust of wind.

The snap of the closed door made Dylan and Laura jump, and then Dylan's own swiftness kicked in and he was by her side, his hand on her elbow. Tears pooled in her eyes and she was shaking. He felt gut-punched, so impotent and filled with a murderous impulse that he shifted his gaze to the door, grateful it was closed.

The grinding sound of spurting gravel and rubber on stone told him Frank was leaving. The air lightened, and Jillian began shoving her little dimpled hand down the front of Laura's shirt, oblivious to the drama that had just unfolded second by painful second.

Dylan felt like he'd just been through a witchcraft trial that had ended with acquittal.

Mike's shoulders were flexed, arms arced in a pose of a fighter, his eyes twitching. He looked at Laura, then Dylan, then Jillian, and back to Laura, whose body still trembled as Dylan's flesh connected.

And then he realized she was shaking from *laughter*.

"Oh. My. God," she whooped, the sound making Jillie's face twist with confused fright, Dylan instinctively reaching for the little girl, who clung to him like a monkey, her little curls bouncing against his cheek as she turned her head to look at her mama from the safety of a non-hysterical parent's grasp.

"He—oh, God—he thought he could—Mike!" she gasped, bending in half to laugh, the cackling like nothing Dylan had ever heard before. Over her prone figure his eyes locked with Mike's and they shrugged simultaneously, eyes wide with curious befuddlement.

"He actually," she wheezed, "thought he could prey on me and scare me into coughing up money...or something...because he disapproved of my lifestyle choices!" Laura's face was a dangerous shade of red, and as she continued to shake. Dylan feared she was about to truly hyperventilate and pass out.

Mike caught it, too, and walked to her, placing one hand on her hip, the other under her elbow, gently guiding her to sit on the couch. He treated her like a wounded animal, careful to lead but not to push. If Dylan weren't holding Jillie, he'd do the same.

Frank's departure left more questions than answers, but as Laura's eyes squeezed out tears of mirth and relief, and as her breathing became steady again, punctuated by aftershocks of uncontrollable giggles, he let a wry smile stretch his own mouth.

It was funny.

In a very, very weird sort of way.

Mike walked in the kitchen, the sound of running water the only other noise beyond Laura's chokes and laughter. Jillian watched her mother like an anthropological specimen, with a mature detachment that made Dylan quirk an eyebrow and puzzle over the scene.

405

Re-entering the room with three glasses of water, Mike handed one to Dylan and pressed another on Laura, who looked up, startled, as if she'd forgotten he was there. She gulped the water down in one go, let out a small burp, then laughed again.

"I'm ridiculous," she declared.

Both men nodded.

"Mama dick!" Jillian shouted, clapping. That was one way to say "ridiculous."

The room erupted with giggles in baritones and basses, altos and sopranos, and by the time they all recovered it was done.

Done.

Frank had exorcised himself from their internal boxes of fear, his moralistic judgment like a scouring pad.

And yet the scratches remained.

CHAPTER FIVE

ALEX

Dinner with his *mom* was never an emotional land mine for Josie, thankfully. They'd enjoyed numerous meals in restaurants ranging from a great Turkish place in Arlington to a so-so Indian joint in South Boston, but dinner with his *stepfather* included could be...interesting.

At least John wore pants this time.

"Hey!" Josie said in a voice filled with friendliness, reaching up for a hug from John. "Where are the bagpipes?" The long-running joke about John's Scottish roots had become a new feature again as the Outlander series by Diana Gabaldon became a crazy hit on television, leading to multiple requests for his stepdad to play bagpipes at various events.

Including fan parties for something called "The Wedding Episode," which Josie had insisted Alex watch, and which turned him into a Jamie fan, in more ways than one.

John's obsessive need to practice—wearing a kilt in the most traditional way possible—meant that coming home for a visit could involve a glimpse of a wee couple stones more than he or Josie wanted to see. Especially when his mom and John had a high bar that bisected the open-concept kitchen and dining area, and John would climb up to sit and...

Chat.

Appetite gone.

Noi, the purebred Husky John and his mother had rescued from a shelter a few years ago, incessantly pushed at Josie's crotch, even as they dined at the table. A huge farmer's table, it easily seated twelve, though the four of them were clustered at one end, John at the head, Meribeth across from Josie and Alex.

A muffled movement under the table told Alex his mom had gently nudged Noi, who came out with his head down and tail in a position that indicated assent. He knew who the top dog in the house was.

And she smiled pleasantly across the table at Josie.

"You and Alex seem to be meshing well," his mom said as she spun the stem of her wine glass slowly in front of her, almost hypnotic in her motion, as if she were treating a client. Alex suppressed a groan.

"He's a lousy roommate, but a great partner," Josie said, putting her hand on his thigh and squeezing a little too hard, her eyes on his mom.

"What's that supposed to mean?" He looked at her with mock surprise. He knew exactly what she meant. He was a slob. And she was right. Dr. Perfect couldn't be on 24/7 in his personal life, right?

"It means you need to stop leaving your dirty socks on the counter next to the coffee machine," Josie said with a shudder, laughing. Her hand dove between his legs, making a slow trek toward his growing erection.

We're playing that game? He moved his foot close to hers and pushed lightly. She pushed back, cheeks rounding with a smile, eyes lowering from his mom's.

Then I'll join. He reached over and imitated her. Those cheeks reddened.

"Alex!" Meribeth said, making him retract his hand out of some instinct long buried in him, like he was a chastened boy reaching for an illicit chocolate chip cookie.

Hmmm, Josie was a treat, after all. And, as he put his palm against the soft, worn fabric of her snug jeans, he remembered that she was his. All his. And he could taste her at will.

And without recrimination.

"I didn't raise you to throw your nasty socks on the kitchen counter!" Meribeth said in joking horror. She drained her glass and John filled it silently, pouring the Chardonnay in her wine glass with a silent grin. Josie liked John more than she thought she would. He was quirky and sharp, non-judgmental in a way that made it a bit hard to understand his boundaries, but once she'd gotten over the fact that her categorization-happy brain couldn't fit him neatly into a box, she had relaxed.

"The socks are the least of it," Josie said with a mutter, biting her lips as the laugh tried to escape. "He pulls the shower curtain in the wrong direction and insists on using a hand towel as a bath mat."

"What's wrong with that?" John and Meribeth said in unison, making Alex's deep laugh shake the room. Something nudged at his crotch and he leaned back, enjoying the sheepish look on Josie's face as her hand suggested that while he might be a terrible roommate, maybe he wasn't too bad as a lover...

And then he saw both her hands fly up in the air as she covered her mouth.

If her hand was there, then what was touching his —

"NO!" he thundered, jumping up, making Josie's wine glass topple. She caught it before it went over, and the dog scampered across the room, meekly settling into its dog bed next to the fireplace, looking up with a guilty eye.

"I've heard of blow jobs and hand jobs, but you may have invented the best *nose* job ever," John said drolly. Meribeth smacked him. Alex simmered in place, embarrassed and a bit disgruntled, his blood rushing. Damn dog.

Josie's face was bright red, and not from the flush of histamine that always pinked her cheeks from white wine. "Oh, Alex," she gasped, descending into giggles.

"Let's go back to talking about my socks on the counter," he grumbled, giving Noi one last glare. The dog's eyes were closed, and he panted, pink tongue hanging out a bit, stark against the white fluff of his fur.

"He needs to go for a walk," Meribeth said absently. "In a few minutes." She turned to Josie. "What about work? How's the career change going?"

Josie recovered from her little giggle fit and sat up, drinking a bit of water. Alex loved to watch her move, and especially enjoyed seeing her interact with his mom.

"Going well, actually. We plan to make some matches soon. But…"

"But?" John asked, eyebrow cocked. "Not enough men?"

"Never enough men," Josie explained, suddenly serious. She could shift into work mode so easily, treating the strangeness of her job as if it were just another corporate venture. As if Good Things Come in Threes were a new web portal for music, or an app for shopping.

"Maybe I should sign up," John offered.

Meribeth just rolled her eyes. "You don't like to share appetizers when we go out for dinner. You really think you're capable of sharing a *woman*?" Her arched tone carried mischief.

"Never tried. I'll put it on my bucket list. Maybe we could sign up and Josie can match us with another guy."

Alex had chosen that exact moment to take an enormous gulp of his wine, and as John's words came out he choked, then sprayed the remains of his dinner.

Everyone looked at him like he was crazy.

"I already share myself with someone else, and I'm looking right at him," Meribeth said sweetly as Alex mopped the mess from his hands.

The table burst into laughter. Minus Alex.

"I know we're grown-ups," Alex started.

"Some of us are," Josie and Meribeth whispered in unison, looking at each other with surprise, then mirth.

Alex cleared his throat pointedly. "But talking about my mother being in a threesome really does cross a line I would prefer to maintain."

John's quiet nod in acucquiescense was enough for Alex.

"And then there's creepy Frank," Josie added, segueing nicely.

"Creepy Frank? Is that the name of a new band?" John asked.

Josie smirked. "I wish. It's Laura's uncle. We think he's reappeared in her life, looking for money."

Meribeth bristled. Alex caught it immediately and frowned. Why would she have that kind of reaction?

"Reappeared? After being gone for long?" Meribeth asked with a fake casualness, as if she were forcing herself to speak neutrally.

Alex's body tightened. Something was suddenly off. He avoided John's eyes but saw his stepfather's hand clench. He felt it, too.

Josie appeared to be oblivious, continuing her story. "It's been a few years. Last time Laura saw him was after her mom died."

"Oh! I'm sorry. I didn't know." Alarm flashed through Meribeth's eyes. "Was she young?"

"Under fifty, I think."

John and Meribeth exchanged a look. "That's young," they said together.

"Car accident," Josie explained. "Her mom had asthma and had an attack that escalated quickly. Lost control of the car, and…" She didn't need to say the rest.

His mom's face crumpled with compassion. "I'm so sorry. There's nothing worse than losing your mom long before you're supposed to."

Alex's eyes searched Josie's face for a reaction, because he knew Josie had a very, very different opinion on his mom's point. But she remained placid. A little too under-reactive, in fact.

"Right," Josie said in a clipped tone. "Anyhow, Frank reappeared this week. Came to work and interrogated me without telling me who he was. He's a real creep, making allusions to how Laura, Mike, and Dylan are living in sin, that the baby is being raised in an immoral home."

Alex's mom's eyes flashed with righteous indignation. "How dare he!"

John shook his head sadly and emptied the wine bottle into his own glass. Wordlessly, he went into the kitchen and emerged with another chilled bottle.

This would be a two-bottle night. Maybe three.

"No kidding!" Josie was raring to go as John filled her glass nice and full. Her comfort zone—discussion centered on anyone but her, and mothers—was established now. "He came to see me and never told me he was Laura's uncle. Wrote her an email but didn't give her contact info. Crashed Mike's office and made veiled threats. Then he finally came to their cabin and spouted all this crap about how the baby was being raised in a depraved home."

"Sounds like a real asshole. Is he looking for money?" John asked, eyes narrowed.

Alex nodded. "And Mike and Dylan have plenty of it."

"Doesn't mean her uncle is entitled to any," John added.

"No," Meribeth said, pensive. "But if he's making morality claims about the baby, that would make any parent's heart shrink with terror." She swallowed, hard, and gave Alex a look he didn't understand. "When someone comes out of the past, unexpected, and makes statements about how you're raising your kid, you freak out."

He strongly suspected that she was not talking about Laura and Jillian.

"Did that...happen?" he asked quietly, his voice so hushed he thought no one could hear him.

Conversation halted, Josie's brows knitted together, John's face suddenly expressionless.

Meribeth reached for John's hand and closed her eyes, trembling slightly as she took a deep breath. Alex's toes began to tingle, his thighs tight and restless, his body itchy and twitchy.

"Your father. Your biological father. He reappeared. Once."

The room telescoped.

"I remember. You told me," he rasped. Josie's hand found his, clasping it tight, and he felt three sets of eyes on him, resting like heavy rocks, pressing him deep into his chair.

"It was years ago. you were...fourteen? Fifteen?" Meribeth's eyes traveled up, as if retrieving the memory. "He was in town for a business conference and asked to see me. The internet was gaining popularity and he'd found me online. Knew I had a son. Had backtracked the dates and..."

"Of course he knew you had a son!" Alex said. "You told him!"

Her mouth twisted with bitterness and she reached for her wine, draining it in an impressive feat of continuous swallows, like an Oxford student drinking a yard of ale uninterrupted.

"I did. At the time. He didn't believe me. And so when you were a teen he looked me up, saw pictures of you, and...put it all together."

John just nodded. She'd met him right after, Alex knew, when she'd consulted a lawyer about custody and protecting Alex from becoming the rope in a tug of war that never materialized.

"You never told me?" Josie said to him, clearly disappointed.

"He...it wasn't like that, Josie. He wasn't trying to get custody of Alex. Didn't even want to see him." His mom looked at Alex closely, knowing the words hurt. "He just wanted to make sure the opposite, in fact."

"Opposite?"

"He had a life where he didn't want me to find him," Alex ground out, the words hard to say. His turn to gulp his glass of wine.

414

"He...what?" Josie's confusion was palpable. "Then why did he find you?" she asked Meribeth, who shrugged.

"Booty call gone wrong," John said, voice dripping with sarcasm.

Alex's neck snapped toward his mom, who winced. "Really?"

"Sorry, Merry. I shouldn't have said that," John whispered in his mom's ear. She looked like she wanted a hole to swallow her up.

Alex could use one of those too right now.

Josie just sighed in understanding.

Noi's nose nudging his crotch at that exact moment was the most pleasant interruption he could have possibly conjured.

"Someone needs to go for a walk," he announced, jumping up.

"And so does the dog," John said quietly. He then shouted, "OW!" and looked at Meribeth, who had quite obviously just kicked him under the table.

Alex really didn't care. He grabbed the leash off the wall and reached for Noi, whose yeti-like tail wagged so hard and covered so much territory it could trigger an avalanche.

"I'll come with you," Josie said, jumping up from the table then coming to a woozy stop.

"Too much wine?" Meribeth's smile made her dimples come out, and for a brief second Alex caught a glimpse of the shy, beautiful seventeen-year-old girl she had been when his father had—

"I'm fine," Josie insisted, coming to Alex's side and reaching for the leash.

Noi took off with a snap that jerked Josie off her feet as he bounded for the door, quickly held open by

John so the dog and woman didn't go crashing through the glass.

"Who's walking who?" John called out as Alex followed Josie, laughing as he jogged to catch up.

"Whom."

"Whom? When did you become Grammar Girl?" Her arm was wiggling like a wet noodle, but she seemed determined to hang on to the dog's leash. Alex carefully unwound it and took over.

Noi slowed down.

"How did you do that?" Josie squeaked, clearly baffled.

"He can sense power. Dominance." He jokingly puffed up his chest. "An alpha."

She snorted. The dog lifted his leg and a stream of pee shot out, the sound distinct in the darkness.

"Or he just needed to pee really badly," she noted.

"That too," Alex grumbled. The cool night air should have grounded him, but he felt a deep sense of unease after the conversation at the table. Generally speaking, his mom didn't mention his biological father very often. In fact, it had been years. While he knew the story she described, he'd tucked it away into a part of his brain that he didn't air out very often, preferring to think of the rejection as an aberration, as a flaw in his sperm donor's personality and absolutely, positively not a reflection on Alex as a human being.

Because that would be emotionally unbearable.

"I'm sorry," Josie said, out of breath and panting to walk in double time as she struggled to keep up with the giant, overexcited dog and long-legged Alex. "You never told me that story about your bio—"

"I'm sure you have plenty of stories about your mom you've kept inside," he answered with a little too much bitterness. Regret flushed through his pulsing

416

veins immediately, but some part of him couldn't apologize. It felt like weakness. Like he really was someone you pushed aside, like a kid you don't want to acknowledge.

She flinched.

He had a dual reaction, like something inside him split, the fury and pain on one side and his rational, compassionate side on the other. Cold, calculated glee formed inside him, tender shoots of an evil seed sprouting from the look of hurt on her face. For some reason, it felt good to see her have such a strong reaction to him.

It felt powerful.

The other side rushed in, shoving the bad away and pulling her against his chest, hundred-pound Husky on a leash be damned.

"*I'm* sorry." His stomach was on fire and his legs shook slightly from a combination of suppressed rage and shocked intensity. He'd really been that evil side, enjoyed it for those few seconds—and that was the most disturbing part of the whole story about his bio dad.

How little he really knew himself.

Her arms stayed motionless by her sides, and that same bitter seed that had begun to unfold inside him now tasted like poison. His breath rasped against her neck as he curled down to hold her, her palms tentative as they linked loosely around his waist. *That's right*, he thought. *Trust me.*

Because God knows I'm not sure I trust myself.

On the surface, this was nothing. They'd made two sniping comments at each other, and an outsider would say he was overreacting, overly fearful that his sharp words were taken the wrong way by an overwrought woman.

Alex and Josie weren't just anyone, though. Within the parameters of their relationship, he'd just screwed up, big time.

Worse? That damn sense of evil glory within.

Feeling powerless was a tremendous weapon. When people can make you feel powerless, it's so tempting to turn to the darkness within to fight back. Alex had little experience with this.

Josie, he knew, was a master.

The realization struck him like a lightning bolt.

"I would never do to a child what my father did to me," he said softly, his breath pushing thin strands of her hair over her ear.

"I know," she replied, arms reaching out to him for comfort.

"You've been that child, too," he added. "Rejected just for being there."

She froze.

"Rejected for just *being*," he said with a groan, a raw feeling in the back of his throat as the words came out.

Her head bobbed with a nod against his chest.

"My mom shielded me from that," he continued. "But yours *caused* it."

Josie took in a shaky, deep breath, still silent.

"I want you to feel so loved by me that you have enough inside you. That the empty cup is overflowing. That every day you know I loved you more than I thought I was capable of. And that when I die—"

She looked up in alarm, eyes shining with unspilled tears, Noi beginning to whine and tug at the leash looped through Alex's hand.

"—you have so much love stored within you it lasts until the next life we live, so we can find each other."

The tears dropped down her round cheeks now, spilling down her neckline.

"This life isn't good enough for you? You're staking a claim on eternity?" she asked with a loving smile.

"If I could bite you and make our love immortal, I would," he joked, breaking the tension. Normally, Josie was the one who descended into jokes when the emotions got to be too much. This time, he was the one who broke first.

They were rubbing off on each other.

"I draw the line at sparkles and werewolves," she said as she pulled back and wove her fingers with his, her bones so birdlike under his grasp. Noi yanked, hard, on the leash, and he let the beast lead them to the path where John had found them last winter, nearly, ahem...in a delicate position.

Josie's eyes lit up as she recognized the path, then she frowned. "Dog," she said.

Alex laughed. "Yeah, we won't replicate our... *outdoor sport* from last winter. Not with Noi as an audience."

As if he understood their words, the big white puffball stopped in his tracks and looked at Alex, cocking its head.

"He knows we're talking about sex," Josie said.

Noi shook himself like he was wet, turned his head with a sniff, and pulled them onto the dirty path.

Alex felt completely wiped, like someone really had drained him of his blood. Explaining love was so far beyond his grasp. His understanding of how intimacy worked was something he invented as he went along. Josie was so hard to figure out, and although they'd spent so much time together, and two months actually living together, he felt as if she were still a mystery. A language he couldn't yet speak but was starting to read, single word by single word, parsing out meaning from a handful of vocabulary that he hoped was enough to gain meaning.

"I love you," he called out to her as Noi raced ahead, chasing some smaller animal.

"I love you, too!" she cried.

Marry me, he nearly shouted back, then dug his heels in as his body came to a reeling halt from the thought that slammed against his skull.

Marry.

Me.

The surreal sense of the two selves receded, his stronger side emerging. Love always won, didn't it?

It had to.

The alternative was just too painful.

Formalizing a life with Josie—an entire lifetime, measured in years, not months. Decades, not years. He could imagine it so easily that the life he lived before meeting her seemed more washed out. Faded. As if it were real but in sepia tones, a little less shiny. A lot less loving.

If he asked her to marry him, right here, right now, as she ran behind him to catch up, he could imagine her reaction. Surprise. Horror. Withdrawal. She wasn't ready, even if he was.

And he was.

Like birth, though, timing was everything. Allow life to unfold on its own timeline and the result was always better. Rush anything and complications could emerge.

Complications were something they could do without. More than enough of those already.

Noi's nose was buried deep in a bush as he rustled some tiny creatures out of the foliage, the furry bodies

420

a blur as they scampered up a pine tree, needles splintering down like poking rain on Alex's head. Illuminated by streetlights above him, on the road, he could see the white dog, could feel his muscled pull against the tether of the leash. Josie's cold hands wrapped around his waist from behind, her frozen little ice-cube fingers sneaking under his shirt to tickle him like a cadaver's bones in motion.

He made a sound like a teenage girl squealing. It was so abrupt that Noi's neck snapped up and he sniffed, looking at Alex with curious wonder.

"That cold?" Josie asked. Even in the mild late-spring weather, on the verge of summer, she managed to be cold most nights. Fingers and toes, mostly.

"It's like you're stroking me with a Popsicle," he said with a shiver. Noi made a huffing bark sound. *That's right, boy*, Alex thought. *Defend me from the Icicle Fingers of Doom.*

"I suppose that means," she said teasingly, her fingers at his jeans button, "you would prefer I not put them—ah, you're so warm," she groaned as her tentacles of cold wrapped around his soft penis, sending a rapid chill from feet to thighs, up his spine, making him convulse.

"By all that is holy, what in the hell? That's torture!" he said through gritted teeth. "I can't believe I ever thought about marrying a woman who would be so cruel!"

The words were out before he could think. Her hand paused.

Her hand paused for a *long* time.

And then she touched him, stroked him with her small, skillful fist, the heat and blood flowing where his body needed it most in that moment. Noi tugged on the leash and Alex's grip slackened as he was distracted. The dog shot off into the bushes.

Alex was about to shoot something off, too.

A distant part of his brain told him to chase Noi, that he wasn't smart around the road above, that he would jump in the murky spring waters of the recently melted lake and get filthy.

Josie was getting filthy, too, in an entirely different —and achingly better—way.

He turned around, facing her, instinct overcoming his pleasure. She looked down, hand determined to finish its task.

Knees bent slightly, he braced himself as her other hand slowly lowered his zipper, unclasped the button, and then she spoke with perfectly articulated words:

"Just don't ask me to obey."

JOSIE

Josie held Noi's leash like it was a rabid skunk. "I cannot believe he got into the lake," she *tsked*.

"I knew this would happen," Alex muttered, giving her a disapproving side-eye. "It's all your fault."

"My fault?" They trudged up the steps to Meribeth and John's house. Alex opened the front door for her, Noi walking slowly, as if he knew he were about to be chastened.

Or worse—bathed.

"I should never have let go of the leash."

"That's right—*your* fault."

"You had me by the balls, Josie. Literally."

She turned bright red and looked at a spot over his shoulder. He turned around.

Meribeth.

With eyebrows so far up her face they might as well have been a hat.

"What are you—oh, no! What happened to Noi?" she asked, bending down awkwardly to check out the coffee-colored dog.

Who chose that exact moment to shake himself vigorously, spraying mud spatters all over Meribeth's face, chest, and arms.

Josie's eyes widened with horror. Alex stood stock-still and speechless. John entered the room just as Noi shook, his collar jingling with the effort, and all the humans just stared.

If that had just happened to Josie's mother, Marlene would have taken to screaming, blaming Josie, shaming Josie, threatening to get rid of the dog and finding three past transgressions to rub in Josie's face, too.

With that kind of baggage burrowed deep in her psyche, Josie found it hard even to look at Meribeth, whose mouth was in an "O" of surprise, little mud smudges dotting her lipsticked lips.

And then she began to giggle. Meribeth's head bent down, her chest shaking, the draping folds of her multicolored jacket shimmering with motion.

"Oh, my," she gasped as she laughed. "I should have known better than to bend down and greet a muddy dog."

Josie's face morphed into confusion.

Blaming *herself*? In what universe did a mother blame herself for something like this?

Alex and John reached down to help Meribeth stand, each taking one arm. "You know," John said though a mixture of laughter and snickering, "we did just clean the hot tub yesterday. I can fire it up. You take a quick shower and we can jump in."

That sounded like a big cue for Josie and Alex to leave.

Besides, they had some unfinished business. Well, Alex had finished. Josie, on the other hand…

Marriage? Alex's talk about marriage made her insides turn to pudding. She knew that they were on that journey, but figured it was a three-thousand-mile journey and they were still on their first tank of gas— not getting ready for the final leg before reaching the destination.

"You kids want to join us?" Meribeth asked, holding her hands out from her body, laughter dying down. She looked at Josie in earnest. "It's a nice night to relax and get wet."

Alex turned a choking laugh into a fake cough. Josie loved how dirty his mind was.

"Um, no…thanks. Thanks, Mom," he said, wrapping an arm around Josie's shoulders. "In fact, I have to be at the hospital at seven, so we need to go home and get to bed."

Hell yes, we do, Josie thought. *And by the way, Alex, not only will I not obey, I'm keeping my last name.*

John looked pleased with Alex's explanation. *You old horn dog*, Josie thought, then realized John wasn't that old. Not really.

Alex's phone buzzed, and Josie made a fake weeping sound as he checked it. The only time he received calls was from his mom (who was right in front of him), her (ditto) or—

"Shit. A patient emergency."

Meribeth frowned. Josie wanted to cry for real. Seriously? Her clit was an emergency, too.

They said their goodbyes, and within twenty minutes Josie found herself alone in their apartment, a quick kiss on the cheek delivered in the front seat of the still-running car about as much action as she was getting tonight.

She cast a reluctant glance at the drawer in the bedside table.

Time to make her own *bzzzz*.

* * *

Alex slipped between the sheets like a sex thief in the night, there to steal an orgasm or three from her. Swollen and spent from taking matters into her own hands (quite literally), she merely snuggled against his warm, naked form and settled back into sleep.

His nose nudged against her inner thighs and she murmured, "Seriously? Your timing sucks. I just took care of things—" she opened one eye and waited a beat for focus to come into play so she could read the bedside clock "—three hours ago."

"That was just the warmup. The actual game is about to start." His tongue licked slowly along the crevice between her thighbone and—

"Oh!"

"You're so slick," he said in amazement, the words muffled by, well, *her*.

"Orgasms tend to do that," she answered with a laugh that turned to a groan. "And you don't have to d o *that*," she whispered, guiding his chin up. He followed, nude body like a muscled statue come to life, all hot flame and taut skin.

"I want you in me," she whispered, body primed, her mind playing images of his body entwined with hers, the movie in her imagination about to unroll in real time.

"Already?"

"Yes."

And so it was done, with fluidity that seemed too good to be true, his enormity touching both her cervix and soul with a completeness that made her forget that she was ever fragmented. Sex could be touching and silly, playful and messy, awkward and revealing, and it was all of those with Alex.

Sometimes at the same time.

Whatever part of her felt self-conscious could co-exist with the sensual beast she became at times. As an old friend had once said, she could experience *both/and* instead of *either/or*.

When she and Alex were together, the black and white of her life blended into the most spectacular, nuanced shades of grey. Some of which exploded behind her closed eyelids, burst blood vessels in her neck and face, and made her muscles clench so hard it seemed the fibers cried out Alex's name in passion, until her twin strands of DNA curled in and under like her body, all lust and need, all animal and faith.

Learning to be *both/and* took courage. Alex's long, hard body separated slowly from hers as he rolled onto his back and leaned toward her, carefully pulling the covers over them, knowing she was always cold. The gesture made her soul sing.

"I love you," he mumbled as sleep took over his body, steady breaths pouring out of his chest within seconds.

"I love you, too," she whispered easily.

So easily.

426

* * *

"He said the word *marriage*?" Laura asked. Josie could hear her friend on the other end of the call, brewing coffee. Josie was stuck in the office, her morning spent talking with some software developer who was designing the database they would use to match people. If she heard him talk about Netflix and relational data one more time she was going to go hire a yenta to just hand-match people for her.

"Yes."

"Did you faint?"

Obligatory eye roll, even if Laura couldn't see it. "No."

"SQUEE! You're gonna marry Alex, you're gonna marry Alex!"

"Guh! Guh!" Josie heard Jillian squealing in the background.

Laura sighed. "At least you can get married to the person you love."

"So can you!" Where was this coming from?

"Not *both* of them."

"True. But you can marry *one* of them." Josie's words rang hollow.

A long sigh filled the phone, a pain-infused sound that made Josie feel helpless. This morning she'd been abandoned by Alex for a twin c-section gone wrong, and today she had called Laura to talk.

She hadn't meant to poke a bear.

"I can't, you know? Marry one. Because then it's picking a favorite, and neither one of them is my favorite. I love them both."

"You don't favor one of them over the other? Not even a tiny bit? It's okay if you do," Josie said in her best non-judgmental, soothing voice.

427

A harsh laugh was the only response. "Darla and I talked about this at lunch. It's...hard to explain to someone who's not...you know," Laura answered, a soft slurp echoing on the phone as she—Josie imagined —drank her coffee.

"I told you having lunch with Darla would help!" Josie crowed triumphantly.

"You were right," Laura muttered.

"I'm sorry—what was that?" Josie asked loudly. "You said something and I didn't quite hear it."

"You were right."

"Again?"

"Shut up."

"Tut up!" Jillian screeched in the background.

"Damn it," Laura mumbled.

"Jammit! Jammit!"

Josie laughed so hard she began to cough uncontrollably.

"Now I'm a hypocrite," Laura whined, "because I'm always after the guys not to curse in front of her."

"You're not a hypocrite," Josie gasped. "You're only human."

"And a woman who can't marry the loves of her life."

"Why all the talk about marriage? It's not just because Alex mentioned it."

"No. It's not," Laura admitted.

"It's the Frank mess, isn't it? You're talking about legalities, visited a lawyer..."

"Yes," Laura said, her exhale stretching like verbal taffy. "He made that stupid comment about sin, and how Jillian's not being raised properly, and it got my mind spinning a million miles an hour. So I talked Mike and Dylan's collective ears off for days, and we realized that if I died, Jillian's biological father would get custody of her, but if I go on and have more kids with both guys, then—"

Josie got it instantly.

"—if a bio dad and I died, the other dad would be —"

"Screwed," Josie said with a low whistle.

"Huh. Well, sort of. Technically, Dylan's biological children would go to his parents. And Mike's would —"

She shivered. "Go to his. But he hasn't talked to them in years!"

"The law doesn't care," Laura said in a low voice. "And Frank is *my* next of kin."

"What? I thought your father was."

"Good luck finding him."

Josie frowned. "You're talking about marriage because you're worried Frank would try to get his hands on Jillian for her money?" She tried to keep the incredulity out of her voice, but failed.

"I know! I know it sounds crazy. It is crazy. But it's also...possible? A slim chance means we have to do something to protect Jillie. Mike and Dylan sorted out the money and trusts when she was born, but custody in the event of a nightmare...we never factored that in."

Josie swallowed, hard, and said, "You know Alex and I would raise her. If you...you know."

"Died?"

"If you wanted me to raise her," Josie said, clearing her throat gently. Tears sprang in her eyes, surprising her. In that moment her heart felt too tight and too big all at once, like it was being squeezed and peeled open at the same time. She didn't like thinking about her best friend being dead. But she also realized that her offer was a sign of progress, too.

She and Alex, acting as parents…

"I love you," Laura said sweetly through the phone, her voice shaking slightly. "I know what it means to have you make that offer."

"But you don't think I'm capable of raising a potted plastic plant, much less your child," Josie said, a joke in her voice.

"Ha ha. No, it's that you're not a blood relative. To any of us. Frank, Dylan's parents, even Mike's parents, have more legal claim than you."

"Not fair."

"I know," Laura sighed.

And then it hit Josie. "I think I know a way you can get the highest degree of legal protection for Jillian. And keep her and your future children together in case you and one of the guys dies."

"How?" Laura's eager voice made Josie's heart flail in her chest.

"Have them get married."

"Them? Who—oh. Oh, God…no. Josie, no." A series of weird gasps and groans, chokes and sputtering noises filled Josie's ear. Had Jillian wrestled the phone from Laura?

"Laura?" she asked.

A great whoop of laughter was her reply.

"Josie! Oh, oh, oh you're crazy! Mike and Dylan get *married*?"

"Why not?" she answered, a defensive tone in her voice. "It's legal in Massachusetts. And then each guy would be the legal stepfather to the other's kids."

The laughter stopped abruptly.

"You sure about that?"

"Um, pretty much. That's how it works in hetero marriage, right?"

Laura went quiet. Josie's brain raced. Maybe this could work. Perhaps this was the answer.

"I don't know," Laura said, voice filled with skepticism. "But I do know the number for the lawyer we used for the wills and trusts. I think it's time for a brief consultation."

"Just do me one favor," Josie begged.

"What?"

"Don't tell them this was my idea."

Laura sucked in a sharp dose of air, the sound splitting Josie's eardrum. "Right. Dylan will shit a brick if you bring this up."

"I think he could shit enough to build a tornado shelter with this idea. Then again, it'll be pretty obvious it was my idea, so forget what I said. I'll take the hit."

Laura looked like she was a million miles away. "I still wish I would have them both."

"You *do* have them both," Josie said in a soothing tone. Funny how she couldn't care less about being married to Alex. The institution itself didn't seem to matter to her. If they were together, it was enough, and she didn't need a piece of paper to prove it.

Yet...when she put herself in Laura's shoes, and imagined being told she couldn't marry the person(s) she loved, a fireball of resentment and sorrow filled her.

"If they marry each other it's to show that what all three of you created is so real they have to find a crazy legal maneuver to protect it."

"That's one angle I hadn't thought of." Laura's voice turned from despondent to pensive.

"In the end, it's all about love," Josie said, feeling like a Hallmark card.

"Love. Right." Laura made a dismissive noise. "Then why is this so hard?"

"Because love is never enough."

"Thanks, Ms. Merry Sunshine."

Josie smiled even though Laura couldn't see it. "I don't mean that love isn't amazing. Just that it's work. Hard work. And when you do the hard work together, you create even more love."

Laura went silent. Seconds ticked by, making Josie wonder if she'd said the wrong thing.

A long exhale, and then:

"The Beatles had it wrong."

CHAPTER SIX

DYLAN

"**C**an we go anywhere *but* Jeddy's for once?" Alex asked in a voice that brooked no argument. "I do not relish hearing Madge talk about the latest unicorn butt plug she bought."

"How about we just talk while we lift? Blow out our bodies then hang in the sauna?" Dylan answered as he finished putting forty-fives on the olympic bar, locking in a good three hundred pounds for squats. To start.

"They have a killer smoothie bar here, too," Mike added.

"What about an espresso bar?" Alex asked.

Dylan forced himself to take a deep, invigorating breath. Nothing like being in a gym to give you the feeling like you were swimming through testosterone soup. He considered himself a fairly strong guy, but felt like a wimp as he took a good look around the room.

He was smack-dab average.

"You need protein and amino acids after you blow out your quads, dude," Mike said, wiping his face with a hand towel. He'd looked like he'd just gone for a five-mile sprint in the rain, and his biceps bulged, veins like extension cords slid under tanned skin.

"And caffeine," Alex answered mildly.

Dylan laughed. "Last thing you want after you puke your guts out from doing squats is caffeine."

Alex began to fidget nervously, making Dylan laugh inside. Laura and Josie joked about Dr. Perfect and how unflappable he was. Good to see the man could be rattled.

Without having to run into a parking sign to do it.

The scar above Alex's eye was mild, but Dylan could find it easily, and as Mike eased into the squat cage, Alex spotting him, Dylan marveled at how different life was now for everyone.

Every damn one of them.

Including Frank.

Mike made it through seven squats before Dylan and Alex helped lift the bar for him. Alex took some of the weight off and did his own lunges, making it through three sets of increasing weight, though never reaching Mike's power.

Dylan, on the other hand, blew Mike out of the water.

"How in the hell does he *do* that?" Dylan heard Alex's voice rise with surprise.

"He eats his Wheaties," Mike joked. Dylan was shorter than Mike but came damn close to matching him in weight, muscled body holding so much restrained molecular power. He couldn't move, couldn't think, couldn't grin—as much as he wanted to —but instead popped back up to rack the bar and move slowly until the black pinpricks left his vision.

The adrenaline rush was worth it.

Gotta love endorphins. Even the ones that didn't involve sex.

But *especially* the ones that *did* involve sex.

Guzzling half his bottle of water, Dylan took in the room while Mike racked weights for Alex, who had something to prove.

"You okay, doc?" Dylan joked. "Don't want you to tear a nail on those surgeon's hands." He actually liked Alex. Stand-up guy. But he had to bust his balls a little, right? The three of them spent so much time chatting at Jeddy's and being directed by women that it was good to be in a man's world (female lifters excepted). Even just for a few hours.

"You're the one who was a model, Dylan," Alex said in a low voice as he bent down in the squat cage, squaring his shoulders under the bar and wrapping his wrists up to put his palms, then fingers, on the gnarled metal. "You know more about buffed nails and body paint than I do."

Mike's howl of laughter seemed to fuel Alex, and damn if the guy didn't come a little too close for comfort to Dylan's highest weight and rep set. Shit. He needed to up his game and lift more.

Staggering out of the cage after two sets and a failed rep that required Mike and Dylan to grab the pole, Alex looked purple. Little broken blood vessels around his eyes told Dylan the guy had been saving face. Ah, damn.

"You pushed too hard," Mike said quietly, careful not to let any of the other lifters in the gym hear.

Alex nodded as he sucked down water Mike had mixed with an electrolyte solution. "I know. Stupid," he added, shaking his head. "But look who I'm lifting with."

Mike and Dylan nodded. They got it.

You had to at least try.

They grabbed their car keys and phones from the little cubbies in the free-weight room. The walk to the smoothie bar made Dylan feel like he was marching on down-filled pillows, the push of blood to the surface of his skin such a fucking awesome rush. He could forget about anything in those moments of extraordinary strength.

Anything except Frank.

Smoothies ordered, the trio drank more water and rested on barstools at the juice counter.

Bzzz. Alex jumped and felt his own ass like a man going off to prison and touching a woman for the last time in his life. Frantic and weirdly rushed.

"What the fuck?" a disembodied man's voice muttered.

"Is that me?" Alex hissed. "I'm on call for a case."

"Me," Dylan said, grabbing his phone. A swipe and —score!

"Nick's report!" Dylan crowed as a tray filled with large shake glasses teeming with greenish-grey sludge was delivered to them.

"What's in there?" Alex asked Mike as Dylan read the email from the private investigator:

Dylan,

See attached.

Nick

"Talkative guy," Mike mumbled as Dylan opened the PDF, turning his phone sideways so they could read the tiny print a little bit better.

The report was astounding. Arrest records in one, two, three—Dylan couldn't keep up—states, all for fraud or larceny or petty theft. Most involved cons, which didn't surprise him. Frank set up fake charities and scammed people. Frank trained a fleet of kids to steal dogs and waited for the owners to post a reward and brought them back, caught only when one of the kids stole the same dog twice and Frank showed up again for a reward.

And then—

Mike's low whistle pierced the juice counter's sitting area. "He defrauded an heiress?"

"Don't forget the DUIs," Alex added, pointing to the screen. "In one...two...three different states?"

"You would never guess," Dylan said, handing off the phone to Mike and drinking half his smoothie in one series of gulps. The cold, slightly chalky drink made him crave coffee suddenly.

Damn Alex. He was right.

"What do you mean?" Alex asked Dylan, mesmerized by what he was reading on the phone's screen.

"Frank. He's so...slick. Smooth. Like a well-preserved middle-aged man. More George Clooney than Bernie Madoff, you know?"

"Bernie Madoff was pretty damn slick, too. Fooled a lot of smart people," Mike said.

"True. Frank's just—he seems above a DUI. Or stealing dogs." Dylan shook his head. "Who the hell steals someone's dog for money?"

"The same kind of guy who sniffs out his niece after she's settled into a great life with two billionaires," Alex pointed out.

Dylan felt like a balloon with a slow leak.

"At least we know now," Mike added. He pointed to the phone. "We need to print that out and study it. I'll bring it to our lawyer and get his opinion. And we need to talk to Laura about it."

"No!" Dylan could imagine it all seven steps ahead, how Laura would freak out, the way she'd feel guilty again, then angry, how this information would give them a leg up when it came to dealing with Frank but, really, no new answers. They'd suspected Frank was a slimeball. Nick's report confirmed it.

"Why not?" Mike and Alex asked in unison.

"Is there anything violent in there?" he asked rhetorically. Mike shook his head. "Nothing about kids?"

"Other than acting like Fagin from Oliver Twist and gathering a bunch of street urchins to go out and steal people's dogs, no," Alex said, scrolling through the report.

"Good. Then he's just a garden-variety con man. He doesn't want custody of Jillie. He wants money. He can threaten and cajole, tease and manipulate, and mindfuck Laura, but he can't really do anything."

Mike looked at him, jaw tight. "Good points."

"Frank is the kind of guy who gets other people to do his bidding for him. He comes in for the kill when it suits him, and he's looking for easy pickings. He's not going to sweat. He's not going to push and persevere. Once things get difficult, he's outta there. Look," Dylan said, taking the phone from Alex, "at what he's actually done. He finds a way to prey on other people's emotions and then gets what he can when they're weak."

"We're not weak," Mike protested.

"But Laura is," Dylan explained. "She's a lot stronger than she was years ago, but Frank has this ability to find some sweet part of her that wants to be good, and liked, and loved. And he plucks it like a banjo, damn it."

"You're right," Mike said, clearly hating that it was true.

"Then you need to figure out his weakness, and his price. Pair them together," Alex declared.

Mike gave Alex a look of calculated admiration. "That's smart. But how?"

"First, I'd call your lawyer and have him review that." Alex pointed to the phone. "Then, find out how you can buy Frank off while making a subtle threat."

Dylan's eyebrow arched. "Threat?"

"A subtle one. Nothing too specific. Does he have any outstanding warrants anywhere?"

"You seem to know an awful lot about the criminal mind," Dylan said with a mock-suspicious tone.

Alex laughed. "You get interviewed by cops in the ER often enough, you pick up a few things."

"Threaten Frank with being ratted out wherever he might have warrants, give him some money, and—"

Dylan was cut off by Mike's joyful whoop. "Yes! An outstanding warrant for failure to appear in court for a DUI. In Connecticut," Mike hissed.

Alex's eyes shone with glee. "You got him. Nail the bastard. Give him a small check and a big hint that you know about Connecticut and that asshole will be gone, quick. He doesn't care about Laura or Jillian." His eyes clouded with some emotion Dylan didn't quite understand, but he suddenly had the sense that they weren't only talking about Frank.

Mike grabbed his own phone and autodialed his lawyer. "On it already."

Dylan raised his empty glass to Alex. "To finding someone's weakness and exploiting it."

Alex thought for a second, then said, "No. To stopping the assholes who use that technique against good people."

Dylan could drink to *that*.

MIKE

Jeddy's it was. At the rate they ate here, Mike was seriously considering making Madge an offer on the place. Owning a restaurant wasn't high on his list of life goals, but maybe they could build an apartment over it and never have to cook again.

"What are you smirking about?" Dylan asked as he shoved hip-first into the booth, knocking against Mike's elbow.

"Shit!" Mike hissed as hot coffee slid over the webbing of his thumb. He set the coffee cup down quickly and sucked on the heated flesh.

"Sorry." Dylan fished a few ice chips out of his water glass and handed them to Mike, wrapped in a flimsy napkin. The cold rush of the ice made Mike's anger die down fast.

Laura watched from across the table, clearly amused. "You two are a well-oiled machine."

Both of them looked up at her as she spooned a thick chunk of peanut-butter-sauce-covered vanilla ice cream into her mouth, rotating the spoon and licking it suggestively, pretending to deep-throat. Who knew a long sundae spoon could go *that* far in?

Mike's pants tightened. Dylan shifted uncomfortably next to them. About that imaginary apartment upstairs...

"You auditioning for a porn movie?" a rather unwelcome voice screeched from Mike's right. Josie appeared, dragging a bemused Alex.

"I thought we were going to Kendall Square for a movie," Alex said, brow furrowed, shooting daggers at Josie.

"Food first."

"But we're miles from Kendall Square..." The look that passed between them made Mike sit up. Good thing he was capable now.

"Why are Josie and Alex here?" Mike asked Laura, who batted her eyelashes and fished around her sundae glass for a cherry and proceeded to—

Oh, my...

"I can tie a knot in a cherry stem with my tongue, too, you know," Josie said defensively.

Laura winked, her mouth contorting in several muscled directions, all of which made Mike's cock thicken.

Laura's lips spread in a wide grin seconds later and she pulled the cherry stem out of her mouth.

Double knotted.

"Show-off," Josie muttered.

"Marry me," Dylan gasped.

"Took the words right out of my mouth," Mike added.

"Speaking of marriage..." Laura said, making all four sets of eyes glue themselves to hers. Mike cocked one eyebrow, broke away from Laura, and looked pointedly at Dylan.

The hair on his arms stood at attention, the ripple traveling up over his shoulders and between the blades under his neck, down to his sacrum, a chill and fire settling there as if waiting for what was about to come.

Waiting for orders to know what to do next.

Dylan looked at Alex, who was bending down to sit, Josie having shoved Laura over against the booth's wall. "You two have something you want to share."

Blood drained out of Josie's face like a vampire had just exsanguinated her.

Alex chuckled, but Mike knew it was laughter without amusement. Could tell it was a touchy subject and wished Dylan hadn't made the joke. But he had, and now the issue hung over them like a stinky fart.

"Uh, no. Not yet." He gave Josie's hand an obvious squeeze, but she might as well have been a plastic blow-up sex doll. Her expression said she would have been happier with that right now.

"'Yet'? Not 'yet'? You just moved in!"

"Two months ago."

"I swear it's only been two hours."

"Time flies when you're having fun."

"Actually, time flies when you're having sex. Otherwise, time doesn't fly. It crawls with agonizing slowness, as evidenced by this conversation," Dylan said dryly.

"We need to talk about marriage," Laura said softly. Mike hated being across the table from her, and reached reflexively for her hand.

Dylan beat him to it.

"Whose marriage?" He exchanged a look with Mike that made Mike's heart explode. They'd had endless private conversations about this—okay, not *endless*. Maybe three or so, which felt endless in manspeak. He and Dylan didn't really talk about their feelings the way Laura did with each of them. They just...*were*. A decision between them took two or three sentences. Not two or three days and thousands of blabbered words.

This decision, though...who could Laura marry?

You only get one spouse, right?

"Um, yours, actually," Josie said. Alex gave Mike a look that didn't make sense, until it suddenly did. Gotcha. Alex knew something they didn't, and it was about to be revealed.

"Why am I here, again?" Alex asked.

"Decoration," Josie replied.

"Moral support," Laura added.

The gooseflesh on Mike's arms spread to his entire body, and his eyes narrowed involuntarily. "Support?"

"We have a plan," Laura and Josie said simultaneously.

Dylan, Mike, and Alex all groaned in reply just as Madge appeared.

"Did you guys order before we got here?" Alex asked, incredulous as Madge unloaded plate after plate of fried green tomatoes, pistachio crepes, and ah— lobster cakes.

"As if you need to order when I know my sweet Alex is coming," Madge said.

"We have the bat signal for you," Laura said with a smile.

Alex stuffed a cake in his mouth and wisely said nothing. Mike's appetite disappeared the second the talk of marriage erupted.

He thought it was about to overflow, too. Who would Laura choose? Society and law only permitted a person to marry one other person. Forcing her to choose could irreparably damage their threesome. Then again, it could also strengthen the paternity issue.

Frank's sudden appearance complicated everything. His subtle threat to take Jillian should something happen to Laura had plagued her and it was painful to have their loving construct fraying at the edges because of the combination of Frank and a

443

society that didn't have a word—much less legal protections—for their kind of love.

"Here's what we pieced together," Josie mumbled through a mouthful of crepe. "We know who Jillian's biological father is—"

Alex began choking on his cake. "We do?" he gasped.

"We can look it up on a birth certificate. And a lawyer will have to," she added, pointedly looking at both Dylan and Mike. Appetite went from zero to negative ten, and Mike's mouth quirked at one side as he watched Dylan drop his fork, leaving a half-eaten fried green tomato.

"Okay, so...what does that have to do with marriage?" Dylan challenged.

"In theory," Laura said quietly, "if I married the man who isn't Jillie's father, then he gets stepfather protection if something happens to me."

A cold rush flushed through Mike. He'd suspected Jillie's lighter complexion meant...

"But that won't work," Alex said mildly, recovering from his choke. "If you're planning on more kids, I mean."

Josie nodded. Mike's skin began to feel like cotton, the conversation bizarre and surreal, as if they were talking about cross-pollinating garden flowers, or deciding where to add a deck to the cabin.

His family's fate was being deconstructed over coconut shrimp and peanut butter cup sundaes.

"Pull back and explain it to me like I'm stupid," Dylan said.

"We. Already. Are," Josie said slowly. "That's my default mode with you."

Dylan shot her a nasty look and made a rolling motion with his hand, urging her to continue.

"If you have another child and that child is by the same father, then you're fine. But what if Laura has children by both of you? Then if she di—were gone," Josie said, catching herself, "the non-biological father of the kids wouldn't have any legal rights whatsoever to visitation or custody. Imagine if Laura and *one* of you died."

"Why are we imagining all this death?" Mike asked, his voice a chilly whisper, like a cold finger sliding down the spine.

Everyone stopped mid-bite.

"It's Frank, isn't it?" he asked. "Not that you think he's going on a killing spree," he said with a derisive snort. "It's more…estate planning got moved up a few notches on the list of Stuff We Should Do Someday."

Laura's mournful eyes told him he'd hit the nail on the head. The urge to hold her, raw and needful, tingled inside him and would not go away.

He drained his now-tepid cup of coffee and started to push Dylan out of the booth, thumbing toward the bathroom.

The rush of cold blood racing through his body pumped into his thighs, his calves, through his abs, and up to his throat as he moved past Dylan, walking numbly to the bathroom, where he found the men's room empty. Thank God. Mike slumped against the wall and stared at his own reflection.

What the fuck? he mouthed to himself. He looked like Mike—blonde, tall, lanky, a little hunched over from being the tallest guy in the room most of his life. His shirt looked like it had the day he bought it at the mall, his jeans were old and well worn, a relic from college. Most of what he saw in the mirror had been part of who he was for most of his life—body, clothes, emotional state—and yet he felt like he was

445

experiencing a metamorphosis right now, second by second.

Word by word.

Marriage. Jealousy flared within. If he were Jillian's biological father, then it made sense for Dylan to marry Laura. Made perfect sense. Couldn't argue with it.

So why did he feel like smashing his fist through that mirror?

The door creaked and Mike straightened himself, walking to the urinal and unzipping as someone entered the bathroom.

"Come here often?" asked a familiar voice. Dylan stood in front of the urinal next to him, unzipped, and they voided their bladders in unison.

Mike started laughing, his stream jumping up in concert with his amusement.

"Dude, aim!" Dylan said, alarmed. "I don't need your pee all over me. Get enough of that already from changing the baby."

"Can't help it," Mike said, finishing up quickly. "I just...I can't believe we're in here peeing together while they talk about our future like we're playing Barbie and Ken."

"And Ken. You forgot. Two Kens." Dylan shook off, zipped up, and began washing his hands. Mike joined him at the second sink and caught his eye in the mirror.

"I never forget there are two Kens."

Dylan's turn to laugh. "And now we're describing our intimate relationships in terms of plastic dolls." He sighed heavily. "When did we reach this new kind of low?"

"When Frank appeared and threatened everything."

Dylan made a sour face. "I don't... That guy hasn't technically threatened anything. Not really. And you know—and I know—we could hand him six figures and he'd go away."

Mike wiped his hands and tossed the crumpled towel in the trash. "Three points!" he whispered, then turned to Dylan, serious. "And he'd be back again after blowing it."

"So? Big fucking deal. We have plenty of money."

"We don't have enough to make his re-entry stop freaking her out." Mike sighed. "Plus, as much as I hate the guy, Frank's appearance forces us to look at all this. We've been living in a bubble of our own creation. We need some legal protections."

"We have that! We set up our wills and trusts so Laura and Jillian are taken care of forever."

"Financially. Sure—we did. But legally...these custody issues are serious. And we want more kids."

Mike looked at Dylan evenly, watching carefully. He'd expected an argument there. "You do want more after all, don't you?" Mike tried to keep his surprise out of his voice.

Dylan smiled without showing teeth. "Yeah...just on a different timetable than you and Laura. Maybe wait a few more years. But...yeah. I mean, Jillie's probably..."

Don't say it, Mike thought. No one had said it, and as long as none of them did, it was somehow easier to live in the bubble. Having their perfect little life intruded upon by external forces was one thing.

Undermining it from within was another.

"Jillian," Mike said as Dylan finished cleaning up and headed toward the door, "is *our* daughter. Ours." He halted Dylan's progress with a firm hand on his shoulder.

447

Dylan turned around, eyes hooded and closed off. "You and I know that within the emotional reality of our relationship at home, with Laura and Jillie. But out here?" Dylan let out a harsh snort. "Out here in the real world we have genetics. Biology. Law. Societal norms."

Mike closed his eyes, the hand on Dylan's shoulder less fierce. Warmer. His partner's neck muscles were steel bands.

"I know."

"I know, too. And now we have to face that. If Laura has kids by both of us, it causes legal issues. I think Laura and Josie talked about this—"

"You think?" Mike laughed.

Dylan gave him an amused look, and the bands of steel loosened microscopically. "And they've analyzed all the possibilities and decided our fate."

"It should be you," Mike blurted out, the words like a dagger stabbing his heart. They were the right words.

"And then what, Mike?" Dylan spat. "If I died and Laura died, then any kid I had with Laura wouldn't be yours. You'd have no claim. They'd be split up. I mean, if they had long enough together you might have a tiny chance claiming they were bonded, but..."

Mike's throat closed off. Just puckered closed. He was right. Dylan's parents would legally have the strongest claim to Dylan's kids, and Mike's parents—

Oh, shit.

The stricken look he sent Dylan's way was reflected in his eyes. "Yeah, Mike. That's what they're out there saying. We have to figure out a way around all this."

"Josie and Alex? Can we leave our kids to them?" Mike rasped as his throat pried open, muscle by muscle.

Dylan shrugged. "Who knows?" An evil grin spread across his face. "Did you see Josie pale when we talked about her and Alex getting married?"

"Yeah?"

"I think she'll shit her pants if we go out there and tell her we want to leave our kids to them."

Mike's laughed felt tinny, like it was coming from three dimensions away, but it was real. It warmed him.

"You know," he said quietly, "we never talked about getting married with Jill.'

Dylan jolted, as if zapped by a small current. "Jesus," he said with a slight hiss. "You're right. The topic never came up. Not even at the end."

Mike nodded. "She never brought it up."

"Neither did we."

"Then why now, with Laura? It's not just because of the baby," Mike rushed to comment, but he could tell Dylan understood. Dylan always understood.

With a series of rapid blinks, Dylan thought for a moment, then said, "Because it's different with Laura."

Mike's throat tightened, not with grief for Jill, but with love for Laura. "It *is* different, isn't it? Wanting to marry Laura doesn't diminish Jill, and yet..."

The concerned look Dylan gave him made Mike flash back to two years ago, to the unremitting grief after Jill's death, to how hopeless it all seemed right before they'd met Laura.

She had brought them so much more than love.

Laura was pure joy.

Dylan clasped his arm and looked deep into his eyes. "It'll be okay. I think you're feeling like Laura's felt since Frank appeared. Unmoored. Unsure."

449

A sinking feeling floated from throat to belly. Damn if Dylan wasn't right.

"God, I...I had no idea it felt like this." He ran his hand through his hair. "You feel like this, too?"

Blinking rapidly, Dylan gave Mike a sheepish look. "Not as bad, I think, because I do have my parents. You and Laura don't. Mom and Dad have a relationship with Jillie and they will with future kids. If worse came to worst and we died, they'd come through. I have that. You and Laura don't."

That gave Mike pause. Never thought of it that way before. And while Dylan's mom and dad were perfectly fine, they weren't exactly over the moon about Mike.

Would they let him continue to have a relationship with a child who turned out to be Dylan's biologically, unless compelled to do so by a court?

"My head hurts," Mike confessed.

"Mine too. And not just from listening to Josie's yammering." Dylan pushed the bathroom door opened and motioned for Mike to exit. "Let's go face whatever scheme they've concocted."

CHAPTER SEVEN

DYLAN

"**Y**ou want them to do *what*?" Alex hissed at Josie as Dylan reached the table, unnerved from his conversation with Mike but grimly determined to face this mess head-on. He didn't like any of it. Not one bit, but fuck if this wasn't the way life worked, right?

You couldn't plan for it. It just all happened at once.

"What does someone want us to do? Sorry, Josie," Dylan said with mischief, "we're a threesome. Not a fivesome. No experiments with you two." He gave Alex an over-the-top lascivious wink just as Madge came over to clear the empty plates.

Alex looked like he was having a stroke. Madge just howled with laughter and said, "Five pieces of cheesecake coming up."

No one argued, though Laura gave her empty sundae glass a guilty look. It made Dylan smile. She felt as if her body post-baby was less attractive, but Dylan felt otherwise. More to hold. More to love. More to feel, hot flesh and curves so voluptuous and enveloping when her legs were tight around his hips, or slung over his shoulders, open and—

"...so we think you and Mike should get married." Laura's words rang out, whispered as she leaned across the table.

We. You. Mike. Laura was saying the words, so she didn't mean that she and Mike should get married. She didn't say *you* and *me*, so she didn't mean Dylan and Laura should get married.

Who the fuck was getting married, then?

"WHAT?" Mike thundered. "You want me to marry DYLAN?"

That cleared things up.

All conversation in the half-full diner came to a deadly halt. The muffled sounds of food sizzling on the grill came through, the pneumatic wheeze of a bus's brakes outside, the sound of a crosswalk beeping...

Not even an inhale could be detected from the fifty-plus people in the restaurant.

"Well, that's discreet," Alex mumbled.

"Fuck discretion," Mike roared, and stood, shoving Dylan out of the booth, making his hip twist and his thigh scream, and he was roughly manhandled, nearly poured out onto the floor, Mike's body outside before Dylan could register what had just happened.

"He took that well," Josie said, slinging an arm around Laura's shoulders.

Laura stared at the scratched tabletop, just blinking silently. Madge appeared and threw five plates of varying cheesecakes on the table, plunked down a pile of chilled forks, and said nothing.

Nothing.

Ah, fuck, Dylan thought. *This is bad.*

Everyone ignored the sweets in front of them. Alex tried hard to look everywhere but at Dylan, finally twisting in his seat as if he could catch a glimpse of

Mike, who was long out of sight of the restaurant's window.

"He okay?"

"Would you be okay if your girlfriend suggested you marry a man?"

"No." The word came out of Alex like a gunshot.

"There's your answer." Dylan was spinning on the inside. Absolutely spinning. Of all the scenarios he'd imagined since the topic of custody and what-ifs came up, marrying Mike had been—well, not dead last. Just...not. Not at all. Never an option, never a thought, nope, nada.

Fin.

Stunned, he looked at Laura, who was doing her best Alex imitation and staring so hard at the salt shaker Dylan thought she might animate it via pure telekinetic will.

"What," he finally said, looking right at the person he knew was responsible for this hare-brained idea, "made Josie think of this whopper?"

Alex gave him a hard look, the kind you have when you're watching someone you're not sure about.

Smart man.

Josie looked like she was holding her breath, eyes wide with something less than terror, but more than apprehension. She plunged a long-handled spoon into a wet sundae and stirred the soupy mess.

But said nothing.

Laura reached across the table for Dylan's hand, turning simultaneously backwards, toward the door, as if connecting in the flesh with Dylan would make their third magically appear. The look on her face as she twisted back to look at Dylan made it clear she really expected...something.

This was Mike, though. Dylan sighed, letting a little of the tension in his chest release. Mike was long gone by now, a mile down the road, running his heart out. Pounding out the confusion and pain.

Not that Dylan didn't have his fair share, but running off like that wasn't how he handled conflict. He faced it, head-on.

Laura leaned across the table and gave him a hard look. "It was my idea."

"Yours?" His own explosion was more contained than Mike's, but no less emotional. Her face was hard, eyes narrowed, the skin underneath pulled high and tight, like she dared him to question her.

He took the dare.

"You think me and Mike are gay?"

Her face crinkled in a look of utter disbelief. "What? No! Of course not."

"Well," he said slowly, like he was explaining this to their one year old, "when two men get married legally, it's gay marriage."

"The label doesn't make you gay," Josie said, interrupting.

"*Nothing* makes me gay."

"Why are you so touchy about the gay label?" Josie asked mildly, head tilted like she was questioning an experiment volunteer.

"Because it's not the right word to describe my sexuality. Why are you so touchy about letting Alex marry you?"

That shut her up.

"Explain," he growled at Laura, who jumped slightly in her seat, startled, as he squeezed her hand hard and pulled his own back. Right now, touching her felt like a violation. A sick feeling filled the back of his throat, coating his stomach, burying deep in his bones.

He didn't like any of this. Not Frank, not Mike's reaction, not the talk about custody of Jillie, his parents, biological fathers—

None of it.

And certainly not the idea that neither he nor Mike would marry Laura, but instead that they would—

"No," he whispered.

Laura's confusion filled her flushed cheeks, eyes wild with panic, calming periodically and ramping back up to something just shy of anxiety. "No? You don't want me to explain?"

"No, I don't want to marry Mike."

Closing her eyes, Laura took a deep sigh, then said, "If we go on and have more kids, and I have kids by both of you, legally I'm their mother, and legally the biological father is their father. But—"

He felt like this was déjà vu, like Laura, Josie, and Alex had been eavesdropping on his conversation with Mike just minutes ago in the bathroom. When did legalities become so important?

When Frank showed his fucking face in their goddamn house.

"I know," he said. "The non-biological father would have no legal rights over the other children if you and one of us died."

"Yes," Laura and Josie said in unison. Alex just stared dumbly at Dylan and gave a single-shoulder shrug, as if to say, *Sorry, bro.*

Yeah. Right. Sorry.

He had let himself imagine marrying Laura, and had tortured himself by thinking about Mike not marrying Laura. Pretzeling his mind in every contorted way you could imagine, he'd tried to think of a way to have a long-term show of commitment to her and one that protected custody of Jillian and their future kids.

He had never—not once—thought about marrying Mike.

"My parents will pass out. We're Catholic!" he groaned.

"Your parents are Catholic. You're lapsed," Josie pointed out.

He gave her a look that made her mouth snap shut like a coin purse.

"You know, for once could you just shut it? We're talking about my life here. Not your helpful little sarcastic do-bee mouth."

"Dylan." Alex's voice was calm but firm. "Let's go for a walk."

"I don't—"

Alex stood, then splayed his hands across the spare end of the table. "I think you need some air."

The room felt like it was on fire, the oxygen seeping out, his internal sense of self gasping for air, stifled and unable to think. Like he was caught in a raging house fire without any equipment. Attacking Josie would be easy. Comforting, even. But Alex wasn't about to let that happen, and from the way Laura was looking at him, maybe stepping away from the epicenter of this seismic shift was a good thing.

He said nothing, just stood and marched outside, Alex on his heels. As he pushed the glass door open, a shower of color greeted them both, filling the sidewalks and the streets.

A rainbow of brightness, people dressed in costume, riding decorated bikes, carrying folded-up banners, all headed for the T station to take the subway into Boston.

"What's this?" he said to no one in particular, though Alex was closest.

"SUPPORT GAY MARRIAGE," one of the signs screamed, carried in the arms of a woman who could have easily been Dylan's mom, white-haired, wrinkled, yet walking with a ramrod straight backbone and a look of grit and determination, her arm around a man about Dylan's age, with facial features that instantly told Dylan he was her son.

"Pride," Alex said with a sly smile. He was clearly trying not to laugh. "They're on their way to the Pride Parade."

The gay rights parade. That's right. Dylan had forgotten that was today.

His eyes took in the line of signs. "Stand On the Side of Love," one of them said. "Love knows no gender," another called out in rainbow colors. "Love people, not genitals," said yet another. The flow of signs and costumes and—*smiles!* So many smiles, grins, and laughter filling the scene, and all making Dylan's fury and confusion die down slowly, tamped by the sheer weight of love out here.

Alex gave a rowdy group of college students a thumbs-up as they strolled past, making them cheer and wave.

"Support gay marriage," Dylan mumbled.

"You don't have to do it," Alex said in a neutral tone, running a hand through his hair, sheltering his eyes with an outstretched palm as the sun burst out from behind a cloud. The two men backed up a foot or so, closer to Jeddy's, as a huge group poured out of a bus on the corner. People dressed in pirate costumes tumbled out of the bus.

"Do what? Protect my and Mike's rights to Jillian?" Dylan sighed. "Until the law catches up to threesomes, we don't seem to have a choice."

"You always have a choice," Alex said reasonably, placing a friendly hand on Dylan's shoulder, turning to look at him.

"Out and proud!" one of the college kids screamed, giving Alex and Dylan two thumbs up. To Alex's credit, he didn't flinch, didn't pull away from Dylan. Just laughed.

"They think we're a couple," Dylan said seriously. "You don't care?"

"Why should I care what the world thinks? I'm secure in knowing who and what I want. People will think what they want to think. Can't control that. All you can control is what you do and why you do it. If you need to marry Mike to secure Jillian's future, then that's what you do. On the outside, it means one thing. To you, it means something completely different."

"I know that."

"But can you *live* it?"

Just then, Mike burst through the throng of people, a vision in pale blue amidst a sea of primary colors. He jogged over to them, carefully making his way through the crowd, his face covered in sweat, pits soaked through and neckline wet.

Dylan knew him so well.

Mike was barely panting, though Dylan imagined he'd run a few miles in the short period of time he'd been gone. Alex acted like it was no big deal for Mike to reappear, and let go of Dylan's shoulder, crossing his arms over his chest and taking in the people.

"So," Mike said, huffing out the last little bit of exerted breath in him.

"So?" Dylan asked.

Mike's eyes burned, his nostrils flared, but it wasn't with anger. Something deeper and unknown, something that made Dylan's inner self go calm, was in those eyes.

And then:

"You ready to make an honest man out of me?"

MIKE

The actual process of marrying Dylan turned out to be remarkably unremarkable. Thank God for that, too, because if it had been too complicated he might very well have exploded and disintegrated into a million tiny pieces, carried off in the wind.

Instead, he signed his name a few times, filled out a million forms, went to the town hall for a license, and took care of it all before a judge.

Wham, bam, thank you...*man*.

Married. Not to Laura. And Dylan wasn't, either. But in a court of law, they were now the legal stepfather to each other's children, and that provided a modicum of protection. Mike had consulted with a family law attorney who had thrown out points of law and terminology like *psychological father* and *stepparent rights* and *next of kin*, and who had concluded that while they did not *need* to marry, it couldn't hurt to bolster a case should the worst-case scenario happen, should Laura and one of the fathers died.

All this for a one-in-a-million chance of the worst possible outcome in life *ever*.

It hardly seemed worth it until he realized: he, Laura, and Dylan were long shots, too.

459

And so he was married.

No rings. No celebration. Nothing to indicate this was a special occasion—on that, he and Dylan had agreed. This was a contractual formality, a point of law, a *marriage of convenience*, and by God, that's all it was going to be.

He loved Dylan, but he adored Laura, and the ache inside him persisted. He wanted more. The piece of paper now on file with the town clerk didn't remove his ability to find that *more* with her, Dylan, and Jillie, but it left a bad taste in his mouth anyhow.

"Have a great honeymoon!" the town clerk's office worker called out as they exited the building, his pleasant wave making Mike's guts tighten. Dylan snorted. Laura groaned but said nothing.

Jillian waved back and squealed.

At least the whole family had been there.

His family of creation, that is. His family of origin was a whole other story. He snorted as he imagined making that phone call.

Hi, Mom and Dad. I just got married! Her *name? Her name is Dylan.*

Giving Dylan the side eye as Laura corralled them all, Jillie in her arms, he relaxed his shoulders. Being married to Dylan wasn't the worst thing in the world, right?

"Doing taxes just got more complicated," Dylan said with a laugh.

Ah, God.

"Stand close! Let's get a nice wedding photo of the happy couple!" Laura chirped, holding up her smartphone and tapping the screen a few times.

Out of the corner of Mike's eye he saw movement, his mouth frozen in a smile for Laura's sake, teeth grinding together so hard he could crack walnuts.

A white van. An antenna. Something black and machinelike, moving toward them. Mike's arm was around Dylan's for the picture and he felt his partner stiffen, the two turning toward the motion in unison.

A camera.

A video camera.

A big one, too, from a news station.

"Fuck," Dylan said, drawing out the word, just as Laura turned around to see what they were staring at.

"Oh, no!" she gasped, pulling Jillian in to her chest, covering her face.

"Get in the Jeep," Mike snapped. He didn't have to say it again, all the adults scrambling in, Dylan on one side of the back seat, protecting Jillie from the camera.

"Mike! Dylan! How's the happy day? Did I hear someone say 'wedding'?" The same news reporter Mike saw on the morning news channels was clip-clopping over on high heels that looked like rock-climbing crampons.

Fuck. The hulk inside him roared to life, his insides like a Bessemer furnace fed a half-ton of coal, the embers about to fire up and flame in glory and destructive heat. A series of clicks, snaps, and mutters from the back seat told him Dylan or Laura was putting Jillian in her carseat, and then the snap of two car doors shutting entered his consciousness, his foot easing off the brake, Jeep in reverse, his impulse to floor it tempered only by the fact that a second news van had pulled in, half blocking him.

If he didn't maneuver very, very carefully, he would have more than a gay marriage announcement in the news within the hour.

The slow, tedious process of moving the Jeep out of the parking spot gave the two cameramen plenty of time to capture them in the Jeep, though Laura threw a blanket over Jillian. A few months ago the baby would have thought it was a game, but toddlerhood had turned Jillian into an independent being with her own very firm ideas about how the world worked, and it did not include being covered.

Thrusting the blanket to the floor, Jillian looked right at the bright lights on the cameras.

"Jillie," Mike heard Dylan say as the Jeep's bumper cleared the second white news van, as two reporters with microphones now dodged the line between getting the story and not being run over, as the two cameramen clearly experienced a different, more adventurous line. On multiple occasions, as the seconds rolled out with agonizing slowness, Mike was certain he'd run over someone's foot, or would pin one of the men carrying the bulky cameras under a tire.

Thankfully, no. Cleared of the vehicles and the people, he pulled out of the parking lot with painful slowness, caught at the right turn by gridlock in the street, held up by a red light.

His teeth were grinding so hard they'd surely become bone dust soon, and Jillian began to wail. "No bankee! No bankee!"

Mike caught a glimpse of Laura trying to play "peekaboo" and failing, covering Jillie here and there. The two female reporters with microphones now held up cell phones, obviously snapping photo after photo as he sat there, rage flowing through his veins like blood.

Finally, traffic cleared, and he pulled out, signaled right at the light, and headed for the Mass Pike.

Dylan's sigh of relief matched Laura's, but no such sound could come out of Mike.

"What in the hell just happened?" Laura asked in a breathless voice, mindlessly stroking Jillian's hair to the point of the baby's annoyance.

"Mama, top!" she shouted, pulling her head away. Mike saw Laura fold her hands in her lap and pick at a cuticle.

"We just got stalked," Mike said in a bitter voice. "Someone tipped them off."

"No, it's my fault," Laura declared in a shaky voice. "I made that 'married' comment in the parking lot a little too loudly, and I'll bet the camera people just happened to be there for—"

"For what?" Dylan said. "For nothing. You saw the town hall. It was dead. Empty. No election, no event, no scandal."

"*We're* the scandal," Mike muttered as he floored it, ripping the accelerator up to seventy-five miles per hour cruising. His eyes jumped to the rearview mirror to find Jillian's eyes drooping, ready for a nap. Perfect timing. The longest part of the drive home was on Route 2, with smooth sailing.

By the time they got home, he could put in a call to their lawyer and see about damage control.

"Frank," Dylan muttered. "I'll bet this was all him."

Laura just stared out the window, wringing her hands now that Jillian was slumping against one side of her carseat. Mike saw Dylan reach across the baby to hold Laura's hand. She grasped it like a lifeline. Mike smiled, a sad stretching of muscle triggered more by relief than anything else.

The drive home was quiet. Too quiet.

Just married.

CHAPTER EIGHT

DYLAN

The first thing Dylan did when he got home was to call Nick, to find out if he could learn who had tipped off the news reporters. He suspected Frank, but wanted to know as much as possible before letting the accusations fly.

The news coverage of his wedding was about as bad as he'd anticipated.

His *wedding*.

His…whatever.

Dylan Mike and Laura took Cyndi's time with Jillian to regroup and examine the news online and on television.

"Date with a bachelor won by the billionaire!" screamed one headline, a front-and-center photo of an oiled-up Dylan in suspenders and a firefighter's pants, strolling down the charity auction runway. The picture itself was surreal—had he really been *that* guy? Two or so years felt like a lifetime ago as he watched Laura and Mike huddle over the laptop on the kitchen bar.

"We have a hashtag," Mike declared, shocked.

"What is it?"

Mike sighed but said nothing. Laura just frowned.

Dylan walked over and looked at the Twitter account.

#billionairebisexuals

"Oh, great," he sputtered, not sure whether to laugh or punch something.

"Oh, there's another one," Laura muttered. He looked again.

#billionairesandwich

As in: Hey @lauramichaels you go girl *#billionairesandwich*

He and Mike shared a scorching look as Mike closed the laptop with a sharp slam.

They'd been the butt of jokes and scrutinized by the media before. As long as no one listened to commuter radio for the next few weeks, and Josie and Darla screened calls and online threats, they should be fine. Dylan thought about Frank, considered what Nick had told them, and turned to Mike.

"We just need to buy him off."

"And then what?" Laura protested. "He'll create another mess like this and come back for more?"

"Tell her," Mike demanded. "We need to tell her what we learned about him."

"You learned something about Frank and didn't tell me?" Laura descended on Dylan and came at him so fast he had to work hard not to flinch.

"Yes." Admitting the truth was better than lying.

"Why?" Anger was easier to deal with than hurt, too—and he did flinch at the tone in Laura's voice.

"Because," Mike said, enveloping her in a half-hug, pulling her soft, sweet body into his side and making Dylan's throat tighten with need, "we didn't know what to do with the information and we needed to let it percolate a bit."

She let a puff of air out through her nose, lips too tight to open. "You mean," she said in a voice pulled tighter than a violin string, "you are both pulling this overprotective husband bullshit."

"You're my overprotective husband?" Dylan cracked as he looked at Mike with exaggerated glee. "There's finally a pro to this whole marriage thing!"

And that was when Laura crumpled, leaving Dylan feeling like the complete and utter ass Josie always said he was.

Hurting Laura's feelings was bad enough.

Making Josie be *right* was intolerable.

"I want to marry *you*!" Laura said fiercely, sitting on the ground now, head between her knees, hands buried in her curly golden locks. She wouldn't look at him or Mike, and Dylan knew that if she did, her eyes would be red and would make his heart feel like someone had put it through a document shredder.

"*Both* of you," she added with a sob so distinct it made Dylan glad Cyndi had taken Jillian out for a long day of errands and baby gymnastics.

"You're supposed to be my husbands. Not each other's husband! If anyone has a right to an overbearing, overprotective, stupid thug of an inconsiderate, pompous husband, it's *me*!"

"Are you the pompous one, or am I?" Dylan asked Mike out of the corner of his mouth.

And that was when Laura threw a stuffed teddy bear at him. The kind with a big, heavy music box in it. It clipped him in the head and made him see stars.

"I think that means *you're* the pompous one," Mike said too casually, dodging a foot to the left as a softer stuffed snake flailed uselessly in the air as it missed its intended target.

"She's never thrown things at us before like this!" Dylan said, rubbing his temple. Damn bear had a wallop to it. He never liked that animal anyway.

"Quit talking about me like I'm not even here!" she screamed. "You two don't need me! You just act like I don't have a say in anything and then you go off and get married and I'm alone and will only ever have Jillie and my cats and oh my God..."

Mike studied Laura with extreme concern. "What the hell?" he whispered to Dylan.

"I don't know. The last time I saw her like this was when she was—"

"PREGNANT!"

LAURA

Laura's single, shouted word echoed through the house like an alarm.

She'd guessed, based only on being a week late, but her cycles had come back a few months ago, right as rain. A week's delay might not mean anything, but the swollen breasts, the moodiness, the feeling of full-body flushing and a sense of inner sweetness, like she had a secret, made her realize what was going on.

It wasn't official, but it was pretty damn close.

"You're pregnant?" Mike asked softly, his face turning gentle and loving.

"You're pregnant?" Dylan asked with disbelief, jaw hanging open like a ventriloquist's dummy. His hair was messy and eyes wide and open, not shut off and angry like she'd feared.

"I don't, I... Well, I'm late."

Dylan frowned, letting a great burst of air out in what could have been a sigh but sounded like an indictment. "Just because you're late doesn't mean you're pregnant." But he didn't even seem to be able to convince himself.

"Have you tested yet?" Mike asked, crossing the room to place a warm, reassuring palm on her forearm.

"No."

And with that, he sprinted out the door.

"What the—?" She looked at Dylan, who just shrugged.

"Drugstore!" Mike called back, leaving her alone with the one man who wanted her to be pregnant about as much as—

Her phone rang. The number was one she didn't recognize. Without thinking, she answered and said, "This is Laura."

"Laura." The voice was unmistakable.

"Hi Frank," she said flatly. Dylan's nostrils flared, his head tilting, jaw working like an auger.

"I wanted to say my goodbyes."

"Goodbye?" She frowned, giving Dylan a look that asked, *Did you do this?*

He just shrugged, a *who, me?* gesture that made her want to throttle him. Why didn't anyone tell her anything anymore?

"Ah, yes. I have business that will take me out of the area for a very long time, and I simply wanted to visit in person, but regret that I cannot."

Wow. What a mouthful of manure. She wondered how he could stand himself.

"You're leaving? For good?" She didn't even try to keep the hope out of her voice.

"Yes, my dear. Kiss that baby for me and know that you are a very good mother. Just like your own mother was." *Click.*

That was it?

That was *IT*?

"What," she snapped at Dylan as she set her phone down on the couch, "did you do to Frank?"

"We didn't hurt him," Dylan protested. "We just met with the lawyer and decided that maybe Frank needed some incentive to get out of our lives."

Her eyes narrowed. Dylan wasn't telling her the whole truth.

"Incentive? You mean money?"

"Something like that."

"AND THIS IS WHY YOU TWO DRIVE ME NUTS!" Laura shouted, feeling like her flesh was going to rip off her bones and strangle Dylan all by its fluffy self.

"I thought you just said you wished you could have an overprotective husband!"

"Don't throw my words back at me!"

Bzzzz.

Laura's phone.

"Hey, chickie," Josie said as Laura picked up. Her heart was pounding so hard she could feel it behind her eyeballs. "What's up?"

"I'm pregnant and I can't marry my husbands and now they're making fun at me and—"

"Whoa, whoa, whoa," Josie said swiftly. "That's a lot to handle! You need me to come over?"

"No!" Laura wailed, completely disgusted with herself. She knew she was out of control, knew she was behaving like a completely raving idiot, and yet she couldn't stop. "No! I want you to meet me at Jeddy's."

"Of course you do," Josie said sourly. "Can't we meet somewhere else, for once?"

"Can I just have one thing I want"—sob—"for once?" Laura gasped.

470

"Yep. You're *definitely* pregnant," Josie declared. "Congratulations!"

"Jeddy's. In an hour. No men. Do not bring Alex. Do you hear me?"

Click.

Laura shot Dylan a look designed to set his hair on fire, grabbed her purse and keys, and stormed out of the house.

Men.

Can't live with them, can't marry both of them.

MIKE

The phone was slick against his ear, nerves making him sweat.

"Thank you, Alex. The jeweler is right there next to the hospital, and if you wouldn't mind getting the ring…" *Ring.* The word felt funny playing on his lips, like it was tickling him. "I can't make it there before they close." Mike checked the time. No way.

"No problem, Mike. Happy to do it. I can zip over there now and once I finish this paperwork, I'll get it to you."

"Great."

"Congrats."

Mike could hear the wistful tone in Alex's voice, and his smile turned from elation to something a bit more introspective. Poor guy. He and Josie would have their time someday. Mike didn't say a word about Laura's suspicions of pregnancy. He knew that Alex wanted a family with Josie, and maybe engagement and a new baby would rub it in a little too much.

"Thanks. So, the ring? Where should we meet to get it? I want to do this sooner rather than later." Mike and Dylan had talked about this—how they wanted one ring to use when they proposed to Laura. one ring with a beautiful pearl in the center, representing her.

And two big, billionaire-sized diamonds flanking it.

They planned to propose at the sex cabin, under the summer's moon, with champagne and rose petals, the whole romantic scene. Ask her to marry them—in their hearts. Offer a big ceremony for close friends, perhaps in an exotic Caribbean location. Or Hawaii. Or Thailand.

Who cared?

Just being married—in spirit—as a triad was what Mike wanted.

The fact that Laura was probably pregnant made the timeline move up. If he and Dylan proposed now, it had more meaning. More grace.

More...just *more*.

"Want to meet at Jeddy's?" Mike asked.

Alex groaned. "If Madge sees me walk in with a jeweler's bag she'll have another heart attack from sheer glee."

"I don't want to be responsible for killing Madge," Mike said dryly. "That old bat would haunt me through five more lifetimes if I did that."

"Eh, I'm kidding. I'll just hide the box in my pocket. Sure. Let's meet at Jeddy's. Josie's at the office working on some late project with her developer, yammering on about regression analysis and correlation for matching people up."

"Sexy," Mike said with a laugh.

Alex joined him. "Nothing sexier than a woman who can talk math."

Mike could think of a few sexier things, but wisely kept his mouth shut. "See you in a few." Alex hung up. Good man. Nice to turn to someone other than Dylan when he needed a bit of assistance.

Mike put his phone down and stared at the glowing lights of the drugstore. He'd already rushed in and bought four tests—one of each kind they sold—and now he pulled out of the parking lot to race to Route 2 and get into Cambridge. He figured Laura was weepy and Dylan could handle her for the extra time.

This was worth it.

Bzzz. His phone rang as he got on the entrance ramp. Dylan.

"What's up?" Mike asked.

"Laura and I had a...I don't even know what the fuck it was. A fight, I guess." The poor guy sounded like he'd been hit with a bulldozer. "Anyhow, Laura left. She's on her way to Jeddy's."

"Jeddy's? SHIT!"

"Why shit?" Dylan sounded alarmed. Mike *felt* alarmed.

"Because I called Alex and he's getting the ring from the jeweler's and we're meeting at—"

"Jeddy's. Jesus. Can't we get a little more original?"

"I doubt Laura's going to beg Josie to meet her in the free-weight room at the gym," Mike said with a snort.

"Only if they start serving coconut shrimp at the juice bar. Damn. You need me to race there right now, don't you? Get the ring, propose to Laura—at *Jeddy's*?" Dylan's howl of protest mixed with the kind of breathless, gasping laughter that Mike felt inside, too, but couldn't quite express.

"I guess so."

"Let me give Cyndi a quick call and make sure she can keep Jillian longer."

Mike thought about that for a second. "Why not bring her?"

"Cyndi?"

"No, doofus. Jillian. Have her be there. Make it about us. All of us."

Dylan inhaled slowly, then said, "Done. I'll be late, but let's do it." Mike expected him to hang up, but he stayed on the line, his breath coming in even patterns, his silence saying so much. "You ready to do this?"

"I married *you*, didn't I? How could proposing to Laura be any harder? Hopefully there won't be any camera crews around."

"I'm not worried about that. Frank tipped them off, and he's long gone, so—"

"Frank tipped them off? You sure about that?" This was news to Mike.

"Yeah. Nick got back to me damn fast. Turns out he knows one of the cameraman—"

"You sure *he* didn't tip them off?"

"Turns out Nick's gay. Went on and on about his own husband and how great it was that we—you know. So...no. Nick didn't tip them off."

"Gotcha."

Awkward silence filled the air, and then:

"He dug around, and it was Frank who tipped off the press."

"Nice. He must have done it before we talked to him. Asshole. Good thing he's gone."

"Oh, he's long gone after the way we handled him."

474

Mike grinned. This was what Dylan and Mike had started to tell Laura before she freaked. Going to Frank with a very comfortable figure in the form of a cashier's check, plus a printout of the outstanding warrant for his arrest in Connecticut, had been blindingly simple. The man had taken the check and the papers, scanned both, and reached out to shake each of their hands.

Then he'd walked out of Mike's office.

Simple.

Too bad Laura couldn't be so uncomplicated.

"How we gonna do this?" Dylan asked Mike, whose chest was warming with joy as he picked up speed on the highway, careful not to go too much over the speed limit yet feeling pushed by an unseen force to get to Laura quickly. To find her. To look her in the eye and propose to spend the rest of their lives together.

The only way they knew how.

CHAPTER NINE

JOSIE

Madge had seated her as if she were expected, a quick hug and a carafe of coffee her greeting. The place was half full tonight, filled with a hodgepodge of people with vaguely familiar faces and a large group at a horseshoe booth reminiscing about college from thirty years ago.

The hot coffee felt good. Josie's thigh moved against the white plastic bag she carried, and she looked at it with a mixture of excitement and guilt.

Pregnancy tests. If Laura wasn't quite sure, it couldn't hurt to run into the bathroom at the restaurant and pee on a stick, right?

Josie chilled out and drank her coffee, her body relaxing in waves. When was the last time she just sat around? Everything in her world was about Alex or the business. Long gone were the days of curling up on the couch and binge-watching a season of television, or wasting hours listening to music while cooking. Lately, their idea of dinner (when Alex wasn't gone) was sandwiches and salads, or worse—frozen dinners.

Starting a new business, starting a new life as roommates...lovers...significant others... *whateverthefuckyoucalledthis*—it was overwhelming.

No wonder her shoulders were practically glued to her ears all the time from tension.

Every time the front door swung open she looked up, like a dog trained by a bell. Not Laura. Not the second time. Third time a group of loud college guys came in, and the fourth—what looked like a small Girl Scout troop.

The fifth bell was—Alex?

He walked in and searched the room, clearly intent on finding someone specific. She knew, though, it wasn't her he sought.

One eyebrow shot up, involuntary but appropriate. Who was he meeting? Madge? But he hadn't said anything about seeing Madge and Ed, so—

"Josie?" he called out in a voice that told her he was just as surprised to see her. "What are you doing here?"

"What are *you* doing *here*?" she countered, standing as he drew close. To be eye to eye she would need to stand on the seat of the booth, and the thought crossed her mind. He wore scrubs and a look of exhaustion on his face, hair messy and eyes tired. He'd just finished up a little more than twenty-four hours at work and she didn't expect him at home for quite some time. She reached up on tiptoes and he bent down for a great big hug.

One that made the inside of her hip feel like it was being gouged by a rock.

"Is that a sledgehammer in your pocket or are you just happy to see me?" she joked as her slim little hand reached into his front pocket and pulled out—

A jeweler's box.

She froze. He was frozen, too, looking over her shoulder and down behind her, brows drawn together and eyes ablaze with intelligence and disbelief.

"What is that?" they both said in unison. Her fingers fumbled the box, but she kept hold of it.

This was the size of an engagement ring.

"Oh, Alex," she murmured, body stinging with cold and hot electric wires that charged at random. "Oh, my God." Her hand flew to her mouth and she dropped down on her heels, the feeling like being dropped on her head.

But he wasn't listening.

ALEX

A lex had rushed into Jeddy's searching for Mike, to deliver the ring and be on his way, back home for a shower and, he hoped, a late-night frolic with his beloved.

Instead, he found his beloved staring at him from a booth, a bit slack-jawed with an expression that mirrored his.

"Josie?" he called out. "What are you doing here?"

"What are *you* doing *here*?" she countered. He crossed the room and reached for her, that small, warm body like part of his beating heart. He closed his eyes and inhaled deeply, enjoying the scent of her, eyes opening to pull back and—

What was on the booth in that white bag?

He blinked rapidly, widening his eyes on purpose to make sure lack of sleep wasn't making his eyes play tricks on him.

Oh. Oh, my.

Pregnancy tests.

There were pregnancy tests spilling out of a drugstore bag on the booth next to his girlfriend.

"Is that a sledgehammer in your pocket or are you just happy to see me?" she joked as her slim little hand reached into his front pocket and pulled out—

Laura's ring.

Shit.

She froze. A million thoughts traveled through his mind at the speed of light, most of them involving little brown-haired babies. Josie was pregnant? They were going to have a baby?

His face spread with the most amazing smile he'd ever felt in his life, as if it were connected directly to his heart.

"What is that?" they asked in unison.

He looked down. Josie was juggling Laura's ring like it was a hot potato.

"Oh, Alex," she murmured. "Oh, my God." Her hand flew to her mouth.

Double shit.

"Oh, um. That's...that's, um..." His words didn't just fail him. They fled his body like rats on a sinking ship. God damn it—of all the times to have his mind go blank, to try to explain what was going on, and yet —she had some explaining to do, too!

Baby! They'd made a baby! His mother would be a grandma. Grandpa Ed would meet his first great-grandchild. Alex would help make an entire human being with the woman he adored most in life.

"I...I know what it is, Alex," Josie whispered, so somberly it jolted him out of his baby reverie. Fuck. Now Mike and Dylan's surprise would be ruined because he'd—

"You bought this for me," she added. It wasn't a question.

"Uh," he stammered. That was *not* what he expected her to say.

As she opened the box with shaking hands, tears filled her eyes. "Oh!" she gasped, looking up, a blend of terror and joy in those eyes, the look one he could describe on his deathbed in sixty or seventy years, so crystal clear to him as if it were painted on his soul by Michelangelo.

A hand reached out and snatched the box from Josie, closing it. "Thanks!" Mike had appeared out of nowhere, his other hand clapping Alex on the back. "I appreciate it. Laura's going to love this." And with that, he winked at Josie.

Alex swore he felt the earth move as Josie's heart snapped shut, closing up like a potato bug being poked in the stomach.

"Ha!" she said, the sound like someone being gut-punched, the air forced out by pain. "That's a beautiful ring. Of course," she said, clearing her throat, clearly struggling for composure. "Of course she'll love it."

Unsure what he was watching, Alex knew one thing: she was upset, and if he wasn't completely off-base, he would swear she was also...

Disappointed?

She wouldn't look at Alex. Pulled away, but not to the booth where she'd just been sitting. Just pulled away, like an animal that needed to have four paths of escape to feel safe.

He wanted to wrap his arms around her, to make her feel protected and sure, to cradle the new life inside her—their baby. If she was mad at her erroneous impression that he would ever be so presumptuous as to propose to her now—when she had made it abundantly clear in a thousand different ways that she wasn't ready for marriage—he needed to talk to her, to soothe her, to make everything smooth between the two of them.

"Josie," he said softly.

She wouldn't look at him.

His eyes skittered over the pregnancy tests in the bag behind her, then he took a careful inventory of her face. The understandable assumption that the ring in his pocket was for her and her anger made him—

And then her eyes met his, and something in him melted and exploded at the same time, because she wasn't angry.

She was *sad*.

LAURA

The gas station bathroom had turned out to be the last place on earth where she should have tested her urine to figure out whether she was going crazy or really pregnant.

Then again, the toilet was so nasty it wasn't hard to straddle the porcelain bowl and aim for the end of the little plastic stick.

Which, sixty seconds later, gave her the answer.

Pregnant.

Two more tests later and she was sure.

The wind whooshed out of her. A wildfire flush ripped across her pale skin as the truth began to sink in. She really was pregnant. A trembling hand reached up and brushed her long, blonde hair off her face, tucking it behind her ear. She looked pale, though the blinking, half-dead fluorescent light in the nasty bathroom might have accounted for some of that. A roiling feeling of nausea hit her—and it wasn't the pregnancy.

Damn was she fertile, because *hello*? Still nursing and on the pill? Did Mike and Dylan have supersperm?

Apparently so.

At least *one* of them did.

After she washed her hands and carefully threw out all the tests, she climbed back in the car and headed toward Jeddy's. Ridiculously late at this point, she sent Josie a quick text while she was at a stoplight.

By the time she got to Jeddy's, she could see Josie talking with Alex. Alex? Good grief, were they joined at the hip? She'd told Josie absolutely no testicles at this meal. Ovaries only.

Ovaries, estrogen, and lots of ice cream.

As she yanked the front door open and prepared to pretend to be okay with Alex's presence, that flush she'd felt earlier turned into a full-blown creepy-crawly feeling, like being gently stroked with a paintbrush.

Josie.

Alex.

Mike.

Dylan.

Jillian?

Why were they all here, of all places?

Dylan looked at her with those soft puppy-dog eyes that she loved so much, his body bent protectively around Jillian, who was in his arms and playing peekaboo with Madge. The old waitress used a cloth napkin to cover her face and reveal it, much to Jillian's delight, squeals of laughter filling the restaurant.

Sweaty, confused, and bubbling over with emotion, Laura took in the scene. Mike and Dylan walked close to her, while Josie hung behind, moving off to a corner, face impossible to read.

What was going on?

Mike gave Dylan one of those looks that drove her nuts all the time, the exchange of glances that was some form of shorthand. Madge took Jillian from Dylan and gave him a wink.

No, really.

What.

Was.

This?

"Mama! Mama!" Jillie shrieked, her voice still happy but beginning to take on that edge toddlers get when they realize they might not get what they want immediately. Madge frowned, shrugged, then brought the baby to Laura, handing her off.

She seemed so little, yet so gigantic compared to the tiny newborn she'd been a little over a year ago. Time really flew, didn't it?

Lately at the speed of a supersonic jet.

Alex stayed in place and looked awkward, eyes shifting between Laura and Josie, his mouth turning down with a slight frown when he looked at Josie. Had something gone wrong? Why was Josie standing apart from him, her face a mask, but her eyes so red?

Was Madge sick? Had something happened to Ed? Jillian played with the necklace around Laura's neck and moved just enough to make Laura's stomach feel off, a tendril of nausea making its way up.

And then.

Mike and Dylan moved within a few feet of her and Jillie, Mike's eyes glistening with...was he crying? Nearly crying? Dylan looked nervous, giving Jillian a wink and stopping to study Laura's face, his head at an angle, his eyes steady and true.

484

"What are you—"

They both dropped down, each on bended knee.

Oh, God.

"Laura," they asked in unison, "will you marry us?" The words echoed like a chime that hits the perfect frequency, all sweetness and light, all love and comfort in one clear note.

Mike held out a ring, with two enormous diamonds on either side of a pearl the color of her hair. His hand was suspended in thin air, Dylan gently taking the box from Mike and standing, slowly. Mike rose as well, and they closed the gap between them.

She was completely stunned.

"This is the part where you answer them," Madge shouted. In a dim, distant part of her mind, Laura knew that other patrons were watching, with various smiles of amusement or confusion dotting their features. How often do two men propose to the same woman?

With one ring?

"I…I… Oh my God, yes! Yes, of course, yes! But we can't actually be married!" she protested. The room erupted into applause as she said yes, the rest of her words drowned out by catcalls and cheers.

"Yes, we can," Dylan said firmly, eyes firm and loving. "The real marriage is the one the three of us forge together." And with that, he kissed her, Jillian's little fingers slipping into her hair, her babbles a sweet backdrop to the taste of her one true love.

Her *other* one true love interrupted them with hands on her shoulders, his sun-kissed hair pressing into the family crowd. "That's *my* wife you're kissing," Mike said with a mock growl, dropping the jokes as he turned Laura toward him and slipped the ring on her trembling hand. It fit perfectly.

Her arms slipped around his neck and his kiss tasted like love and dreams, his hands like anchors and tethers, Dylan's arms enveloping them both until Jillian said, "Top it! Top it!" and the three broke apart, breathless with glee.

"This wasn't the first proposal I've ever seen here at Jeddy's. Not even the first time I've ever seen two guys propose to the same girl in one day. But I'll be damned if I've ever seen two men propose to the same woman and have them all marry each other!" Madge crowed. "That deserves a big meal, on the house!"

Madge turned to Alex and said with a half-grin, "Same for you too, sport. When you decide to make a decent woman out of Josie, I'll give you whatever you want."

The look on Josie's face made Laura's joy fade.

She'd never seen Josie look so *sad*.

JOSIE

When she'd seen the ring in Alex's pocket, her first thought had been horror. Mind-grinding terror that made everything in her seize up.

And then she realized how fucking *fake* that was.

She wasn't really terrified to marry Alex. She was afraid of *wanting* to marry Alex. Those were two completely different emotions, and being able to distinguish between them was critical.

Had she really just developed a *habit* of freaking out at the idea of marriage? Trained her mind to think she didn't want to marry Alex, when in fact, she did?

And desperately so?

While she'd been shocked to hold that ring in her hands and think it was from him, and that he was about to propose, what had been more shocking was having it removed by Mike. Learning that the ring wasn't for her. Comprehending that Alex had just been carrying it for Mike and Alex wasn't planning to ask her to marry him.

Her heart felt like someone had chainsawed it out of her chest.

She had no right to feel like this. None. Pushing Alex away because of her fear of commitment had practically become the Official Josie Mendham National Sport. She could have her own flag and uniform, if she kept it up like this. If anyone deserved the one-two punch of finding that box in his pocket and having it turn out to be for someone else, it was Josie.

So why was she so distraught?

Clamming up and shutting down was her default. As time passed, though, and she became more comfortable and trusting of Alex, she found that withdrawing emotionally didn't work. It was no longer a sanctuary. Building an emotional fortress around herself didn't help.

Didn't work.

In fact, it caused more damage than good, and left her with an ache for those long, strong arms that were a better wall than anything she could ever create.

Sensing this, Alex walked across the room as the fellow diners cheered for Laura, Mike, and Dylan. Her eyes tracked his smooth movement across the linoleum floor, how his legs carried him toward her with such confidence. Assurance.

Permanence.

"You are not okay," he whispered as one arm reached around her for an embrace, the other cradling her jaw, fingers light and gentle against the back of her head, her ear tickled by the long surgeon's hand.

"How'd you guess?"

"You look like you wish you had ruby slippers and could click the heels furiously."

"I think I'd rather have a house fall on me. I'm more the Wicked Witch type and less the Dorothy type," she joked, but a sob caught in her throat and ruined her ruse.

"It's fine," he said soothingly in her ear. "The tears are normal. They happen to women in your...women like..." The stumbling over his words was odd. Alex didn't generally—

Wait.

Women in your *what*?

"Women like...?" She drew out the question, pulling back to look into eyes that radiated so much love she thought she might go blind.

His palm flattened against her belly. "In your condition." He bent down and kissed her cheek, a small bit of wetness registering in her mind. When he pulled back, she saw why.

A single tear had fallen from those loving eyes.

"Condition?" she choked out, completely confused. What condition?

Now his eyes clouded slightly, the confusion shared. "You, um..." His gaze turned to the booth. "You had a bag of tests next to you, and one fell out. You're pregnant—or think you are, right? I'm going to be a dad." The tears in his eyes filled in, and the expression on his face made her feel like a goddess. A slow caress from ribs to belly button made her melt in place.

Or maybe that was simply shock.

"PREGNANT?" she shrieked, laughing and crying at the same time. He thought she was pregnant? One half of her mind registered his dismay as her words and braying giggles hit him. Oh, shit. Alex *wanted* her to be pregnant?

The other half realized his dismay matched her own—over the ring.

She *wanted* him to propose.

His hands tightened on her body, pulling her closer, yet his face was a mask of an attempt to cover up the churning ocean of emotion inside him. Josie could feel it. See it.

And hated herself for doing this to him.

"You're not pregnant?" His hand withdrew from her belly. She missed it instantly.

"No, Alex," she answered with a weak smile. "Laura is."

"Oh."

His single-word reply felt like a gunshot.

"And that ring wasn't for me," she said, trying so hard not to say the words, scrambling inside her emotional core to cover the resentment she felt that he hadn't planned to propose.

His head snapped back with surprise. "No—I thought you didn't want to get married!" His voice grew progressively louder at the end of the sentence, the word "married" carrying through the room.

Laura, Mike, Dylan, and Madge all turned to look at them.

"I never said that," she replied in a low voice. "I just wasn't ready...now."

"Your *now* and my *now* are about a thousand years apart," he cracked. The sarcasm was new for him. Suddenly, it seemed Alex could build walls, too.

Josie had two choices, and, as more eyes fell on her and Alex, she felt time slip into a slower pace, her heart acutely aware of each microsecond, of how Alex's soul was closing off to her, and she chose the path that made her most vulnerable.

Most trusting.

Most raw.

"No," she rasped, looking him in the eye, the world around them turning to a blur. "Our nows are in sync. If that ring had been for me, if you had intended to propose, that would have made me very, very happy."

Watching Alex respond to her words was like seeing winter turn to spring in triple time, hope blossoming on his face, in his skin, infused in the way his muscles altered their grip on her.

"You—really?" The incredulity in his voice made her smile.

"Yes. Really." The heat of his body against hers filled her with everything she ever needed.

Until he dropped, suddenly, on one knee before her.

Laura, Mike, Dylan, Jillian, and Madge edged closer, now less than two yards away, their eyes the only thing Josie could see in her peripheral vision. She saw Laura reach up and grab Dylan's bicep, registered Jillian's wiggliness and Madge's keen sense of attention.

"Josephine Elizabeth Mendham, I..." He gave a self-deprecating laugh. "I wish I had a ring for this."

Madge stepped closer and tapped him on his shoulder, making Josie look at the old woman. Alex turned to her, befuddled.

When Madge spoke, her voice was thick with emotion, one wrinkled finger pointing to the other hand. "Here." Madge worked to pull a ring off her finger, carefully passing it to a dazed Alex. Madge put her hands on Alex's shoulders and bent over to whisper face to face. Josie heard every word.

"Eddie told me a long time ago that I am his memory now, Alex." Madge cleared her throat, and tears grew fat on the lower edge of her eyes, spilling over as she continued. "This was your grandmother's ring. Eddie gave it to me and told me that he wanted the first grandchild who married to have it."

Josie looked at the simple diamond ring, a single marquis-cut stone buried in a thin silver band.

Alex's jaw tightened, and Josie saw his throat move as he struggled to maintain composure, eyes flipping from the ring now in his hand to Madge's tearful face.

"Thank you," he whispered, eyes searching Madge's face. "I...I remember the ring... Grandma wore it through everything, even when she gardened or washed the dishes. I didn't know Grandpa wanted it to go to—"

Madge smiled, the movement making tears travel down her cheek and neck, wetting her uniform's collar. "Now you do." She turned to Josie and gave her a huge hug, whispering, "And now the ring is in the rightful woman's hands."

Josie joined in the waterworks as Madge pulled away and made a grand gesture with her arm.

"What the hell are you waiting for, kiddo?" Madge asked Alex, nudging him with her knee. "The lady is waiting!"

Mike fished a handkerchief out of his back pocket and handed it to Laura. Josie wanted to say something, to do something, but when her eyes met Alex's again she just—

He was the only person there.

"Will you, Josie, be my wife?" He held the ring out in the soft palm of his hand, the diamond glittering like a beacon.

Go toward the light, Josie. Go toward the light.

"Yes!" she gasped. He reached for her left hand and slid the ring on her finger, the band too loose yet, somehow, just perfect.

Dr. and Mrs. Perfect.

More cheers filled the room, and Madge announced that cake was on the house for everyone. Laura bum-rushed Josie with a hug, the two descending into giggles and tears, finally just jumping up and down in place screaming, "Can you believe it?" over and over.

Mike, Dylan, and Alex all shook each other's hands and grinned like fools.

Jillian screamed, "Mama! Mama!" until finally, Laura had to leave Josie, who was quickly scooped up into a kiss that made her toes tingle, her future husband looking like the most incredible soul in the world.

Because he was.

"How about a double wedding?" Laura asked, Jillian now in her arms.

"You *have* a double wedding," Josie joked, pointing to Mike and Dylan.

"Ha ha. I mean it," Laura said, her face flushed with happiness. "We could have something private. Away from cameras. Combine our fun."

"We can't seem to shake you two anyhow, and Josie's practically joined to Laura at the hip," Dylan said dryly.

Alex squeezed her hand. "I'm game for anything. We can elope, run off to Vegas, do the big church wedding in Ohio—"

"Dear God, no," Josie moaned. "No Ohio."

"Okay...but my mom has to be there. She'll kill me if I get married without her," Alex explained.

"We need a place in the woods," Mike said adamantly. "Lots of nature. Peaceful, and out of the way."

Madge shepherded them into the biggest booth in the place, grabbing a high chair for Jillian. As Laura clicked the baby in place and fished through the diaper bag for cereal, her new ring nearly blinded Josie. By comparison, her own ring was tiny.

But there was no comparison.

Ever.

"I have a huge, extended family," Alex warned.

"Me, too," Dylan said sheepishly, with the perma-grin shared by all three men. Josie wanted to laugh, but this humming feeling, like she was being run by an electric current of love, made her gooey and soft inside.

She liked it.

"My family is tiny," Josie said, thinking. "Darla. Aunt Cathy."

"Don't forget your mom," Laura said, then winced, throwing her hands up defensively. "Don't hate me for mentioning her!"

"I know." Josie sighed and looked at Alex. "You'll have to meet her eventually."

Alex kissed her temple. "I'm sure I'll love her."

Josie gave him an exaggerated once-over. "And she will love you. In all the wrong ways."

"My only family is Frank, and he's certainly not invited," Laura said. "So I have no one coming."

Mike and Dylan instinctively hugged her, the pile of arms and heads adorable.

"We're your family now," they said in unison.

493

"Besides, I don't have any family coming, either," Mike added.

"We need a wedding place that can handle extended family, is in the woods, and isn't too far from a major airport," Dylan declared as he pulled back. "That's a challenge."

Madge came over as Dylan spoke, her arms loaded with a giant tray of water, coffee, and cake. She set the tray down and delivered the food quickly, her face plastered with the same goofy grin everyone else had.

Food disbursed, she stopped suddenly, eyes widening.

Alex half stood, alarmed by the change in her. "Madge, is something wrong?"

She laughed and waved a hand at him. "No! The opposite." She snapped her fingers. "I've got it."

"Got what?"

Madge leaned down and placed a loving hand on Alex's shoulder, facing the rest of the group. "I know the perfect place for the wedding. My daughter owns this campground up in Maine..."

:)

The next book in the Her Billionaires series is titled *It's Always Complicated*.

If you've followed Laura, Mike, Dylan, Josie, and Alex through the 1,500 pages of the series so far, you'll love *It's Always Complicated*, which blends characters from three of my series: the Her Billionaires series, the Random series, and the Obedient series.

Look for it on your favorite retailer's site.

It's Always Complicated

Please join my mailing list at: jkentauthor.com to learn about other books, new releases, and sales.

Thank you SO MUCH for reading this book. Please consider writing a review wherever you read it, to help share this series with other readers.

Also by Julia Kent

Shopping for a Billionaire Boxed Set (Parts 1-5) (a New York Times Bestseller!)
Shopping for a Billionaire's Fiancee
Shopping for a CEO (A USA Today Bestseller!)
Shopping for a Billionaire's Wife (a USA Today Bestseller!)

Her Billionaires: Boxed Set (a New York Times Bestseller!)
It's Complicated
Completely Complicated
It's Always Complicated

Random Acts of Crazy (a New York Times Bestseller!)
Random Acts of Trust
Random Acts of Fantasy
Random Acts of Hope
Randomly Ever After: Sam and Amy
Random Acts of Love
Random on Tour: Los Angeles
Merry Random Christmas

Maliciously Obedient (a USA Today Bestseller!)
Suspiciously Obedient
Deliciously Obedient

ABOUT THE AUTHOR

Text JKentBooks to 77948 and get a text message on release dates!

New York Times and *USA Today* bestselling author Julia Kent turned to writing contemporary romance after deciding that life is too short not to have fun. She writes romantic comedy with an edge, and new adult books that push contemporary boundaries. From billionaires to BBWs to rock stars, Julia finds a sensual, goofy joy in every book she writes, but unlike Trevor from *Random Acts of Crazy*, she has never kissed a chicken.

She loves to hear from her readers by email at jkentauthor@gmail.com, on Twitter @jkentauthor, and on Facebook at facebook.com/jkentauthor

Visit her website at http://jkentauthor.com